Thieves' World™

First Blood

TOR BOOKS BY LYNN ABBEY

Sanctuary

Thieves' World: Turning Points

Thieves' World: First Blood

Thieves' World™

First Blood

Edited by
Robert Lynn Asprin
and Lynn Abbey
Single-Volume Compilation by
Lynn Abbey

TOR®

A TOM DOHERTY ASSOCIATES BOOK

NEW YORK

THIEVES' WORLD™: FIRST BLOOD

Copyright © 2003 by Robert Lynn Asprin, Lynn Abbey, and Thieves' World 2000

Thieves' World™ and Sanctuary™ are trademarks belonging to Lynn Abbey and are used with permission.

"Thieves' World" copyright © 1979 by Robert Lynn Asprin
"Tales from the Vulgar Unicorn" copyright © 1980 by Robert Lynn Asprin

All rights reserved, including the right to reproduce this book, or portions thereof, in any form.

Maps by Mark Stein Studios

This book is printed on acid-free paper.

A Tor Book
Published by Tom Doherty Associates, LLC
175 Fifth Avenue
New York, NY 10010

www.tor.com

Tor® is a registered trademark of Tom Doherty Associates, LLC.

Library of Congress Cataloging-in-Publication Data

Thieves' world : first blood / edited by Robert Lynn Asprin and Lynn Abbey.—1st ed.
      p.   cm.
   "A Tor book"—T.p. verso
   ISBN 0-312-87488-X
   1. Fantasy fiction, American.   I. Title: First blood.   II. Asprin, Robert.   III. Abbey, Lynn.

PS648.F3T475 2003
813'.0876608—dc21
                                                                          2003054335

First Edition: December 2003

Printed in the United States of America

0 9 8 7 6 5 4 3 2 1

Copyright Acknowledgments

To the many *Thieves' World* fans who've
waited for the wheel to come 'round again,
and to all the authors who've made
Sanctuary the city that it is

You're all invited to a readers' gathering at
http://groups.yahoo.com/group/thieves-world

Contents

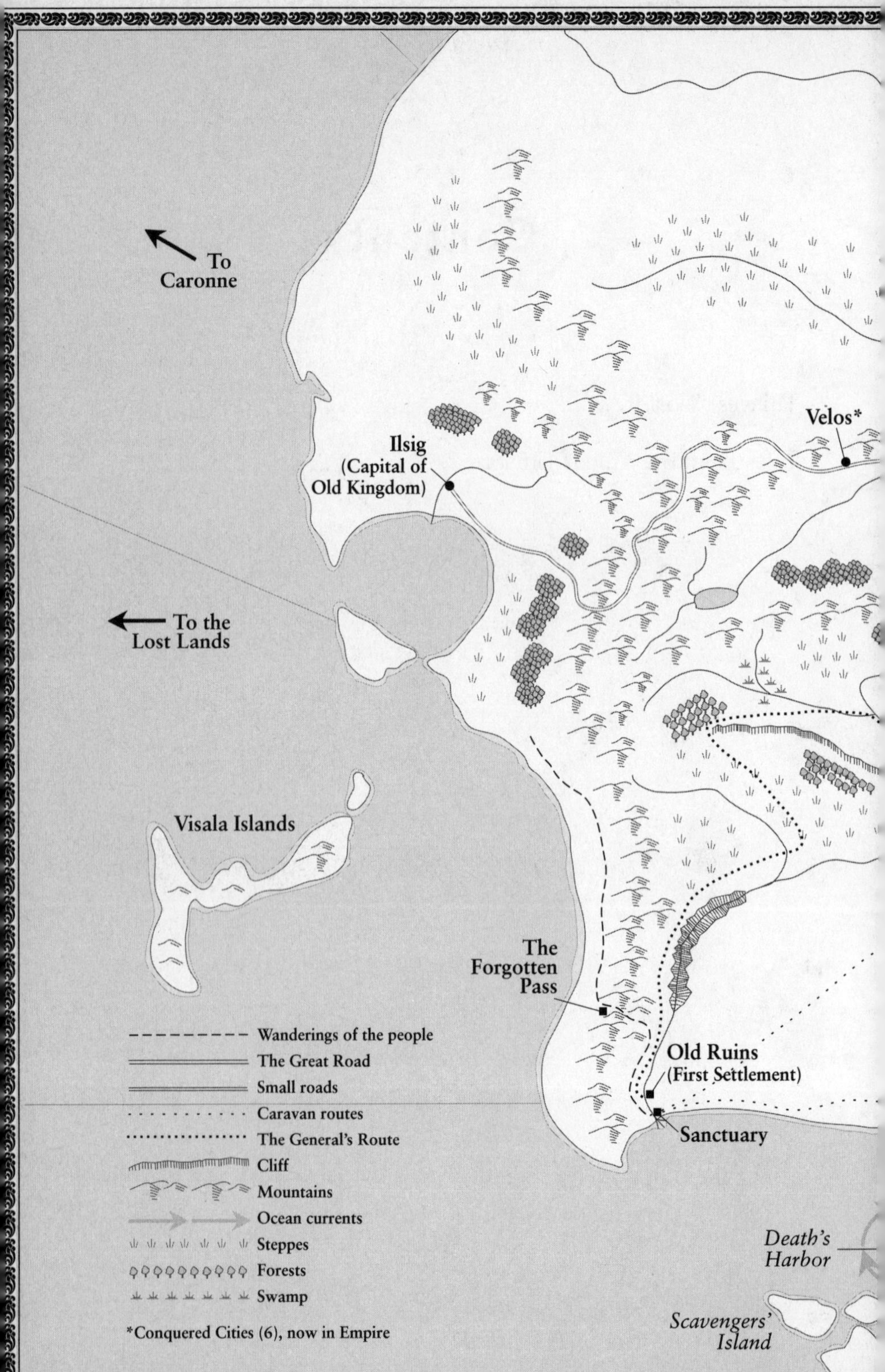
To Caronne
To the Lost Lands
Ilsig (Capital of Old Kingdom)
Velos*
Visala Islands
The Forgotten Pass
Old Ruins (First Settlement)
Sanctuary
Death's Harbor
Scavengers' Island
Wanderings of the people
The Great Road
Small roads
Caravan routes
The General's Route
Cliff
Mountains
Ocean currents
Steppes
Forests
Swamp
*Conquered Cities (6), now in Empire
Mark Stein Studios, 2003

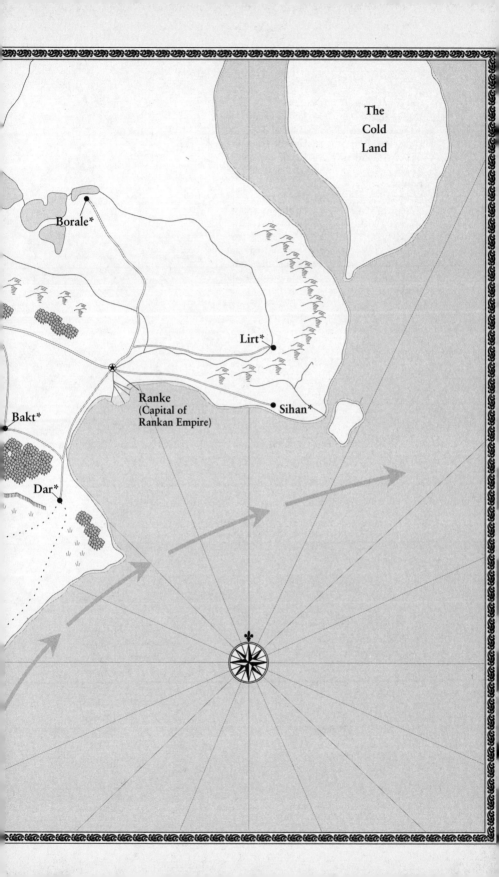

The
Cold
Land

Borale*

Lirt*

Ranke
(Capital of
Rankan Empire)

Sihan*

Bakt*

Dar*

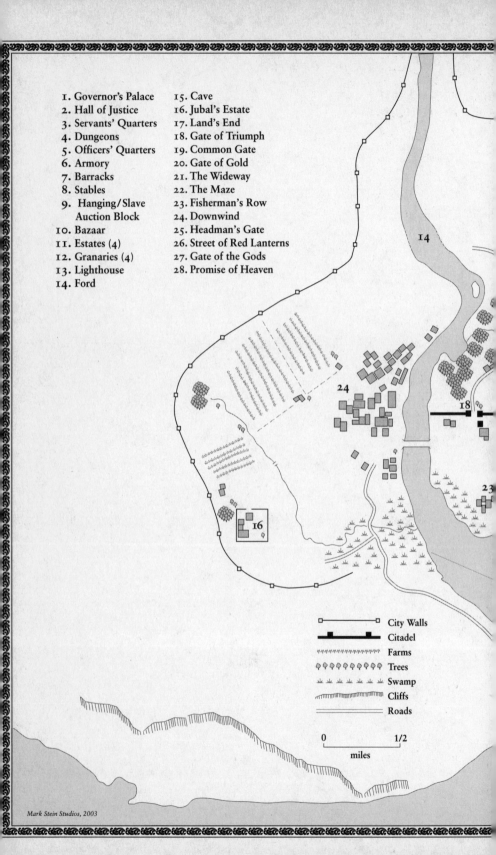

1. Governor's Palace
2. Hall of Justice
3. Servants' Quarters
4. Dungeons
5. Officers' Quarters
6. Armory
7. Barracks
8. Stables
9. Hanging/Slave Auction Block
10. Bazaar
11. Estates (4)
12. Granaries (4)
13. Lighthouse
14. Ford

15. Cave
16. Jubal's Estate
17. Land's End
18. Gate of Triumph
19. Common Gate
20. Gate of Gold
21. The Wideway
22. The Maze
23. Fisherman's Row
24. Downwind
25. Headman's Gate
26. Street of Red Lanterns
27. Gate of the Gods
28. Promise of Heaven

City Walls
Citadel
Farms
Trees
Swamp
Cliffs
Roads

0   1/2
miles

Mark Stein Studios, 2003

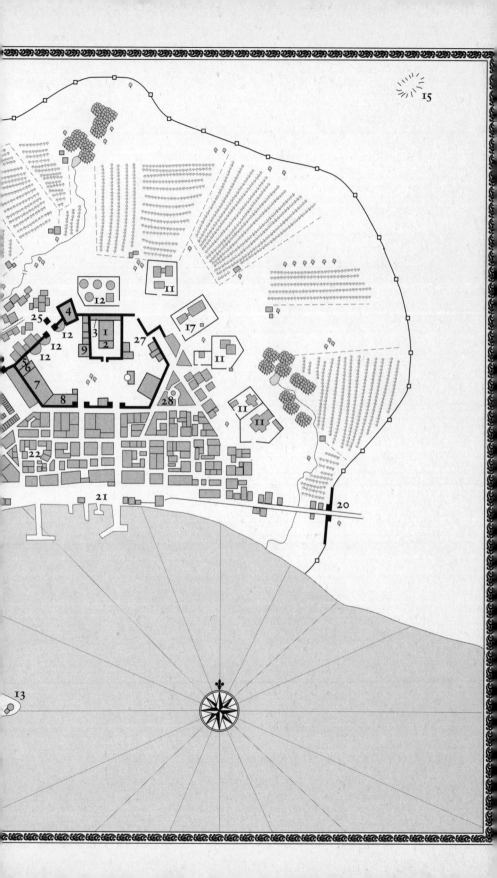

Thieves' World

Editor's Note

The perceptive reader may notice small inconsistencies in the characters appearing in these stories. Their speech patterns, their accounts of certain events, and their observations on the town's pecking order vary from time to time.

These are not inconsistencies!

The reader should consider the contradictions again, bearing three things in mind.

First: Each story is told from a different viewpoint, and different people see and hear things differently. Even readily observable facts are influenced by individual perceptions and opinions. Thus, a minstrel narrating a conversation with a magician would give a different account than would a thief witnessing the same exchange.

Second: The citizens of Sanctuary are by necessity more than a little paranoid. They tend to either omit or slightly alter information in conversation. This is done more reflexively than out of premeditation, as it is essential for survival in this community.

Finally, Sanctuary is a fiercely competitive environment. One does not gain employment by admitting to being "the second-best swordsman in town." In addition to exaggerating one's own status, it is commonplace to downgrade or ignore one's closest competitors. As a result, the pecking order of Sanctuary will vary depending on who you talk to . . . or more important, who you believe.

Introduction

Robert Aspirin

One
The Emperor

"But surely Your Excellency can't dispute the facts of the matter!"

The robed figure of the emperor never slackened its pacing as the new leader of the Rankan Empire shook his head in violent disagreement.

"I do not dispute the facts, Kilite," he argued, "but neither will I order the death of my brother."

"*Step*brother," his chief adviser corrected pointedly.

"The blood of our father flows in both our veins," the emperor countered, "and I'll have no hand in spilling it."

"But Your Excellency," Kilite pleaded, "Prince Kadakithis is young and idealistic . . ."

". . . and I am not," the emperor finished. "You belabor the obvious, Kilite. That idealism is my protection. He would no more lead a rebellion against the emperor—against his brother—than I would order his assassination."

"It is not the prince we fear, Your Excellency, it's those who would use

him." The adviser was adamant. "If one of his many false-faced followers succeeded in convincing him that your rule was unjust or inhumane,
that idealism would compel him to move against you even though he
loves you dearly."

The emperor's pacing slowed until finally he was standing motionless,
his shoulders drooping slightly.

"You're right, Kilite. All my advisers are right." There was weary resig-
nation in his voice. "Something must be done to remove my brother from
the hotbed of intrigue here at the capital. If at all possible, however, I
would hold any thoughts of assassination as a last resort."

"If Your Excellency has an alternate plan he wishes to suggest, I would
be honored to give it my appraisal," Kilite offered, wisely hiding his feelings of triumph.

"I have no immediate plan," the emperor admitted. "Nor will I be
able to give it my full concentration until another matter is settled which
weighs heavily on my mind. Surely the empire is safe from my brother
for a few more days?"

"What is the other decision demanding your attention?" the adviser
asked, ignoring his ruler's attempt at levity. "If it is something I might
assist you in resolving . . ."

"It is nothing. A minor decision, but an unpleasant one nonetheless. I
must appoint a new military governor for Sanctuary."

"Sanctuary?" Kilite frowned.

"A small town at the southern tip of the empire. I had a bit of trouble
finding it myself—it's been excluded from the more recent maps. Whatever reason there was for the town's existence has apparently passed. It is
withering and dying, a refuge for petty criminals and down-at-the-heels
adventurers. Still, it's part of the empire."

"And they need a new military governor," Kilite murmured softly.

"The old one's retiring." The emperor shrugged. "Which leaves me
with a problem. As a garrisoned empire town, they are entitled to a governor of some stature—someone who knows the empire well enough to
serve as their representative and go-between with the capital. He should
be strong enough to uphold and enforce the law—a function I fear where
the old governor was noticeably lax."

Without realizing it, he began to pace again.

"My problem is that such a man could be better utilized elsewhere in the empire. It seems a shame to waste someone on such an insignificant, out-of-the-way assignment."

"Don't say 'out-of-the-way,' Your Excellency." Kilite smiled. "Say 'far from the hotbed of intrigue.'"

The emperor looked at his adviser for a long moment. Then both men began to laugh.

Two
The Town

Hakiem the Storyteller licked the dust from his lips as he squinted at the morning sun. It was going to be hot again today—a wine day, if he could afford wine. The little luxuries, like wine, that he allowed himself were harder to come by as the caravans became fewer and more infrequent.

His fingers idly seeking a sand flea that had successfully found its way inside his rags, he settled himself wearily in his new roost at the edge of the bazaar. Previously, he had frequented the large wharf until the fishermen drove him off, accusing him of stealing. Him! With all the thieves that abounded in this town, they chose him for their accusations.

"Hakiem!"

He looked about him and saw a band of six urchins descending on him, their eyes bright and eager.

"Good morning, children." He grimaced, exposing his yellow teeth. "What do you wish of old Hakiem?"

"Tell us a story," they chorused, surging around him.

"Be off with you, sand fleas!" he moaned, waving an arm. "The sun will be hot today. I'll not add to the dryness of my throat telling you stories for free."

"Please, Hakiem?" one whined.

"We'll fetch you water," promised another.

"I have money."

The last offer caught at Hakiem's attention like a magnet. His eyes fastened hungrily on the copper coin extended in a grubby hand. That coin and four of its brothers would buy him a bottle of wine.

Where the boy had gotten it mattered not—he had probably stolen it. What concerned Hakiem was how to transfer the wealth from the boy to himself. He considered taking it by force, but decided against it. The bazaar was rapidly filling with people, and open bullying of children would doubtless draw repercussions. Besides, the nimble urchins could outrun him with ease. He would just have to earn it honestly. Disgusting, the depths to which he had sunk.

"Very well, Ran-tu." He smiled, extending his hand. "Give me the money, and you shall have any story you wish."

"After I hear the story," the boy announced haughtily. "You shall have the coin . . . if I feel the story is worth it. It is the custom."

"So it is." Hakiem forced a smile. "Come, sit here beside me so you can hear every detail."

The boy did as he was told, blissfully unaware that he was placing himself within Hakiem's long, quick reach.

"Now then, Ran-tu, what story do you wish to hear?"

"Tell us about the history of our city," the boy chirped, forgetting his pretended sophistication for the moment.

Hakiem grimaced, but the other boys jumped and clapped their hands with enthusiasm. Unlike Hakiem, they never tired of hearing this tale. "Very well," Hakiem sighed. "Make room here!"

He shoved roughly at the forest of small legs before him, clearing a small space in the ground, which he swept smooth with his hand. With quick, practiced strokes, he outlined the southern part of the continent and formed the north-south mountain range.

"The story begins here, in what once was the kingdom of Ilsig, west of the Queen's Mountains."

". . . which the Rankans call the World's End Mountains . . ." supplied an urchin.

". . . and the mountain men call Gunderpah . . ." contributed another.

Hakiem leaned back on his haunches and scratched absently.

"Perhaps," he said, "the young gentlemen would like to tell the story while Hakiem listens."

"No, they wouldn't," insisted Ran-tu. "Shut up, everyone. It's my story! Let Hakiem tell it."

Hakiem waited until silence was restored, then nodded loftily to Ran-tu and continued.

"Afraid of invasion from the then young Rankan Empire across the mountains, they formed an alliance with the mountain tribes to guard the only known pass through the mountains."

He paused to draw a line on his map indicating the pass.

"Lo, it came to pass that their fears were realized. The Rankans turned their armies toward Ilsig, and they were forced to send their own troops into the pass to aid the mountain men in the kingdom's defense."

He looked up hopefully and extended a palm as a merchant paused to listen, but the man shook his head and moved on.

"While the armies were gone," he continued, scowling, "there was an uprising of slaves in Ilsig. Body servants, galley slaves, gladiators, all united in an effort to throw off the shackles of bondage. Alas . . ."

He paused and threw up his hands dramatically.

". . . the armies of Ilsig returned early from their mountain campaign and put a swift end to the uprising. The survivors fled south . . . here . . . along the coast."

He indicated the route with his fingers.

"The kingdom waited for a while, expecting the errant slaves to return of their own volition. When they didn't, a troop of cavalry was sent to overtake them and bring them back. They overtook the slaves here, forcing them back into the mountains, and a mighty battle ensued. The slaves were triumphant, and the cavalry was destroyed."

He indicated a point in the southern portion of the mountain range.

"Aren't you going to tell about the battle?" Ran-tu interrupted.

"That is a story in itself . . . requiring separate payment." Hakiem smiled.

The boy bit his lip and said nothing more.

"In the course of their battle with the cavalry, the slaves discovered a pass through the mountains, allowing them to enter this green valley where game was plentiful and crops sprang from the ground. They called it Sanctuary."

"The valley isn't green," an urchin interrupted pointedly.

"That's because the slaves were dumb and overworked the land," countered another.

"My dad used to be a farmer, and he didn't overwork the land!" argued a third.

"Then how is it you had to move into town when the sands took your farm?" countered the second.

"I want to hear my story!" barked Ran-tu, suddenly towering above them.

The group subsided into silence.

"The young gentleman there has the facts of the matter right," smiled Hakiem, pointing a finger at the second urchin. "But it took time. Oh my, yes, lots of time. As the slaves exhausted the land to the north, they moved south, until they reached the point where the town stands today. Here they met a group of native fishermen, and between fishing and farming managed to survive in peace and tranquility."

"That didn't last long," snorted Ran-tu, momentarily forgetting himself.

"No," agreed Hakiem. "The gods did not will it so. Rumors of a discovery of gold and silver reached the kingdom of Ilsig and brought intruders into our tranquility. First adventurers, and finally a fleet from the kingdom itself to capture the town and again bring it under the kingdom's control. The only fly in the kingdom's victory wine that day was that most of the fishing fleet was out when they arrived, and, realizing the fate of the town, took refuge on Scavengers' Island to form the nucleus of the Cape Pirates, who harass ships to this day."

A fisherman's wife passed by and, glancing down, recognized the map in the dust, smiled, and tossed two copper coins to Hakiem. He caught them neatly, elbowing an urchin who tried to intercept them, and secreted them in his sash.

"Blessings on your house, mistress," he called after his benefactor.

"What about the empire?" Ran-tu prompted, afraid of losing his story.

"What? Oh, yes. It seems that one of the adventurers pushed north seeking the mythical gold, found a pass through the Civa, and eventually joined the Rankan Empire. Later, his grandson, now a general in the empire, found his ancestor's journals. He led a force south over his grandfather's old route and recaptured the town. Using it as a base, he launched a naval attack around the cape and finally captured the kingdom of Ilsig, making it a part of the empire forever."

"Which is where we are today," one of the urchins spat bitterly.

"Not quite," corrected Hakiem, his impatience to be done with the story yielding to his integrity as a tale-spinner. "Though the kingdom surrendered, for some reason the mountain men continued to resist the empire's attempts to use the Great Pass. That was when the caravan routes were established."

A faraway look came into his eyes.

"Those were the days of Sanctuary's greatness. Three or four caravans a week laden with treasure and trade goods. Not the miserable supply caravans you see today—great caravans that took half a day just to enter town."

"What happened?" asked one of the awestruck urchins.

Hakiem's eyes grew dark. He spat in the dust.

"Twenty years ago, the empire succeeded in putting down the mountain men. With the Great Pass open, there was no reason to risk major caravans in the bandit-ridden sands of the desert. Sanctuary has become a mockery of its past glory, a refuge for the scum who have nowhere else to go. Mark my words, one day the thieves will outnumber the honest citizenry, and then . . ."

"One side, old man!"

A sandaled foot came down on the map, obliterating its outlines and scattering the urchins.

Hakiem cowered before the shadow of one of the Hell Hounds, the five new elite guards who had accompanied the new governor into town.

"Zalbar! Stop that!"

The unsmiling giant froze at the sound of the voice and turned to face the golden-haired youth who strode onto the scene.

"We're supposed to be governing these people, not bludgeoning them into submission."

It seemed strange, seeing a lad in his late teens chastising a scarred veteran of many campaigns, but the larger man merely dropped his eyes in discomfort.

"Apologies, Your Highness, but the emperor said we were to bring law and order to this hellhole, and it's the only language these blackguards understand."

"The emperor—my brother—put me in command of this town to govern it as I see fit, and my orders are that the people are to be treated kindly as long as they do not break the laws."

"Yes, Your Highness."

The youth turned to Hakiem. "I hope we did not disturb your story. Here—perhaps this will make up for our intrusion."

He pressed a gold coin into Hakiem's hand.

"Gold!" Hakiem sneered. "Do you think one miserable coin can make up for scaring those precious children?"

"What?" roared the Hell Hound. "Those gutter-rats? Take the prince's money and be thankful I—"

"Zalbar!"

"But, Your Highness, this man is only playing on your—"

"If he is, it's mine to give. . . ."

He pressed a few more coins into Hakiem's outstretched hand.

"Now come along. I want to see the bazaar."

Hakiem bowed low, ignoring the Hell Hound's black glare. When he straightened, the urchins were clustered about him again.

"Was that the prince?"

"My dad says he's the best thing for this town."

"My dad says he's too young to do a good job."

"Izzat so!?"

"The emperor sent him here to get him out of the way."

"Sez who?"

"Sez my brother! He's been bribing guards here all his life and never had any trouble till the prince came. Him and his whores and his Hell Hounds."

"They're going to change everything. Ask Hakiem. . . . Hakiem?"

The urchins turned to their chosen mentor, but Hakiem had long since departed with his new wealth for the cool depths of a tavern.

Three
The Plan

"As you already know, you five men have been chosen to remain with me here in Sanctuary after the balance of the honor guard returns to the capital."

Prince Kadakithis paused to look each man in the face before he continued. Zalbar, Bourne, Quag, Razkuli, and Annan. Each of them a seasoned veteran, they doubtless knew their work better than the prince knew his. Kadakithis' royal upbringing came to his rescue, helping him to hide his nervousness as he met their gazes steadily.

"As soon as the ceremonies are completed tomorrow, I will be swamped with problems in clearing up the backlog of cases in the civil court. Realizing that, I thought it best to give you your briefing and assignments now, so that you will be able to proceed without the delay of waiting for specific instructions."

He beckoned the men forward, and they gathered around the map of Sanctuary hung on the wall.

"Zalbar and I have done some preliminary scouting of the town. Though this briefing should familiarize you with the basic lay of the land, you should each do your own exploring and report any new observations to each other. Zalbar?"

The tallest of the soldiers stepped forward and swept his hand across the map.

"The thieves of Sanctuary drift with wind like the garbage they are—" he began.

"Zalbar!" the prince admonished. "Just give the report without asides or opinions."

"Yes, Your Highness," the man replied, bowing his head slightly. "But there is a pattern here which follows the winds from the east."

"The property values change because of the smells," Kadakithis reported. "You can say that without referring to the people as garbage. They are still citizens of the empire."

Zalbar nodded and turned to the map once more.

"The areas of least crime are here, along the eastern edge of town," he announced, gesturing. "These are the richest mansions, inns, and temples, which have their own defenses and safeguards. West of them, the town consists predominantly of craftsmen and skilled workers. The crime in this area rarely exceeds petty theft."

The man paused to glance at the prince before continuing.

"Once you cross the Processional, however, things get steadily worse. The merchants vie with each other as to who will carry the widest selection of stolen or illicit goods. Much of their merchandise is supplied by smugglers who openly use the wharves to unload their ships. What is not purchased by the merchants is sold directly at the bazaar."

Zalbar's expression hardened noticeably as he indicated the next area.

"Here is a tangle of streets known simply as the Maze. It is acknowledged by all to be the roughest section of town. Murder and armed robbery are commonplace occurrences day or night in the Maze, and most honest citizens are afraid to set foot there without an armed escort. It has been brought to our attention that none of the guardsmen in the local garrison will enter this area, though whether this is out of fear or if they have been bribed . . ."

The prince cleared his throat noisily. Zalbar grimaced and moved on to another area.

"Outside the walls to the north of town is a cluster of brothels and gaming houses. There are few crimes reported in this area, though we believe this is due more to a reluctance on the part of the inhabitants to deal with authorities than from any lack of criminal activity. To the far west of town is a shantytown inhabited by beggars and derelicts known as the Downwinders. Of all the citizens we've encountered so far, they seem the most harmless."

His report complete, Zalbar returned to his place with the others as the prince addressed them once again.

"Your priorities until new orders are issued will be as follows," he announced, eyeing the men carefully. "First, you are to make a concentrated effort to reduce or eliminate petty crime on the east side of town. Second, you will close the wharves to the smuggler traffic. When that is done, I will sign into law certain regulations enabling you to move against the brothels. By that time, my court duties should have eased to a point where we can formulate a specific plan of action for dealing with the Maze. Any questions?"

"Are you anticipating any problems with the local priesthood over the ordered construction of new temples to Savankala, Sabellia, and Vashanka?" Bourne asked.

"Yes, I am," the prince acknowledged. "But the difficulties will probably be more diplomatic than criminal in nature. As such, I will attend to it personally, leaving you free to pursue your given assignments."

There were no further questions, and the prince steeled himself for his final pronouncement.

"As to how you are to conduct yourselves while carrying out your orders . . ." Kadakithis paused dramatically while sweeping the assemblage with a hard glare. "I know you men are all soldiers and used to meeting opposition with bared steel. You are certainly permitted to fight to defend yourselves if attacked or to defend any citizen of this town. However, I will not tolerate brutality or needless bloodshed in the name of the empire. Whatever your personal feelings may be, you are not to draw a sword on any citizen unless they have proven—I repeat, *proven*—themselves to be criminal. The townsfolk have already taken to calling you Hell Hounds. Be sure that title refers only to the vigor with which you pursue your duties and not to your viciousness. That is all."

There were mutters and dark glances as the men filed out of the room. While the Hell Hounds' loyalty to the empire was above question, Kadakithis had pause to wonder if in their own minds they truly considered him a representative of that empire.

Sentences of Death

John Brunner

One

It was a measure of the decline in Sanctuary's fortunes that the scriptorium of Master Melilot occupied a prime location fronting on Governor's Walk. The nobleman whose grandfather had caused a fine family mansion to be erected on the site had wasted his substance in gambling, and at last was reduced to eking out his days in genteel drunkenness in an improvised fourth story of wattle and daub, laid out across the original roof, while downstairs Melilot installed his increasingly large staff and went into the book—as well as the epistle—business. On hot days the stench from the bindery, where size was boiled and leather embossed, bid fair to match the reek around Shambles Cross.

Not all fortunes, be it understood, were declining. Melilot's was an instance. Ten years earlier he had owned nothing but his clothing and a scribe's compendium; then he worked in the open air, or huddled under some tolerant merchant's awning, and his customers were confined to poor litigants from out of town who needed a written summary of their

cases before appearing in the Hall of Justice, or suspicious illiterate purchasers of goods from visiting traders who wanted written guarantees of
quality.

On a never-to-be-forgotten day, a foolish man instructed him to write
down matter relevant to a lawsuit then in progress, which would
assuredly have convinced the judge had it been produced without the
opposition being warned. Melilot realized that, and made an extra copy.
He was richly rewarded.

Now, as well as carrying on the scribe's profession—by proxy,
mostly—he specialized in forgery, blackmail, and mistranslation. He was
exactly the sort of employer Jarveena of Forgotten Holt had been hoping
for when she arrived, particularly since his condition, which might be
guessed at from his beardless face and roly-poly fatness, made him indifferent to the age or appearance of his employees.

The services offered by the scriptorium, and the name of its proprietor,
were clearly described in half a dozen languages and three distinct modes
of writing on the stone face of the building, a window and a door of
which had been knocked into one large entry (at some risk to the stabil-
ity of the upper floors) so that clients might wait under cover until someone who understood the language they required was available.

Jarveena read and wrote her native tongue well: Yenized. That was
why Melilot had agreed to hire her. No competing service in Sanctuary
could offer so many languages now. But two months might go by—
indeed, they just had done so—without a single customer's asking for a
translation into or from Yenized, which made her pretty much of a status
symbol. She was industriously struggling with Rankene, the courtly version of the common dialect, because merchants liked to let it be thought
their goods were respectable enough for sale to the nobility even if they
had come ashore by night from Scavengers' Island, and she was making
good headway with the quotidian street-talk in which the poorer clients
wanted depositions of evidence or contracts of sale made out. Nonetheless she was still obliged to take on menial tasks to fill her time.

It was noon, and another such task was due.

Plainly, it was of little use relying on inscriptions to reach those who
were most in need of a scribe's assistance; accordingly Melilot maintained a squad of small boys with peculiarly sweet and piercing voices,
who paraded up and down the nearby streets advertising his service by

shouting, wheedling, and sometimes begging. It was a tiring occupation, and the children frequently grew hoarse. Thrice a day, therefore, someone was commanded to deliver them a nourishing snack of bread and cheese and a drink made of honey, water, a little wine or strong ale, and assorted spices. Since her engagement, Jarveena had been least often involved in other duties when the time for this one arrived. Hence she was on the street, distributing Melilot's bounty, when an officer whom she knew by name and sight turned up, acting in a most peculiar manner. He was Captain Aye-Gophlan, from the guard post at the corner of the Processional.

He scarcely noticed her as he went by, but that was less than surprising. She looked very much like a boy herself—more so, if anything, than the chubby-cheeked blond urchin she was issuing rations to. When Melilot took her on she had been in rags, and he had insisted on buying her new clothes of which, inevitably, the price would be docked from her minuscule commission on the work she did. She didn't care. She only insisted in turn that she be allowed to choose her garb: a short-sleeved leather jerkin cross-laced up the front; breeches to midcalf; boots to tuck the breeches into; a baldric on which to hang her scribe's compendium with its reed-pens and ink-block and water-pot and sharpening knife and rolls of rough reed-paper; and a cloak to double as covering at night. She had a silver pin for it—her only treasure.

Melilot had laughed, thinking he understood. He owned a pretty girl a year shy of the fifteen Jarveena admitted to, who customarily boxed the ears of his boy apprentices when they waylaid her in a dark passageway to steal a kiss, and that was unusual enough to demand explanation.

But that had nothing to do with it. No more did the fact that with her tanned skin, thin build, close-cropped black hair, and many visible scars, she scarcely resembled a girl regardless of her costume. There were plenty of ruffians—some of noble blood—who were totally indifferent to the sex of the youngsters they raped.

Besides, to Jarveena such experiences were survivable; had they not been, she would not have reached Sanctuary. So she no longer feared them.

But they made her deeply—bitterly—angry. And someday one who deserved her anger more than any was going to pay for at least one of his countless crimes. She had sworn so . . . but she had been only nine then, and with the passage of time the chance of vengeance grew more and more remote. Now she scarcely believed in it. Sometimes she dreamed of doing to another what had been done to her, and woke moaning with shame, and she could not explain why to the other apprentice scribes sharing the dormitory that once had been the bedroom of the noble who now snored and vomited and groaned and snored under a shelter fit rather for hogs than humans the wrong side of his magnificently painted ceiling.

She regretted that. She liked most of her companions; some were from respectable families, for there were no schools here apart from temple schools whose priests had the bad habit of stuffing children's heads with myth and legend as though they were to live in a world of make-believe instead of fending for themselves. Without learning to read and write at least their own language they would be at risk of cheating by every smart operator in the city. But how could she befriend those who had led soft, secure lives, who at the advanced age of fifteen or sixteen had never yet had to scrape a living from gutters and garbage piles?

Captain Aye-Gophlan was in mufti. Or thought he was. He was by no means so rich as to be able to afford clothing apart from his uniforms, of which it was compulsory for the guards to own several—this one for the emperor's birthday, that one for the feast of the regiment's patron deity, another for day-watch duty, yet another for night-watch duty, another for funeral drill. . . . The common soldiers were luckier. If they failed in their attire, the officers were blamed for stinginess. But how long was it since there had been enough caravans through here for the guard to keep up the finery required of them out of bribes? Times indeed were hard when the best disguise an officer on private business could contrive was a plum-blue overcloak with a hole in it exactly where his crotch armor could glint through.

Seeing him, Jarveena thought suddenly about justice. Or more nearly, about getting even. Perhaps there was no longer any hope of bringing to account the villain who had killed her parents and sacked their estate, enslaved the able-bodied, turned loose his half-mad troops on children to glut the lust of their loins amid the smoke and crashing of beams as the village its inhabitants called Holt vanished from the stage of history.

But there were other things to do with her life. Hastily she snatched back the cup she had already allowed to linger too long in the grasp of this, luckily the last of Melilot's publicity boys. She cut short an attempt at complaint with a scowl which drew her forehead skin down just far enough to reveal a scar normally covered by her forelock.

That was a resource she customarily reserved until all else failed. It had its desired effect; the boy gulped and surrendered the cup and went back to work, pausing only to urinate against the wall.

Two

Just as Jarveena expected, Aye-Gophlan marched stolidly around the block, occasionally glancing back as though feeling insecure without his regular escort of six tall men, and made for the rear entrance to the scriptorium—the one in the crooked alley where the silk-traders were concentrated. Not all of Melilot's customers cared to be seen walking in off a populous and sunny roadway.

Jarveena thrust the wine jar, dish, and cup she was carrying into the hands of an apprentice too young to argue, and ordered them returned to the kitchen—next to the bindery, with which it shared a fire. Then she stole up behind Aye-Gophlan and uttered a discreet cough.

"May I be of assistance, Captain?"

"Ah—!" The officer was startled; his hand flew to something stick-shaped under his cloak, no doubt a tightly rolled scroll. "Ah . . . Good day to you! I have a problem concerning which I desire to consult your master."

"He will be taking his noon meal," Jarveena said in a suitably humble tone. "Let me conduct you to him."

Melilot never cared to have either his meals or the naps which followed them interrupted. But there was something about Aye-Gophlan's behavior which made Jarveena certain that this was an exceptional occasion.

She opened the door of Melilot's sanctum, announced the caller rapidly enough to forestall her employer's rage at being distracted from the immense broiled lobster lying before him on a silver platter, and wished there were some means of eavesdropping on what transpired.

But he was infinitely too cautious to risk that.

At best Jarveena had hoped for a few coins by way of bonus if Aye-Gophlan's business proved profitable. She was much surprised, therefore, to be summoned to Melilot's room half an hour later.

Aye-Gophlan was still present. The lobster had grown cold, untouched, but much wine had been consumed.

On her entrance, the officer gave her a suspicious glare.

"This is the fledgling you imagine could unravel the mystery?" he demanded.

Jarveena's heart sank. What devious subterfuge was Melilot up to now? But she waited meekly for clear instructions. They came at once, in the fat man's high and slightly whining voice.

"The captain has a writing to decipher. Sensibly, he has brought it to us, who can translate more foreign tongues than any similar firm! It is possible that it may be in Yenized, with which you are familiar . . . though, alas, I am not."

Jarveena barely suppressed a giggle. If the document were in any known script or language, Melilot would certainly recognize it—whether or not he could furnish a translation. That implied—hmm! A cipher! How interesting! How did an officer of the guard come by a message in code he couldn't read? She looked expectant, though not eager, and with much reluctance Aye-Gophlan handed her the scroll.

Without appearing to look up, she registered a tiny nod from Melilot. She was to agree with him.

But—

What in the *world?* Only a tremendous self-control prevented her from letting fall the document. Merely glancing at it made her dizzy, as though her eyes were crossing against her will. For a second she had seemed to read it clearly, and a heartbeat later . . .

She took a firm grip on herself. "I believe this to be Yenized, as you suspected, sir," she declared.

"Believe?" Aye-Gophlan rasped. "But Melilot swore you could read it instantly!"

"Modern Yenized I can, Captain," Jarveena amplified. "I recognize this as a high and courtly style, as difficult for a person like myself as imperial Rankene would be for a herdsman accustomed to sleeping with the swine." It was always politic to imply one's own inferiority when talking to someone like this. "Luckily, thanks to my master's extensive library, I've gained a wider knowledge of the subject in recent weeks; and with the help of some of the books he keeps I would expect to get at least its gist."

"How long would it take?" Aye-Gophlan demanded.

"Oh, one might safely say two or three days," Melilot interpolated in a tone that brooked no contradiction. "Given that it's so unusual an assignment, there would naturally be no charge except on production of a satisfactory rendering."

Jarveena almost dropped the scroll a second time. Never in living memory had Melilot accepted a commission without taking at least half his fee in advance. There must be something quite exceptional about this sheet of paper—

And of course there was. It dawned on her that moment, and she had to struggle to prevent her teeth from chattering.

"Wait here," the fat man said, struggling to his feet. "I shall return when I've escorted the captain out."

The moment the door closed she threw the scroll down on the table next to the lobster—wishing, irrelevantly, that it were not still intact, so she might snatch a morsel without being detected. The writing writhed into new patterns even as she tried not to notice.

Then Melilot was back, resuming his chair, sipping from his half-full wine cup.

"You're astute, you little weasel!" he said in a tone of grudging admiration. "Are you quick-witted enough to know precisely why neither he nor I—nor you!—can read that writing?"

Jarveena swallowed hard. "There's a spell on it," she offered after a pause.

"Yes! Yes, there is! Better than any code or cipher. Except for the eyes of the intended recipient, it will never read the same way twice."

"How is it that the captain didn't realize?"

Melilot chuckled. "You don't have to read and write to become a captain of the guard," he said. "He can about manage to tell whether the clerk who witnesses his mark on the watch-report is holding the page right side up; but anything more complicated and his head starts to swim anyway."

He seized the lobster, tore off a claw, and cracked it between his teeth; oil ran down his chin and dripped on his green robe. Picking out the meat, he went on. "But what's interesting is how he came by it. Make a guess."

Jarveena shook her head.

"One of the imperial bodyguards from Ranke, one of the detachment who escorted the prince along the Generals' Road, called to inspect the local guardhouse this morning at dawn. Apparently he made himself most unpopular, to the point that, when he let fall that scroll without noticing, Aye-Gophlan thought more of secreting it than giving it back. Why he's ready to believe that an imperial officer would carry a document in Old High Yenized, I can't guess. Perhaps that's part of the magic."

He thrust gobbets of succulent flesh into his mouth and chomped for a while. Jarveena tried not to drool.

To distract herself by the first means to mind, she said, "Why did he tell you all this . . . ? Ah, I'm an idiot. He didn't."

"Correct." Melilot looked smug. "For that you deserve a taste of lobster. Here!" He tossed over a lump that by his standards was generous, and a chunk of bread also; she caught both in midair with stammered thanks and wolfed them down.

"You need to have your strength built up," the portly scribe went on. "I have a very responsible errand for you to undertake tonight."

"Errand?"

"Yes. The imperial officer who lost the scroll is called Commander Nizharu. He and his men are billeted in pavilions in the courtyard of the Governor's Palace; seemingly he's afraid of contamination if they have to go into barracks with the local soldiery.

"After dark this evening you are to steal in and wait on him, and inquire whether he will pay more for the return of his scroll and the name of the man who filched it, or for a convincing but fraudulent translation which will provoke the unlawful possessor into some rash action. For all I can guess," he concluded sanctimoniously, "he may have let it fall deliberately. *Hmm?*"

Three

It was far from the first time since her arrival that Jarveena had been out after curfew. It was not even the first time she had had to scamper in shadow across the broad expanse of Governor's Walk in order to reach and scramble over the palace wall, nimble as a monkey despite the mass of scar tissue where her right breast would never grow. Much practice enabled her to whip off her cloak, roll it into a cylinder not much thicker than a money belt, fasten it around her, and rush up the convenient hand- and toeholds in the outer wall which were carefully not repaired, and for a fat consideration, when the chief mason undertook his annual repointing.

But it was definitely the first time she had had to contend with crack soldiers from Ranke on the other side. One of them, by ill chance, was relieving himself behind a flowering shrub as she descended, and needed to do no more than thrust the haft of his pike between her legs. She gasped and went sprawling.

But Melilot had foreseen all this, and she was prepared with her story and the evidence to back it up.

"Don't hurt me, please! I don't mean any harm!" she whimpered, making her voice as childish as possible. There was a torch guttering in a sconce nearby; the soldier heaved her to her feet by her right wrist, his grip as cruel as a trap's, and forced her toward it. A sergeant appeared from the direction of the pavilions which since her last visit had sprouted like mushrooms between the entry to the Hall of Justice and the clustered granaries on the northwest side of the grounds.

"What you got?" he rumbled in a threatening bass voice.

"Sir, I mean no harm! I have to do what my mistress tells me, or I'll be nailed to the temple door!"

That took both of them aback. The soldier somewhat relaxed his fingers and the sergeant bent close to look her over better in the wan torchlight.

"By that, I take it you serve a priestess of Argash?" he said eventually.

It was a logical deduction. On the twenty-foot-high fane of that divinity his most devoted followers volunteered, when life wearied them, to be hung up and fast unto death.

But Jarveena shook her head violently.

"N-no, sir! Dyareela!"—naming a goddess banned these thirty years owing to the bloodthirstiness of her votaries.

The sergeant frowned. "I saw no shrine to *her* when we escorted the prince along Temple Avenue!"

"N-no, sir! Her temple was destroyed, but her worshipers endure!"

"Do they now!" the sergeant grunted. "Hmm! That sounds like something the commander ought to know!"

"Is that Commander Nizharu?" Jarveena said eagerly.

"What? How do you know his name?"

"My mistress sent me to him! She saw him early today when he was abroad in the city, and she was so taken with his handsomeness that she resolved at once to send a message to him. But it was all to be in secret!" Jarveena let a quaver enter her voice. "Now I've let it out, and she'll turn me over to the priests of Argash, and . . . Oh, I'm done for! I might as well be dead right now!"

"Dying can wait," the sergeant said, reaching an abrupt decision. "But the commander will definitely want to know about the Dyareelans. I thought only madmen in the desert paid attention to that old bitch nowadays. . . . Hello, what's this at your side?" He lifted it into the light. "A writing case, is it?"

"Yes, sir. That's what I mainly do for my mistress."

"If you can write, why deliver messages yourself? That's what I always say. Oh, well, I guess you're her confidante, are you?"

Jarveena nodded vigorously.

"A secret shared is a secret no longer, and here's one more proof of the proverb. Oh, come along!"

By the light of two lamps filled, to judge by their smell, with poor-grade fish oil, Nizharu was turning the contents of his pavilion upside down, with not even an orderly to help him. He had cleared out two brass-bound wooden chests and was beginning on a third, while the bedding from his field couch of wood and canvas was strewn on the floor, and a dozen bags and pouches had been emptied and not repacked.

He was furious when the sergeant raised the tent flap and roared that he was not to be disturbed. But Jarveena took in the situation at a glance and said in a clear firm voice, "I wonder if you're looking for a scroll."

Nizharu froze, his face turned so that light fell on it. He was as fair a man as she had ever seen: his hair like washed wool, his eyes like chips of summer sky. Under a nose keen as a bird's beak, his thin lips framed well-kept teeth marred by a chip off the right upper front incisor. He was lean and obviously very strong, for he was turning over a chest that must weigh a hundred pounds and his biceps were scarcely bulging.

"Scroll?" he said softly, setting down the chest. "What scroll?"

It was very hard for Jarveena to reply. She felt her heart was going to stop. The world wavered. It took all her force to maintain her balance. Distantly she heard the sergeant say, "She didn't mention any scroll to us!"

And, amazingly, she was able to speak for herself again.

"That's true, Commander," she said. "I had to lie to those men to stop them killing me before I got to you. I'm sorry." Meantime she was silently thanking the network of informers who kept Melilot so well supplied with information that the lie had been credible even to these strangers. "But I think this morning you mislaid a scroll . . . ?"

Nizharu hesitated a single moment. Then he rapped, "Out! Leave the boy here!"

Boy? Oh, miracle! If Jarveena had believed in a deity, now was when she would have resolved to make sacrifice for gratitude. For that implied he hadn't recognized her.

She waited while the puzzled sergeant and soldier withdrew, mouth dry, palms moist, a faint singing in her ears. Nizharu slammed the lid of the chest he had been about to overturn, sat down on it, and said, "Now explain! And the explanation had better be a good one!"

It was. It was excellent. Melilot had devised it with great care and drilled her through it a dozen times during the afternoon. It was tinged with just enough of the truth to be convincing.

Aye-Gophlan, notoriously, had accepted bribes. (So had everyone in the guard who might possibly be useful to anybody wealthier than himself, but that was by the by.) It had consequently occurred to Melilot—a most loyal and law-abiding citizen, who as all his acquaintance would swear had loudly welcomed the appointment of the prince, the new governor, and looked forward to the city being reformed—it had occurred to him that perhaps this was part of a plan. One could scarcely conceive of a high-ranking imperial officer being so casual with what was obviously a top-secret document. *Could* one?

"Never," murmured Nizharu, but sweat beaded his lip.

Next came the tricky bit. Everything depended on whether the commander wanted to keep the mere existence of the scroll a secret. Now he knew Aye-Gophlan had it, it was open to him to summon his men and march down to the guardhouse and search it floor to rooftree, for—according to what Jarveena said, at any rate—Aye-Gophlan was far too cautious to leave it overnight in the custody of a mere scribe. He would return on his next duty-free day, the day after tomorrow or the day after that, depending on which of his fellow officers he could exchange with.

But Melilot had deduced that if the scroll were so important that Nizharu kept it by him even when undertaking a mundane tour of inspection, it must be very private indeed. He was, apparently, correct. Nizharu listened with close attention and many nods to the alternative plan of action.

For a consideration, Melilot was prepared to furnish a false translation designed to jar Aye-Gophlan into doing something for which Nizharu could safely arrest him, without it ever being known that he had enjoyed temporary possession of a scroll which by rights should have remained in the commander's hands. Let him only specify the terms, and it would be as good as done.

When she—whom Nizharu still believed a he, for which she was profoundly glad—finished talking, the commander pondered awhile. At length he started to smile, though it never reached his eyes, and in firm clear terms expressed his conditions for entering into a compact along the lines Melilot proposed. He capped all by handing over two gold coins, of a type she did not recognize, with a promise that he would have her (his) hide if they did not both reach Melilot, and a large silver token of the kind used at Ilsig for himself.

Then he instructed a soldier she had not met to escort her to the gate and across Governor's Walk. But she gave the man the slip as soon as they were clear of the palace grounds and rushed toward the back entry, via Silk Corner.

Melilot being rich, he could afford locks on his doors; he had given her a heavy bronze key, which she had concealed in her writing case. She fumbled it into the lock, but before she could turn it the door swung wide and she stepped forward as though impelled by another person's will.

This was the street—or rather alley. This was the door with its over-hanging porch. Outside everything was right.

But inside everything was absolutely, utterly, unqualifiedly *wrong*.

Four

Jarveena wanted to cry out, but found herself unable to draw enough breath. A vast sluggishness took possession of her muscles, as though she were descending into glue. Taking one more step, she knew, would tire her to the point of exhaustion; accordingly she concentrated merely on looking about her, and within seconds was wishing that she hadn't.

A wan, greyish light suffused the place. It showed her high stone walls on either side, a stone-flagged floor underfoot, but nothing above except drifting mist that sometimes took on an eerie pale color: pinkish, bluish, or the sickly phosphorescent shade of dying fish. Before her was nothing but a long table, immensely and ridiculously long, such that one might seat a full company of soldiers at it. A shiver tried to crawl down her spine, but failed thanks to the weird paralysis that gripped her. For what she was seeing matched in every respect the descriptions, uttered in a whisper, which she had heard of the home of Enas Yorl. In all the land there were but three Great Wizards powerful enough not to care that their true names were noised abroad: one was at Ranke and served the needs of the court; one was at Ilsig and accounted the most skillful; the third, by reason of some scandal, made do with the slim pickings at Sanctuary, and that was Enas Yorl.

But how could he be here? His palace was on—or, more exactly, below—Pyrtanis Street, where the city petered out to the southeast of Temple Avenue.

Except . . .

The thought burgeoned from memory and she fought against it, and failed. Someone had once explained to her:

Except when it is somewhere else.

Abruptly it was as though the table shrank, and from an immense distance its farther end drew close and along with it a high-backed, throne-like chair in which sat a curious personage. He was arrayed in an enormously full, many-layered cloak of some dull brown stuff, and wore a high-crowned hat whose broad brim somehow contrived to shadow his face against even the directionless grey light that obtained here.

But within that shadow two red gleams like embers showed, approximately where a human's eyes would be.

This individual held in his right hand a scroll, partly unrolled, and with his left he was tapping on the table. The proportions of his fingers were abnormal, and one or two of them seemed either to lack, or to be overprovided with, joints. One of his nails sparkled luridly, but that ceased after a little.

Raising his head, after a fashion, he spoke.

"A girl. Interesting. But one who has . . . suffered. Was it punishment?"

It felt to Jarveena as though the gaze of those two dull red orbs could penetrate her flesh as well as her clothing. She could say nothing, but had nothing to say.

"No," pronounced the wizard—for surely it must be none other. He let the scroll drop on the table, and it formed itself into a tidy roll at once, while he rose and approached her. A gesture, as though to sketch her outline in the air, freed her from the lassitude that had hampered her limbs. But she had too much sense to break and run.

Whither?

"Do you know me?"

"I . . ." She licked dry lips. "I think you may be Enas Yorl."

"Fame at last," the wizard said wryly. "Do you know why you're here?"

"You . . . Well, I guess you set a trap for me. I don't know why, unless it has to do with that scroll."

"Hmm! A perceptive child!" Had he possessed eyebrows, one might have imagined the wizard raising them. And then at once: "Forgive me. I should not have said 'child.' You are old in the ways of the world, if not in years. But after the first century, such patronizing remarks come easy to the tongue. . . ." He resumed his chair, inviting Jarveena with a gesture to come closer. She was reluctant.

For when he rose to inspect her, he had been squat. Under the cloak he was obviously thickset, stocky, with a paunch. But by the time he regained his seat, it was equally definite that he was thin, light-boned, and had one shoulder higher than the other.

"You have noticed," he said. His voice too had altered; it had been baritone, while now it was at the most flattering a countertenor. "Victims of circumstance, you and I both. It was not I who set a trap for you. The scroll did."

"For me? But *why*?"

"I speak with imprecision. The trap was set not for you qua you. It was set for someone to whom it meant the death of another. I judge that you qualify, whether or not you know it. Do you? Make a guess. Trust your imagination. Have you, for example, recognized anybody who came to the city recently?"

Jarveena felt the blood drain from her cheeks. She folded her hands into fists.

"Sir, you are a great magician. I recognized someone tonight. Someone I never dreamed of meeting again. Someone whose death I would gladly accomplish, except that death is much too good for him."

"Explain!" Enas Yorl leaned an elbow on the table, and rested his chin on his fist . . . except that neither the elbow nor the chin, let alone the fist, properly corresponded to such appellations.

She hesitated a second. Then she cast aside her cloak, tore loose the bow that held the cross-lacing of her jerkin at her throat, and unthreaded it so that the garment fell wide to reveal the cicatrices, brown on brown, which would never fade, and the great foul keloid like a turd where her right breast might have been.

"Why try to hide anything from a wizard?" she said bitterly. "He commanded the men who did this to me, and far far worse to many others. I thought they were bandits! I came to Sanctuary hoping that here if anywhere I might get wind of them—how could bandits gain access to Ranke or the conquered cities? But I never dreamed they would present themselves in the guise of imperial guards!"

"*They* . . . ?" Enas Yorl probed.

"Ah . . . No. I confess: it's only one that I can swear to."

"How old were you?"

"I was nine. And six grown men took pleasure of me, before they beat me with wire whips and left me for dead."

"I see." He retrieved the scroll and with its end tapped the table absently. "Can you now divine what is in this message? Bear in mind that it forced me hither."

"Forced? But I'd have thought—"

"I found myself here by choice? Oh, the contrary!" A bitter laugh rang out, acid-shrill. "I said we're both victims. Long ago when I was young I was extremely foolish. I tried to seduce away the bride of someone more powerful than me. When he found out, I was able to defend myself, but . . . Do you understand what a spell is?"

She shook her head.

"It's . . . activity. As much activity as a rock is passivity, which is conscious of being a rock but of nothing else. A worm is a little more aware; a dog or horse, much more; a human being, vastly more—but not infinitely more. In wildfire, storms, stars, can be found processes which with no consciousness of what they are act upon the outside world. A spell is such a process, created by an act of will, having neither aim nor purpose save what its creator lends. And to me my rival bequeathed . . . But no matter. I begin to sound as though I pity myself, and I know my fate is just. Shall we despise justice? This scroll can be an instrument of it. Written on it are two sentences.

"Of death."

While he spoke, there had been further changes under his concealing garb. His voice was now mellow and rich, and his hands, although very slender, possessed the ordinary number of joints. However, the redness still glowed.

"If one sentence is upon Commander Nizharu," Jarveena said firmly, "may it be executed soon."

"That could be arranged." A sardonic inflection colored the words. "At a price."

"The scroll doesn't refer to him? I imagined—"

"You imagined it spelt his doom, and that was why he was so anxious about its loss? In a way that's correct. In a way . . . And I can make certain that that shall be the outcome. At a price."

"What—price?" Her voice quavered against her will.

He rose slowly from his chair, shaking his cloak out to its fullest; it swept the floor with a faint rustling sound.

"Need you ask, of one who so plainly is obsessed by lust for women? That was the reason for my downfall. I explained."

Ice seemed to form around her heart. Her mouth was desert on the instant.

"Oh, why be so timid?" purred Enas Yorl, taking her hand in his. "You've endured many worse bedfellows. I promise."

It was true enough that the only means she had found to cross the weary leagues between Forgotten Holt and Sanctuary had been to yield her body: to merchants, mercenaries, grooms, guardsmen . . .

"Tell me first," she said with a final flare of spirit, "whose deaths are cited in the document."

"Fair," said the wizard. "Know, then, that one is an unnamed man, who is to be falsely convicted of the murder of another. And that the other is the new governor, the prince."

Thereupon the light faded, and he embraced her unresisting.

Five

She woke late, at least half an hour past dawn. She was in her own bed; the dormitory was otherwise empty. All her limbs were pervaded by a delicious languor. Enas Yorl had kept his promise. If he had been equally skilled when he was younger, small wonder his rival's bride had preferred him to her husband!

Reluctantly opening her eyes, she saw something on the rough pillow. Puzzled, she looked again, reached out, touched: green, iridescent, powdery—

Scales!

With a cry she leapt from the bed, just as Melilot marched in, redfaced with fury.

"So there you are, you little slut! Where were you all night? I watched until I could stay awake no longer! By now I was sure you'd been taken by the guard and thrown in jail! *What did Nizharu say?*"

Naked, bewildered, for a long moment Jarveena was at a loss. Then her eye fell on something infinitely reassuring. On the wooden peg over her bed hung her cloak, jerkin, and breeches, and also her precious writing-case, just as though she herself had replaced them on retiring.

Seizing the case, she opened the compartment where she hid such things, and triumphantly produced the gold she had accepted from the commander—but not the silver he had allotted to herself.

"He paid this for a false rendering of the scroll," she said. "But you're not to make one."

"What?" Snatching the coins, Melilot made to bite them, but checked.

"How would you like to be scribe by appointment to the governor's household?"

"Are you crazed?" The fat man's eyes bulbed.

"Not in the least." Heedless of his presence, Jarveena reached under the bed for her chamber pot and put it to its appropriate use. Meantime she explained the plot she had hatched.

"But this means you're claiming to have read the scroll," Melilot said slowly as he tried to digest her proposals. "It's enchanted! How could you?"

"Not I, but Enas Yorl."

Melilot's mouth worked and all his color drained away. "But his palace is guarded by basilisks!" he exclaimed at last. "You'd have been struck to stone!"

"It doesn't quite work like that," Jarveena said, pulling on her breeches, giving silent thanks that she could do so briskly. That dreadful paralysis would haunt her dreams for years. "To settle the argument, though, why don't you bring the scroll? I mean, why don't we go and take another look at it?"

They were in his sanctum a couple of minutes later.

"It's perfectly clear," Melilot said slowly when he had perused the document twice. "It's very stilted—formal Rankene—and I don't know anybody here or in the conquered cities who would use it for a letter. But it says exactly what you said it would."

A tremor of awe made his rolls of fat wobble.

"You're satisfied it's the same scroll? There's been no substitution?" Jarveena pressed.

"Yes! It's been all night in a locked chest! Only magic can account for what's happened to it!"

"Then," she said with satisfaction, "let's get on with the job."

Each noon, in the grounds of the Governor's Palace before the Hall of Justice, the guard was inspected and rotated. This ceremony was open to the public—to everybody, in principle, but in practice only to those who could afford to bribe the gate guards. Hence most of the spectators were of the upper class, hangers-on of the nobility, or making an appearance at the law courts. Not a few bore a general resemblance, in figure or clothing and in their retinue, to Melilot, who was in any case a frequent visitor when transcripts of evidence were in demand.

Therefore his presence and Jarveena's were unremarkable. Moreover word had got about that today was the last day when the crack imperial guards would perform the ceremonial drill before fifteen of them were ordered back to Ranke. There was a much larger throng than usual awaiting the appearance of the governor, one of whose customary chores this was whenever he was in residence.

It was a warm, dry, dusty day. The sun cast strong dark shadows. Tents, pavilions, stone walls seemed all of a substance. So in a way did people, especially those in armor. Under closed visors, any soldier might have been mistaken for any other of like stature.

Strictly it was not the turn of a guard detachment from the watch-house on the Processional to take over from the Hell Hounds. But a few bribes, and a sharp order from Aye-Gophlan, and the problem had been sorted out.

Jarveena composed her features and did her best to look as though she were just another casual passerby impressed by the standard of marching of troops from the capital, rather than a person whose dearest ambition for revenge bid fair to be fulfilled.

But her mouth kept wanting to snarl open like a wolf's.

The relieving guard marched in from the direction of Governor's Walk, exchanged salutes and passwords with the imperial troops, and formed up in the center of the courtyard. Attended by two armed orderlies, Commander Nizharu formally recognized his successor and took station at his side for the governor's inspection. As soon as it was over, the departing troops would retire by squads and march away with flying colors.

Less than ten minutes later, amid a ripple of applause at the precision drill of the Hell Hounds, the prince was leaving the parade ground arm-in-arm with Nizharu. The latter was being posted back to the capital, but five of his comrades were to establish a bodyguard of local soldiers for the governor, trained to imperial standards.

So rumor said. Rumor had been known to lie.

With some care and ingenuity, Melilot had smiled and shoved his way to the front of the crowd, and as the two approached and all were bowing, he said very loudly and clearly, "Why, Commander! What good luck! Now is my chance to return the scroll you dropped yesterday morning!"

Nizharu had raised his visor because of the heat. It could clearly be seen that his face grew pasty-pale. "I—I know nothing of any scroll!" he barked as soon as he could gather his wits.

"No? Oh, in that case, if it isn't yours, I'm sure the prince will accept it from me with a view to tracing its rightful owner!"

Fat though he was, Melilot could act briskly when he must. He whipped the scroll from under his robe and thrust it into Jarveena's eager hand. A heartbeat later, she was on her bended knee before the prince, gazing up into his handsome, youthful, and somewhat vacuous face.

"Read, Your Highness!" she insisted fiercely, and almost forced him to take hold of it.

The instant the prince caught its tenor, he froze. Nizharu did the opposite. Spinning on his heel, he shouted for his men and broke into a run.

The knife which Jarveena carried in her writing-case served other purposes than the sharpening of reed pens. She withdrew it with a practiced flick, aimed, *threw*.

And, howling, Nizharu measured his length on the ground, pierced behind the right knee where there was only leather, not metal, to protect him. The crowd shouted in alarm and seemed on the brink of panic, but the incoming guard had been warned. Throwing back his visor, Captain Aye-Gophlan ordered his men to surround and arrest Nizharu, and in a fine towering rage the prince bellowed at the onlookers to explain why.

"This message is from a traitor at the imperial court! It instructs Nizharu to assign one of his guards to murder me as soon as he has found someone on whom the charge can be falsely pinned! And it says that the writer is enchanting the message to prevent the wrong person's reading it—but there's no difficulty in reading this! It's the court writing I was first taught as a child!"

"We—ah—arranged for the magic to be eliminated," hinted Melilot. And added quickly, "Your Highness!"

"How came you by it?"

"It was dropped by Nizharu when he inspected our guardhouse." That was Aye-Gophlan, marching smartly forward. "Thinking it important, I consulted Master Melilot, whom I've long known to be loyal and discreet."

"And as for me . . ." Melilot gave a deprecating shrug. "I have certain *contacts*, let us say. It put me to no trouble to counteract the spell."

True, thought Jarveena, and marveled at how cleverly he lied.

"You shall be well rewarded," declared the prince. "And, after due trial, so shall he be! Attempting the life of one of the imperial blood— why, it's as heinous a crime as anyone might name! It was a miracle that he let fall the scroll. Surely the gods are on my side!" Raising his voice

again: "Tonight let all make sacrifice and give thanks! Under divine protection I have survived a dastardly assassin!"

If all gods, Jarveena thought, are no better than Melilot, I'm content to
be an unbeliever. But I do look forward to watching Nizharu fry.

Six

"In view of how you must be feeling, Jarveena," said a soft voice at her
side, "I compliment you on the way you are concealing your emotions."

"It's not difficult," she answered with bitterness. The crowd was dispersing around them, heading away from the execution block where,
according to the strict form, traitor Nizharu had paid for his many
crimes by beating, hanging, and lastly burning.

And then she started. The person who had addressed her was nobody
she recognized: tall, stooped, elderly, with wisps of grey hair, carrying a
market basket . . .

Where eyes should be, a glint of red.

"Enas Yorl?" she whispered.

"That same." With a dry chuckle. "Inasmuch as I can ever make the
statement. . . . Are you content?"

"I—I guess I'm not." Jarveena turned away and began to follow the
drift of the crowd. "I ought to be! I begged the privilege of writing the
authorization for his execution in my own hand, and I thought I might
include mention of my parents, my friends, the villagers he slaughtered
or enslaved, but my formal Rankene isn't good enough. so I had to make
do copying a draft by Melilot!" She tossed her head. "And i hoped to
stand up in open court, swear to what he did, watch the faces of the people change as they realized what a filthy villain came hither disguised as
an imperial officer. . . . They said there was no need for any other evidence after Aye-Gophlan's and Melilot's and the prince's."

"To speak after princes is a dangerous habit," opined the wizard. "But
at all events, it appears to have dawned on you that revenge is never what
you hope for. Take my own case. He who did to me what you know of
was so determined to wreak his vengeance that he created one spell more
than he could handle. To each he was obliged to cede a certain portion of

his will; for as I told you, spells have no aim or purpose of their own. He thereby deprived himself of ordinary sense, and to his death sat blubbering and moaning like an infant."

"Why do you tell me this?" cried Jarveena. "I want to make the most of my moment of satisfaction, even if it can't be as rich and memorable as I dreamed."

"Because," said the wizard, taking her arm by fingers whose touch evoked extraordinary thrills all over her, "you paid a fair and honest price for the service I undertook. I shall not forget you. Scarred and branded you may be without; within you are beautiful."

"Me?" said Jarveena with genuine astonishment. "As well call a toad beautiful, or a mud wall!"

"As you like," Enas Yorl answered with a shrug. The movement revealed that he was no longer quite what he had been earlier. "At all events, there is a second reason."

"What?"

"You read the writing on the scroll, and previously I had described it to you. Nonetheless you're acting as though you have forgotten something."

For a brief moment she failed to take his point. Then her hand flew to her open mouth.

"Two deaths," she whispered.

"Yes, indeed. And I scarcely need tell you to whom a traitor in the imperial court would apply for a spell powerful enough to drag me into the matter willy-nilly. I could make the paper legible. I could not evade the consequences of undoing a colleague's work."

"Whose death? *Mine?*"

"It would be politic to minimize the danger, as for instance by taking employment with a seafarer. Many merchant-captains would be glad of a skillful clerk, and after your apprenticeship with Melilot you're well equipped for such a post. Moreover, your present master is inclined to jealousy. You are half his age, yet already he regards you as a rival."

"He dissembles well," muttered Jarveena, "but now and then he's acted in a fashion that makes me believe you."

"He might regard you more kindly were you to become a sort of foreign agent for him. I'm sure you could contrive—for a reasonable fee—to supply him with commercially valuable information. He would scarcely object to adding other strings to his bow: trading in spices, for instance."

For a while Jarveena had seemed enlivened by his discourse. Now she fell back into gloom.

"Why should I want to make myself rich, let alone him? Ever since I can remember I've had a purpose in life. It's gone—carried to the sky with the stench of Nizharu!"

"It takes a very rich person to commission a spell."

"What would I want with magic?" she said contemptuously.

A second later, and it was as though fire coursed all over her body, out-lining every mark that defaced her, every whiplash, every burn, every cut and scratch. She had forgotten until now, but sometime during that extraordinary night when she had lain with him, he had taken the trou-ble to trace her whole violent life story from the map of her skin.

Now she also remembered thinking that it must be for some private magical reason. Could she have been wrong? Could it have been simpler than that—could it just have been that he sympathized with one whom life had scarred in another way?

"You might wish," he was saying calmly, "to cleanse your body of the past as I think you have now begun to cleanse your mind."

"Even . . . ?" She could not complete the question save by raising her hand to the right side of her chest.

"In time. You are young. Nothing is impossible. But one thing is much too possible. We've spoken of it. Now, act!"

They were almost at the gate, and the crowd was pressing and jostling; people were setting their hands to their money belts and pouches, for these were prime conditions for theft.

"I take it you'd not have spoken up unless you had a new employer in mind for me?" Jarveena said at length.

"You're most perceptive."

"And if there were not some long-term advantage in it for yourself?"

Enas Yorl sighed. "There is a long-term purpose to everything. If there were not, spells would be impossible."

"So there was a purpose behind Nizharu's dropping of the scroll?"

"Dropping . . . ?"

"Oh! Why didn't I think of that?"

"In time. I'm sure you would have done. But you came to Sanctuary so recently, you could scarcely be expected to know that in his boyhood Aye-Gophlan was counted among the smartest dips and cutpurses in the city.

How else do you think he managed to buy himself a commission in the guards? Does he talk as though he came from a wealthy background?"

They were at the gate, and being squeezed through. Clutching her writing-case tightly with one hand, keeping the other folded over the silver pin that fastened her cloak in a roll around her waist, Jarveena thought long and long.

And came to a decision.

Even though her main purpose in life up to now had vanished, there was no reason why she should not find another and maybe better ambition. If that were so, there were good reasons to try and prolong her life by quitting Sanctuary.

Although . . .

She glanced around in alarm for the magician, thinking them separated in the throng, and with relief was able to catch him by the arm.

"Will distance make any difference? I mean, if the doom is on me, can I flee from it?"

"Oh, it's not on you. It's merely that there were two deaths in the charm, and only one has happened. Any day of any year, any number die in any city of this size. It's probable that the spell will work itself out locally; when there's a thunderstorm, the lightning strikes beneath it, not a hundred leagues away. Not inconceivably the other death may be that of someone who was as guilty as Nizharu in the sack of Forgotten Holt. He had soldiers with him, did he not?"

"Yes, they were all soldiers, whom I long mistook for bandits . . . ! Oh, what a pass this land has come to! You're quite right! I'm going away, as far as I can, whether or not it means I can outrun my death!"

She caught his hand, gave it a squeeze, and leaned close. "Name the ship that I must look for!"

The day the ship sailed it was unsafe for Enas Yorl to venture on the street; occasionally the changes working in him cycled into forms that nobody, not with the kindest will in the world, could mistake for human. He was therefore obliged to watch the tiring way, making use of a scrying glass, but he was determined to make certain that nothing had gone wrong with his scheme.

All turned out well. He tracked the ship, with Jarveena at her stern, until sea mists obscured her, and then leaned back in what, for the time being, could not exactly be a chair as most people thought of chairs.

"And with you no longer around to attract it," he murmured to the air, "perhaps luck may lead that second death-sentence to be passed on one who wearies beyond measure of mad existence, sport of a hundred mindless spells, this miserable, this pitiable Enas Yorl."

Yet some hope glimmered, like the red pits he had to wear for eyes, in the knowledge that at least one person in the world thought more kindly of him than he did himself. At length, with a snorting laugh, he covered the scrying glass and settled down resignedly to wait out the implacable transformation, a little comforted by knowing that so far he had never been the same shape twice.

The Face of Chaos

Lynn Abbey

The cards lay facedown in a wide crescent on the black-velvet-covered table Illyra used for her fortune-telling. Closing her eyes, she touched one at random with her index finger, then overturned it. The Face of Chaos, a portrait of man and woman as seen in a broken mirror. She had done a card-reading for herself; an attempt to penetrate the atmosphere of foreboding that had hung over the ramshackle cloth-and-wood structure she and Dubro, the bazaar smith, called home. Instead it had brought only more anxiety.

She went to another small table to apply a thick coating of kohl to her eyelids. No one would visit a young, pretty S'danzo to have their fortune told, and no stranger could enter her home for any other reason. The kohl and the formless S'danzo costume concealed her age in the dimly lit room, but if some love-deluded soldier or merchant moved too close, there was always Dubro under the canopy a few steps away. One sight of the brawny, sweating giant with his heavy mallet ended any crisis.

"Sweetmeats! Sweetmeats! Always the best in the bazaar. Always the best in Sanctuary!"

The voice of Haakon the vendor reached through the cloth-hung doorway. Illyra finished her toilette quickly. Dark masses of curly hair were secured with one pin under a purple silk scarf that contrasted garishly with each of the skirts, the shawl, and the blouse she wore. She reached deep within those skirts for her purse and removed a copper coin.

It was still early enough in the day that she might venture outside their home. Everyone in the bazaar knew she was scarce more than a girl, and there would be no city folk wandering about for another hour, at least.

"Haakon! Over here!" she called from under the canopy where Dubro kept his tools. "Two . . . no, three, please."

He lifted three of the sticky treats onto a shell that she held out for them, accepting her copper coin with a smile. In an hour's time, Haakon would want five of the same coin for such a purchase, but the bazaar folk sold the best to each other for less.

She ate one, but offered the other two to Dubro. She would have kissed him, but the smith shrank back from public affection, preferring privacy for all things which pass between a man and woman. He smiled and accepted them wordlessly. The big man seldom spoke; words came slowly to him. He mended the metalwares of the bazaar folk, improving many as he did so. He had protected Illyra since she'd been an orphaned child wandering the stalls, turned out by her own people for the irredeemable crime of being a half-caste. Bright-eyed, quick-tongued Illyra spoke for him now whenever anything needed to be said, and in turn, he still took care of her.

The sweetmeats gone, Dubro returned to the fire, lifting up a barrel hoop he had left there to heat. Illyra watched with never-sated interest as he laid it on the anvil to pound it back into a true circle for Jofan, the wineseller. The mallet fell, but instead of the clear, ringing sound of metal on metal, there was a hollow clang. The horn of the anvil fell into the dirt.

Even Haakon was wide-eyed with silent surprise. Dubro's anvil had been in the bazaar since . . . since Dubro's grandfather for certain, and perhaps longer—no one could remember before that. The smith's face darkened to the color of the cooling iron. Illyra placed her hands over his.

"We'll get it fixed. We'll take it up to the Court of Arms this afternoon. I'll borrow Moonflower's ass and cart. . . ."

"No!" Dubro exploded with one tortured word, shook loose her hands, and stared at the broken piece of his livelihood.

"Can't fix an anvil that's broken like that one," Haakon explained softly to her. "It'll only be as strong as the seam."

"Then we'll get a new one," she responded, mindful of Dubro's bleak face and her own certain knowledge that no one else in the bazaar possessed an anvil to sell.

"There hasn't been a new anvil in Sanctuary since before Ranke closed down the sea trade with Ilsig. You'd need four camels and a year to get a mountain-cast anvil like that one into the bazaar—if you had the gold."

A single tear smeared through the kohl. She and Dubro were well off by the standards of the bazaar. They had ample copper coins for Haakon's sweetmeats and fresh fish three times a week, but a pitifully small hoard of gold with which to convince the caravan merchants to bring an anvil from distant Ranke.

"We've got to have an anvil!" she exclaimed to the unlistening gods, since Dubro and Haakon were already aware of the problem.

Dubro kicked dirt over his fire and strode away from the small forge.

"Watch him for me, Haakon. He's never been like this."

"I'll watch him—but it will be your problem tonight when he comes home."

A few of the city folk were already milling in the aisles of the bazaar; it was high time to hide in her room. Never before in her five years of working the S'danzo trade within the bazaar had she faced a day when Dubro did not lend his calm presence to the stream of patrons. He controlled their coming and going. Without him, she did not know who was waiting, or how to discourage a patron who had questions but no money. She sat in the incense-heavy darkness waiting and brooding.

Moonflower. She would go to Moonflower, not for the old woman's broken-down cart, but for advice. The old woman had never shunned her the way the other S'danzo had. But Moonflower wouldn't know about fixing anvils, and what could she add to the message so clearly conveyed by the Face of Chaos? Besides, Moonflower's richest patrons arrived early in the day to catch her best "vibrations." The old woman would not appreciate a poor relation taking up her patrons' valuable time.

No patrons of her own yet, either. Perhaps the weather had turned bad. Perhaps, seeing the forge empty, they assumed that the inner chamber was empty also. Illyra dared not step outside to find out.

She shuffled and handled the deck of fortune-telling cards, acquiring a measure of self-control from their worn surfaces. Palming the bottom card, Illyra laid it faceup on the velvet.

"Five of Ships," she whispered.

The card was a stylized scene of five small fishing boats, each with its net cast into the water. Tradition said that the answer to her question was in the card. Her gift would let her find it—if she could sort out the many questions floating in her thoughts.

"Illyra the fortune-teller?"

Illyra's reverie was interrupted by her first patron before she had gained a satisfactory focus in the card. This first woman had problems with her many lovers, but her reading was spoiled by another patron stepping through the door at the wrong time. This second patron's reading was disrupted by the fish-smoker looking for Dubro. The day was everything the Face of Chaos had promised.

The few readings that were not disrupted reflected her own despair more than the patron's. Dubro had not returned, and she was startled by any sound from the outside canopy. Her patrons sensed the confusion and were unsatisfied with her performance. Some refused to pay. An older, more experienced S'danzo would know how to handle these things, but Illyra only shrank back in frustration. She tied a frayed rope across the entrance to her fortune-telling room to discourage anyone from seeking her advice.

"Madame Illyra?"

An unfamiliar woman's voice called from outside, undaunted by the rope.

"I'm not seeing anyone this afternoon. Come back tomorrow."

"I can't wait until tomorrow."

They all say that, Illyra thought. Everyone else always knows that they are the most important person I see and that their questions are the most complex. But they are all very much the same. Let the woman come back.

The stranger could be heard hesitating beyond the rope. Illyra heard the sound of rustling cloth—possibly silk—as the woman finally turned away. The sound jarred the S'danzo to alertness. Silken skirts meant wealth. A flash of vision illuminated Illyra's mind—this was a patron she could not let go elsewhere.

"If you can't wait, I'll see you now," she yelled.

"You will?"

Illyra untied the rope and lifted the hanging cloth to let the woman enter. She had surrounded herself with a shapeless, plain shawl; her face was veiled and shadowed by a corner of the shawl wound around her head. The stranger was certainly not someone who came to the S'danzo of the bazaar often. Illyra retied the rope after seating her patron on one side of the velvet-covered table.

A woman of means who wishes to be mysterious. That shawl might be plain, but it is too good for someone as poor as she pretends to be. She wears silk beneath it, and smells of roses, though she has tried to remove her perfume. No doubt she has gold, not silver or copper.

"Would you not be more comfortable removing your shawl? It is quite warm in here," Illyra said, after studying the woman.

"I'd prefer not to."

A difficult one, Illyra thought.

The woman's hand emerged from the shawl to drop three old Ilsig gold coins onto the velvet. The hand was white, smooth, and youthful. The Ilsig coins were rare now that the Rankan Empire controlled Sanctuary. The woman and her questions were a welcome relief from Illyra's own thoughts.

"Well, then, what is your name?"

"I'd prefer not to say."

"I must have some information if I'm to help you," Illyra said as she scooped the coins into a worn piece of silk, taking care not to let her fingers touch the gold.

"My ser . . . There are those who tell me that you alone of the S'danzo can see the near future. I must know what will happen to me tomorrow night."

The question did not fulfill Illyra's curiosity or the promise of mystery, but she reached for her deck of cards.

"You are familiar with these?" she asked the woman.

"Somewhat."

"Then divide them into three piles and choose one card from each pile—that will show me your future."

"For tomorrow night?"

"Assuredly. The answer is contained within the moment of the question. Take the cards."

The veiled woman handled the cards fearfully. Her hands shook so badly that the three piles were simply unsquared heaps. The woman was

visibly reluctant to touch the cards again and gingerly overturned the top
card of each rather than handle them again.

Lance of Flames.

The Archway.

Five of Ships, reversed.

Illyra drew her hands back from the velvet in alarm. The Five of
Ships—the card had been in her own hands not moments before. She did
not remember replacing it in the deck. With a quivering foreknowledge
that she would see a part of her own fate in the cards, Illyra opened her
mind to receive the answer. And closed it almost at once.

Falling stones, curses, murder, a journey without return. None of the
cards was particularly auspicious, but together they created an image of
malice and death that was normally hidden from the living. The
S'danzo never foretold death when they saw it, and though she was but
half S'danzo and shunned by them, Illyra abided by their codes and
superstitions.

"It would be best to remain at home, especially tomorrow night.
Stand back from walls which might have loose stones in them. Safety lies
within yourself. Do not seek other advice—especially from the priests of
the temples."

Her visitor's reserve crumbled. She gasped, sobbed, and shook with
unmistakable terror. But before Illyra could speak the words to calm her,
the black-clad woman dashed away, pulling the frayed rope from its
anchorage.

"Come back!" Illyra called.

The woman turned while still under the canopy. Her shawl fell back to
reveal a fair-skinned blond woman of a youthful and delicate beauty. A
victim of a spurned lover? Or a jealous wife?

"If you had already seen your fate, then you should have asked a different question, such as whether it can be changed," she chided softly,
guiding the woman back into the incense-filled chamber.

"I thought if you saw differently . . . But Molin Torchholder will have
his way. Even you have seen it."

Molin Torchholder. Illyra recognized the name. He was the priestly
temple builder within the Rankan prince's entourage. She had another
friend and patron living within his household. Was this the woman of
Cappen Varra's idylls? Had the minstrel finally overstepped himself?

"Why would the Rankan have his way with you?" she asked, prying gently.

"They have sought to build a temple for their gods."

"But you are not a goddess, nor even Rankan. Such things should not concern you."

Illyra spoke lightly, but she knew, from the cards, that the priests sought her as part of some ritual—not in personal interest.

"My father is rich—proud and powerful among those of Sanctuary who have never accepted the fall of the Ilsig kingdom and will never accept the empire. Molin has singled my father out. He has demanded our lands for his temple. When we refused, he forced the weaker men not to trade with us. But my father would not give in. He believes the gods of Ilsig are stronger, but Molin has vowed revenge rather than admit failure."

"Perhaps your family will have to leave Sanctuary to escape this foreign priest, and your home be torn down to build their temple. But though the city may be all you know, the world is large, and this place but a poor part of it."

Illyra spoke with far more authority than she actually commanded. Since the death of her mother, she had left the bazaar itself only a handful of times and had never left the city. The words were part of the S'danzo oratory Moonflower had taught her.

"My father and the others must leave, but not me. I'm to be part of Molin Torchholder's revenge. His men came once to my father's house. The Rankan offered us my full bride-price, though he is married. Father refused the 'honor.' Molin's men beat him senseless and carried me screaming from the house.

"I fought with him when he came to me that night. He will not want another woman for some time. But my father could not believe I had not been dishonored. And Molin said that if I would not yield to him, then no living man should have me."

"Such are ever the words of scorned men," Illyra added gently.

"No. It was a curse. I know this for certain. Their gods are strong enough to answer when they call. Last night two of their Hell Hounds appeared at our estate to offer new terms to my father. A fair price for our land, safe conduct to Ilsig—but I am to remain behind. Tomorrow night they will consecrate the cornerstone of their new temple with a virgin's death. I am to be under that stone when they lay it."

Though Illyra was not specifically a truth-seer, the tale tied all the horrific visions into a whole. It would take the gods to save this woman from the fate Molin Torchholder had waiting for her. It was no secret that the empire sought to conquer the Ilsig gods as they had conquered their armies. If the Rankan priest could curse a woman with unbreachable virginity, Illyra didn't think there was much she could do.

The woman was still sobbing. There was no future in her patronage, but Illyra felt sorry for her. She opened a little cabinet and shook a good-sized pinch of white powder into a small liquid-filled vial. "Tonight, before you retire, take this with a glass of wine."

The woman clutched it tightly, though the fear did fade from her eyes.

"Do I owe you more for this?" she asked.

"No, it is the least I could do for you."

There was enough of the cylantha powder to keep the woman asleep for three days. Perhaps Molin Torchholder would not want a sleeping virgin in his rite. If he did not mind, the woman would not awaken to find out.

"I can give you much gold. I could bring you to Ilsig."

Illyra shook her head. "There is but one thing I wish—and you do not have it," she whispered, surprised by the sudden impulsiveness of her words. "Nor all the gold in Sanctuary will find another anvil for Dubro."

"I do not know this Dubro, but there is an anvil in my father's stables. It will not return to Ilsig. It can be yours, if I'm alive to tell my father to give it to you."

The impulsiveness cleared from Illyra's mind. There were reasons now to soothe the young woman's fears.

"It is a generous offer," she replied. "I shall see you then, three days hence at your father's home—if you will tell me where it is."

And if you do, she added to herself, then it will not matter if you survive or not.

"It is the estate called Land's End, behind the temple of Ils, Himself."

"Whom shall I ask for?"

"Marilla."

They stared at each other for a few moments; then the blond woman made her way into the afternoon-crowded bazaar. Illyra knotted the rope across the entrance to her chambers with distracted intensity.

How many years—five at least—she had been answering the banal questions of city folk who could not see anything for themselves. Never, in all that time, had she asked a question of a patron, or seen such a death, or one of her own cards in a reading. And in all the years of memory within the S'danzo community within the bazaar, never had any of them crossed fates with the gods.

No, I have nothing to do with gods. I do not notice them, and they do not see me. My gift is S'danzo. I am S'danzo. We live by fate. We do not touch the affairs of gods.

But Illyra could not convince herself. The thought circled in her mind that she had wandered beyond the realms of her people and gifts. She lit the incense of gentle-forgetting, inhaling it deeply, but the sound of Dubro's anvil breaking and the images of the three cards remained ungentle in her thoughts. As the afternoon waned, she convinced herself again to approach Moonflower for advice.

Three of the obese S'danzo woman's children squalled at each other in the dust while her dark-eyed husband sat in the shade holding his hands over his eyes and ears. It was not an auspicious moment to seek the older woman's counsel. The throngs of people were leaving the bazaar, making it safe for Illyra to wander among the stalls looking for Dubro.

"Illyra!"

She had expected Dubro's voice, but this one was familiar also. She looked closely into the crowd at the wineseller's.

"Cappen Varra?"

"The same," he answered, greeting her with a smile. "There was a rope across your gate today, and Dubro was not busy at his fire—otherwise I should have stopped to see you."

"You have a question?"

"No, my life could not be better. I have a song for you."

"Today is not a day for songs. Have you seen Dubro?"

"No. I'm here to get wine for a special dinner tomorrow night. Thanks to you, I know where the best wine in Sanctuary is still to be found."

"A new love?"

"The same. She grows more radiant with each day. Tomorrow the master of the house will be busy with his priestly functions. The household will be quiet."

"The household of Molin Torchholder must agree with you then. It is good to be in the grace of the conquerors of Ilsig."

"I'm discreet. So is Molin. It is a trait which seems to have been lost among the natives of Sanctuary—S'danzo excepted, of course. I'm most comfortable within his house."

The seller handed him two freshly washed bottles of wine, and with brief farewells, Illyra saw him on his way. The wineseller had seen Dubro earlier in the day. He offered that the smith was visiting every wineseller in the bazaar and not a few of the taverns outside it. Similar stories waited for her at the other winesellers. She returned to the forge home in the gathering twilight and fog.

Ten candles and the oil stove could not cut through the dark emptiness in the chamber. Illyra pulled her shawls tightly around her and tried to nap until Dubro returned. She would not let herself think that he would not return.

"You have been waiting for me."

Illyra jumped at the sound. Only two of the candles remained lit; she had no idea how long she had slept, only that her home quivered with shadows and a man, as tall as Dubro but of cadaverous thinness, stood within the knotted rope.

"Who are you? What do you want?" She flattened against the back of the chair.

"Since you do not recognize me, then say, I have been looking for you."

The man gestured. The candles and stove rekindled and Illyra found herself staring at the blue-starred face of the magician Lythande.

"I have done nothing to cross you," she said, rising slowly from her chair.

"And I did not say that you had. I thought you were seeking me. Many of us have heard you calling today."

He held up the three cards Marilla had overturned and the Face of Chaos.

"I—I had not known my problems could disturb your studies."

"I was reflecting on the legend of the Five Ships—it was comparatively easy for you to touch me. I have taken it to myself to learn things for you.

"The girl Marilla appealed first to her own gods. They sent her to you since for them to act on her fate would rouse the ire of Sabellia and Savankala. They have tied your fates together. You will not solve your own troubles unless you can relieve hers."

"She is a dead woman, Lythande. If the gods of Ilsig wish to help her, they will need all their strength—and if that isn't enough, then there is nothing I can do for her."

"That is not a wise position to take, Illyra," the magician said with a smile.

"That is what I *saw*. S'danzo do not cross fates with the gods."

"And you, Illyra, are not S'danzo."

She gripped the back of the chair, angered by the reminder but unable to counter it.

"They have passed the obligation to you," he said.

"I do not know how to break through Marilla's fate," Illyra said simply. "I *see*, they must *change*."

Lythande laughed. "Perhaps there *is* no way, child. Maybe it will take two sacrifices to consecrate the temple Molin Torchholder builds. You had best hope there is a way through Marilla's fate."

A cold breeze accompanied his laughter. The candles flickered a moment, and the magician was gone. Illyra stared at the undisturbed rope.

Let Lythande and the others help her if it's so important. I want only the anvil, and that I can have regardless of her fate.

The cold air clung to the room. Already her imagination was embroidering upon the consequences of enraging any of the powerful deities of Sanctuary. She left to search for Dubro in the fog-shrouded bazaar.

Fog tendrils obscured the familiar stalls and shacks of the daytime bazaar. A few fires could be glimpsed through cracked doorways, but the area itself had gone to sleep early, leaving Illyra to roam through the moist night alone.

Nearing the main entrance she saw the bobbing torch of a running man. The torch and runner fell with an aborted shout. She heard lighter footsteps running off into the unlit fog. Cautiously, fearfully, Illyra crept toward the fallen man.

It was not Dubro, but a shorter man wearing a blue hawk-mask. A dagger protruded from the side of his neck. Illyra felt no sorrow at the death of one of Jubal's bullyboys, only relief that it had not been Dubro. Jubal was worse than the Rankans. Perhaps the crimes of the man behind the mask had finally caught up with him. More likely someone had risked venting a grudge against the seldom-seen former gladiator. Anyone who dealt with Jubal had more enemies than friends.

As if in silent response to her thoughts, another group of men appeared out of the fog. Illyra hid among the crates and boxes while five men without masks studied the dead man. Then, without warning, one of them threw aside his torch and fell on the warm corpse, striking it again and again with his knife. When he had had his fill of death, the others took their turns.

The bloody hawk-mask rolled to within a hand-span of Illyra's foot. She held her breath and did not move, her eyes riveted in horror on the unrecognizable body in front of her. She wandered away from the scene blind to everything but her own disbelieving shock. The atrocity seemed to be the final senseless gesture of the Face of Chaos in a day that had unraveled her existence.

She leaned against a canopy post fighting waves of nausea, but Haakon's sweetmeats had been the only food she had eaten all day. The dry heaving of her stomach brought no relief.

" 'Lyra!"

A familiar voice roared behind her and an arm thrown protectively around her shoulder broke the spell. She clung to Dubro with clenched fingers, burying her convulsive sobs in his leather vest. He reeked of wine and the salty fog. She savored every breath of him.

" 'Lyra, what are you doing out here?" He paused, but she did not reply. "Did you begin to think I'd not come back to you?"

He held her tightly, swaying restlessly back and forth. The story of the hawk-masked man's death fell from her in racked gasps. It took Dubro only a moment to decide that his beloved Illyra had suffered too much in his absence and to repent that he had gotten drunk or sought work outside the bazaar. He lifted her gently and carried her back to their home, muttering softly to himself as he walked.

Not even Dubro's comforting arms could protect Illyra from the nightmare visions that stalked her sleep once they had returned to their home. He shook off his drunkenness to watch over her as she tossed and fretted on the sleeping linens. Each time he thought she had settled into a calm sleep, the dreams would start again. Illyra would awaken sweating and incoherent from fear. She would not describe her dreams to him when he asked. He began to suspect that something worse than the murder had taken place in his absence, though their home showed no sign of attack or struggle.

Illyra did try to voice her fears to him at each waking interlude, but the mixture of visions and emotions found no expression in her voice. Within her mind, each redreaming of the nightmare brought her closer to a single image that both collected her problems and eliminated them. The first rays of a feeble dawn had broken through the fog when she had the final synthetic experience of the dream.

She saw herself at a place the dream spirit said was the estate called Land's End. The estate had been long abandoned, with only an anvil chained to a pedestal in the center of a starlit courtyard to show that it had been inhabited. Illyra broke the chain easily and lifted the anvil as if it had been paper. Clouds rushed in as she walked away and a moaning wind began to blow dust devils around her. She hurried toward the doorway where Dubro waited for his gift.

The steel cracked before she had traveled half the distance, and the anvil crumbled completely as she transferred it to him. Rain began to fall, washing away Dubro's face to reveal Lythande's cruel, mocking smile. The magician struck her with the card marked with the Face of Chaos. And she died, only to find herself captive within her body, which was being carried by unseen hands to a vast pit. The dissonant music of priestly chants and cymbals surrounded her. Within the dream, Illyra opened her dead eyes to see a large block of stone descending into the pit over her.

"I'm already dead!" she screamed, struggling to free her arms and legs from invisible bindings. "I can't be sacrificed—I'm already dead!"

Her arms came free. She flailed wildly. The walls of the pit were glassy and without handholds. The lowered stone touched her head. She shrieked as the life left her body for a second time. Her body released her spirit, and she rose up through the stone, waking as she did.

"It was a dream," Illyra said before Dubro could ask.

The solution was safe in her mind now. The dream would not return. But it was like a reading with the cards. In order to understand what the dream spirit had given her, she would have to meditate upon it.

"You said something of death and sacrifice," Dubro said, unmollified by her suddenly calmed face.

"It was a dream."

"What sort of dream? Are you afraid that I will leave you or the bazaar now that I have no work to do?"

"No," she said quickly, masking the fresh anxiety his words produced. "Besides, I have found an anvil for us."

"In your dream with the death and sacrifice?"

"Death and sacrifice are keys the dream spirit gave me. Now I must take the time to understand them."

Dubro stepped back from her. He was not S'danzo, and though bazaar folk, he was not comfortable around their traditions or their gifts. When Illyra spoke of "seeing" or "knowing," he would draw away from her. He sat, quiet and sullen, in a chair pulled into the corner most distant from her S'danzo paraphernalia.

She stared at the black-velvet covering of her table well past the dawn and the start of a gentle rain. Dubro placed a shell with a sweetmeat in it before her. She nodded, smiled, and ate it, but did not say anything. The smith had already turned away two patrons when Illyra finished her meditation.

"Are you finished, now, 'Lyra?" he asked, his distrust of S'danzo ways not overshadowing his concern for her.

"I think so."

"No more death and sacrifice?"

She nodded and began to relate the tale of the previous day's events. Dubro listened quietly until she reached the part about Lythande.

"In my home? Within these walls?" he demanded.

"I saw him, but I don't know how he got in here. The rope was untouched."

"No!" Dubro exclaimed, beginning to pace like a caged animal. "No, I want none of this. I will not have magicians and sorcerers in my home!"

"You weren't here, and I did not invite him in." Illyra's dark eyes flashed at him as she spoke. "And he'll come back again if I don't do these things, so hear me out."

"No, just tell me what we must do to keep him away."

Illyra dug her fingernails into the palm of one hand hidden in the folds of her skirts. "We will have to—to stop the consecration of the cornerstone of the new temple for the Rankan gods."

"'Gods,' 'Lyra, you would not meddle with the gods? Is this the meaning you found in 'death and sacrifice'?"

"It is also the reason Lythande was here last night."

"But, 'Lyra . . ."

She shook her head, and he was quiet.

He won't ask me what I plan to do, she thought as he tied the rope across the door and followed her toward the city. As long as everything is in my head, I'm certain everything is possible and that I will succeed. But if I spoke of it to anyone—even him—I would hear how little hope I have of stopping Molin Torchholder or of changing Marilla's fate.

In the dream, her already dead body had been offered to Sabellia and Savankala. Her morning's introspection had convinced her that she was to introduce a corpse into Molin Torchholder's ceremonies. They passed the scene of the murder, but Jubal's men had reclaimed their comrade. The only other source of dead men she knew of was the Governor's Palace, where executions were becoming a daily occurrence under the tightening grip of the Hell Hounds.

They passed by the huge charnel house just beyond the bazaar gates. The rain held the death smells close by the half-timbered building. Could Sabellia and Savankala be appeased with the mangled bones and fat of a butchered cow? Hesitantly she mounted the raised wooden walk over the red-brown effluvia of the building.

"What do the Rankan gods want from this place?" Dubro asked before setting foot on the walkway.

"A substitute for the one already chosen."

A man emerged from a side door pushing a sloshing barrel, which he dumped into the slow-moving stream. Shapeless red lumps flowed under the walkway between the two bazaar folk. Illyra swayed on her feet.

"Even the gods of Ranke would not be fooled by these." Dubro lowered his hand toward the now-ebbing stream. "At least offer them the death of an honest man of Ilsig."

He held out a hand to steady her as she stepped back on the street, then led the way past the Serpentine to the Governor's Palace. Three men hung limply from the gallows in the rain, their crimes and names inscribed on placards tied around their necks. Neither Illyra nor Dubro had mastered the arcane mysteries of script.

"Which one is most like the one you need?" Dubro asked.

"She should be my size, but blond," Illyra explained while looking at the two strapping men and one grandfatherly figure hanging in front of them.

Dubro shrugged and approached the stern-faced Hell Hound standing guard at the foot of the gallows.

"Father," he grunted, pointing at the elderly corpse.

"It's the law—to be hanged by the neck until sundown. You'll have to come back then."

"Long walk home. He's dead now—why wait?"

"There is *law* in Sanctuary now, peon, Rankan law. It will be respected without exception."

Dubro stared at the ground, fumbling with his hands in evident distress. "In the rain I cannot see the sun—how shall I know when to return?"

Guard and smith stared at the steely-gray sky, both knowing it would not clear before nightfall. Then, with a loud sigh, the Hell Hound walked to the ropes, selected and untied one, which dropped Dubro's "father" into the mud.

"Take him and begone!"

Dubro shouldered the dead man, walking to Illyra, who waited at the edge of the execution grounds.

"He's—he's—" she gasped in growing hysteria.

"Dead since sunrise."

"He's covered with filth. He reeks. His face . . ."

"You wanted another for the sacrifice."

"But not like that!"

"It is the way of men who have been hanged."

They walked back toward the charnel house, where Sanctuary's undertakers and embalmers held sway. There, for five copper coins, they found a man to prepare the body. For another coin he would have rented them a cart and his son as a digger to take the unfortunate ex-thief to the common field outside the Gate of Triumph for proper burial. Illyra and Dubro made a great show of grief, however, and insisted that they would bury their father with their own hands. Wrapped in a nearly clean shroud, the old man was bound to a plank. Illyra held the foot end, Dubro the other. They made their way back to the bazaar.

"Do we take the body to the temple for the exchange?" he asked as they pushed aside their chairs to make room for the plank.

Illyra stared at him, not realizing at first that his faith in her had made the question sincere. "During the night the Rankan priests will leave the Governor's Palace for the estate called Land's End. They will bear Marilla with them. We will have to stop them and replace Marilla with our corpse, without their knowledge."

The smith's eyes widened with disillusion. " 'Lyra, it is not the same as stealing fruit from Blind Jakob! The girl will be alive. He is dead. Surely the priests will see."

She shook her head, clinging desperately to the image she had found in meditation. "It rains. There will be no moonlight, and their torches will give more smoke that light. I gave the girl cylantha. They will have to carry her as if she were dead."

"Will she take the drug?"

"Yes!"

But Illyra wasn't sure—couldn't be sure—until they actually saw the procession. So many questions: if Marilla had taken the drug, if the procession was small, unguarded, and slowed by its burden, if the ritual was like the one in her dream. The cold panic she had felt as the stone descended on her returned. The Face of Chaos loomed, laughing, in her mind's eye.

"Yes! She took the drug last night," she said firmly, dispelling the Face by force of will.

"How do you know this?" Dubro asked incredulously.

"I *know*."

There was no more discussion as Illyra threw herself into the preparation of a macabre feast that they ate on a table spread over their dead guest. The vague point of sundown passed, leaving Sanctuary in a dark rainy night, as Illyra had foreseen. The continuing rain bolstered her confidence as they moved slowly through the bazaar and out the Common Gate.

They faced a long, but not difficult, walk beyond the walls of the city. As Dubro pointed out, the demoiselles of the Street of Red Lanterns had to follow their path each night on their way to the Promise of Heaven. The ladies giggled behind their shawls at the sight of the two bearing what was so obviously a corpse. But they did nothing to hinder them, and it was far too early for the more raucous traffic returning from the Promise.

Huge piles of stone in a sea of muddy craters marked the site of the new temple. A water-laden canopy covered sputtering braziers and torches; otherwise the area was quiet and deserted.

It is the night of the Ten-Slaying. Cappen Varra told me the priests would be busy. Rain will not stop the dedication. Gods do not feel rain! Illyra thought, but again did not know and sat with her back to Dubro quivering more from doubt and fear than from the cold water dripping down her back.

While she sat, the rain slowed to a misty drizzle and gave promise of stopping altogether. She left the inadequate shelter of the rockpile to venture nearer the canopy and braziers. A platform had been built above the mud at the edge of a pit with ropes dangling on one side that might be used to lower a body into the pit. A great stone was poised on logs opposite, ready to crush anything below. At least they were not too late—no sacrifice had taken place. Before Illyra had returned to Dubro's side, six torches appeared in the mist-obscured distance.

"They are coming," Dubro whispered as she neared him.

"I see them. We have only a few moments now."

From around her waist she unwound two coils of rope taken from the bazaar forge. She had devised her own plan for the actual exchange, as neither the dream spirit nor her meditations had offered solid insight or inspiration.

"They will most likely follow the same path we did, since they are carrying a body also," she explained as she laid the ropes across the mud, burying them slightly. "We will trip them here."

"And I will switch our corpse for the girl?"

"Yes."

They said nothing more as each crouched in a mud hole waiting, hoping, that the procession would pass between them.

The luck promised in her dream held. Molin Torchholder led the small procession, bearing a large brass and wood torch from Sabellia's temple in Ranke itself. Behind him were three chanting acolytes bearing both incense and torches. The last two torches were affixed to a bier carried on the shoulders of the last pair of priests. Torchholder and the other three trod over the ropes without noticing them. When the first pallbearer was between the ropes Illyra snapped them taut. The burdened priests heard the smack as the ropes lifted from the mud, but were tripped before they could react. Marilla and the torches fell toward Dubro, the priests toward Illyra. In the dark commotion, Illyra got safely to a nearby pile of building stones, but without being able to see if Dubro had accomplished the exchange.

"What's wrong?" Torchholder demanded, hurrying back with his torch to light the scene.

"The damned workmen left the hauling ropes strewn about," a mud-splattered priest exclaimed as he scrambled out of the knee-deep mud hole.

"And the girl?" Molin continued.

"Thrown over there, from the look of it."

Lifting his robes in one hand, Molin Torchholder led the acolytes and priests to the indicated mud pit. Illyra heard sounds she prayed were Dubro making his own way to the safe shadows.

"A hand here."

"Damned Ilsig mud. She weighs ten times as much now."

"Easy. A little more mud, a little sooner won't affect the temple, but it's an ill thought to rouse the Others." Torchholder's calm voice quieted them all.

The torches were relit. From her hideout, Illyra could see a mud-covered shroud on the bier. Dubro had succeeded somehow: she did not allow herself to think anything else.

The procession continued on toward the canopy. The rain had stopped completely. A sliver of moonlight showed through the dispersing clouds. Torchholder loudly hailed the break in the clouds as an omen of the forgiving, sanctifying, presence of Vashanka and began the ritual. In due time the acolytes emptied braziers of oil onto the shroud, setting it and the corpse on fire. They lowered the flaming bier into the pit. The acolytes threw symbolic armloads of stone after it. Then they cut the ropes that held the cornerstone in its place at the edge. It slid from sight with a loud, sucking sound.

Almost at once, Torchholder and the other two priests left the platform to head back toward the palace, leaving only the acolytes to perform a nightlong vigil over the new grave. When the priests were out of sight Illyra scrambled back to the mud holes and whispered Dubro's name.

"Here," he hissed back.

She needed only one glance at his moon-shadowed face to know something had gone wrong.

"What happened?" she asked quickly, unmindful of the sound of her voice. "Marilla? Did they bury Marilla?"

There were tears in Dubro's eyes as he shook his head. "Look at her!" he said, his voice barely under control.

A mud-covered shroud lay some paces away. Dubro would neither face it nor venture near it. Illyra approached warily.

Dubro had left the face covered. Holding her breath, Illyra reached down to peel back the damp, dirty linen.

For a heartbeat, she saw Marilla's sleeping face. Then it became her own. After a second of self-recognition, the face underwent a bewildering series of changes to portraits of people from her childhood and others whom she did not recognize. It froze for a moment in the shattered image of the Face of Chaos, then was still with pearly-white skin where there should have been eyes, nose, and mouth.

Illyra's fingers stiffened. She opened her mouth to scream, but her lungs and throat were paralyzed with fright. The linen fell from her unfeeling hands, but did not cover the hideous thing that lay before her.

Get away! Get away from this place!

The primitive imperative rose in her mind and would not be appeased by anything less than headlong flight. She pushed Dubro aside. The acolytes heard her as she blundered through the mud, but she ignored them. There were buildings ahead—solid stone buildings outlined in the moonlight.

It was a manor house of an estate long since abandoned. Illyra recognized it from her dream, but her panic and terror had been sated in the headlong run from the faceless corpse. An interior door hung open on rusty hinges that creaked when she pushed the door. She was unsurprised to see an anvil sitting on a plain wooden box in the center of a courtyard that her instincts told her was not entirely deserted.

I'm only prolonging it now. The anvil, and the rest, they are there for me.

She stepped into the courtyard. Nothing happened. The anvil was solid and far too heavy for her to lift.

"You've come to collect your reward?" a voice called.

"Lythande?" she whispered, waiting for the cadaverous magician to appear.

"Lythande is elsewhere."

A hooded man stepped into the moonlight.

"What has happened? Where is Marilla? Her family?"

The man gestured to his right. Illyra followed his movement and saw the tumbledown headstones of an old graveyard.

"But . . . ?"

"The priests of Ils seek to provoke the new gods. They created the homunculus, disguising it to appear as a young woman to an untrained observer. Had it been interred in the foundation of the new temple, it would have created a disruptive weakness. The anger of Savankala and Sabellia would reach across the desert. That is, of course, exactly what the priests of Ils wanted.

"We magicians—and even you gifted S'danzo—do not welcome the meddling feuds of gods and their priests. They tamper with the delicate balances of fate. Our work is more important than the appeasement of deities, so this time, as in the past, we have intervened."

"But the temple? They should have buried a virgin, then?"

"A forged person would arouse the Rankan gods, but not an imperfect virgin. When the temple of Ils was erected, the old priests sought a royal soul to inter beneath the altar. They wanted the youngest, and most loved, of the royal princes. The queen was a sorceress of some skill herself. She disguised an old slave, and his bones still rest beneath the altar."

"So the gods of Ilsig and Ranke are equal?"

The hooded man laughed. "We have seen to it that all gods within Sanctuary are equally handicapped, my child."

"And what of me? Lythande warned me not to fail."

"Did I not just say that our purpose—and therefore your purpose—was accomplished? You did not fail, and we repay, as Marilla promised, with a black-steel anvil. It is yours."

He laid a hand on the anvil and disappeared in a wisp of smoke.

" 'Lyra, are you all right? I heard you speaking with someone. I buried that girl before I came looking for you."

"Here is the anvil."

"I do not want such an ill-gotten thing."

Dubro took her arm and tried to lead her out of the courtyard.

"I have paid too much already!" she shouted at him, wresting away from his grasp. "Take it back to the bazaar—then we will forget all this ever happened. Never speak of it to anyone. But don't leave the anvil here, or it's all worth nothing!"

"I can never forget your face on that dead girl . . . thing."

Illyra remained silently staring at the still-muddy ground. Dubro went to the anvil and brushed the water and dirt from its surface. "Someone has carved a symbol in it. It reminds me of one of your cards. Tell me what it means before I take it back to the bazaar with us."

She stood by his side. A smiling Face of Chaos had been freshly etched into the worn surface of the metal.

"It is an old S'danzo sign of good luck."

Dubro did not seem to hear the note of bitterness and deceit in her voice. His faith in Illyra had been tried but not shattered. The anvil was heavy, an ungainly bundle in his arms.

"Well, it won't get home by itself, will it?" He stared at her as he started walking.

She touched the pedestal and thought briefly of the questions still whirling in her head. Dubro called again from outside the courtyard. The entire length of Sanctuary lay between them and the bazaar, and it was not yet midnight. Without glancing back, she followed him out of the courtyard.

The Gate of the Flying Knives

Poul Anderson

Again penniless, houseless, and ladyless, Cappen Varra made a brave
sight just the same as he wove his way amidst the bazaar throng. After
all, until today he had for some weeks been in, if not quite of, the household of Molin Torchholder as much as he could contrive. Besides the
dear presence of ancilla Danlis, he had received generous reward from
the priest-engineer whenever he sang a song or composed a poem. That
situation had changed with suddenness and terror, but he still wore a
bright green tunic, scarlet cloak, canary hose, soft half-boots trimmed in
silver, and plumed beret. Though naturally heartsick at what had happened, full of dread for his darling, he saw no reason to sell the garb yet.
He could raise enough money in various ways to live on while he
searched for her. If need be, as often before, he could pawn the harp that
a goldsmith was presently redecorating.

If his quest had not succeeded by the time he was reduced to rags, then
he would have to suppose Danlis and the Lady Rosanda were forever
lost. But he had never been one to grieve over future sorrows.

Beneath a westering sun, the bazaar surged and clamored. Merchants,
artisans, porters, servants, slaves, wives, nomads, courtesans, entertain-

ers, beggars, thieves, gamblers, magicians, acolytes, soldiers, and who knew what else mingled, chattered, chaffered, quarreled, plotted, sang, played games, drank, ate, and who knew what else. Horsemen, camel drivers, wagoners pushed through, raising waves of curses. Music tinkled and tweedled from wineshops. Vendors proclaimed the wonders of their wares from booths, neighbors shouted at each other, and devotees chanted from flat rooftops. Smells thickened the air, of flesh, sweat, roast meat and nuts, aromatic drinks, leather, wool, dung, smoke, oils, cheap perfume.

Ordinarily, Cappen Varra enjoyed this shabby-colorful spectacle. Now he single-mindedly hunted through it. He kept full awareness, of course, as everybody must in Sanctuary. When light fingers brushed him, he knew. But whereas aforetime he would have chuckled and told the pickpurse, "I'm sorry, friend; I was hoping I might lift somewhat off you," at this hour he clapped his sword in such forbidding wise that the fellow recoiled against a fat woman and made her drop a brass tray full of flowers. She screamed and started beating him over the head with it.

Cappen didn't stay to watch. On the northern edge of the bazaar he found what he wanted: the home of Illyra the fortune-teller and Dubro the smith. Reek from a nearby tannery well-nigh drowned the incense she burned in a curious holder, and would surely overwhelm any of her herbs. She herself also lacked awesomeness, such as most seeresses, mages, conjurers, scryers, and the like affected. She was too young; she would have looked almost wistful in her flowing, gaudy S'danzo garments, had she not been so beautiful.

Cappen gave her a bow in the manner of Caronne. "Good day, Illyra the lovely," he said.

She smiled from the cushion whereon she sat. "Good day to you, Cappen Varra." They had had a number of talks, usually in jest, and he had sung for her entertainment. He had hankered to do more than that, but she seemed to keep all men at a certain distance, and a hulk of a black-smith who evidently adored her saw to it that they respected her wish.

"Nobody in these parts has met you for a fair while," she remarked. "What fortune was great enough to make you forget old friends?"

"My fortune was mingled, inasmuch as it left me without time to come down here and behold you, my sweet," he answered out of habit.

Lightness departed from Illyra. In the olive countenance, under the chestnut mane, large eyes focused hard on her visitor. "You find time when you need help in disaster," she said.

He had not patronized her before, or indeed any fortune-teller or thaumaturge in Sanctuary. In Caronne, where he grew up, most folk had no use for magic. In his later wanderings he had encountered sufficient strangeness to temper his native skepticism. As shaken as he already was, he felt a chill go along his spine. "Do you read my fate without even casting a spell?"

She smiled afresh, but bleakly. "Oh, no. It's simple reason. Word did filter back to the Maze that you were residing in the Jewelers' Quarter and a frequent guest at the mansion of Molin Torchholder. When you appear on the heels of a new word—that last night his wife was reaved from him—plain to see is that you've been affected yourself."

He nodded. "Yes, and sore afflicted. I have lost—" He hesitated, unsure whether it would be quite wise to say "—my love" to this girl whose charms he had rather extravagantly praised.

"—your position and income," Illyra snapped. "The high priest cannot be in any mood for minstrelsy. I'd guess his wife favored you most, anyhow. I need not guess you spent your earnings as fast as they fell to you, or faster, were behind in your rent, and were accordingly kicked out of your choice apartment as soon as rumor reached the landlord. You've returned to the Maze because you've no place else to go, and to me in hopes you can wheedle me into giving you a clue—for if you're instrumental in recovering the lady, you'll likewise recover your fortune, and more."

"No, no, no," he protested. "You wrong me."

"The high priest will appeal only to his Rankan gods," Illyra said, her tone changing from exasperated to thoughtful. She stroked her chin. "He, kinsman of the emperor, here to direct the building of a temple which will overtop that of Ils, can hardly beg aid from the old gods of Sanctuary, let alone from our wizards, witches, and seers. But you, who belong to no part of the empire, who drifted hither from a kingdom far in the West . . . you may seek anywhere. The idea is your own; else he would furtively have slipped you some gold, and you have engaged a diviner with more reputation than is mine."

Cappen spread his hands. "You reason eerily well, dear lass," he conceded. "Only about the motives are you mistaken. Oh, yes, I'd be glad to stand high in Molin's esteem, be richly rewarded, and so forth. Yet I feel for him; beneath that sternness of his, he's not a bad sort, and he bleeds. Still more do I feel for his lady, who was indeed kind to me and who's been snatched away to an unknown place. But before all else—" He grew quite earnest. "The Lady Rosanda was not seized by herself. Her ancilla has also vanished, Danlis. And—Danlis is she whom I love, Illyra, she whom I meant to wed."

The maiden's look probed him further. She saw a young man of medium height, slender but tough and agile. (That was due to the life he had had to lead; by nature he was indolent, except in bed.) His features were thin and regular on a long skull, clean-shaven, eyes bright blue, black hair banged and falling to the shoulders. His voice gave the language a melodious accent, as if to bespeak white cities, green fields and woods, quicksilver lakes, blue sea, of the homeland he left in search of his fortune.

"Well, you have charm, Cappen Varra," she murmured, "and how you do know it." Alert: "But coin you lack. How do you propose to pay me?"

"I fear you must work on speculation, as I do myself," he said. "If our joint efforts lead to a rescue, why, then we'll share whatever material reward may come. Your part might buy you a home on the Path of Money." She frowned. "True," he went on, "I'll get more than my share of the immediate bounty that Molin bestows. I will have my beloved back. I'll also regain the priest's favor, which is moderately lucrative. Yet consider. You need but practice your art. Thereafter any effort and risk will be mine."

"What makes you suppose a humble fortune-teller can learn more than the prince governor's investigator guardsmen?" she demanded.

"The matter does not seem to lie within their jurisdiction," he replied.

She leaned forward, tense beneath the layers of clothing. Cappen bent toward her. It was as if the babble of the marketplace receded, leaving these two alone with their wariness.

"I was not there," he said low, "but I arrived early this morning after the thing had happened. What's gone through the city has been rumor, leakage that cannot be caulked, household servants blabbing to friends outside and they blabbing onward. Molin's locked away most of the facts till he can discover what they mean, if ever he can. I, however, I came on the scene while chaos still prevailed. Nobody kept me from talking to folk, before the lord himself saw me and told me to begone. Thus I know about as much as anyone, little though that be."

"And—?" she prompted.

"And it doesn't seem to have been a worldly sort of capture, for a worldly end like ransom. See you, the mansion's well guarded, and neither Molin nor his wife have ever gone from it without escort. His mission here is less than popular, you recall. Those troopers are from Ranke and not subornable. The house stands in a garden, inside a high wall whose top is patrolled. Three leopards run loose on the grounds after dark.

"Molin had business with his kinsman the prince, and spent the night at the palace. His wife, the Lady Rosanda, stayed home, retired, later came out and complained she could not sleep. She therefore had Danlis wakened. Danlis is no chambermaid; there are plenty of those. She's amanuensis, adviser, confidante, collector of information, ofttimes guide or interpreter—oh, she earns her pay, does my Danlis. Despite she and I having a dawntide engagement, which is why I arrived then, she must now be out of bed at Rosanda's whim, to hold milady's hand or take dictation of milady's letters or read to milady from a soothing book—but I'm a spendthrift of words. Suffice to say that they two sought an upper chamber which is furnished as both solarium and office. A single staircase leads thither, and it is the single room at the top. There is a balcony, yes; and, the night being warm, the door to it stood open, as well as the windows. But I inspected the façade beneath. That's sheer marble, undecorated save for varying colors, devoid of ivy or of anything that any climber might cling to, save he were a fly.

"Nevertheless . . . just before the east grew pale, shrieks were heard, the watch pelted to the stair and up it. They must break down the inner door, which was bolted. I suppose that was merely against chance interruptions, for nobody had felt threatened. The solarium was in disarray; vases and things were broken; shreds torn off a robe and slight traces of blood lay about. Aye, Danlis, at least, would have resisted. But she and her mistress were gone.

"A couple of sentries on the garden wall reported hearing a loud sound as of wings. The night was cloudy-dark and they saw nothing for certain. Perhaps they imagined the noise. Suggestive is that the leopards

were found cowering in a corner and welcomed their keeper when he
would take them back to their cages.

"And this is the whole of anyone's knowledge, Illyra," Cappen ended.
"Help me, I pray you, help me get back my love!"

She was long quiet. Finally she said, in a near whisper, "It could be a
worse matter than I'd care to peer into, let alone enter."

"Or it could not," Cappen urged.

She gave him a quasi-defiant stare. "My mother's people reckon it
unlucky to do any service for a *suvesh*—a person not of their tribe—
without recompense. Pledges don't count."

Cappen scowled. "Well, I could go to a pawnshop and— But no, time
may be worth more than rubies." From the depths of unhappiness, his
grin broke forth. "Poems also are valuable, right? You S'danzo have your
ballads and love ditties. Let me incite a poem, Illyra, that shall be yours
alone."

Her expression quickened. "Truly?"

"Truly. Let me think. . . . Aye, we'll begin thus." And, venturing to
take her hands in his, Cappen murmured:

> *My lady comes to me like break of day.*
> *I dream in darkness if it chance she tarries,*
> *Until the banner of her brightness harries*
> *The hosts of Shadowland from off the way—*

She jerked free and cried, "No! You scoundrel, that has to be something you did for Danlis—or for some earlier woman you wanted in
your bed—"

"But it isn't finished," he argued. "I'll complete it for you, Illyra."

Anger left her. She shook her head, clicked her tongue, and sighed.
"No matter. You're incurably yourself. And I . . . am only half S'danzo.
I'll attempt your spell."

"By every love goddess I ever heard of," he promised unsteadily, "you
shall indeed have your own poem after this is over."

"Be still," she ordered. "Fend off anybody who comes near."

He faced about and drew his sword. The slim, straight blade was
hardly needed, for no other enterprise had site within several yards of
hers, and as wide a stretch of paving lay between him and the fringes of
the crowd. Still, to grasp the hilt gave him a sense of finally making

progress. He had felt helpless for the first hours, hopeless, as if his dear had actually died instead of—of what? Behind him he heard cards riffled, dice cast, words softly wailed.

All at once Illyra strangled a shriek. He whirled about and saw how the blood had left her olive countenance, turning it grey. She hugged herself and shuddered.

"What's wrong?" he blurted in fresh terror.

She did not look at him. "Go away," she said in a thin voice. "Forget you ever knew that woman."

"But—but what—"

"Go away, I told you! Leave me alone!"

Then somehow she relented enough to let forth: "I don't know. I dare not know. I'm just a little half-breed girl who has a few cantrips and a tricksy second sight, and—and I saw that this business goes outside of space and time, and a power beyond any magic is there—Enas Yorl could tell more, but he himself—" Her courage broke. "Go away!" she screamed. "Before I shout for Dubro and his hammer!"

"I beg your pardon," Cappen Varra said, and made haste to obey.

He retreated into the twisting streets of the Maze. They were narrow; most of the mean buildings around him were high; gloom already filled the quarter. It was as if he had stumbled into the same night where Danlis had gone . . . Danlis, creature of sun and horizons. . . . If she lived, did she remember their last time together as he remembered it, a dream dreamed centuries ago?

Having the day free, she had wanted to explore the countryside north of town. Cappen had objected on three counts. The first he did not mention; that it would require a good deal of effort, and he would get dusty and sweaty and saddle-sore. She despised men who were not at least as vigorous as she was, unless they compensated by being venerable and learned.

The second he hinted at. Sleazy though most of Sanctuary was, he knew places within it where a man and a woman could enjoy themselves, comfortably, privately—his apartment, for instance. She smiled her negation. Her family belonged to the old aristocracy of Ranke, not the newly rich, and she had been raised in its austere tradition. Albeit her father had fallen on evil times and she had been forced to take service, she kept her pride, and proudly would she yield her maidenhead to her bridegroom. Thus far she had answered Cappen's ardent declarations with the admission that she liked him and enjoyed his company and wished he would change the subject. (Buxom Lady Rosanda seemed as if she might be more approachable, but there he was careful to maintain a cheerful correctness.) He did believe she was getting beyond simple enjoyment, for her patrician reserve seemed less each time they saw each other. Yet she could not altogether have forgotten that he was merely the bastard of a minor nobleman in a remote country, himself disinherited and a foot-loose minstrel.

His third objection he dared say forth. While the hinterland was comparatively safe, Molin Torchholder would be furious did he learn that a woman of his household had gone escorted by a single armed man, and he no professional fighter. Molin would probably have been justified, too. Danlis smiled again and said, "I could ask a guardsman off duty to come along. But you have interesting friends, Cappen. Perhaps a warrior is among them?"

As a matter of fact, he knew any number, but doubted she would care to meet them—with a single exception. Luckily, Jamie the Red had no prior commitment, and agreed to join the party. Cappen told the kitchen staff to pack a picnic hamper for four.

Jamie's girls stayed behind; this was not their sort of outing, and the sun might harm their complexions. Cappen thought it a bit ungracious of the Northerner never to share them. That put him, Cappen, to considerable expense in the Street of Red Lanterns, since he could scarcely keep a paramour of his own while wooing Danlis. Otherwise he was fond of Jamie. They had met after Rosanda, chancing to hear the minstrel sing, had invited him to perform at the mansion, and then invited him back, and presently Cappen was living in the Jewelers' Quarter. Jamie had an apartment nearby.

Three horses and a pack mule clopped out of Sanctuary in the new-born morning, to a jingle of harness bells. That merriment found no echo in Cappen's head; he had been drinking past midnight, and in no case enjoyed rising before noon. Passive, he listened to Jamie:

"—Aye, milady, they're mountaineers where I hail from, poor folk but free folk. Some might call us barbarians, but that might be unwise in our hearing. For we've tales, songs, laws, ways, gods as old as any in the world, and as good. We lack much of your Southern lore, but how much of ours do you ken? Not that I boast, please understand. I've seen wonders in my wanderings. But I do say we've a few wonders of our own at home."

"I'd like to hear of them," Danlis responded.

"We know almost nothing about your country in the empire—hardly more than mentions in the chronicles of Venafer and Mattathan, or the *Natural History of Kahayavesh*. How do you happen to come here?"

"Oh—ah, I'm a younger son of our king, and I thought I'd see a bit of the world before settling down. Not that I packed any wealth along to speak of. But what with one thing and another, hiring out hither and yon for this or that, I get by." Jamie paused. "You, uh, you've far more to tell, milady. You're from the crown city of the empire, and you've got book learning, and at the same time you come out to see for yourself what land and rocks and plants and animals are like."

Cappen decided he had better get into the conversation. Not that Jamie would undercut a friend, nor Danlis be unduly attracted by a wild highlander. Nevertheless—

Jamie wasn't bad-looking in his fashion. He was huge, topping Cappen by a head and disproportionately wide in the shoulders. His loose-jointed appearance was deceptive, as the bard had learned when they sported in a public gymnasium; those were heavy bones and oak-hard muscles. A spectacular red mane drew attention from boyish face, mild blue eyes, and slightly diffident manner. Today he was plainly clad, in tunic and cross-gaitered breeks; but the knife at his belt and the ax at his saddlebow stood out.

As for Danlis, well, what could a poet do but struggle for words which might embody a ghost of her glory? She was tall and slender, her features almost cold in their straight-lined perfection and alabaster hue—till you observed the big grey eyes, golden hair piled on high, curve of lips whence came that husky voice. (How often he had lain awake yearning for her lips! He would console himself by remembering the strong, delicately blue-veined hand that she did let him kiss.) Despite waxing warmth and dust puffed up from the horses' hoofs, her cowled riding habit remained immaculate and no least dew of sweat was on her skin.

By the time Cappen got his wits out of the blankets wherein they had still been snoring, talk had turned to gods. Danlis was curious about those of Jamie's country, as she was about most things. (She did shun a few subjects as being unwholesome.) Jamie in his turn was eager to have her explain what was going on in Sanctuary. "I've heard but the one side of the matter, and Cappen's indifferent to it," he said. "Folk grumble about your master—Molin, is that his name—?"

"He is not my master," Danlis made clear. "I am a free woman who assists his wife. He himself is a high priest in Ranke, also an engineer."

"Why is the emperor angering Sanctuary? Most places I've been, colonial governments know better. They leave the local gods be."

Danlis grew pensive. "Where shall I start? Doubtless you know that Sanctuary was originally a city of the kingdom of Ilsig. Hence it has built temples to the gods of Ilsig—notably Ils, Lord of Lords, and his queen Shipri the All-Mother, but likewise others—Anen of the Harvests, Thufir the tutelary of pilgrims—"

"But none to Shalpa, patron of thieves," Cappen put in, "though these days he has the most devotees of any."

Danlis ignored his jape. "Ranke was quite a different country, under quite different gods," she continued. "Chief of these are Savankala the Thunderer, his consort Sabellia, Lady of Stars, their son Vashanka the Ten-Slayer, and his sister and consort Azyuna—gods of storm and war. According to Venafer, it was they who made Ranke supreme at last. Mattathan is more prosaic and opines that the martial spirit they inculcated was responsible for the Rankan Empire finally taking Ilsig into itself."

"Yes, milady, yes, I've heard this," Jamie said, while Cappen reflected that if his beloved had a fault, it was her tendency to lecture.

"Sanctuary has changed from of yore," she proceeded. "It has become polyglot, turbulent, corrupt, a canker on the body politic. Among its most vicious elements are the proliferating alien cults, not to speak of necromancers, witches, charlatans, and similar predators on the people. The time is overpast to restore law here. Nothing less than the imperium can do that. A necessary preliminary is the establishment of the imperial deities, the gods of Ranke, for everyone to see: symbol, rallying point, and actual presence."

"But they *have* their temples," Jamie argued.

"Small, dingy, to accommodate Rankans, few of whom stay in the city for long," Danlis retorted. "What reverence does that inspire, for the pantheon and the state? No, the emperor has decided that Savankala and Sabellia must have the greatest fane, the most richly endowed, in this entire province. Molin Torchholder will build and consecrate it. Then can the degenerates and warlocks be scourged out of Sanctuary. Afterward the prince governor can handle common felons."

Cappen didn't expect matters would be that simple. He got no chance to say so, for Jamie asked at once, "Is this wise, milady? True, many a soul hereabouts worships foreign gods, or none. But many still adore the old gods of Ilsig. They look on your, uh, Savankala as an intruder. I intend no offense, but they do. They're outraged that he's to have a bigger and grander house than Ils of the Thousand Eyes. Some fear what Ils may do about it."

"I know," Danlis said. "I regret any distress caused, and I'm sure Lord Molin does too. Still, we must overcome the agents of darkness, before the disease that they are spreads throughout the empire."

"Oh, no," Cappen managed to insert, "I've lived here awhile, mostly down in the Maze. I've had to do with a good many so-called magicians, of either sex or in between. They aren't that bad. Most I'd call pitiful. They just use their little deceptions to scrabble out what living they can, in this crumbly town where life has trapped them."

Danlis gave him a sharp glance. "You've told me people think ill of sorcery in Caronne," she said.

"They do," he admitted. "But that's because we incline to be rationalists, who consider nearly all magic a bag of tricks. Which is true. Why, I've learned a few sleights myself."

"You have?" Jamie rumbled in surprise.

"For amusement," Cappen said hastily, before Danlis could disapprove. "Some are quite elegant, virtual exercises in three-dimensional geometry." Seeing interest kindle in her, he added, "I studied mathematics in boyhood; my father, before he died, wanted me to have a gentleman's education. The main part has rusted away in me, but I remember useful or picturesque details."

"Well, give us a show, come luncheon time," Jamie proposed.

Cappen did, when they halted. That was on a hillside above the White Foal River. It wound gloaming through farmlands whose intense green denied that desert lurked on the rim of sight. The noonday sun baked strong odors out of the earth: humus, resin, juice of wild plants. A solitary plane tree graciously gave shade. Bees hummed.

After the meal, and after Danlis had scrambled off to get a closer look at a kind of lizard new to her, Cappen demonstrated his skill. She was especially taken—enchanted—by his geometric artifices. Like any Rankan lady, she carried a sewing kit in her gear; and being herself, she had writing materials along. Thus he could apply scissors and thread to paper. He showed how a single ring may be cut to produce two that are interlocked, and how a strip may be twisted to have but one surface and one edge, and whatever else he knew. Jamie watched with pleasure, if with less enthusiasm.

Observing how delight made her glow, Cappen was inspired to carry on the latest poem he was composing for her. It had been slower work than usual. He had the conceit, the motif, a comparison of her to the dawn, but hitherto only the first few lines had emerged, and no proper structure. In this moment—

> —the banner of her brightness harries
> The hosts of Shadowland from off the way
> That she now wills to tread—for what can stay
> The triumph of that radiance she carries?

Yes, it was clearly going to be a rondel. Therefore the next two lines were:

> My lady comes to me like break of day.
> I dream in darkness if it chance she tarries.

He had gotten that far when abruptly she said: "Cappen, this is such a fine excursion, such splendid scenery. I'd like to watch sunrise over the river tomorrow. Will you escort me?"

Sunrise? But she was telling Jamie, "We need not trouble you about that. I had in mind a walk out of town to the bridge. If we choose the proper route, it's well guarded everywhere, perfectly safe."

And scant traffic moved at that hour; besides, the monumental statues along the bridge stood in front of bays which they screened from passersby— "Oh, yes, indeed, Danlis, I'd love to," Cappen said. For such an opportunity, he could get up before cockcrow.

—When he reached the mansion, she had not been there.

Exhausted after his encounter with Illyra, Cappen hied him to the Vulgar Unicorn and related his woes to One-Thumb. The big man had come on shift at the inn early, for a fellow boniface had not yet recovered from the effects of a dispute with a patron. (Shortly thereafter, the patron was found floating facedown under a pier. Nobody questioned One-Thumb about this; his regulars knew that he preferred the establishment safe, if not always orderly.) He offered taciturn sympathy and the loan of a bed upstairs. Cappen scarcely noticed the insects that shared it.

Waking about sunset, he found water and a washcloth, and felt much refreshed—hungry and thirsty, too. He made his way to the taproom below. Dusk was blue in windows and open door, black under the rafters. Candles smeared weak light along the counter and main board and on lesser tables at the walls. The air had grown cool, which allayed the stenches of the Maze. Thus Cappen was acutely aware of the smells of beer—old in the rushes underfoot, fresh where a trio of men had settled down to guzzle—and of spitted meat, wafting from the kitchen.

One-Thumb approached, a shadowy hulk save for highlights on his bald pate. "Sit," he grunted. "Eat. Drink." He carried a great tankard and a plate bearing a slab of roast beef on bread. These he put on a corner table, and himself on a chair.

Cappen sat also and attacked the meal. "You're very kind," he said between bites and draughts.

"You'll pay when you get coin, or if you don't, then in songs and magic stunts. They're good for trade." One-Thumb fell silent and peered at his guest.

When Cappen was done, the innkeeper said, "While you slept, I sent out a couple of fellows to ask around. Maybe somebody saw something that might be helpful. Don't worry—I didn't mention you, and it's natural I'd be interested to know what really happened."

The minstrel stared. "You've gone to a deal of trouble on my account."

"I told you, I want to know for my own sake. If deviltry's afoot, where could it strike next?" One-Thumb rubbed a finger across the toothless part of his gums. "Of course, if you should luck out—I don't expect it, but in case you do—remember who gave you a boost." A figure appeared in the door and he went to render service.

After a bit of muttered talk, he led the newcomer to Cappen's place. When the minstrel recognized the lean youth, his pulse leaped. One-Thumb would not have brought him and Hanse together without cause; bard and thief found each other insufferable. They nodded coldly but did not speak until the tapster returned with a round of ale.

When the three were seated, One-Thumb said, "Well spit it out, boy. You claim you've got news."

"For him?" Hanse flared, gesturing at Cappen.

"Never mind who. Just talk."

Hanse scowled. "I don't talk for a single lousy mugful."

"You do if you want to keep on coming in here."

Hanse bit his lip. The Vulgar Unicorn was a rendezvous virtually indispensable to one in his trade.

Cappen thought best to sweeten the pill: "I'm known to Molin Torch-holder. If I can serve him in this matter, he won't be stingy. Nor will I. Shall we say—hmm—ten gold royals to you?"

The sum was not princely, but on that account plausible. "Awright, awright," Hanse replied. "I'd been casing a job I might do in the Jewelers' Quarter. A squad of the watch came by toward morning and I figured I'd better go home, not by the way I came, either. So I went along the Avenue of Temples, as I might be wanting to stop in and pay my respects to some god or other. It was a dark night, overcast, the reason I'd been out where I was. But you know how several of the temples keep lights going. There was enough to see by, even upward a ways. Nobody else was in sight. Suddenly I heard a kind of whistling, flapping noise aloft. I looked and—"

He broke off.

"And what?" Cappen blurted. One-Thumb sat impassive.

Hanse swallowed. "I don't swear to this," he said. "It was still dim, you realize. I've wondered since if I didn't see wrong."

"What was it?" Cappen gripped the table edge till his fingernails whitened.

Hanse wet his throat and said in a rush: "What it seemed like was a huge black thing, almost like a snake, but bat-winged. It came streaking from, oh, more or less the direction of Molin's, I'd guess now that I think back. And it was aimed more or less toward the temple of Ils. There was something that dangled below, as it might be a human body or two. I didn't stay to watch, I ducked into the nearest alley and waited. When I came out, it was gone."

He knocked back his ale and rose. "That's all," he snapped. "I don't want to remember the sight any longer, and if anybody ever asks, I was never here tonight."

"Your story's worth a couple more drinks," One-Thumb invited.

"Another evening," Hanse demurred. "Right now I need a whore. Don't forget those ten royals, singer." He left, stiff-legged.

"Well," said the innkeeper after a silence, "what do you make of this latest?"

Cappen suppressed a shiver. His palms were cold. "I don't know, save that what we confront is not of our kind."

"You told me once you've got a charm against magic."

Cappen fingered the little silver amulet, in the form of a coiled snake, he wore around his neck. "I'm not sure. A wizard I'd done a favor for gave me this, years ago. He claimed it'd protect me against spells and supernatural beings of less than godly rank. But to make it work, I have to utter three truths about the spellcaster or the creature. I've done that in two or three scrapes, and come out of them intact, but I can't prove the talisman was responsible."

More customers entered, and One-Thumb must go to serve them. Cappen nursed his ale. He yearned to get drunk and belike the landlord would stand him what was needful, but he didn't dare. He had already learned more than he thought the opposition would approve of—whoever or whatever the opposition was. They might have means of discovering this.

His candle flickered. He glanced up and saw a beardless fat man in an ornate formal robe, scarcely normal dress for a visit to the Vulgar Unicorn. "Greetings," the person said. His voice was like a child's.

Cappen squinted through the gloom. "I don't believe I know you," he replied.

"No, but you will come to believe it, oh, yes, you will." The fat man sat down. One-Thumb came over and took an order for red wine—"a decent wine, mine host, a Zhanuvend or Baladach." Coin gleamed forth.

Cappen's heart thumped. "Enas Yorl?" he breathed.

The other nodded. "In the flesh, the all-too mutable flesh. I do hope my curse strikes again soon. Almost any shape would be better than this. I hate being overweight. I'm a eunuch, too. The times I've been a woman were better than this."

"I'm sorry, sir," Cappen took care to say. Though he could not rid himself of the spell laid on him, Enas Yorl was a powerful thaumaturge, no mere prestidigitator.

"At least I've not been arbitrarily displaced. You can't imagine how annoying it is, suddenly to find oneself elsewhere, perhaps miles away. I was able to come here in proper wise, in my litter. *Faugh*, how can anyone voluntarily set shoes to these open sewers they call streets in the Maze?"

The wine arrived. "Best we speak fast and to the point, young man, that we may finish and I get home before the next contretemps."

Enas Yorl sipped and made a face. "I've been swindled," he whined. "This is barely drinkable, if that."

"Maybe your present palate is at fault, sir," Cappen suggested. He did not add that the tongue definitely had a bad case of logorrhea. It was an almost physical torture to sit stalled, but he had better humor the mage.

"Yes, quite probably. Nothing has tasted good since— Well. To business. On hearing that One-Thumb was inquiring about last night's incident, I sent forth certain investigators of my own. You will understand that I've been trying to find out as much as I can." Enas Yorl drew a sign in the air. "Purely precautionary. I have no desire whatsoever to cross the Powers concerned in this."

A wintry tingle went through Cappen. "You know who they are, what it's about?" His tone wavered.

Enas Yorl wagged a finger. "Not so hasty, boy, not so hasty. My latest information was of a seemingly unsuccessful interview you had with Illyra the seeress. I also learned you were now in this hostel and close to its landlord. Obviously you are involved. I must know why, how, how much—everything."

"Then you'll help—sir?"

A headshake made chin and jowls wobble. "Absolutely not. I told you I want no part of this. But in exchange for whatever data you possess, I am willing to explicate as far as I am able, and to advise you. Be warned: my advice will doubtless be that you drop the matter and perhaps leave town."

And doubtless he would be right, Cappen thought. It simply happened to be counsel that was impossible for a lover to follow . . . unless—O kindly gods of Caronne, no, no!—unless Danlis was dead.

The whole story spilled out of him, quickened and deepened by keen questions. At the end, he sat breathless while Enas Yorl nodded.

"Yes, that appears to confirm what I suspected," the mage said most softly. He stared past the minstrel, into shadows that loomed and flickered. Buzz of talk, clink of drinking ware, occasional gust of laughter among customers seemed remoter than the moon.

"What was it?" broke from Cappen.

"A sikkintair, a Flying Knife. It can have been nothing else."

"A—what?"

Enas focused on his companion. "The monster that took the women," he explained. "Sikkintairs are an attribute of Ils. A pair of sculptures on the grand stairway of his temple represent them."

"Oh, yes, I've seen those, but never thought—"

"No, you're not a votary of any gods they have here. Myself, when I got word of the abduction, I sent my familiars scuttling about and cast spells of inquiry. I received indications . . . I can't described them to you, who lack arcane lore. I established that the very fabric of space had been troubled. Vibrations had not quite damped out as yet, and were centered on the temple of Ils. You may, if you wish a crude analogy, visualize a water surface and the waves, fading to ripples and finally to naught, when a diver has passed through."

Enas Yorl drank more in a gulp than was his wont. "Civilization was old in Ilsig when Ranke was still a barbarian village," he said, as though to himself; his gaze had drifted away again, toward darkness. "Its myths depicted the home of the gods as being outside the world—not above, not below, but outside. Philosophers of a later, more rationalistic era elaborated this into a theory of parallel universes. My own researches— you will understand that my condition has made me especially interested in the theory of dimensions, the subtler aspects of geometry—my own researches have demonstrated the possibility of transference between these different spaces.

"As another analogy, consider a pack of cards. One is inhabited by a king, one by a knight, one by a deuce, et cetera. Ordinarily none of the figures can leave the plane on which it exists. If, however, a very thin piece of absorbent material soaked in a unique kind of solvent were laid between two cards, the dyes that form them could pass through: retaining their configuration, I trust. Actually, of course, this is a less than ideal comparison, for the transference is accomplished through a particular contortion of the continuum—"

Cappen could endure no more pedantry. He crashed his tankard down on the table and shouted, "By all the hells of all the cults, will you get to the point?"

Men stared from adjacent seats, decided no fight was about to erupt, and went back to their interests. These included negotiations with street-walkers who, lanterns in hand, had come in looking for trade.

Enas Yorl smiled. "I forgive your outburst, under the circumstances," he said. "I too am occasionally young.

"Very well. Given the foregoing data, including yours, the infrastructure of events seems reasonably evident. You are aware of the conflict over a proposed new temple, which is to outdo that of Ils and Shipri. I do not maintain that the god has taken a direct hand. I certainly hope he feels that would be beneath his dignity; a theomachy would not be good for us, to understate the case a trifle. But he may have inspired a few of his more fanatical priests to action. He may have revealed to them, in dreams or vision, the means whereby they could cross to the next world and there make the sikkintairs do their bidding. I hypothesize that the Lady Rosanda—and, to be sure, her coadjutrix, your inamorata—are incarcerated in that world. The temple is top full of priests, deacons, acolytes, and lay people for hiding the wife of a magnate. However, the gate need not be recognizable as such."

Cappen controlled himself with an inward shudder and made his trained voice casual: "What might it look like, sir?"

"Oh, probably a scroll, taken from a coffer where it had long lain forgotten, and now unrolled—yes, I should think in the sanctum, to draw power from the sacred objects and to be seen by as few persons as possible who are not in the conspiracy—" Enas Yorl came out of his abstraction. "Beware! I deduce your thought. Choke it before it kills you."

Cappen ran sandy tongue over leathery lips. "What . . . should we . . . expect to happen, sir?"

"That is an interesting question," Enas Yorl said. "I can but conjecture. Yet I am well acquainted with the temple hierarchy and—I don't think the archpriest is privy to the matter. He's too aged and weak. On the other hand, this is quite in the style of Hazroah, the high flamen. Moreover, of late he has in effect taken over the governance of the temple from his nominal superior. He's bold, ruthless—should have been a soldier— Well, putting myself in his skin, I'll predict that he'll let Molin stew awhile, then cautiously open negotiations—a hint at first, and always a claim that this is the will of Ils.

"None but the emperor can cancel an undertaking for the imperial deities. Persuading him will take much time and pressure. Molin is a Rankan aristocrat of the old school; he will be torn between his duty to his gods, his state, and his wife. But I suspect that eventually he can be worn down to the point where he agrees that it is, in truth, bad policy to exalt Savankala and Sabellia in a city whose tutelaries they have never been. He in his turn can influence the emperor as desired."

"How long would this take, do you think?" Cappen whispered. "Till the women are released?"

Enas Yorl shrugged. "Years, possibly. Hazroah may try to hasten the process by demonstrating that the Lady Rosanda is subject to punishment. Yes, I should imagine that the remains of an ancilla who had been tortured to death, delivered on Molin's doorstep, would be a rather strong argument."

His look grew intense on the appalled countenance across from him. "I know," he said. "You're breeding fever dreams of a heroic rescue. It cannot be done. Even supposing that somehow you won through the gate and brought her back, the gate would remain. I doubt Ils would personally seek revenge; besides being petty, that could provoke open strife with Savankala and his retinue, who're formidable characters themselves. But Ils would not stay the hand of the Flamen Hazroah, who is a most vengeful sort. If you escaped his assassins, a sikkintair would come after you, and nowhere in the world could you and she hide. Your talisman would be of no avail. The sikkintair is not supernatural, unless you give that designation to the force which enables so huge a mass to fly; and it is from no magician, but from the god.

"So forget the girl. The town is full of them." He fished in his purse and spilled a handful of coins on the table. "Go to a good whorehouse, enjoy yourself, and raise one for poor old Enas Yorl."

He got up and waddled off. Cappen sat staring at the coins. They made a generous sum, he realized vaguely: silver lunars, to the number of thirty.

One-Thumb came over. "What'd he say?" the taverner asked.

"I should abandon hope," Cappen muttered. His eyes stung; his vision blurred. Angrily, he wiped them.

"I've a notion I might not be smart to hear more." One-Thumb laid his mutilated hand on Cappen's shoulder. "Care to get drunk? On the house. I'll have to take your money or the rest will want free booze too, but I'll return it tomorrow."

"No, I—I thank you, but—but you're busy, and I need someone I can talk to. Just lend me a lantern, if you will."

"That might attract a robber, fellow, what with those fine clothes of yours."

Cappen gripped sword hilt. "He'd be very welcome, the short while he lasted," he said in bitterness.

He climbed to his feet. His fingers remembered to gather the coins.

Jamie let him in. The Northerner had hastily thrown a robe over his massive frame; he carried the stone lamp that was a night-light. "*Shhsh*," he said. "The lassies are asleep." He nodded toward a closed door at the far end of this main room. Bringing the lamp higher, he got a clear view of Cappen's face. His own registered shock. "Hey-o, lad, what ails you? I've seen men poleaxed who looked happier."

Cappen stumbled across the threshold and collapsed in an armchair. Jamie barred the outer door, touched a stick of punk to the lamp flame and lit candles, filled wine goblets. Drawing a seat opposite, he sat down, laid red-furred right shank across left knee, and said gently, "Tell me."

When it had spilled from Cappen, he was a long span quiet. On the walls shimmered his weapons, among pretty pictures that his housemates had selected. At last he asked low, "Have you quit?"

"I don't know, I don't know," Cappen groaned.

"I think you can go on a ways, whether or no things are as the witch-master supposes. We hold where I come from that no man can flee his weird, so he may as well meet it in a way that'll leave a good story. Besides, this may not be our deathday; and I doubt yon dragons are unkillable, but it could be fun finding out; and chiefly, I was much taken with your girl. Not many like her, my friend. They also say in my homeland, 'Waste not, want not.'"

Cappen lifted his glance, astounded. "You mean I should try to free her?" he exclaimed.

"No, I mean *we* should." Jamie chuckled. "Life's gotten a wee bit dull for me of late—aside from Butterfly and Light-of-Pearl, of course. Besides, I could use a share of reward money."

"I . . . I want to," Cappen stammered. "How I want to! But the odds against us—"

"She's your girl, and it's your decision. I'll not blame you if you hold back. Belike, then, in your country, they don't believe a man's first troth is to his woman and kids. Anyway, for you that was no more than a hope."

A surge went through the minstrel. He sprang up and paced, back and forth, back and forth. "But what could we do?"

"Well, we could scout the temple and see what's what," Jamie proposed. "I've been there once in a while, reckoning 'twould do no hurt to give those gods their honor. Maybe we'll find that indeed naught can be done in aid. Or maybe we won't, and go ahead and do it."

Danlis—

Fire blossomed in Cappen Varra. He was young. He drew his sword and swung it whistling on high. "Yes! We will!"

A small grammarian part of him noted the confusion of tenses and moods in the conversation.

The sole traffic on the Avenue of Temples was a night breeze, cold and sibilant. Stars, as icy to behold, looked down on its broad emptiness, on darkened buildings and weatherworn idols and rustling gardens. Here and there flames cast restless light, from porticoes or gables or ledges, out of glass lanterns or iron pots or pierced stone jars. At the foot of the grand staircase leading to the fane of Ils and Shipri, fire formed halos on the enormous figures, male and female in robes of antiquity, that flanked it.

Beyond, the god-house itself loomed, porticoed front, great bronze doors, granite walls rising sheer above to a gilt dome from which light also gleamed; the highest point in Sanctuary.

Cappen started up. "Halt," said Jamie, and plucked at his cloak. "We can't walk straight in. They keep guards in the vestibule, you know."

"I want a close view of those sikkintairs," the bard explained.

"Um, well, maybe not a bad idea, but let's be quick. If a squad of the watch comes by, we're in trouble." They could not claim they simply wished to perform their devotions, for a civilian was not allowed to bear more arms in this district than a knife. Cappen and Jamie each had that, but no illuminant like honest men. In addition, Cappen carried his rapier, Jamie a claymore, a visored conical helmet, and a knee-length byrnie. He had, moreover, furnished spears for both.

Cappen nodded and bounded aloft. Halfway, he stopped and gazed. The statue was a daunting sight. Of obsidian polished glassy smooth, it might have measured thirty feet were the tail not coiled under the narrow body. The two legs which supported the front ended in talons the length of Jamie's dirk. An up-reared, serpentine neck bore a wickedly lanceolate head, jaws parted to show fangs that the sculptor had rendered in diamond. From the back sprang wings, batlike save for their sharp-pointed curvatures, which if unfolded might well have covered another ten yards.

"Aye," Jamie murmured, "such a brute could bear off two women like an eagle a brace of leverets. Must take a lot of food to power it. I wonder what quarry they hunt at home."

"We may find out," Cappen said, and wished he hadn't.

"Come." Jamie led the way back, and around to the left side of the temple. It occupied almost its entire ground, leaving but a narrow strip of flagstones. Next to that, a wall enclosed the flower-fragrant sanctum of Eshi, the love goddess. Thus the space between was gratifyingly dark; the intruders could not now be spied from the avenue. Yet enough light filtered in that they saw what they were doing. Cappen wondered if this meant she smiled on their venture. After all, it was for love, mainly. Besides, he had always been an enthusiastic worshiper of hers, or at any rate of her counterparts in foreign pantheons; oftener than most men had he rendered her favorite sacrifice.

Jamie had pointed out that the building must have lesser doors for utilitarian purposes. He soon found one, bolted for the night and between windows that were hardly more than slits, impossible to crawl through. He could have hewn the wood panels asunder, but the noise might be heard. Cappen had a better idea. He got his partner down on hands and knees. Standing on the broad back, he poked his spear through a window and worked it along the inside of the door. After some fumbling and whispered obscenities, he caught the latch with the head and drew the bolt.

"*Hoosh*, you missed your trade, I'm thinking," said the Northerner as he rose and opened the way.

"No, burglary's too risky for my taste," Cappen replied in feeble jest. The fact was that he had never stolen or cheated unless somebody deserved such treatment.

"Even burgling the house of a god?" Jamie's grin was wider than necessary.

Cappen shivered. "Don't remind me."

They entered a storeroom, shut the door, and groped through murk to the exit. Beyond was a hall. Widely spaced lamps gave bare visibility. Otherwise the intruders saw emptiness and heard silence. The vestibule and nave of the temple were never closed; the guards watched over a priest always prepared to accept offerings. But elsewhere hierarchy and staff were asleep. Or so the two hoped.

Jamie had known that the holy of holies was in the dome, Ils being a sky god. Now he let Cappen take the lead, as having more familiarity with interiors and ability to reason out a route. The minstrel used half his mind for that and scarcely noticed the splendors through which he passed. The second half was busy recollecting legends of heroes who incurred the anger of a god, especially a major god, but won to happiness in the end because they had the blessing of another. He decided that future attempts to propitiate Ils would only draw the attention of that august personage; however, Savankala would be pleased, and, yes, as for native deities, he would by all means fervently cultivate Eshi.

A few times, which felt ghastly long, he took a wrong turning and must retrace his steps after he had discovered that. Presently, though, he found a staircase which seemed to zigzag over the inside of an exterior wall. Landing after landing passed by—

The last was enclosed in a very small room, a booth, albeit richly ornamented—

He opened the door and stepped out—

Wind searched between the pillars that upheld the dome, through his clothes and in toward his bones. He saw stars. They were the brightest in heaven, for the entry booth was the pedestal of a gigantic lantern. Across a floor tiled in symbols unknown to him, he observed something large at each cardinal point—an altar, two statues, and the famous Thunderstone, he guessed; they were shrouded in cloth of gold. Before the eastern object was stretched a band, the far side of which seemed to be aglow.

He gathered his courage and approached. The thing was a parchment, about eight feet long and four wide, hung by cords from the upper corners to a supporting member of the dome. The cords appeared to be glued fast, as if to avoid making holes in the surface. The lower edge of the scroll, two feet above the floor, was likewise secured; but to a pair of anvils surely brought here for the purpose. Nevertheless the parchment flapped and rattled a bit in the wind. It was covered with cabalistic signs.

Cappen stepped around to the other side, and whistled low. That held a picture, within a narrow border. Past the edge of what might be a pergola, the scene went to a meadowland made stately by oak trees standing at random intervals. About a mile away—the perspective was marvelously executed—stood a building of manorial size in a style he had never seen before, twistily colonnaded, extravagantly sweeping of roof and eaves, bloodred. A formal garden surrounded it, whose paths and topiaries were of equally alien outline; fountains sprang in intricate patterns. Beyond the house, terrain rolled higher, and snowpeaks thrust above the horizon. The sky was deep blue.

"What the pox!" exploded from Jamie. "Sunshine's coming out of that painting. I *feel* it."

Cappen rallied his wits and paid heed. Yes, warmth as well as light, and . . . and odors? And were those fountains not actually at play?

An eerie thrilling took him. "I . . . believe . . . we've . . . found the gate," he said.

He poked his spear cautiously at the scroll. The point met no resistance; it simply moved on. Jamie went behind. "You've not pierced it," he reported. "Nothing sticks out on this side which, by the way, is quite solid."

"No," Cappen answered faintly, "the spearhead's in the next world."

He drew the weapon back. He and Jamie stared at each other.

"Well?" said the Northerner.

"We'll never get a better chance," Cappen's throat responded for him. "It'd be blind foolishness to retreat now, unless we decide to give up the whole venture."

"We, uh, we could go tell Molin, no, the prince what we've found."

"And be cast into a madhouse? If the prince *did* send investigators anyway, the plotters need merely take this thing down and hide it till— the squad has left. No." Cappen squared his shoulders. "Do what you like, Jamie, but I am going through."

Underneath, he heartily wished he had less self-respect, or at least that he weren't in love with Danlis.

Jamie scowled and sighed. "Aye, right you are, I suppose. I'd not looked for matters to take so headlong a course. I awaited that we'd simply scout around. Had I foreseen this, I'd have roused the lassies to bid them, well, goodnight." He hefted his spear and drew his sword. Abruptly he laughed. "Whatever comes, 'twill not be dull!"

Stepping high over the threshold, Cappen went forward.

It felt like walking through any door, save that he entered a mild summer's day. After Jamie had followed, he saw that the vista in the parchment was that on which he had just turned his back: a veiled mass, a pillar, stars above a nighted city. He checked the opposite side of the strip, and met the same designs as had been painted on its mate.

No, he thought, not its mate. If he had understood Enas Yorl aright, and rightly remembered what his tutor in mathematics had told him about esoteric geometry, there could be but a single scroll. One side of it gave on this universe, the other side on his, and a spell had twisted dimensions until matter could pass straight between.

Here too the parchment was suspended by cords, though in a pergola of yellow marble, whose circular stairs led down to the meadow. He imagined a sikkintair would find the passage tricky, especially if it was burdened with two women in its claws. The monster had probably hugged them close to it, come in at high speed, folded its wings, and glided between the pillars of the dome and the margins of the gate. On the outbound trip, it must have crawled through into Sanctuary.

All this Cappen did and thought in half a dozen heartbeats. A shout yanked his attention back. Three men who had been idling on the stairs had noticed the advent and were on their way up. Large and hard-featured, they bore the shaven visages, high-crested morions, gilt cuirasses, black tunics and boots, shortswords, and halberds of temple guards. "Who in the Unholy's name are you?" called the first. "What're you doing here?"

Jamie's qualms vanished under a tide of boyish glee. "I doubt they'll believe any words of ours," he said. "We'll have to convince them a different way. If you can handle him on our left, I'll take his *feres*."

Cappen felt less confident. But he lacked time to be afraid; shuddering would have to be done in a more convenient hour. Besides, he was quite a good fencer. He dashed across the floor and down the stair.

The trouble was, he had no experience with spears. He jabbed. The halberdier held his weapon, both hands close together, near the middle of the shaft. He snapped it against Cappen's, deflected the thrust, and nearly tore the minstrel's out of his grasp. The watchman's return would have skewered his enemy, had the minstrel not flopped straight to the marble.

The guard guffawed, braced his legs wide, swung the halberd back for an axhead blow. As it descended, his hands shifted toward the end of the helve.

Chips flew. Cappen had rolled downstairs. He twirled the whole way to the ground and sprang erect. He still clutched his spear, which had bruised him whenever he crossed above it. The sentry bellowed and hopped in pursuit. Cappen ran.

Behind them, a second guard sprawled and flopped, diminuendo, in what seemed an impossibly copious and bright amount of blood. Jamie had hurled his own spear as he charged and taken the man in the neck. The third was giving the Northerner a brisk fight, halberd against claymore. He had longer reach, but the redhead had more brawn. Thump and clatter rang across the daisies.

Cappen's adversary was bigger than he was. This had the drawback that the former could not change speed or direction as readily. When the guard was pounding along at his best clip, ten or twelve feet in the rear, Cappen stopped within a coin's breadth, whirled about, and threw his shaft. He did not do that as his comrade had done. He pitched it between the guard's legs. The man crashed to the grass. Cappen plunged in. He didn't risk trying for a stab. That would let the armored combatant grapple him. He wrenched the halberd loose and skipped off.

The sentinel rose. Cappen reached an oak and tossed the halberd. It lodged among boughs. He drew blade. His foe did the same.

Shortsword versus rapier—*much* better, though Cappen must have a care. The torso opposing him was protected. Still, the human anatomy has more vulnerable points than that. "Shall we dance?" Cappen asked.

As he and Jamie approached the house, a shadow slid across them. They glanced aloft and saw the gaunt black form of a sikkintair. For an instant, they nerved themselves for the worst. However, the Flying Knife simply caught an updraft, planed high, and hovered in sinister magnificence. "Belike they don't hunt men unless commanded to," the Northerner speculated. "Bear and buffalo are meatier."

Cappen frowned at the scarlet walls before him. "The next question," he said, "is why nobody has come out against us."

"Um, I'd deem those wights we left scattered around were the only fighting men here. What task was theirs? Why, to keep the ladies from escaping, if those are allowed to walk outdoors by day. As for yon manse, while it's plenty big, I suspect it's on loan from its owner. Naught but a few servants need be on hand—and the women, let's hope. I don't suppose anybody happened to see our little brawl."

The thought that they might effect the rescue—soon, safely, easily—went through Cappen in a wave of dizziness. Afterward—he and Jamie had discussed that. If the temple hierophants, from Hazroah on down, were put under immediate arrest, that ought to dispose of the vengeance problem.

Gravel scrunched underfoot. Rose, jasmine, honeysuckle sweetened the air. Fountains leaped and chimed. The partners reached the main door. It was oaken, with many glass eyes inset; the knocker had the shape of a sikkintair.

Jamie leaned his spear, unsheathed his sword, turned the knob left-handed, and swung the door open. A maroon sumptuousness of carpet, hangings, upholstery brooded beyond. He and Cappen entered. Inside were quietness and an odor like that just before a thunderstorm.

A man in a deacon's black robe came through an archway, his tonsure agleam in the dimness. "Did I hear— Oh!" he gasped, and scuttled backward.

Jamie made a long arm and collared him. "Not so fast, friend," the warrior said genially. "We've a request, and if you oblige, we won't get stains on this pretty rug. Where are your guests?"

"What, what, what," the deacon gobbled.

Jamie shook him, in leisured wise lest he quite dislocate the shoulder. "Lady Rosanda, wife to Molin Torchholder, and her assistant Danlis. Take us to them. Oh, and we'd liefer not meet folk along the way. It might get messy if we did."

The deacon fainted.

"Ah, well," Jamie said. "I hate the idea of cutting down unarmed men, but chances are they won't be foolhardy." He filled his lungs. *"Rosanda!"* he bawled. *"Danlis! Jamie and Cappen Varra are here! Come on home!"*

The volume almost bowled his companion over. "Are you mad?" the minstrel exclaimed. "You'll warn the whole staff—" A flash lit his mind: if they had seen no further guards, surely there were none, and nothing corporeal remained to fear. Yet every minute's delay heightened the danger of something else going wrong. Somebody might find signs of invasion back in the temple; the gods alone knew what lurked in this realm. . . . Yes, Jamie's judgment might prove mistaken, but it was the best he could have made.

Servitors appeared, and recoiled from naked steel. And then, and then—

Through a doorway strode Danlis. She led by the hand, or dragged, a half-hysterical Rosanda. Both were decently attired and neither looked abused, but pallor in cheeks and smudges under eyes bespoke what they must have suffered.

Cappen came nigh dropping his spear. "Beloved!" he cried. "Are you hale?"

"We've not been ill-treated in the flesh, aside from the snatching itself," she answered efficiently. "The threats, should Hazroah not get his way, have been cruel. Can we leave now?"

"Aye, the soonest, the best," Jamie growled. "Lead them on ahead, Cappen." His sword covered the rear. On his way out, he retrieved the spear he had left.

They started back over the garden paths. Danlis and Cappen between them must help Rosanda along. That woman's plump prettiness was lost in tears, moans, whimpers, and occasional screams. He paid scant attention. His gaze kept seeking the clear profile of his darling. When her grey eyes turned toward him, his heart became a lyre.

She parted her lips. He waited for her to ask in dazzlement, *"How did you ever do this, you unbelievable, wonderful men?"*

"What have we ahead of us?" she wanted to know.

Well, it was an intelligent query. Cappen swallowed disappointment and sketched the immediate past. Now, he said, they'd return via the gate to the dome and make their stealthy way from the temple, thence to Molin's dwelling for a joyous reunion. But then they must act promptly—yes, roust the prince out of bed for authorization—and occupy the temple and arrest everybody in sight before new trouble got fetched from this world.

Rosanda gained some self-control as he talked. "Oh, my, oh, my," she wheezed, "you unbelievable, wonderful men."

An ear-piercing trill slashed across her voice. The escapers looked behind them. At the entrance to the house stood a thickset middle-aged person in the scarlet robe of a ranking priest of Ils. He held a pipe to his mouth and blew.

"Hazroah!" Rosanda shrilled. "The ringleader!"

"The high flamen—" Danlis began.

A rush in the air interrupted. Cappen flung his vision skyward and knew the nightmare was true. The sikkintair was descending. Hazroah had summoned it.

"Why, you son of a bitch!" Jamie roared. Still well behind the rest, he lifted his spear, brought it back, flung it with his whole strength and weight. The point went home in Hazroah's breast. Ribs did not stop it. He spouted blood, crumpled, and spouted no more. The shaft quivered above his body.

But the sikkintair's vast wings eclipsed the sun. Jamie rejoined his band and plucked the second spear from Cappen's fingers. "Hurry on, lad," he ordered. "Get them to safety."

"Leave you? No!" protested his comrade.

Jamie spat an oath. "Do you want the whole faring to've gone for naught? Hurry, I said!"

Danlis tugged at Cappen's sleeve. "He's right. The state requires our testimony."

Cappen stumbled onward. From time to time he glanced back.

In the shadow of the wings, Jamie's hair blazed. He stood foursquare, spear grasped as a huntsman does. Agape, the Flying Knife rushed down upon him. Jamie thrust straight between those jaws, and twisted.

The monster let out a saw-toothed shriek. Its wings threshed, made thundercrack, it swooped by, a foot raked. Jamie had his claymore out. He parried the blow.

The sikkintair rose. The shaft waggled from its throat. It spread great ebon membranes, looped, and came back earthward. Its claws were before it. Air whirred behind.

Jamie stood his ground, sword in right hand, knife in left. As the talons smote, he fended them off with the dirk. Blood sprang from his thigh, but his byrnie took most of the edged sweep. And his sword hewed. The sikkintair ululated again. It tried to ascend, and couldn't. Jamie had crippled its left wing. It landed—Cappen felt the impact through soles and bones—and hitched itself toward him. From around the spear came a geyser hiss.

Jamie held fast where he was. As fangs struck at him, he sidestepped, sprang back, and threw his shoulders against the shaft. Leverage swung jaws aside. He glided by the neck toward the forequarters. Both of his blades attacked the spine.

Cappen and the women hastened on.

They were almost at the pergola when footfalls drew his eyes rearward. Jamie loped at an overtaking pace. Behind him, the sikkintair lay in a heap.

The redhead pulled alongside. "*Hai*, what a fight!" he panted. "Thanks for this journey, friend! A drinking bout's worth of thanks!"

They mounted the death-defiled stairs. Cappen peered across miles. Wings beat in heaven, from the direction of the mountains. Horror stabbed his guts. "Look!" He could barely croak.

Jamie squinted. "More of them," he said. "A score, maybe. We can't cope with so many. An army couldn't."

"That whistle was heard farther away than mortals would hear," Danlis added starkly.

"What do we linger for?" Rosanda wailed. "Come, take us home!"

"And the sikkintairs follow?" Jamie retorted. "No. I've my lassies, and kinfolk, and—" He moved to stand before the parchment. Edged metal dripped in his hands; red lay splashed across helm, ring mail, clothing, face. His grin broke forth, wry. "A spaewife once told me I'd die on the far side of strangeness. I'll wager she didn't know her own strength."

"You assume that the mission of the beasts is to destroy us, and when that is done they will return to their lairs." The tone Danlis used might have served for a remark about the weather.

"Aye, what else? The harm they'd wreak would be in a hunt for us. But put to such trouble, they could grow furious and harry our whole world. That's the more likely when Hazroah lies skewered. Who else can control them?"

"None that I know of, and he talked quite frankly to us." She nodded. "Yes, it behooves us to die where we are." Rosanda sank down and blubbered. Danlis showed irritation. "Up!" she commanded her mistress. "Up and meet your fate like a Rankan matron!"

Cappen goggled hopelessly at her. She gave him a smile. "Have no regrets, dear," she said. "You did well. The conspiracy against the state has been checked."

*The far side of strangeness—check—chessboard—that version of chess where you pretend the right and left sides of the board are identical on a cylinder—*tumbled through Cappen. The Flying Knives drew closer fast. *Curious aspects of geometry—*

Lightning-smitten, he knew . . . or guessed he did . . . "No, Jamie, we go!" he yelled.

"To no avail save reaping of innocents?" The big man hunched his shoulders. "Never."

"Jamie, let us by! I can close the gate. I swear I can—I swear by—by Eshi—"

The Northerner locked eyes with Cappen for a span that grew. At last: "You are my brother in arms." He stood aside. "Go on."

The sikkintairs were so near that the noise of their speed reached Cappen. He urged Danlis toward the scroll. She lifted her skirt a trifle, revealing a dainty ankle, and stepped through. He hauled on Rosanda's wrist. The woman wavered to her feet but seemed unable to find her direction. Cappen took an arm and passed it into the next world for Danlis to pull. Himself, he gave a mighty shove on milady's buttocks. She crossed over.

He did. And Jamie.

Beneath the temple dome, Cappen's rapier reached high and slashed. Louder came the racket of cloven air. Cappen severed the upper cords. The parchment fell, wrinkling, crackling. He dropped his weapon, a-clang, squatted, and stretched his arms wide. The free corners he seized. He pulled them to the corners that were still secured, to make a closed band of the scroll.

From it sounded monstrous thumps and scrapes. The sikkintairs were crawling into the pergola. For them the portal must hang unchanged, open for their hunting.

Cappen gave that which he held a half-twist and brought the edges back together.

Thus he created a surface which had but a single side and a single edge. Thus he obliterated the gate.

He had not been sure what would follow. He had fleetingly supposed he would smuggle the scroll out, held in its paradoxical form, and eventually glue it—unless he could burn it. But upon the instant that he completed the twist and juncture, the parchment was gone. Enas Yorl told him afterward that he had made it impossible for the thing to exist.

Air rushed in where the gate had been, crack and hiss. Cappen heard that sound as if it were an alien word of incantation: "Möbius-s-s."

Having stolen out of the temple and some distance thence, the party stopped for a few minutes of recovery before they proceeded to Molin's house.

This was in a blind alley off the avenue, a brick-paved recess where flowers grew in planters, shared by the fanes of two small and gentle gods. Wind had died away, stars glimmered bright, a half-moon stood above easterly roofs and cast wan argence. Afar, a tomcat serenaded his intended.

Rosanda had gotten back a measure of equilibrium. She cast herself against Jamie's breast. "Oh, hero, hero," she crooned, "you shall have reward, yes, treasure, ennoblement, everything!" She snuggled. "But nothing greater than my unbounded thanks. . . ."

The Northerner cocked an eyebrow at Cappen. The bard shook his head a little. Jamie nodded in understanding, and disengaged. "Uh, have a care, milady," he said. "Pressing against ring mail, all bloody and sweaty too, can't be good for a complexion."

Even if one rescues them, it is not wise to trifle with the wives of magnates.

Cappen had been busy himself. For the first time, he kissed Danlis on her lovely mouth; then for the second time; then for the third. She responded decorously.

Thereafter she likewise withdrew. Moonlight made a mystery out of her classic beauty. "Cappen," she said, "before we go on, we had better have a talk."

He gaped. "What?"

She bridged her fingers. "Urgent matters first," she continued crisply. "Once we get to the mansion and wake the high priest, it will be chaos at first, conference later, and I—as a woman—excluded from serious discussion. Therefore best I give my counsel now, for you to relay. Not that Molin or the prince are fools; the measures to take are for the most part obvious. However, swift action is desirable, and they will have been caught by surprise."

She ticked her points off. "First, as you have indicated, the Hell Hounds"—her nostrils pinched in distaste at the nickname—"the imperial elite guard should mount an immediate raid on the temple of Ils and arrest all personnel for interrogation, except the archpriest. He's probably innocent, and in any event it would be inept politics. Hazroah's death may have removed the danger, but this should not be taken for granted. Even if it has, his coconspirators ought to be identified and made examples of.

"Yet, second, wisdom should temper justice. No lasting harm was done, unless we count those persons who are trapped in the parallel universe; and they doubtless deserve to be."

They seemed entirely males, Cappen recalled. He grimaced in compassion. Of course, the sikkintairs might eat them.

Danlis was talking on:"—humane governance and the art of compromise. A grand temple dedicated to the Rankan gods is certainly required, but it need be no larger than that of Ils. Your counsel will have much weight, dear. Give it wisely. I will advise you."

"Uh?" Cappen said.

Danlis smiled and laid her hands over his. "Why, you can have unlimited preferment, after what you did," she told him. "I'll show you how to apply for it."

"But—but I'm no blooming statesman!" Cappen stuttered.

She stepped back and considered him. "True," she agreed. "You're valiant, yes, but you're also flighty and lazy and— Well, don't despair, I will mold you."

Cappen gulped and shuffled aside. "Jamie," he said, "uh, Jamie, I feel wrung dry, dead on my feet. I'd be worse than no use, I'd be a drogue on things just when they have to move fast. Better I find me a doss, and you take the ladies home. Come over here and I'll tell you how to convey the story in fewest words. Excuse us, ladies. Some of those words you oughtn't to hear."

A week thence, Cappen Varra sat drinking in the Vulgar Unicorn. It was midafternoon and none else were present but the associate tapster, his wound knitted.

A man filled the doorway and came in, to Cappen's table. "Been casting about everywhere for you," the Northerner grumbled. "Where've you been?"

"Lying low," Cappen replied. "I've taken a place here in the Maze which'll do till I've dropped back into obscurity, or decide to drift elsewhere altogether." He sipped his wine. Sunbeams slanted through windows; dust motes danced golden in their warmth; a cat lay on a sill and purred. "Trouble is, my purse is flat."

"We're free of such woes for a goodly while." Jamie flung his length into a chair and signaled the attendant. "Beer!" he thundered.

"You collected a reward, then?" the minstrel asked eagerly.

Jamie nodded. "Aye. In the way you whispered I should, before you left us. I'm baffled why and it went sore against the grain. But I did give

Molin the notion that the rescue was my idea and you naught but a hanger-on whom I'd slip a few royals. He filled a box with gold and silver money, and said he wished he could afford ten times that. He offered to get me Rankan citizenship and a title as well, and make a bureaucrat of me, but I said no, thanks. We share, you and I, half and half. But right this now, drinks are on me."

"What about the plotters?" Cappen inquired.

"Ah, those. The matter's been kept quiet, as you'd await. Still, while the temple of Ils can't be abolished, seemingly it's been tamed." Jamie's regard sought across the table and sharpened. "After you disappeared, Danlis agreed to let me claim the whole honor. She knew better— Rosanda never noticed—but Danlis wanted a man of the hour to carry her redes to the prince, and none remained save me. She supposed you were simply worn out. When last I saw her, though, she . . . *umm* . . . she 'expressed disappointment.'" He cocked his ruddy head. "Yon's quite a girl. I thought you loved her."

Cappen Varra took a fresh draught of wine. Old summers glowed along his tongue. "I did," he confessed. "I do. My heart is broken, and in part I drink to numb the pain."

Jamie raised his brows. "What? Makes no sense."

"Oh, it makes very basic sense," Cappen answered. "Broken hearts tend to heal rather soon. Meanwhile, if I may recite from a rondel I completed before you found me—

> "*Each sword of sorrow that would maim or slay,*
> *My lady of the morning deftly parries.*
> *Yet gods forbid I be the one she marries!*
> *I rise from bed the latest hour I may.*
> *My lady comes to me like break of day;*
> *I dream in darkness if it chance she tarries.*"

A Few Remarks

by Furtwan Coinpinch, Merchant

The first thing I noticed about him, just that first impression you understand, was that he couldn't be a poor man. Or boy, or youth, or whatever he was then. Not with all those weapons on him. From the shagreen belt he was wearing over a scarlet sash—a violently scarlet sash!—swung a curved dagger on his left hip and on the right one of those Ilbarsi "knives" long as your arm. Not a proper sword, no. Not a military man, then. That isn't all, though. Some few of us know that his left buskin is equipped with a sheath; the slim thing and knife hilt appear to be only a decoration. Gift from a woman, I heard him tell Old Thumpfoot one afternoon in the bazaar. I doubt it.

(I've been told he has another sticker strapped less than comfortably to his inner thigh, probably the right. Maybe that's part of the reason he walks the way he does. Cat-supple and yet sort of stiff of leg all at once. A tumbler's gait—or a punk's swagger. Don't tell him I said!)

Anyhow, about the weapons and my first impression that he couldn't be poor. There's a throwing knife in that leather and copper armlet on his right upper arm, and another in the long bracer of black leather on that same arm. Both are short. The stickers I mean, not the bracers or the arms either.

All that armament would be enough to scare anybody on a dark night, or even a moonbright one. Imagine being in the Maze or someplace like that and out of the shadows comes this young bravo, swaggering, wearing all that sharp metal! Right at you out of the shadows that spawned him. Enough to chill even one of those Hell Hounds. Even one of you-know-who's boys in the blue hawk-masks might step aside.

That was my impression. Shadowspawn. About as pleasant as gout or dropsy.

Shadowspawn

Andrew Offutt

His mop of hair was blacker than black and his eyes nearly so, under brows that just missed meeting above a nose not quite falcate. His walk reminded some of one of those red-and-black gamecocks brought over from Mrsevada. They called him Shadowspawn. No compliment was intended, and he objected until Cudget told him it was good to have a nickname, although he wished his own weren't Cudget Swearoath. Besides, Shadowspawn had a romantic and rather sinister sound, and that appealed to his ego, which was the largest thing about him. His height was almost average and he was rangy, wiry; swiftly wiry, with those bulgy rocks in his biceps and calves that other males wished they had.

Shadowspawn. It was descriptive enough. No one knew where he'd been spawned, which was shadowy, and he worked among shadows. Perhaps it was down in the shadows of the "streets" of Downwind and maybe it was over in Syr that he'd been birthed. It didn't matter. He belonged to Sanctuary and wished it belonged to him. He acted as if it did. If he knew or suspected that he'd come out of Downwind, he was sure he had risen above it. He just didn't have time for those street gangs of which surely he'd have been chieftain.

He was no more sure of his age than anyone else. He might have lived a score of years. It might have been fewer. Had a creditable mustache before he was fifteen.

The raven-wing hair, tending to an indecisive curl, covered his ears without reaching his shoulders. He'd an earring under that hair, on the left. Few knew it. Had it done at fourteen, to impress her who took his virginity that year. (She was two-score-and-two then, married to a man like a building stone with a belly. She's a hag with a belly out to here, now.)

"The lashes under those thick glossy brows of his are so black and thick they look almost kohled, like a woman's or a priest over in Yenized," a man called Weasel told Cusharlain, in the Vulgar Unicorn. "Some fool made that remark once, in his presence. The fellow wears the scar still and knows he's lucky to be wearing tongue and life. Should have known that a bravo who wears two throwing knives on his right arm is dangerous, and left-handed. And with a name like Shadowspawn . . . !"

His name was not Shadowspawn, of course. True, many did not know or no longer remembered his name. It was Hanse. Just Hanse. Not Hanse Shadowspawn; people called him the one or the other or nothing at all.

He seemed to wear a cloak about him at all times, a thoughtful S'danzo told Cusharlain. Not a cloak of fabric; this one concealed his features, his mind. Eyes hooded like a cobra's, some said. They weren't, really. They just did not seem directed outward, those glittering black onyxes he had for eyes. Perhaps their gaze was fixed on the plank-sized chips on his shoulders. Mighty easily knocked off.

By night he did not swagger, save when he entered a public place. Night of course was Hanse's time, as it had been Cudget's. By night . . . "Hanse walks like a hungry cat," some said, and they might shiver a bit. In truth he did not. He *glided*. His buskins' soft soles lifting only a finger's breadth with each step. They came down on the balls of the feet, not the heels. Some made fun of that—not to Hanse—because it made for a sinuous glide strange in appearance. The better-born watched him with an aesthetic fascination. And some horripilation. Among females, highborn or otherwise, the fascination was often layered with interest, however unwilling. Most then said the predictable: a distasteful, rather sexy animal, that Hanse, that Shadowspawn.

It had been suggested to him that a bit of committed practice could make him a real swordslinger: he was a natural. Employment, a uniform . . . Hanse was not interested. Indeed he sneered at soldiers, at uniforms. And now he hated them, with a sort of unreasoning reason.

These things Cusharlain learned, and he began to know him called Shadowspawn. And to dislike him. Hanse sounded the sort of too-competent young snot you would step aside for—and hate yourself for doing it.

"Hanse is a bastard!" This from Shive the Changer, with a thump of his fist on the broad table on which he dealt with such as Hanse, changing loot into coin.

"Ah." Cusharlain looked innocently at him. "You mean by nature."

"Probably by birth too. A bastard both by birth and by nature! Better that all such cocky snotty stealthy arrogant bravos were stillborn!"

"He's bitten you then, Shive?"

"A bravo and a lowborn punk he is, and that's all."

"Punk?"

"Well . . . perhaps a cut above punk." Shive touched his mustachios, which he kept curled like the horns of a mountain goat. "Cudget was a damned good thief. The sort of fellow who made the trade honorable. An art form. A pleasure doing business with. And Hanse was his apprentice, or nearly, sort of . . . and he has the potential of being an even better thief. Not man—thief." Shive wagged a finger made shiny by wax. "The potential, mind you. He'll never realize it." The finger paused on its way back to stroke one mustachio.

"You think not," Cusharlain said, drawing Shive out, pulling words from a man who knew how to keep his mouth shut and was alive and wealthy because he did.

"I think not. He'll absorb a foot or so of sharp metal long before. Or dance on the air."

"As, I remind you, Cudget did," Cusharlain said, noting that within the trade no one said "hanged."

Shive took umbrage. "After a long career! And Cudget was respected! He's respected still."

"Umm. Pity you admire the master but not the apprentice. He could use you, surely. And you him. If he's a successful thief, there'll be profit for the fence he chooses to—"

"Fence? Fence?"

"Sorry, Shive. The changer he chooses to exchange his . . . goods with, for Rankan coin. There's always a profit to—"

"He cheated me!"

So. At last Shive admitted it. That's how he'd been bitten by this Hanse. Fat and fifty and the second-most-experienced changer in Sanctuary, Shive had been cheated by a cocky youngster.

"Oh," Cusharlain said. He rose, showing Shive a satirical little smile. "You know, Shive . . . you shouldn't admit that. You are after all a man with some twenty years' experience . . . and he has only that many years of life, if not less."

Shive stared after the customs inspector. An Aurveshan raised in Sanctuary and now employed by their mutual conqueror, Ranke. As well as by an informal league of changers and Sanctuary's foremost thieves; those so successful they employed other thieves. With a distinct curl of his lip—a cultivated artificial maneuver—and a brush of his double-curled left mustachio, Shive returned his attention to the prying of a nice ruby from its entirely too recognizable setting.

Just now Cusharlain's prowling the Maze was in service of still another employer, for he was an ambitious and ever-hungry man. An amenable man, to opportunities for profit and new contracts. Today he was merely collecting information about the former apprentice of Cudget Swearoath, who had been swung shortly after the new prince governor came out from Ranke to "whip this Thieves' World of a town into shape." Above bribery, beyond threat, the (very) young ass actually meant to govern Sanctuary! To clean it up! Young Kadakithis, whom they called Kittycat!

So far he had angered the priesthood and every thief and changer in Sanctuary. And a good three-fifths of the taverners. And even a number of the garrison soldiers, with those baby-clean, revoltingly competent Hell Hounds of his. Some of the old villa dwellers thought he was just wonderful.

Probably wets his bed, Cusharlain thought with a jerk of his head—at the same time as he expertly twitched his robe's hem away from the touch of a legless beggar. Cusharlain knew very well that the fellow's legs were single-strapped up under his long, long, tattered coat. Well, and well. So one boy of nineteen or twenty, a thief, hated another, a half-brother of the emperor sent out here because it was the anus of the empire, good and far from the Rankan imperial seat! This the customs inspector had learned today, while gathering information for his secretive and clandestine employer. Hanse, Hanse. In all his life this Hanse had held regard for one person other than his cocky self: Cudget Swearoath. Respected senior thief. And Cudget had been arrested, which certainly would not have happened in the old days. The days B.D.P., Cusharlain thought; Before this Damned Prince! Far more incredibly, if there could be grades of incredibility, Cudget had been hanged!

Prince Stupid!

"Ah, the lad knows he can't hope to do injury on the prince," someone had told the night proprietor of the Golden Lizard, who had told Cusharlain's old friend Gelicia, proprietor of the popular House of Mermaids. "He schemes to steal from the very prince governor, and make a quick large profit in the doing."

Cusharlain stared at her. "This young gamecock means to try to rob the very palace?" he said, feeling stupid instantly; so she'd said, yes. "Don't scoff, Cusher," Gelicia said, waving a doughy hand well leavened with rings. This noon she was wearing apple green and purple and purple and lavender and mauve and orange, all in a way that exposed a large portion of her unrivaled bosom, which resembled two white cushions for a large divan and which Cusharlain was singularly uninterested in viewing.

"If it can be done, Shadowspawn'll do it," she said. "Oh, go ahead, tip yourself some more wine. Did you hear about the ring he tugged from under Corlas's pillow—while Corlas's head was on it, sleeping? You know, Corlas the camel dealer. Or've you heard tell of how our boy Hanse clumb up and stole the eagle off the roof of Barracks Three for a lark?"

"I wondered what had happened to that!"

She nodded wisely with a trebling of chin and a flashing swing of earrings whose diameter was the same as his wine cup—which was of silver. Her wine cup, that is; the one he was using.

"Shadowspawn," she said, "as Eshi is my witness. Had a prodigal offer from some richie up in Twand, too—and do you know Hanse wouldn't take it? Said he liked having the thing. Pisses on it every morning on rising, he says."

Cusharlain smiled. "And . . . if it can't be done? Reaching the palace, I mean."

Gelicia's shrug imparted to her bosom a quake of seismic proportions. "Why then Sanctuary will be minus one more cockroach, and no one'll miss him. Oh, my Lycansha will moon for a while, but she'll soon be over it."

"Lycansha? Who's Lycansha?"

Nine rings flashed on Gelicia's hands as she sketched a form in the air exactly as a man would have done. "Ah, the sweetest little Cadite oral-submissive you ever laid eyes on, who fancies that leanness and those mid-night eyes of his, Cusher. Like to . . . meet her? She's at liberty just now."

"I'm on business, Gelicia." His sigh was carefully elaborate.

"Asking about our little Shadowspawn?" Gelicia's meaty face took on a businesslike expression, which some would have called crafty-furtive.

"Aye."

"Well. Whoever you're reporting to, Cusher—you haven't talked to me!"

"Of course not, Gelicia! Don't be silly. I haven't talked with anyone with a name, or an address, or a face. I enjoy my . . . relationship with some of you more enterprising citizens"—he paused for her mirthful snort—"and have no wish to jeopardize it. Or to lose the physical attrib-utes necessary to my availing myself of your dear girls from time to time."

Her snickering laugh rose and went on up to whoops about the time he reached the street, assuring him that eventually the successful Gelicia had got his parting joke. Red Lanterns was a quiet neighborhood this time of day, after the sweeping up of the dust and tracks of last night's customers. Now sheets were being washed. A few deliveries made. A couple of workmen were occupied with a broken door hasp at a House down the street.

Cusharlain squinted upward. The Enemy, a horrid white ball in a hor-rid sky going the color of turmeric powder laced with saffron, was high, nigh to passing noon. One-Thumb should be stirring himself about now. Cusharlain decided to go and have a talk with him, too, and maybe he could get his report made by sunset. His employer did not seem as long on patience as on funds. The customs inspector of a fading city whose chief business was theft and the disposal of its product had learned the former, and was ever at work on increasing his share of the latter.

———

"Did what?" the startlingly good-looking woman said. "Roaching? What's roaching mean?"

Her companion, who was only little older than her seventeen or eighteen years, stiffened his neck to keep from looking anxiously around. "Sh—not so loud. When do cockroaches come out?"

She blinked at the dark, so intense young man. "Why—at night."

"So do thieves."

"Oh!" She laughed, struck her hands together with a jangling of bangles—gold, definitely—and touched his arm. "Oh, Hanse, I know so little! You know just about everything, don't you." Her face changed. "My, these hairs are soft." And she left her hand on that arm with its dark, dark hairs.

"The streets are my home," he told her. "They birthed me and gave me suck. I know quite a bit, yes."

He could hardly believe his luck, sitting here in a decent tavern out of the Maze with this genuinely beautiful Lirain who was . . . by the Thousand Eyes and by Eshi, too, could it be?—one of the concubines the prince governor had brought over from Ranke! And she's obviously fascinated with me, Hanse thought. He acted as if he sat here in the Golden Oasis every afternoon with such as she. What a coincidence, what great good fortune to have run into her in the bazaar that way! Run into her indeed! She had been hurrying and he'd been turning, glancing back at one of those child-afrighters of Jubal's, and they had slammed together and had to cling to each other to avoid falling. She had been so apologetic and in seeming need to make amends and—here they were, Hanse and a palace conky unguarded or watched, and a beauty at that—and wearing enough to support him for a year. He strove to be oh so cool.

"You certainly do like my gourds, don't you?"

"Wha—"

"Oh, don't dissemble. I'm not mad. Really, Hanse. If I didn't want 'em looked at I'd cover 'em in high-necked homespun."

"Uh . . . Lirain, I've seen one other pearl-sewn halter of silk in my life, and it didn't have those swirls of gold thread, or so many pearls. I wasn't this close, either." *Damn*, he thought. *Should have complimented her, not let her know my interest is greed for the container!*

"Oh! Here I am, one of seven women for one man and bored, and I thought you were wanting to get into my bandeau, when what you really want is it. What's a poor girl to do, used to the flatteries of courtiers and servants, when she meets a real man who speaks his real thoughts?"

Hanse tried not to let his preening show. Nor did he know how to apologize, or to fancytalk, beyond the level of the Maze. Besides, he thought this pout-lipped beauty with her heart-shaped face and nice woman's belly was having some fun with him. She knew that pout was irresistible!

"Wear high-necked homespun," he said, and while she laughed, "and try not to look that way. This real man knows what you're used to, and that you can't be interested in Hanse the roach!"

Her expression became very serious. "You must not have access to a mirror, Hanse. Why don't you try me?"

Hanse fought his astonishment and made swift recovery. With prickly armpits and outward confidence, he said, "Would you like to take a walk, Lirain?"

"Is there a more private room at the end of it?"

Holding her gaze as she held his, he nodded.

"Yes," she said, that quickly. Concubine of Prince Kadakithis! "Could anything as good as this bandeau be bought in the bazaar?"

He was rising. "Who'd buy it? No," he said, puzzled at the question.

"Then you must buy me the best we can find after a *short* search." She chuckled at the sight of his stricken face. The cocky creature thought she was a whore, to charge him some trifle like any girl! "So that I can wear it back to the palace," she said, and watched understanding brighten that frightening yet sensuous pair of onyxes he wore for eyes, all hard and cold and wary. She slid her hand into his, and they departed the Golden Oasis.

"Of *course* I'm sure, Bourne!" Lirain twitched off the blue-arabesqued bandeau of green silk Hanse had bought her, and hurled it at the man on the divan. He grinned so that his big brown beard writhed. "He has such *needs*! He is never relaxed, and wants and needs so badly, and so wants to be and to do. He is so impressed with who or rather what I am, and yet he would deny under torture that I was anything but another nice tumble. You and I both well know about lowborns who hunger for far more than food! He is completely taken in and he'll be the perfect tool, Bourne. My agent assured me that he is a competent sneak-thief, and that he wants to rob and gain a leg on Prince Kittycat so badly he can taste it. I saw that, right enough. Look, it's perfect!"

"A thief. And competent, you say." Bourne scratched his thigh under the tunic of his Hell Hound's uniform. He glanced around the apartment she occupied on nights when the prince might come—hours from now. "And he has a valuable halter of yours now, to sell. Perhaps to brag about and get you into trouble. That kind of trouble ends in death, Lirain."

"You find it hard to admit that I—a *woman*—have accomplished this, love? Look here, that gourd-holster was stolen today in the marketplace. Sliced through in back and snatched off, in a single act. Some child of about thirteen, a dirty girl who ran off with it like a racing dromedary. I did not tell anyone because I *so* hated its loss and am *so* mortified."

"All right. Maybe. That's not bad—forgot the part about its being sliced in back, lest it turn up whole. Hmm—I guess it won't. Likely perfectly good silk will be dumped while the pearls and gold thread are sold. And how *competent* was he at the couching, Lirain?"

Lirain looked to the heavens. "O Sabellia, and we call Thee the Sharp-Tongued One! Men! Plague and drought, Bourne, can't you be more than a man? He was . . . fair. That's all. I was on business. *We* are on business, love. Our assignment for those 'certain interested nobles' back in Ranke—my hind leg, it's the emperor himself, worried about his half-brother's pretty golden-haired magnetism!—is to embarrass His Pretty Golden-haired Highness Kadakithis! He's been doing that well enough all by himself! Trying to implement civilized law in this roach nest of a town! Continuing to insist that temples to Savankala and Sabellia have to be mightier than the one to the Ils these people worship, and that Vashanka's must be equal to Ils's. Priests hate him and merchants hate him and thieves hate him—and thieves make this town go!"

Bourne nodded—and demonstrated his strength by drawing a fifteen-inch dagger to clean his nails.

Lirain tossed her girdle of silver links onto a pile of cushions and idly fingered her navel. "Now we provide the finishing touch. There will never be a threat to the emperor from this pretty boy's supporters again! We help Hanse the roach into the palace."

"After which he is absolutely on his own," he said, pointing with the dagger. "We've got be uncompromised."

"Oh," she said flaunting, "I shall be a-couching with His Highness! The while, Hanse steals his rod of authority: the Savankh of Ranke, given him personally by the emperor as symbol of full authority here! Hanse will wish to negotiate a private, quiet trade with Kittycat. The rod for a fat ransom, and his safety. We will be busily seeing that word gets around. A thief broke into the palace and stole the Savankh! And the prince governor is the laughingstock of the capital! He'll either rot here—or, worse still, be recalled in disgrace."

The big man lounging so familiarly on her divan nodded slowly. "I do have to point out that you may well rot here with him."

"Oh, no. You and I are promised reprieve from this midden-heap town. And . . . Bourne . . . *particularly* if we heroically regain the Savankh for the honor of the empire. After its theft is just terribly well known, of course."

"Now, that's good!" Bourne's brows tipped up and his lips pursed, a rather obscene spectacle between the bushiness of brown mustache and beard. "And how do we do that? You going to trade this Hanse another halter for it?"

She looked long at him. Coolly, brows arched above blue-lidded eyes. "What's that in your hand, guardian; Hell Hound so loyal to His Highness?"

Bourne regarded the dagger in his big hairy hand, looked at Lirain, and began to smile.

Though hardly beloved nor indeed particularly lovable, Hanse was a member of the community. Though a paid ally, the customs inspector was not. Hanse heard from three sources that Cusharlain had been asking after him, on behalf of someone else. After giving that thought, Hanse traded with a grimy little thief. First Hanse reminded him that he could easily take the five truly fine melons the boy had been so deft as to steal, all in an afternoon. The boy agreed to accept a longish, stiffish piece of braided gold thread, and Hanse gained four melons. With his hilt and then thumb, Hanse made a nice depression in the top of each. Into each he tucked a nice pearl; four of his thirty-four. These he set before the hugely fat and grossly misnamed Moonflower, a S'danzo who liked food, melons, pearls, Hanse, and proving that she was more than a mere charlatan. Many others were. Few had the Gift. Even the cynical Hanse was convinced that Moonflower had.

She sat on a cushioned stool of extra width and sturdy legs. Her pile of red and yellow and green skirts overflowed it, while disguising the fact that so did her vast backside. Her back was against the east wall of the tired building wherein she and her man and seven of their brood of nine dwelt, and wherein her man sold . . . things. Hanse sat cross-legged before her. Looking boyish without his arm sheaths and in a dusty tunic the color of an old camel. He watched a pearl disappear under Moon-flower's shawl into what she called her treasure chest. He watched the melon disappear between her lavender-painted lips. Swiftly.

"You are such a good boy, Hanse." When she talked, Moonflower was a kitten.

"Only when I want something, passionflower."

She laughed and beamed and tousled his hair, for he knew that such talk pleased her. Then he told her the story. Handed her, disguised in carefully smudged russet, a strip of silken cloth: two straps and two cupped circles bearing many thread holes.

"Ah! You've been visiting a lady in the Path of Money! Nice of you to let Moonflower have four of the pearls you've laboriously sliced off this little sheath!"

"She gave it me for services rendered." He waved a hand.

"Oh, of course. Hmm." She folded it, unfolded it, fondled it, drew it through her dimple-backed hands, sniffed and tasted it with a dainty tongue tip. A gross kitten at her divining. She closed her eyes and was very still. As Hanse was, waiting.

"She is indeed a c—what you said," she told him, able to be discreet even though in something approaching a trance. "Oh, Shadowspawn! You are involved in a plot beyond your dreaming. Odd—this must be the emperor I see, watching from afar. And this big man with your . . . acquaintance. A big man with a big beard. In a uniform? I think so. Close to our ruler, both. Yet . . . ahh . . . they are his enemies. Yes. They plot. She is a serpent and he a lion of no little craft. They seek . . . ahh, I see. The prince governor has become faceless. Yes. They seek to cost him face." Her eyes opened to stare wide at him, two big garnets set amid a heavy layer of kohl. "And you, Hanse my sweet, are their *tool*."

They stared at each other for a moment. "Best you vanish for a time, Shadowspawn. You know what becomes of tools once they are no longer needed."

"Discarded," he snarled, not even bemoaning the loss of Lirain's denuded bandeau, which Moonflower made vanish within a shawl-buried, vaster one.

"Or," she said, keeping him fixed by her gaze, "hung up."

Lirain and her (uniformed?) confederate were tools then, Hanse reasoned, prowling the streets. Prince Kadakithis was nice to look at, and charismatic. So his imperial half-brother had sent him way out here, to Sanctuary. Now he wanted him sorely embarrassed here. Hanse could see the wisdom of that, and knew that despite what any might say, the emperor was no fool. So, then. They two plotted. Lirain gained enough knowledge of Hanse to employ Cusharlain to investigate him. She had found a way to effect their meeting. Yes; though it hurt his ego, he admitted to himself that she had made the approach and the decisions. So now he was their tool. A tool of tools!

Robbing Kadakithis, however, had been his goal before he met that cupiditous concubine. So long as she helped, he was quite willing to let her think he was her dupe. He wanted to be their tool, then—insofar as it aided him to gain easy entry to the palace. Forewarned and all that. There was definitely potential here for a clever man, and Hanse deemed himself twice as clever as he was, which was considerably. Finally, being made the tool of plotting tools was far too demeaning for the Hansean ego to accept.

Yes. He would gain the wand. Trade it to the prince governor for gold—no, better make it the less intimidating silver—and freedom. From Suma or Mrsevada or someplace, he'd send a message back, anonymously informing Kadakithis that Lirain was a traitor. Hanse smiled at that pleasant thought. Perhaps he'd just go up to Ranke and tell the emperor what a pair of incompetent agents he had down in Sanctuary. Hanse saw himself richly rewarded, an intimate of the emperor. . . .

And so he and Lirain met again, and made their agreement and plan.

A gate was indeed left open. A guard did indeed quit his post before a door of the palace. It did indeed prove to be unlatched. Hanse locked it after him. Thus a rather thick-waisted Shadowspawn gained entry to the palatial home of the governor of Sanctuary. Dark corridors led him to the appointed chamber. As the prince was not in it, it was not specifically guarded. The ivory rod, carved to resemble rough-barked wood, was indeed there. So, unexpectedly enjoying the royal couch in its owner's absence, was Lirain's sister concubine. She proved not to have been drugged. She woke and opened her mouth to yell. Hanse reduced that to a squeak by punching her in the belly, which was shockingly convex and soft, considering her youth. He held a pillow over her face, sustaining a couple of scratches and a bruised shin. She became still. He made sure that she was limp but quite alive, and bound her with a gaiter off her own sandal. The other he pulled around so as to hold in place the silken garment he stuffed into her mouth, and tied behind her head. He removed the pendant from one ear. All in darkness. He hurried to wrap the rod of authority in the drape off a low table. Hitching up his tunic, he began drawing from around his waist the thirty feet of knotted rope he had deemed wise. Lirain had assured him that a sedative would be administered to the Hell Hounds' evening libation. Hanse had no way of knowing that to be the truth, or that not only had one of those big burly five done the administering, he had drunk no less than the others. Bourne and company slept most soundly. The plan was that Hanse would leave the same way he had entered. Because he knew he was a tool and was suspicious unto caution, Hanse had decided to effect a different exit.

One end of the rope he secured to the table whose drape he'd stolen. The other he tossed out the window. Crosswise, the table would hold the rope without following him through the window.

It proved true. Hanse went out, and down. Slipping out westward to wend his way among the brothels, he was aware of a number of scorpions scuttling up and down his back, tails poised. Evidently the bound occupant of His Highness's bed was not found. Dawn was still only a promise when Hanse reached his second-floor room in the Maze.

He was a long time wakeful. Admiring the symbol of Rankan authority, named for the god they claimed had given it them. Marveling at its unimposing aspect. A twiglike wand not two feet long, of yellowing ivory. He had done it!

Shortly after noon next day, Hanse had a talk with babbly old Hakiem, who had lately done much babbling about what a fine fellow His handsome Highness was, and how he had even spoken with Hakiem, giving him two pieces of good silver as well! Today Hakiem listened to Hanse, and he swallowed often. What could he do save agree?

Carrying a pretty pendant off a woman's earring, Hakiem hied him to the palace. Gained the Presence by sending in one word to the prince, with the pendant. Assured him he had nothing to do with the theft.

Most privily Hakiem stated what he'd been told, and the thief's terms. Ransom.

The prince governor had to pay, and knew it. If he could get the damned Savankh back, he'd never have to let out that it had been stolen in the first place. Taya, who had spent a night in his bed less comfortable than she had expected, had no notion what had been taken. Too, she seemed to believe his promise to stretch or excise various parts of her anatomy should she flap her mouth to anyone at all.

Meanwhile the concubine Lirain and Hell Hound Bourne were jubilant. Plotting. Grinning. Planning the Revelation that would destroy their employer. Indeed, they lost no time in dispatching a message to their other employers, back in Ranke. That was premature, unwise, and downright stupid.

Next came the coincidence, though it wasn't all that much one. Zalbar and Quag were sword-happy hotheads. Razkuli complained of fire in the gut and had the runs besides. That left only two Hell Hounds; whom else would the prince entrust with this mission? After a short testing conference, he chose Bourne to implement the transaction with the thief. Bourne's instructions were detailed and unequivocal: all was to be effected precisely as the thief, through Hakiem, had specified. Bourne would, of course, receive a nice bonus. He was made to understand that it was also to serve as a gag. Bourne agreed, promised, saluted, louted, departed.

Once the villa had commanded a fine view of the sea and naturally terraced landscape flowing a league along the coast to Sanctuary. Once a merchant had lived here with his family, a couple of concubines who counted themselves lucky, servants, and a small army or defense force. The merchant was wealthy. He was not liked and did not care that many did not care for the way he had achieved wealth and waxed richer. One day a pirate attack began. Two days later the gorge that marked the beginning of rough country disgorged barbarians. They also attacked. The merchant's small army proved too small. He and his armed force and servants and unlucky concubines and family were wiped out. The manse he had called Eaglenest was looted and burned. The pirates had not been pirates and the barbarians had not been barbarians—technically, at least: they were mercenaries. Thus, forty years ago, had some redistribution of wealth been achieved by that clandestine alliance of

Sanctuarite nobles and merchants. Others had called Eaglenest "Eaglebeak" then and still did, though now the tumbled ruins were occupied only by spiders, snakes, lizards, scorpions, and snails. As Eaglebeak was said to be haunted, it was avoided.

It was a fine plan for a night meeting and transfer of goods, and to Eaglebeak came Bourne, alone, on a good big prancing horse that swished its tail for the sheer joy and pride of it. The horse bore Bourne and a set of soft saddlebags, weighty and jingling.

Near the scrubby acacia specified, he drew rein and glanced about at a drear pile and scatter of building stones and their broken or crumbled pieces. His long cloak he doffed before he dismounted. Sliding off his horse, he stood clear while he unbuckled his big weapons belt. The belt, with sheathed sword and dagger, he hung on his saddle horn. He removed the laden bags. Made them jingle. Laid them on the ground. Stepping clear of horse and ransom, he held his arms well out from his body while he turned, slowly.

He had shown the ransom and shown himself unarmed. Now a pebble flew from somewhere to whack a big chunk of granite and go skittering. At that signal, Bourne squatted and, on clear ground in the moonlight, emptied both saddlebags in a clinking, chiming, shimmering, glinting pile of silver coinage amid which gleamed a few gold disks. Laboriously and without happiness, Bourne clinked them all back into the pouches of soft leather, each the size of a nice cushion. He paced forward to lay them, clinking, atop a huge square stone against which leaned another. All as specified.

"Very good." The voice, male and young, came out of the shadows somewhere; no valley floor was so jumbled with stones as this once-courtyard of Eaglebeak. "Now get on your horse and ride back to Sanctuary."

"I will not. You have something for me."

"Walk over to the acacia tree, then, and look toward Sanctuary."

"I will walk over to the tree and watch the saddlebags, thanks, thief. If you show up without that rod . . ."

Bourne did that, and the shadows seemed to cough up a man, young and lean and darkly dressed. The crescent moon was behind him so that Bourne could not see his face. The fellow pounced lithely atop a stone, and held high the stolen Savankh.

"I see it."

"Good. Walk back to your horse, then. I will put this down when I pick up the bags."

Bourne hesitated, shrugged, and began ambling toward his horse. Hanse, thinking that he was very clever indeed and wanting all that money in his hands, dropped from his granite dais and hurried to the bags. Sliding his right arm through the connecting strap, he laid down the rod he carried in his left. That was when Bourne turned around and charged. While he demonstrated how fast a big burly man in mail coat could move, he also showed what a dishonest rascal he was. Down his back, inside his mail shirt, on a thong attached to the camel-hair torque he wore, was a sheath. As he charged, he drew a dagger long as his forearm.

His quarry saw that the weight of the silver combined with Bourne's momentum made trying to run not only stupid, but suicidal. Still, he was young, and a thief: supple, clever, and fast. Bourne showed teeth, thinking this boy was frozen with shock and fear. Until Hanse moved, fast as the lizards scuttling among these great stones. The saddlebags slam-jingled into Bourne's right arm, and the knife flew away while he was knocked half around. Hanse managed to hang on to his own balance; he hashed the Hell Hound in the back with his ransom. Bourne fell sprawling. Hanse ran—for Bourne's horse. He knew Bourne could outrun him so long as he was laden with the bags, and he was not about to part with them. In a few bounds, he gained a great rock and from there pounced onto the horse's back, just as he'd seen others do. It was Hanse's first attempt to mount a horse. Inexperience and the weight of his ransom carried him right off the other side.

In odd silence, he rose, on the far side of the horse. Not cursing as anyone might expect. Here came Bourne, and his fist sprouted fifteen inches of sharp iron. Hanse drew Bourne's other dagger from the sheath on the saddle and threw the small flat knife from his buckskin. Bourne went low and left, and the knife clattered among the tumbled stones of Eaglebeak. Bourne kept moving in, attacking under the horse. Hanse struck at him with his own dagger. To avoid losing his face, Bourne had to fall. Under the horse. Hanse failed to check his swipe, and his dagger nicked the inside of the horse's left hind leg.

The animal squealed, bucked, kicked, tried to gallop. Ruins barred him, and he turned back just as Bourne rose. Hanse was moving away fast, hugging one saddlebag to him and half-dragging the other. Bourne and his horse ran into each other. One of them fell backward and the other reared, neighed, pranced—and stood still, as if stricken with guilt. The other, downed painfully in mail for the second time in two minutes, cursed horse, Hanse, luck, gods, and himself. And began getting up.

However badly it had been handled, Bourne had horse, sword, and, a few paces away, the rod of Rankan authority. Hanse had more silver than would comprise Bourne's retirement. Under its weight he could not hope to escape. He could drop it and run or be overtaken. Dragging sword from sheath, Bourne hoped the roach kept running. What fun to carve him for the next hour or so!

Hanse was working at a decision, too, but none of it fell out that way. Perhaps he should have done something about trying to buy off a god or two; perhaps he should have taken better note of the well, this afternoon, and not run that way tonight. He discovered it too late. He fell in.

He was far less aware of the fall than of utter disorientation—and of being banged in every part of his body, again and again, by the sides of the well, which were brick, and by the saddlebags. When his elbow struck the bricks, the bags were gone. Hanse didn't notice their splash; he was busy crashing into something that wasn't water. And he was hurting.

The well's old wooden platform of a cover and sawhorse affair had fallen down inside, or been so hurled by vandals or ghosts. They weren't afloat, those pieces of very old, damp wood; they were braced across the well, at a slant. Hanse hit, hurt, scrabbled, clung. His feet were in water, and his shins. The wood creaked. The well's former cover deflected the head-sized stone Bourne hurled down. The fist-sized one he next threw struck the well's wall, bounced to roll down Hanse's back, caught a moment at his belt, and dropped into the water. The delay in his hearing the splash led Bourne to misconstrue the well's depth. Hanse clung and dangled. The water was cold.

In the circle of dim light above, Hanse saw Bourne's helmeted head. Bourne, peering down into a well, saw nothing.

"If you happen to be alive, thief, keep the saddlebags! No one will ever find you or them—or the Savankh you stole! You treacherously tricked us all, you see, and fled with both ransom and Savankh. Doubtless I will be chastised severely by His Pretty Highness—and once I'm in Ranke again, I'll be rewarded! You have been a fool and a tool, boy, because I've friends back home in Ranke who will be delighted by the way I have brought embarrassment and shame on Prince Kittycat!"

Hanse, hurting and scared that the wood would yield, played dead. Strange how cold water could be, forty feet down in a brick-walled shaft!

Grinning, Bourne walked over and picked up the Savankh, which His Stupid Highness would never see. He shoved it into his belt. Stuck his sword into the ground. And began wrestling a huge stone to drop, just in case, down the well. His horse whickered. Bourne, who had left his sword several feet away, froze. He straightened and turned to watch the approach of two helmeted men. They bore naked swords. One was a soldier. The other was—*the prince governor*?!

"We thank you for letting us hear your confession, Bourne, traitor."

Bourne moved. He gained his sword. No slouch and no fool, he slashed the more dangerous enemy. For an instant the soldier's mail held Bourne's blade. Then the man crumpled. The blade came free and Bourne spun, just in time to catch the prince's slash in the side. Never burly, Kadakithis had learned that he had to put everything he had behind his practice strokes just so that his opponents would notice. He did that now, so wildly and viciously that his blade tore several links of Bourne's mail coat and relocated them in his flesh. Bourne made an awful noise. Horribly shocked and knowing he was hurt, he decided it were best to fly. He staggered as he ran, and the prince let him go.

Kadakithis picked up the fallen rod of authority and slapped it once against his leather-clad leg. His heart beat unconscionably rapidly as he knelt to help the trusted man he'd brought with him. That was not necessary. In falling, the poor wight had smashed his head open on a chunk of marble from a statue. Slain by a god. Kadakithis glanced after Bourne, who had vanished in darkness and the ruins.

The prince governor stood thinking. At last he went to the well. He knelt and called down into blackness.

"I am Prince Kadakithis. I have the wand. Perhaps I speak uselessly to one dead or dying. Perhaps not, in which case you may remain there and die slowly, or be drawn up to die under torture, or . . . you can agree to help me in a little plan I have just devised. Well—speak up!"

No contemplation was required to convince Hanse that he would go along with anything that meant vacating the well and seeing his next birthday. Who'd have thought pretty Prince Kittycat would come out here, and helmeted, too! He wondered at the noises he had heard. And made reply. The wood creaked.

"You need promise only this," Kadakithis called down. "Be silent until you are under torture. Suffer a little, then tell all."

"Suffer? . . . Torture?"

"Come, come, you deserve both. You'll suffer only a little of what you have coming. Don't, and betray these words, roach, and you will die out of hand. No, make that slowly. Nor will anyone believe you, anyhow."

Hanse knew that he was in over his head, both literally and figuratively. Hanging on to creaky old wood that was definitely rotting away by the second, he agreed.

"I'll need help," the prince called. "Hang on."

Hanse rolled his eyes and made an ugly face. He hung on. He waited. Daring not to pull himself up onto the wood. His shoulders burned. The water seemed to grow colder, and the cold rose up in his legs. He hung on. Sanctuary was only about a league away. He hoped Kitty—the prince—galloped. He hung on. Though the sun never came up and the moon's position changed only a little, Hanse was sure that a week or two passed. Cold, dark, and sore, those weeks. Riches! Wealth! Cudget had told him that revenge was a stupid luxury the poor couldn't afford!

Then His Clever Highness was back, with several men of the night watch and a lot of rope. While they hauled up a bedraggled, bruised Shadowspawn, the prince mentioned a call of nature and strolled away amid the clutter of big stones. He did not lift his tunic. He did pause on the other side of a pile of rubble. He gazed earthward, upon a dead traitor, and slowly he smiled in satisfaction. His first kill! Then Kadakithis began puking.

Pitchy torches flickered to create weird, dancing shadows on stone walls grim as death. The walls framed a large room strewn with tables, chains, needles, pincers, gyves, ropes, nails, shackles, hammers, wooden wedges and blocks and splinters, pliers, fascinating gags, mouth and tongue stretchers, heating irons, wheels, two braziers, pulleys. Much of this charming paraphernalia was stained dark here and there. On one of the tables lay Hanse. He was bruised, cut, contused—and being stretched, all in no more than his breechclout. Also present were Prince Kadakithis, his bright-eyed consort, two severe Hell Hounds, his oddly attired old adviser, and three Sanctuarite nobles from the council. And the palace

smith. Massively constructed and black-nailed, he was an imposing substitute for the torturer, who was ill.

He took up a sledgehammer and regarded it thoughtfully. Milady Consort's eyes brightened still more. So did those of Zalbar the Hell Hound.
Hanse discovered that in his present posture a gulp turned his Adam's
apple into a blade that threatened to cut his throat from the inside.

The smith put down the hammer and took up a pair of long-handled
pincers.

"Does he have to keep that there rag on his jewels, Yer Highness?"

"No need to torture him there," Kadakithis said equably. He glanced
at his wife, who'd gone all trembly. "*Yet.* Try a few less horrific measures. *First.*"

"Surely he isn't tall enough," Zalbar said hopefully. He stood about
six inches from the crank of the rack on which Hanse lay, taut.

"Well do *something* to him!" Milady snapped.

The smith surprised everyone. The movement was swift and the crack
loud. He drew back his whip from a white stripe across Hanse's stomach. It went pink, then darker, and began to rise. The smith raised his
brows as if impressed with himself. Struck again, across the captive's
chest. The whip cracked like a slack sail caught in a gust. Chains rattled
and Hanse's eyes and mouth went wide. A new welt began to rise. The
smith added one across the tops of his thighs. An inch from the jewels,
that. Milady Consort breathed through a mouth gone open.

"I don' like whippin' a man," the smith said. "Nor thisun either. Think
I'll just ease this arm out of its socket and turn it around t'other way."

"You needn't walk all the way around to this side," Zalbar rumbled.
"I'll turn the crank."

To the considerable disappointment of Zalbar and Sanctuary's first
lady, Hanse began to talk. He told them about Bourne and Lirain. He
could not tell them of Bourne's death, as he did not know of it.

"The prince governor of Sanctuary," Kadakithis said, "and representative of the emperor of Ranke, is merciful to one who tells him of a plot.
Release him and hold him here—without torture. Give him wine and
food."

"Damn!" Zalbar rumbled.

"Might I be getting back to my wife now, Highness? This job ain't
no work for me, and I got all that anchor chain to work on tomorrow."

Hanse, not caring who released or guarded or fed him, watched the exit of the royal party.

With Zalbar and Quag, the prince went to Lirain's apartment. "Do you stay here," he said, and took Quag's sword. Neither Hell Hound cared for that and Zalbar said so.

"Zalbar: I don't know if you had a big brother you hated or what, you're a mean hothead who really ought to be employed as royal wasp killer. Now stand here and shut up and wait for me." Zalbar came to attention. He and Quag waited, board-stiff save for a rolling of dark eyes, while their charge entered the chamber of his treacherous concubine. And closed the door. Zalbar was sure that a week or two passed before the door opened and Kadakithis called them in. Quag's sword dripped in his hand.

The Hell Hounds hurried within and stopped short. Staring. Lirain lay not dead, but asleep, sprawled naked and dégagé on a rumpled couch, obviously a recent participant in lovemaking. Naked beside her lay Bourne, not alive, and freshly bloodied.

"I've knocked her unconscious," the prince said. "Take her down to the less comfortable bed so recently vacated by that Hanse fellow, who is to be sent to my apartment. Here, Quag—oh." The prince carefully wiped Quag's sword on Lirain's belly and thighs and handed it to his Hell Hound. Both guards, impressed and pleased, saluted. And bowed as well. They looked passing happy with their prince. Prince Kadakithis looked flagrantly happy with himself.

Attired in a soft tunic that proved a thief could be the size of a prince, Hanse sipped wine from a goblet he wished he could conceal and carry off with him. He rolled his eyes to glance around this royal chamber for audiences most private. For that reason the door was open. By it sat a deaf woman plucking a lute.

"Both of us are overdue for sleep, Hanse. The day presses on to midmorning."

"I am . . . more accustomed to night work than y—than His Highness."

The prince laughed. "So you are, Shadowspawn! Amazing how many clever men turn to crime. Broke into the very palace! My very chamber! Enjoyed a royal concubine too, eh?" He sat gazing reflectively at the thief, very aware that they were nearly of an age. Peasant and prince; thief and governor. "Well, soon Lirain will be babbling her head off, and all will know there was a plot—and from home at that! Also that she was dishonoring her royal master's bed with her coconspirator."

"And that His Heroic Highness not only slew the son of a toad, but showed a true noble ruler's mercy by sparing a thief," Hanse said hopefully.

"Yes, Hanse. That is being put into writing at this moment. Ah, and there were witnesses to everything! All of it!"

Hanse was overboldened to say, "Except . . . Bourne's death, my lord prince."

"Hoho! Would you like to know about that, Hanse? You know so much already. We have holds each on the other, you and I. I killed Bourne up at Eaglenest. With one stroke," Kadakithis added. After all, it had been his first.

Hanse stared.

"You do seem to be learning caution, Shadowspawn! I do hope you will accept the employment I'll soon be offering you. You avoid mentioning that when you came out of that well you saw no corpse. No; he tried to flee and died a few feet away. The moment we returned here, I drugged Lirain. Drank it herself; thought she was drinking poison! She has lain with no one this night. I arranged her on the couch. One absolutely loyal man and I went back and fetched Bourne. My lady wife and I placed the corpse beside Lirain. Along with a bladder of the blood of a—appropriately!—pig. I thrust my sword into it before I called in Quag and Zalbar."

Hanse continued to stare. This saffron-haired boy was clever enough to be a thief! Hanse bet he was dissembling still, too; doubtless a favored rug merchant had aided in the bringing of Bourne's corpse into the palace!

The prince saw his stare, read it. "Perhaps I'm not Prince Kittycat after all? I will shortly have high respect in Sanctuary, and wide knowledge of the plot is a weapon against my enemies at home. You are a hero—ah." The prince nodded toward the doorway, beckoned. An oldish man entered to hand him a sheet of parchment. It soon bore the governor's signature and seal. The secretary left. Kadakithis handed the document to Hanse with a small flourish and a smile that Hanse saw was distinctly royal. Hanse glanced at it—very impressive—and looked again at the prince.

"Oh," Kadakithis said, and no more; a prince did not apologize to a thief for forgetting his lack of education. "It says that by my hand and in the name of the emperor in Ranke, you are forgiven of all you may have done up to this day, Hanse. You aren't a quintuple murderer, are you?"

"I've never killed anyone, Highness."

"I have! This very night—last night, rather!"

"Pardon, Highness, but killing's the business of them that rule, not thieves."

Kadakithis looked long and thoughtfully at Hanse after that, and would likely quote Shadowspawn long hence. Hanse had twice to mention the ransom at the bottom of the well.

"Ah! Forgot that, didn't I. It's been a bit busy tonight—last night. I've things to do, Hanse. A busy day ahead on no sleep and much excitement. I fear I can't be bothered thinking about some coins someone may have lost down an old well. If you can get it out, do. And do return here to discuss employment with me."

Hanse rose. He felt the kinship between them and was not comfortable with it. "That . . . will need some . . . some thinking, Prince Governor, sir. I mean . . . *work*. And for you! Uh, yourself, that is—Your Highness. First I have to try to get used to the fact that I can't hate you anymore."

"Well, Hanse, maybe you can help a few others not to. I could use the help. Unless you take it ill of me to remind you that half of salvage *found* in this demesne is the property of the government."

Hanse began to wonder about the possibility of transferring the few gold coins into one saddlebag. If he was able to get the bags out of the well. That would take time, and help. And that would require paying someone. Or cutting someone in. . . .

Hanse left the palace wearing a soft new tunic, eyes narrowed. Planning, calculating. Plotting.

The Price of Doing Business

Robert Lynn Asprin

Jubal was more powerful than he appeared. Not that his form conveyed any softness or weakness. If anything, his shiny ebony skin stretched tight over lithe, firm muscles gave an immediate impression of quick strength, while his scarred, severe facial features indicated a mind which would not hesitate to use that strength to his own advantage.

Rather, it was his wealth and the shrewd mind that had accumulated it which gave Jubal power above and beyond his iron muscles and razor-edged sword. His money, and the fierce entourage of sell-swords it had bought him, made him a formidable force in the social order of Sanctuary.

Blood had been the price of his freedom; great quantities of blood shed by his opponents in the gladiator pits of Ranke. Blood, too, had given him his start at wealth: seizing a poorly guarded slave caravan for later sale at a sinful profit.

Where others might be content with modest gains, Jubal continued to amass his fortune with fanatic intensity. He had learned a dear lesson while glaring through hate-slitted eyes at the crowds who cheered his gory pit victories: swords and those who wielded them were bought and sold, and thus accounted as nothing in the minds of Society. Money and Power, not skill and courage, were what determined one's standing in the social order of men. It was fear that determined who spat and who wiped in his world.

So Jubal stalked the world of merchants as he had stalked the pits, ruthlessly pouncing on each opportunity and vulnerability as he had pitilessly cut down crippled opponents in the past. To enter into a deal with Jubal was to match wits with a mind trained to equate failure with death.

With this attitude, Jubal's concerns prospered and flourished in Sanctuary. With the first of his profits, he purchased one of the old mansions to the west of town. There he resided like a bloated spider in a web, waiting for signs of new opportunities. His fangs were his sell-swords, who swaggered through the streets of Sanctuary, their features disguised by blue hawk-masks. His web was a network of informants, paid to pass the word of any incident, any business deal, or any shift in local politics which might be of interest to their generous master.

Currently the network was humming with word of the cataclysm in town. The Rankan prince and his new ideas were shaking the very roots of Sanctuary's economic and social structure.

Jubal sat at the center of his web and listened.

After a while, the status reports all began to run together, forming one boring monotone.

Jubal slouched in his thronelike chair staring vacantly at one of the room's massive incense burners, bought in an unsuccessful attempt to counter the stench carried from Sanctuary by the easterly winds. Still the reports droned on. Things had been different when he was just beginning. Then he had been able to personally manage the various facets of his growing enterprises. Now he had to listen while others . . . Something in the report caught his attention.

"Who did you kill?" he demanded.

"A blind," Saliman repeated, blinking at the interruption. "An informer who was not an informer. It was done to provide an example . . . as you ordered."

"Of course." Jubal waved. "Continue."

He relied heavily on informants from the town for the data necessary to conduct his affairs. It was known that if one sold false information to

Jubal, one was apt to be found with a slit throat and a copper piece clenched between the teeth. This was known because it happened . . . frequently. What was not widely known was that if Jubal felt his informants needed an example to remind them of the penalty for selling fabrications, he would order his men to kill someone at random and leave the body with the marks of a false informer. His actual informers were not target for these examples—good informants were hard to find. Instead, someone would be chosen who had never dealt with Jubal. As his informants did not know each other's identities, the example would work.

". . . was found this morning," Saliman plodded on in his tireless recitation voice. "The coin was stolen by the person discovering the body, so there will be no investigation. The thief will talk, though, so word will spread."

"Yes, yes." Jubal grimaced impatiently. "Go on with another item."

"There is some consternation along the Avenue of Temples over the new shrines being erected to Savankala and Sabellia—"

"Does it affect our operations?" Jubal interrupted.

"No," Saliman admitted. "But I thought you should know."

"Now I know," Jubal countered. "Spare me the details. Next item."

"Two of our men were refused service at the Vulgar Unicorn last night."

"By who?" Jubal frowned.

"One-Thumb. He oversees the place evenings from—"

"I know who One-Thumb is!" Jubal snapped. "I also know he's never refused service to any of my men as long as they had copper and their manners were good. If he moved against two of mine, it was because of their own actions, not because he has ill feelings toward me. Next item."

Saliman hesitated, to reorganize his thoughts, then continued.

"Increased pressure from the prince's Hell Hounds has closed the wharves to the smugglers. It is rumored they will be forced to land their goods at the Swamp of Night Secrets as they did in the old days."

"An inconvenience which will doubtless drive their prices up," Jubal mused. "How well guarded are their landings?"

"It is not known."

"Look into it. If there's a chance we can intercept a few shipments in the swamp, there'll be no reason to pay their inflated prices at the bazaar."

"But if the smugglers lose shipments, they will raise their prices all the more to recover the loss."

"Of course." Jubal smiled. "Which means when we sell the stolen goods, we will be able to charge higher prices and still undercut the smugglers."

"We shall investigate the possibility. But—"

"But what?" Jubal inquired, studying his lieutenant's face. "Out with it, man. Something's bothering you about my plan, and I want to know what it is."

"I fear we might encounter difficulty with the Hell Hounds," Saliman blurted. "If they have also heard rumors of the new landing sites, they might plan an ambush of their own. Taking a shipment away from smugglers is one thing, but trying to take confiscated evidence away from the Hell Hounds. . . . I'm not sure the men are up to it."

"My men? Afraid of guardsmen?" Jubal's expression darkened. "I thought I was paying good gold to have the finest swords in Sanctuary at my disposal."

"The Hell Hounds are not ordinary guardsmen," Saliman protested. "Nor are they from Sanctuary. Before they arrived, I would have said ours were the finest swords. Now . . ."

"The Hell Hounds!" Jubal snarled. "It seems all anyone can talk about is the Hell Hounds."

"And you should listen." Saliman bristled. "Forgive me, Jubal, but you yourself admit the men you hire are no newcomers to battle. When they speak of a new force at large in Sanctuary, you should listen instead of decrying their judgment or abilities."

For a moment, a spark of anger flared in Jubal's eyes. Then it died, and he leaned forward attentively in his chair.

"Very well, Saliman. I'm listening. Tell me about the Hell Hounds."

"They . . . they are unlike the guardsmen we see in Sanctuary, or even the average soldier of the Rankan army," Saliman explained, groping for words. "They were handpicked from the Royal Elite Guard especially for this assignment."

"Five men to guard a royal prince," Jubal murmured thoughtfully. "Yes, they would have to be good."

"That's right," Saliman confirmed hurriedly. "With the entire Rankan army to choose from, these five were selected for their skill at arms and unswerving loyalty to the empire. Since their arrival in Sanctuary, every effort to bribe or assassinate them has ended in death for whoever attempted it."

"You're right." Jubal nodded. "They could be a disruptive force. Still, they are only men, and all men have weaknesses."

He lapsed into thoughtful silence for several moments.

"Withdraw a hundred silver shaboozh from the treasury," he ordered at last. "Distribute it to the men to spread around town, particularly to those working in the governor's palace. In exchange, I want information about the Hell Hounds, individually and collectively. Listen especially for word of dissent within their own ranks . . . anything that could be used to turn them against one another."

"It shall be done," Saliman responded, bowing slightly. "Do you also wish a magical investigation commissioned?"

Jubal hesitated. He had a warrior's dread of magicians and avoided them whenever possible. Still, if the Hell Hounds constituted a large enough threat . . .

"Use the money for normal informants," he decided. "If it becomes necessary to hire a magician, then I will personally—"

A sudden commotion at the chamber's entryway drew the attention of both men. Two blue-masked figures appeared, dragging a third between them. Despite their masks, Jubal recognized them as Mor-Am and Moria, a brother-and-sister team of sell-swords in his employment. Their apparent captive was an urchin, garbed in the dirty rags common to Sanctuary's street children. He couldn't have been more than ten years of age, but the sizzling invective he screeched as he struggled against his captors marked him as one knowledgeable beyond his years.

"We caught this gutter rat on the grounds," Mor-Am announced, ignoring the boy's protests.

"Probably out to steal something," his sister added.

"I wasn't stealing!" the boy cried, wrenching himself free.

"A Sanctuary street rat who doesn't steal?" Jubal raised an eyebrow.

"Of course I steal!" the urchin spat. "Everyone does. But that's not why I came here."

"Then why did you come?" Mor-Am demanded, cuffing the boy and sending him sprawling. "To beg? To sell your body?"

"I have a message!" the boy bawled. "For Jubal!"

"Enough, Mor-Am," Jubal ordered, suddenly interested. "Come here, boy."

The urchin scrambled to his feet, pausing only to knuckle tears of anger from his eyes. He shot a glare of pure venom at Mor-Am and Moria, then approached Jubal.

"What is your name, boy?" Jubal prompted.

"I—am called Mungo," the urchin stammered, suddenly shy. "Are you Jubal?"

"I am," Jubal nodded. "Well, Mungo, where is this message you have for me?"

"It . . . it's not written down," Mungo explained, casting a hasty glance at Mor-Am. "I was to tell you the message."

"Very well, tell me," Jubal urged, growing impatient. "And also tell me who is sending the message."

"The message is from Hakiem," the boy blurted. "He bids me tell you that he has important information for sale."

"Hakiem?" Jubal frowned.

The old storyteller! He had often been of service to Jubal when people forgot that he could listen as well as talk.

"Yes, Hakiem. He sells stories in the bazaar. . . ."

"I know, I know," Jubal snapped. For some reason, today everyone thought he knew nothing of the people in town. "What information does he have for me, and why didn't he come himself?"

"I don't know what the information is. But it's important. So important that Hakiem is in hiding, afraid for his life. He paid me to fetch you to him, for he feels the information will be especially valuable to you."

"Fetch me to him?" Jubal rumbled, his temper rising.

"One moment, boy," Saliman interceded, speaking for the first time since his report was interrupted. "You say Hakiem paid you? How much?"

"A silver coin," the boy announced proudly.

"Show it to us!" Saliman ordered.

The boy's hand disappeared within his rags. Then he hesitated.

"You won't take it from me, will you?" he asked warily.

"Show the coin!" Jubal roared.

Cowed by the sudden outburst, Mungo extended his fist and opened it, revealing a silver coin nestled in his palm.

Jubal's eyes sought Saliman, who raised his eyebrows in silent surprise and speculation. The fact that the boy actually had a silver coin indicated many things.

First: Mungo was probably telling the truth. Street rats rarely had more than a few coppers, so a silver coin would have had to come from an outside benefactor. If the boy had stolen it, he would himself be in hiding, gloating over his ill-gotten wealth—not displaying it openly as he had just done.

Assuming the boy was telling the truth, then Hakiem's information must indeed be valuable and the danger to him real. Hakiem was not the sort to give away silver coins unless he were confident of recouping the loss and making a healthy profit besides. Even then, he would save the expense and bring the information himself, were he not truly afraid for his life.

All this flashed through Jubal's mind as he saw the coin, and Saliman's reactions confirmed his thoughts.

"Very well. We shall see what information Hakiem has. Saliman, take Mor-Am and Moria and go with Mungo to find the storyteller. Bring him here and—"

"No!" the boy cried, interrupting. "Hakiem will only give the information to Jubal personally, and he is to come alone."

"What?" Saliman exclaimed.

"This sounds like a trap!" Moria scowled.

Jubal waved them to silence as he stared down at the boy. It could be a trap. Then again, there could be another reason for Hakiem's request. The information might involve someone in Jubal's own force! An assassin . . . or worse, an informer! That could explain Hakiem's reluctance to come to the mansion in person.

"I will go," Jubal said, rising and sweeping the room with his eyes. "Alone, with Mungo. Saliman, I will require the use of your mask."

"I want my knife back!" Mungo declared suddenly.

Jubal raised a questioning eyebrow at Mor-Am, who flushed and produced a short dagger from his belt. "We took it from him when we caught him," the sell-sword explained. "A safety precaution. We had no intent to steal it."

"Give it back." Jubal laughed. "I would not send my worst enemy into the streets of Sanctuary unarmed."

"Jubal," Saliman murmured as he surrendered his hawk-mask. "If this should be a trap . . ."

Jubal dropped a hand to his sword hilt.

"If it is a trap," he smiled, "they'll not find me easy prey. I survived five-to-one odds and worse in the pits before I won my freedom."

"But—"

"You are not to follow," Jubal ordered sternly. "Nor allow any other to follow. Anyone who disobeys will answer to me."

Saliman drew a breath to answer, then saw the look in Jubal's eyes and nodded in silent acceptance.

Jubal studied his guide covertly as they left the mansion and headed toward the town. Though he had not shown it openly, he had been impressed with the boy's spirit during their brief encounter. Alone and unarmed in the midst of hostile swords . . . men twice Mungo's age had been known to tremble and grovel when visiting Jubal at his mansion.

In many ways, the boy reminded Jubal of himself as a youth. Fighting and rebellious, with no parents but his pride and stubbornness to guide him, he had been bought from the slave pens by a gladiator trainer with an eye for cold, spirited fighters. If he had instead been purchased by a gentle master . . . if someone interceded in the dubious path Fate had chosen for Mungo . . .

Jubal halted that line of thought with a grimace as he realized where it was leading. Adopt the boy into his household? Ridiculous! Saliman and the others would think he had gone soft in his old age. More important, his competitors would see it as a sign of weakness, an indication that Jubal could be reached by sentimentality . . . that he had a heart. He had risen above his own squalid beginnings; the boy would just have to do the same!

The sun was high and staggering in its heat as Jubal followed the boy's lead into town. Sweat trickled in annoying rivulets from beneath his blue hawk-mask, but he was loath to acknowledge his discomfort by wiping them away. The thought of removing the mask never entered his mind. The masks were necessary to disguise those in his employment who were wanted by the law; to complete the camouflage, all must wear them. To exempt himself from his own rule would be unthinkable.

In an effort to distract himself from his discomfort, Jubal began to peer cautiously at the people about him as they approached the bazaar. Since they had crossed the bridge and placed the hovels of the Downwinders behind them, there was a marked improvement in the quality of clothes and manners of the citizenry.

His eye fell on a magician, and he wondered about the star tattooed on the man's forehead. Then, too, he noted that the mage was engaged in a heated argument with a brightly garbed young bravo who displayed numerous knives, their hilts protruding from arm sheath, sash, and boot top in ominous warning.

"That's Lythande," Mungo informed him, noting his interest. "He's a fraud. If you're looking for a magician, there are better to be had . . . cheaper."

"You're sure he's a fraud?" Jubal asked, amused at the boy's analysis.

"If he were a true magician, he wouldn't have to carry a sword," Mungo countered, pointing to the weapon slung at the magician's side.

"A point well taken," Jubal acknowledged.

"And the man he's arguing with?"

"Shadowspawn," the boy announced loftily. "A thief. Used to work with Cudget Swearoath before the old fool got himself hung."

"A magician and a thief," Jubal murmured thoughtfully, glancing at the two again. "An interesting combination of talents."

"Unlikely!" Mungo scoffed. "Whatever Shadowspawn's last venture was, it was profitable. He's been spending freely and often, so it's unlikely he'll be looking for more work. My guess would be they're arguing over a woman. They each fancy themselves to be a gift from the gods to womankind."

"You seem to be well informed," Jubal commented, impressed anew with the boy's knowledge.

"One hears much in the streets." Mungo shrugged. "The lower one's standing is, the more important information is for survival . . . and few are lower than my friends and I."

Jubal pondered this as the boy led the way past Shambles Cross. Perhaps he had overlooked a valuable information source in the street children when he built his network of informers. They probably would not hear much, but there were so many of them. Together they might be enough to confirm or quash a rumor.

"Tell me, Mungo," he called to his guide. "You know I pay well for information, don't you?"

"Everyone knows that." The urchin turned in to the Maze and skipped lightly over a prone figure, not bothering to see if the man was asleep or dead.

"Then why is it that none of your friends come to me with their knowledge?"

Jubal stepped carefully over the obstacle and cast a wary glance about. Even in broad daylight, the Maze could be a dangerous place for a lone traveler.

"We street rats are close," Mungo explained over his shoulder. "Even closer than the bazaar people or the S'danzo. Shared secrets lose their value, so we keep them for ourselves."

Jubal recognized the wisdom in the urchins' policy, but it only heightened his resolve to recruit the children.

"Talk it over with your friends," he urged. "A full stomach can . . . Where are we going?"

They had left the dank Serpentine for an alley so narrow that Jubal had to edge sideways to follow.

"To meet Hakiem," Mungo called, not slackening his pace.

"But where is he?" Jubal pressed. "I do not know this rat run."

"If you knew it, it would not make a good hiding place." The boy laughed. "It's just a little farther."

As he spoke, they emerged from the crawlspace into a small courtyard.

"We're here," Mungo announced, coming to a halt in the center of the yard.

"Where?" Jubal growled, standing beside him. "There are no doors or windows in these walls. Unless he is hiding in one of those refuse heaps . . ."

He broke off his commentary as the details of their surroundings sank into his mind. No doors or windows! The only other way out of the courtyard was another crawlspace as small as that they had just traversed . . . except that it was blocked by a pile of wooden cartons. They were in a cul-de-sac!

A sudden crash sounded behind them, and Jubal spun to face it, his hand going reflexively to his sword. Several wooden boxes had fallen from the roof of one of the buildings, blocking the entrance.

"It's a trap!" he hissed, backing toward a corner, his eyes scanning the rooftops.

There was a sudden impact on his back. He staggered slightly, then lashed backward with his sword, swinging blind. His blade encountered naught but air, and he turned to face his attacker.

Mungo danced lightly just out of sword range, his eyes bright with triumph and glee.

"Mungo?" Jubal asked, knowing the answer.

He had been wounded often enough to recognize the growing numbness in his upper back. A rasp of pain as he shifted his stance told the rest of the story. The boy had planted his dagger in Jubal's back, and there it remained. In his mind's eye, Jubal could see it protruding from his shoulder at an unnatural angle.

"I told you we were close," Mungo taunted. "Maybe the big folk are afraid of you, but we aren't. You shouldn't have ordered Gambi's death."

"Gambi?" Jubal frowned, weaving slightly. "Who is Gambi?"

For a moment, the boy froze in astonishment. Then his face contorted with rage and he spat.

"He was found this morning with his throat cut and a copper coin in his mouth. Your trademark! Don't you even know who you kill?"

The blind! Jubal cursed himself for not listening closer to Saliman's reports.

"Gambi never sold you *any* information," Mungo shouted. "He hated you for what your men did to his mother. You had no right to kill him as a false informer."

"And Hakiem?" Jubal asked, stalling for time.

"We guessed right about that, didn't we—about Hakiem being one of your informers?" the boy crowed. "He's on the big wharf sleeping off a drunk. We pooled our money for the silver coin that drew you out from behind your guards."

For some reason, this last taunt stung Jubal more than had the dagger thrust. He drew himself erect, ignoring the warm liquid dripping down his back from the knife wound, and glared down at the boy.

"I need no guard against the likes of you!" he boomed. "You think you know killing? A street rat who stabs overhand with a knife? The next time you try to kill a man—if there is another time—thrust underhand. Go between the ribs, not through them! And bring friends—one of you isn't enough to kill a real man."

"I brought friends!" Mungo laughed, pointing. "Do you think they'll be enough?"

Jubal risked a glance over his shoulder. The gutter rats of Sanctuary were descending on the courtyard. Scores of them! Scrabbling over the wooden cases or swarming down from the roofs like spiders. Children in rags—none of them even half Jubal's height, but with knives, rocks, and sharp sticks.

Another man might have broken before those hate-filled eyes. He

might have tried to beg or bribe his way out of the trap, claiming ignorance of Gambi's murder. But this was Jubal, and his eyes were as cold as
his sword as he faced his tormentors.

"You claim you're doing this to avenge one death," he sneered. "How
many will die trying to pull me down?"

"You feel free to kill us one at a time, for no reason," Mungo retorted,
circling wide to join the pack. "If some of us die killing you, then at least
the rest will be safe."

"Only if you kill me," Jubal corrected. Without taking his eyes from
the pack, he reached his left hand over his right shoulder, found the
knife hilt, and wrenched it free. "And for that, you'll need your knife
back!"

Mungo saw the knife coming as Jubal whipped his left hand down and
across his body, but he froze for a split second. In that split second, the
knife took him full in the throat. The world blurred and he went down,
not feeling the fall.

The pack surged forward, and Jubal went to meet them, his sword
flashing in the sun as he desperately tried to win his way to the exit.

A few fell before his first rush—he didn't know how many—but the
rest scattered and closed about him from all sides. Sticks jabbed at his
face faster than he could parry them, and he felt the touch of knives as
small forms darted from behind him to slash and duck away.

Realization came to him that the harassment would bring him down
before he could clear the wooden cases; abandoning his charge, he
paused, whirling and cutting, trying to clear a space around him. The
urchins were sharp-toothed, elusive phantoms, disappearing from in
front of him to worry him from behind. It flashed through his mind that
he was going to die! The survivor of countless gladiator duels was going
to meet his end at the hands of angry children!

The thought drove him to desperate action. With one last powerful
cut, he broke off his efforts at defense and tried to sprint for a wall to get
something solid at his back. A small girl grabbed his ankle and clung
with all her strength. He stumbled, nearly falling, and cut downward
viciously without looking. His leg came free, but another urchin leapt
onto his back, hammering at his head with a rock.

Jubal lurched sideways, scraping the child off along the wall, then
turned to face the pack. A stick pierced his mask, opening a gash in his

forehead which began to drip blood in his eyes. Temporarily blinded, he laid about him wildly with his sword, sometimes striking something solid, sometimes encountering air. A rock caromed off his head, but he was past feeling and continued his sightless, mindless slashing.

Slowly it crept into his fogged brain that there was a new note in the children's screams. At the same time, he realized that his sword had not struck a target for ten or fifteen swings now. Shaking his head to clear it, he focused anew on the scene before him.

The courtyard was littered with small bodies, their blood a bright contrast to their drab rags. The rest of the pack was in full flight, pursued over the rubble piles by . . .

Jubal sagged against the wall, fighting for breath and numb from wounds too numerous to count. He watched as his rescuer strode to his side, sheathing a sword wet with fresh blood.

"Your . . . your name?" he gasped.

"Zalbar," the uniformed figure panted in return. "Bodyguard to His Royal Highness, Prince Kadakithis. Your wounds . . . are they . . . ?"

"I've survived worse." Jubal shrugged, wincing at the pain the movement caused.

"Very well." The man nodded. "Then I shall be on my way."

"A moment," Jubal asked, holding up a restraining hand. "You have saved my life . . . a life I value quite highly. I owe you thanks and more, for you can't spend words. Name your reward."

"That is not necessary." Zalbar sniffed. "It is my duty."

"Duty or not," Jubal argued, "I know no other guardsman who would enter the Maze, much less risk his life to save . . . Did you say a royal bodyguard: Are you . . ."

"A Hell Hound," Zalbar finished with a grim smile. "Yes, I am. And I promise you, the day is not far off when we will not be the only guardsmen in the Maze."

He turned to go, but Jubal stopped him again, removing the hawk-mask to mop the blood from his eyes.

"Wait!" he ordered. "I have a proposal for you. I have need of men such as you. Whatever pay you receive from the empire, I'll double it . . . as well as adding a bonus for your work today. What say you?"

There was no answer. Jubal squinted to get the Hell Hound's face in focus, and found the man was staring at him in frozen recognition.

"You are Jubal!" Zalbar said in a tone that was more statement than question.

"I am." Jubal nodded. "If you know that, you must also know that there is none in Sanctuary who pay higher than I for services rendered."

"I know your reputation," the Hell Hound acknowledged coldly. "Knowing what I do, I would not work for you at any price."

The rebuff was obvious, but Jubal chose to ignore it. Instead, he attempted to make light of the comment.

"But you already have," he pointed out. "You saved my life."

"I saved a citizen from a pack of street rats," Zalbar countered. "As I said before, it's my duty to my prince."

"But—" Jubal began.

"Had I known your identity sooner," the Hell Hound continued, "I might have been tempted to delay my rescue."

This time, the slight could not be ignored. More puzzled than angry, Jubal studied his opponent.

"I sense you are trying to provoke a fight. Did you save me, then, to wreak some vengeance of your own?"

"In my position, I cannot and will not engage in petty brawls," Zalbar growled. "I fight only to defend myself or the citizens of the empire."

"And I will not knowingly raise a sword against one who has saved my life . . . save in self-defense," Jubal retorted. "It would seem, then, that we will not fight each other. Still, it seems you hold some grudge against me. May I ask what it is?"

"It is the grudge I hold against any man who reaps the benefits of Rankan citizenship while accepting none of the responsibility," the Hell Hound sneered. "Not only do you not serve the empire that shelters you, you undermine its strength by openly flaunting your disrespect for its laws in your business dealings."

"What do you know of my business dealings that allows you to make such sweeping judgments?" Jubal challenged.

"I know you make your money in ways decent men would shun," Zalbar retorted. "You deal in slaves and drugs and other high-profit, low-moral commodities . . . but most of all, you deal in death."

"A professional soldier condemns me for dealing in death?" Jubal smiled.

The Hell Hound flushed red at the barb. "Yes. I also deal in death. But a soldier such as myself fights for the good of the empire, not for

selfish gain. I lost a brother and several friends in the mountain campaigns fighting for the empire . . . for the freedoms you and your kind
abuse."

"Imagine that," Jubal mused. "The whole Rankan army defending
us against a few scattered mountain tribes. Why, if you and your
friends hadn't been there, the Highlanders certainly would have swept
down out of the mountains they haven't left for generations and murdered us all in our sleep. How silly of me to think it was the empire trying to extend its influence into one more place it wasn't wanted. I
should have realized it was only trying to defend itself from a ferocious
attacker."

Zalbar swayed forward, his hand going to his sword hilt. Then he
regained his composure and hardened his features.

"I am done talking to you. You can't understand the minds of decent
men, much less their words."

He turned to go, but somehow Jubal was in his path—on his feet now,
though he swayed from the effort. Though the soldier was taller by a
head, Jubal's anger increased his stature to where it was Zalbar who gave
ground.

"If you're done talking, Hell Hound, then it's time I had my say," he
hissed. "It's true I make money from distasteful merchandise. I wouldn't
be able to do that if your 'decent men' weren't willing to pay a hefty
price for it. I don't sell my goods at swordpoint. They come to me—so
many of them, I can't fill the demand through normal channels."

He turned to gesture at the corpse-littered courtyard.

"It's also true I deal in death," he snarled. "Your benevolent Rankan
masters taught me the trade in the gladiator pits of the capital. I dealt in
death then for the cheers of those same 'decent men' you admire so.

"Those 'decent men' allowed me no place in their 'decent' society
after I won my freedom, so I came to Sanctuary. Now I still deal in death,
for that is the price of doing business here—a price I almost paid today."

For a fleeting moment, something akin to sympathy flashed in the Hell
Hound's eyes as he shook his head.

"You're wrong, Jubal," he said quietly. "You've already paid the price
for doing business in Sanctuary. It isn't your life, it's your soul . . . your
humanity. You've exchanged it for gold, and in my opinion, it was a poor
bargain."

Their eyes met, and it was Jubal who averted his gaze first, unsettled by the Hell Hound's words. Looking away, his glance fell on the body of Mungo, the boy he had admired and thought of bringing into his household—the boy whose life he had wanted to change.

When he turned again, the Hell Hound was gone.

Blood Brothers

Joe Haldeman

*Smiling, bowing as the guests leave. A good luncheon, much reassuring
talk from the gentry assembled; the economy of Sanctuary is basically
sound.* Thank you, my new cook . . . he's from Twand, isn't he a marvel?
*The host appears to be rather in need of a new diet than a new cook,
though the heavy brocades he affects may make him look stouter than he
actually is.* Good leave . . . certainly, tomorrow. Tell your aunt I'm
thinking of her.

You will stay, of course, Amar. *One departing guest raises an eyebrow
slightly, our host a boylover?* We do have business.

Enoir, you may release the servants until dawn. Give yourself a free
evening as well. We will be dining in the city.

And thank you for the excellent service. Here.

He laughs. Don't thank me. Just don't spend it all on one woman. *As
the servant master leaves, our host's bluff expression fades to one of
absolute neutrality. He listens to the servant master's progress down the
stone steps, overhears him dismissing the servants. Turns and gestures to
the pile of cushions by the huge fireplace. The smell of winter's ashes
masked by incense fumes.*

I have a good wine, Amar. Be seated while I fetch it.

Were you comfortable with our guests?

Merchants, indeed. But one does learn from other classes, don't you agree?

He returns with two goblets of wine so purple it is almost black. He sets both goblets in front of Amar; choose. Even closest friends follow this ritual in Sanctuary, where poisoning is art, sport, profession. Yes, it was the color that intrigued me. Good fortune.

No, it's from a grove in the mountains, east of Syr. Kalos or something; I could never get my tongue around their barbaric . . . yes. A good dessert wine. Would you care for a pipe?

Enoir returns. Jingling his bell as he walks up the steps.

That will be all for today, thank you. . . .

No, I don't want the hounds fed. Better sport Ilsday if they're famished. We can live with their whimpering.

The heavy front door creaks shut behind the servant master. You don't? You would not be the only noble in attendance. Let your beard grow a day or two, borrow some rag from a servant. . . .

Well, there are two schools of thinking. Hungry dogs are weaker but fight with desperation. And if your dogs aren't fed for a week, there's a week they can't be poisoned by the other teams.

Oh, it does happen—I think it happened to me once. Not a killing poison, just one that makes them listless, uncompetitive. Perhaps a spell. Poison's cheaper.

He drinks deeply, then sets the goblet carefully on the floor. He crosses the room and mounts a step and peers through a slot window cut in the deep wall.

I'm sure we're alone now. Drink up; I'll fetch the *krrf. He is gone for less than a minute, and returns with a heavy brick wrapped in soft leather.*

Caronne's finest, pure black, unadulterated. *He unfolds the package: ebony block embossed all over its surface with a foreign seal.* Try some?

He nods. "A wise vintner who avoids his wares." You have the gold?

He weighs the bag in his hand. This is not enough. Not by half.

He listens and hands back the gold. Be reasonable. If you feel you can't trust my assay, take a small amount back to Ranke; have anyone test it. Then bring me the price we established.

The other man suddenly stands and claws at his falchion, but it barely clears its sheath, then clatters on the marble floor. He falls to his hands and knees, trembling, stutters a few words, and collapses.

No, not a spell, though nearly as swift, don't you think? That's the virtue of coadjuvant poisons. The first ingredient you had along with everyone else, in the sauce for the sweetmeats. Everyone but me. The second part was in the wine, part of its sweetness.

He runs his thumbnail along the block, collecting a pinch of krrf, which he rubs between thumb and forefinger and then sniffs. You really should try it. It makes you feel young and brave. But then you are young and brave, aren't you?

He carefully wraps the krrf up and retrieves the gold. Excuse me. I have to go change. *At the door he hesitates.* The poison is not fatal; it only leaves you paralyzed for a while. Surgeons use it.

The man stares at the floor for a long time. He is conscious of drooling, and other loss of control.

When the host returns, he is barely recognizable. Instead of the gaudy robe, he wears a patched and stained houppelande with a rope for a belt. The pomaded white mane is gone; his bald scalp is creased with a webbed old scar from a swordstroke. His left thumb is missing from the second joint. He smiles, and shows almost as much gap as tooth.

I am going to treat you kindly. There are some who would pay well to use your helpless body, and they would kill you afterward.

He undresses the limp man, clucking, and again compliments himself for his charity, and the man for his well-kept youth. He lifts the grate in the fireplace and drops the garment down the shaft that serves for disposal of ashes.

In another part of town, I'm known as One-Thumb. Here, I cover the stump with a taxidermist's imitation. Convincing, isn't it? *He lifts the man easily and carries him through the main door.* No fault of yours, of course, but you're distantly related to the magistrate who had my thumb off. *The barking of the dogs grows louder as they descend the stairs.*

Here we are. *He pushes open the door to the kennels. The barking quiets to pleading whines. Ten fighting hounds, each in an individual run, up against its feeding trough, slavering politely, yawning gray sharp fangs.*

We have to feed them separately, of course. So they don't hurt each other.

At the far end of the room is a wooden slab at waist level, with channels cut in its surface leading to hanging buckets. On the wall above it, a rack with knives, cleavers, and a saw.

He deposits the mute staring man on the slab and selects a heavy cleaver.

I'm sorry, Amar. I have to start with the feet. Otherwise it's a terrible mess.

There are philosophers who argue that there is no such thing as evil qua evil; that, discounting spells (which of course relieve an individual of responsibility), when a man commits an evil deed he is the victim himself, the slave of his progeniture and nurturing. Such philosophers might profit by studying Sanctuary.

Sanctuary is a seaport, and its name goes back to a time when it provided the only armed haven along an important caravan route. But the long war ended, the caravans abandoned that route for a shorter one, and Sanctuary declined in status—but not in population, because for every honest person who left to pursue a normal life elsewhere, a rogue drifted in to pursue *his* normal life.

Now, Sanctuary is still appropriately named, but as a haven for the lawless. Most of them, and the worst of them, are concentrated in that section of town known as the Maze, a labyrinth of streets and nameless alleys and no churches. There is communion, though, of a rough kind, and much of it goes on in a tavern named the Vulgar Unicorn, which features a sign in the shape of that animal improbably engaging itself, and is owned by the man who usually tends bar on the late shift, an ugly sort of fellow by the name of One-Thumb.

One-Thumb finished feeding the dogs, hosed the place down, and left his estate by way of a long tunnel, that led from his private rooms to the basement of the Lily Garden, a respectable whorehouse a few blocks from the Maze.

He climbed the long steps up from the basement and was greeted by a huge eunuch with a heavy glaive balanced insolently over his shoulder.

"Early today, One-Thumb."

"Sometimes I like to check on the help at the Unicorn."

"Surprise inspection?"

"Something like that. Is your mistress in?"

"Sleeping. You want a wench?"

"No, just business."

The eunuch inclined his head. "That's business."

"Tell her I have what she asked for, and more, if she can afford it. When she's free. If I'm not at the Unicorn, I'll leave word as to where we can meet."

"I know what it is," the eunuch said in a singsong voice.

"Instant maidenhead." One-Thumb hefted the leather-wrapped brick. "One pinch, properly inserted, turns you into a girl again."

The eunuch rolled his eyes. "An improvement over the old method."

One-Thumb laughed along with him. "I could spare a pinch or so, if you'd care for it."

"Oh . . . not on duty." He leaned the sword against the wall and found a square of parchment in his money belt. "I could save it for my off time, though." One-Thumb gave him a pinch. He stared at it before folding it up. "Black . . . Caronne?"

"The best."

"You have that much of it." He didn't reach toward his weapon.

One-Thumb's free hand rested on the pommel of his rapier. "For sale, twenty *grimales*."

"A man with no scruples would kill you for it."

Gap-toothed smile. "I'm doubly safe with you, then."

The eunuch nodded and tucked away the *krrf*, then retrieved the broadsword. "Safe with anyone not a stranger." Everyone in the Maze knew of the curse that One-Thumb expensively maintained to protect his life: if he were killed, his murderer would never die, but live forever in helpless agony:

> *Burn as the stars burn;*
> *Burn on after they die.*
> *Never to the peace of ashes,*
> *Out of sight and succor*
> *From men or gods or ghost:*
> *To the ends of time, burn.*

One-Thumb himself suspected that the spell would only be effective for as long as the sorcerer who cast it lived, but that was immaterial. The reputation of the sorcerer, Mizraith, as well as the severity of the spell, kept blades in sheaths and poison out of his food.

"I'll pass the message on. Many thanks."

"Better mix it with snuff, you know. Very strong." One-Thumb parted a velvet curtain and passed through the foyer, exchanging greetings with some of the women who lounged there in soft veils (the cut and color of the veils advertised price and, in some cases, curious specialties), and stepped out into the waning light of the end of day.

The afternoon had been an interesting array of sensations for a man whose nose was as refined as it was large. First the banquet, with all its aromatic Twand delicacies, then the good rare wine with a delicate tang of half-poison, then the astringent *krrf* sting, the rich charnel smell of butchery, the musty sweat of the tunnel's rock walls, perfume and incense in the foyer, and now the familiar stink of the street. As he walked through the gate into the city proper, he could tell the wind was westering; the earthy smell from the animal pens had a slight advantage over the tanners' vats of rotting urine. He even sorted out the delicate cucumber fragrance of freshly butchered fish, like a whisper in a jabbering crowd; not many snouts had such powers of discrimination. As ever, he enjoyed the first few minutes within the city walls, before the reek stunned even his nose to dullness.

Most of the stalls in the farmers' market were shuttered now, but he was able to trade two coppers for a fresh melon, which he peeled as he walked into the bazaar, the *krrf* inconspicuous under his arm.

He haggled for a while with a coppersmith, new to the bazaar, for a brace of lamps to replace the ones that had been stolen from the Unicorn last night. He would send one of his urchins around to pick them up. He watched the acrobats for a while, then went to the various wine merchants for bids on the next week's ordinaries. He ordered a hundredweight of salt meat, sliced into snacks, to be delivered that night, and checked the guild hall of the mercenaries to find a hall guard more sober than the one who had allowed the lamps to be stolen. Then he went down to the Wideway and had an early dinner of raw fish and crab fritters. Fortified, he entered the Maze.

As the eunuch had said, One-Thumb had nothing to fear from the regular denizens of the Maze. Desperadoes who would disembowel children for sport (a sport sadly declining since the introduction of a foolproof herbal abortifacient) tipped their hats respectfully, or stayed out of his way. Still, he was careful. There were always strangers, often hot to prove themselves, or desperate for the price of bread or wine; and although One-Thumb was a formidable opponent with or without his rapier, he knew he looked rather like an overweight merchant whose ugliness interfered with his trade.

He also knew evil well, from the inside, which is why he dressed shabbily and displayed no outward sign of wealth. Not to prevent violence, since he knew the poor were more often victims than the rich, but to restrict the class of his possible opponents to those who would kill for coppers. They generally lacked skill.

On the way to the Unicorn, on Serpentine, a man with the conspicuously casual air of a beginner pickpocket fell in behind him. One-Thumb knew that the alley was coming up and would be in deep shadow, and it had a hiding niche a few paces inside. He turned in to the alley and, drawing the dagger from his boot, slipped into the niche and set the *krrf* between his feet.

The man did follow, proof enough, and when his steps faltered at the darkness, One-Thumb spun out of the niche behind him, clamped a strong hand over his mouth and nose, and methodically slammed the stiletto into his back, time and again, aiming for kidneys. When the man's knees buckled, One-Thumb let him down slowly, slitting his throat for silence. He took the money belt and a bag of coin from the still-twitching body, cleaned and replaced his dagger, picked up the *krrf*, and resumed his stroll down the Serpentine. There were a few bright spatters of blood on his houppelande, but no one on that street would be troubled by it. Sometimes guardsmen came through, but not to harass the good citizens nor criticize their quaint customs.

Two in one day, he thought; it had been a year or more since the last time that happened. He felt vaguely good about it, though neither man had been much of a challenge. The cutpurse was a clumsy amateur and the young noble from Ranke a trusting fool (whose assassination had been commissioned by one of his father's ministers).

He came up the street south of the Vulgar Unicorn's entrance and let himself in the back door. He glanced at the inventory in the storeroom and noted that it must have been a slow day, and went through to his office. He locked up the *krrf* in a strongbox and then poured himself a small glass of lemony aperitif, and sat down at the one-way mirror that allowed him to watch the bar unseen.

For an hour he watched money and drink change hands. The bartender, who had been the cook aboard a pirate vessel until he'd lost a leg, seemed good with the customers and reasonably honest, though he gave short measures to some of the more intoxicated patrons—probably not out of concern for their welfare. One-Thumb started to pour a third glass of the liqueur and saw Amoli, the Lily Garden's mistress, come into the place, along with the eunuch and another bodyguard. He went out to meet them.

"Wine over here," he said to a serving wench, and escorted the three to a curtained-off table.

Amoli was almost beautiful, though she was scarcely younger than One-Thumb, in a trade that normally aged one rapidly. She came to the point at once: "Kalem tells me you have twenty *grimales* of Caronne for sale."

"Prime and pure."

"That's a rare amount." One-Thumb nodded. "Where, may I ask, did it come from?"

"I'd rather not say."

"You'd better say. I had a twenty-*grimale* block in my bedroom safe. Yesterday it was stolen."

One-Thumb didn't move or change expression. "That's an interesting coincidence."

She snorted. They sat without speaking while a pitcher of wine and four glasses were slipped through the curtain.

"Of course I'm not accusing you of theft," she said. "But you can understand why I'm interested in the person you bought it from."

"In the first place, I didn't buy it. In the second, it didn't come from Sanctuary."

"I can't afford riddles, One-Thumb. Who was it?"

"That has to remain secret. It involves a murder."

"You might be involved in another," she said tightly.

One-Thumb slowly reached down and brought out his dagger. The bodyguards tensed. He smiled, and pushed it across the table to Amoli. "Go ahead, kill me. What happens to you will be rather worse than going without *krrf*."

"Oh—" She knocked the knife back to him. "My temper is short nowadays. I'm sorry. But the *krrf*'s not just for me; most of my women use it, and take part of their pay in it, which is why I like to buy in large amounts." One-Thumb was pouring the wine; he nodded. "Do you have any idea how much of my capital was tied up in that block?"

He replaced the half-full glasses on the round serving tray and gave it a spin. "Half?"

"And half again of that. I will get it back, One-Thumb!" She selected a glass and drank.

"I hope you do. But it can't be the same block."

"Let me judge that—have you had it for more than two days?"

"No, but it must have left Ranke more than a week ago. It came on the Anenday caravan. Hidden inside a cheese."

"You can't know for sure that it was on the caravan all the time. It could have been waiting here until the caravan came."

"I can hear your logic straining, Amoli."

"But not without reason. How often have you seen a block as large as twenty *grimales*?"

"Only this time," he admitted.

"And is a pressed design stamped all over it uniformly, an eagle within a circle?"

"It is. But that only means a common supplier, his mark."

"Still, I think you owe me information."

One-Thumb sipped his wine. "All right. I know I can trust the eunuch. What about the other?"

"I had a vassal spell laid on him when I bought him. Besides . . . show him your tongue, Gage."

The slave opened his mouth and showed pink scar tissue nested in bad teeth. "He can neither speak nor write."

"We make an interesting table," he said. "Missing thumb, tongue, and tamale. What are you missing, Amoli?"

"Heart. And a block of *krrf*."

"All right." He drank off the rest of his small glass and refilled it. "There is a man high in the court of Ranke, old and soon to die. His son, who would inherit his title, is slothful, incompetent, dishonest. The old man's counselors would rather the daughter succeed; she is not only more able, but easier for them to control."

"I think I know the family you speak of," Amoli said.

"When I was in Ranke on other business, one of the counselors got in touch with me, and commissioned me to dispose of this young pigeon, but to do it in Sanctuary. The twenty *grimales* was my pay, and also the goad, the bait. The boy is no addict, but he is greedy, and the price of *krrf* is three times higher in the court of Ranke than it is in the Maze. It was arranged for me to befriend him and, eventually, offer to be his wholesaler.

"The counselor procured the *krrf* from Caronne and sent word to me. I sent back a tempting offer to the boy. He contrived to make the journey to Sanctuary, supposedly to be introduced to the emperor's brother. He'll miss the appointment."

"That's his blood on your sleeve?" the eunuch asked.

"Nothing so direct; that was another matter. When he's supposed to be at the palace tomorrow, he'll be floating in the harbor, disguised as the shit of dogs."

"So you got the *krrf* and the boy's money as well," Amoli said.

"Half the money. He tried to croy me." He refilled the woman's glass. "But you see. There can be no connection."

"I believe there may be. Anenday was when mine disappeared."

"Did you keep it wrapped in a cheese?"

She ignored that. "Who delivered yours?"

"Marype, the youngest son of my sorcerer Mizraith. He does all of my caravan deliveries."

The eunuch and Amoli exchanged glances. "That's it! It was from Marype I bought the block. Not two hours after the caravan came in." Her face was growing red with fury.

One-Thumb drummed his fingers on the table. "I didn't get mine till evening," he admitted.

"Sorcery?"

"Or some more worldly form of trickery," One-Thumb said slowly. "Marype is studying his father's trade, but I don't think he's adept enough to transport material objects . . . could your *krrf* have been an illusion?"

"It was no illusion. I tried a pinch."

"Do you recall from what part of the block you took it?"

"The bottom edge, near one corner."

"Well, we can settle one thing," he said, standing. "Let's check mine in that spot."

She bade the bodyguards stay, and followed One-Thumb. At the door to his office, while he was trying to make the key work, she took his arm and moved softly up against him. "You never tarry at my place anymore. Are you keeping your own woman, out at the estate? Did we do something—"

"You can't have all my secrets, woman." In fact, for more than a year he had not taken a woman normally, but needed the starch of rape. This was the only part of his evil life that shamed him, and certainly not because of the women he had hurt and twice killed. He dreaded weakness more than death, and wondered which part would fail him next.

Amoli idly looked through the one-way mirror while One-Thumb attended to the strongbox. She turned when she heard him gasp.

"Gods!" The leather wrapping lay limp and empty on the floor of the box.

They both stared for a moment. "Does Marype have his father's protection?" Amoli asked.

One-Thumb shook his head. "It was the father that did this."

Sorcerers are not omnipotent. They can be bargained with. They can even be killed, with stealth and surprise. And spells cannot normally be maintained without effort; a good sorcerer might hold six or a dozen at once. It was Mizraith's fame that he maintained past a hundred, although it was well known that he did this by casting secondary spells on lesser sorcerers, tapping their power unbeknownst. Still, gathering all these strings and holding them, as well as the direct spells that protected his life and fortune, used most of his concentration, giving him a distracted air. The unwary might interpret this as senility—a half-century without sleep had left its mark—and might try to take his purse or life, as their last act.

But Mizraith was rarely seen on the streets, and certainly never near the noise and smell of the Maze. He normally kept to his opulent apartments in the easternmost part of town, flanked by the inns of Wideway, overlooking the sea.

One-Thumb warned the pirate cook that he might have to take a double shift, and took a bottle of the finest brandy to give to Mizraith, and a skin of the ordinary kind to keep up their courage as they went to face the man who guarded his life. The emptied skin joined the harbor's flotsam before they'd gone half of Wideway, and they continued in grim silence.

Mizraith's eldest son let them in, not seeming surprised at their visit. "The bodyguards stay here," he said, and made a pass with one hand. "You'll want to leave all your iron here, as well."

One-Thumb felt the dagger next to his ankle grow warm; he tossed it away and also dropped his rapier and the dagger sheathed to his forearm. There was a similar scattering of weapons from the other three. Amoli turned to the wall and reached inside her skirts, inside herself, to retrieve the ultimate birth-control device, a sort of diaphragm with a spring-loaded razor attached (no one would have her without paying in some coin). The hardware glowed dull red briefly, then cooled.

"Is Marype at home?" One-Thumb asked.

"He was, briefly," the older brother said. "You came to see Father, though." He turned to lead them up a winding flight of stairs.

Velvet and silk embroidered in arcane patterns. A golden samovar bubbling softly in the corner; flower-scented tea. A naked girl, barely of child-bearing age, sitting cross-legged by the samovar, staring. A bodyguard much larger than the ones downstairs, but slightly transparent. In the middle of this sat Mizraith, on a pile of pillows, or maybe of gold, bright eyes in dark hollows, smiling openmouthed at something unseeable.

The brother left them there. Magician, guardian, and girl all ignored them. "Mizraith?" One-Thumb said.

The sorcerer slowly brought his eyes to bear on him and Amoli. "I've been waiting for you, Lastel, or what is your name in the Maze, One-Thumb . . . I could grow that back for you, you know."

"I get along well enough—"

"And you brought me presents! A bottle and a bauble—more my age than this sweetmeat." He made a grotesque face at the naked girl and winked.

"No, Mizraith, this woman and I, we both believe we've been wronged by you. Cheated and stolen from," he said boldly, but his voice shook. "The bottle is a gift."

The bodyguard moved toward them, its steps making no noise. "Hold, spirit." It stopped, glaring. "Bring that bottle here."

As One-Thumb and Amoli walked toward Mizraith, a low table materialized in front of him, then three glasses. "You may serve, Lastel." Nothing had moved but his head.

One-Thumb poured each glass full; one of them rose a handspan above the table and drained itself, then disappeared. "Very good. Thank you. Cheated, now? My, oh my. Stolen? Hee. What could you have that I need?"

"It's only we who need it, Mizraith, and I don't know why you would want to cheat us out of it—especially me. You can't have many commissions more lucrative than mine."

"You might be surprised, Lastel. You might be surprised. Tea!" The girl decanted a cup of tea and brought it over, as if in a trance. Mizraith took it and the girl sat at his side, playing with her hair.

"Stolen, eh? What? You haven't told me. What?"

"*Krrf*," he said.

Mizraith gestured negligently with his free hand and a small snowstorm of grey powder drifted to the rug, and disappeared.

"No." One-Thumb rubbed his eyes. When he looked at the pillows, they were pillows; when he looked away, they turned to blocks of gold. "Not conjured *krrf*." It had the same gross effect but no depth, no nuance.

"Twenty *grimales* of black *krrf* from Caronne," Amoli said.

"Stolen from both of us," One-Thumb said. "It was sent to me by a man in Ranke, payment for services rendered. Your son Marype picked it up at the caravan depot, hidden inside a cheese. He extracted it somehow and sold it to this woman, Amoli—"

"Amoli? You're the mistress of a . . . of the Slippery Lily?"

"No, the Lily Garden. The other place is in the Maze, a good place for pox and slatterns."

One-Thumb continued. "After he sold it to her, it disappeared. He brought it to me last night. This evening, it disappeared from my own strongbox."

"Marype couldn't do that," Mizraith said.

"The conjuring part, I know he couldn't—which is why I say that you must have been behind it. Why? A joke?"

Mizraith sipped. "Would you like tea?"

"No. Why?"

He handed the half-empty cup to the girl. "More tea." He watched her go to the samovar. "I bought her for the walk. Isn't that fine? From behind, she could be a boy."

"Please, Mizraith. This is financial ruin for Amoli and a gross insult to me."

"A joke, eh? You think I make stupid jokes?"

"I know that you do things for reasons I cannot comprehend," he said tactfully. "But this is serious—"

"I know that!" He took the tea and fished a flower petal from it; rubbed it away. "More serious than you think, if my son is involved. Did it all disappear? Is there any tiny bit of it left?"

"The pinch you gave to my eunuch," Amoli said. "He may still have it."

"Fetch it," Mizraith said. He stared slack-jawed into his tea for a minute. "I didn't do it, Lastel. Some other did."

"With Marype's help."

"Perhaps unwilling. We shall see . . . Marype is adept enough to have sensed the worth of the cheese, and I think he is worldly enough to recognize a block of rare *krrf*, and know where to sell it. By himself, he would not be able to charm it away."

"You fear he's betrayed you?"

Mizraith caressed the girl's long hair. "We have had some argument lately. About his progress . . . he thinks I am teaching him too slowly, withholding . . . mysteries. The truth is, spells are complicated. Being able to generate one is not the same as being able to control it; that takes practice, and maturity. He sees what his brothers can do and is jealous. I think."

"You can't know his mind directly?"

"No. That's a powerful spell against strangers, but the closer you are to a person, the harder it is. Against your own blood . . . no. His mind is closed to me."

Amoli returned with the square of parchment. She held it out apologetically. "He shared it with the other bodyguard and your son. Is this enough?" There was a dark patch in the center of the square.

He took it between thumb and forefinger and grimaced. "Markmor!" The second-most-powerful magician in Sanctuary—an upstart not even a century old.

"He's in league with your strongest competitor?" One-Thumb said.

"In league or in thrall." Mizraith stood up and crossed his arms. The bodyguard disappeared; the cushions became a stack of gold bricks. He mumbled some gibberish and opened his arms wide.

Marype appeared in front of him. He was a handsome lad: flowing silver hair, striking features. He was also furious, naked, and rampant.

"*Father! I am busy.*" He made a flinging gesture and disappeared.

Mizraith made the same gesture and the boy came back. "We can do this all night. Or you can talk to me."

Noticeably less rampant. "This is unforgivable." He raised his arm to make the pass again; then checked it as Mizraith did the same. "Clothe me." A brick disappeared, and Marype was wearing a tunic of woven gold.

"Tell me you are not in the thrall of Markmor."

The boy's fists were clenched. "I am not."

"Are you quite certain?"

"We are friends, partners. He is teaching me things."

"You know I will teach you everything, eventually. But—"

Marype made a pass and the stack of gold turned to a heap of stinking dung. "Cheap," Mizraith said, wrinkling his nose. He held his elbow a certain way and the gold came back. "Don't you see he wants to take advantage of you?"

"I can see that he wants access to you. He was quite open about that."

"Stefab," Mizraith whispered. "Nesteph."

"You need the help of my brothers?"

The two older brothers appeared, flanking Mizraith. "What I need is some sense out of you." To the others: "Stay him!"

Heavy golden chains bound his wrists and ankles to sudden rings in the floor. He strained and one broke; a block of blue ice encased him. The ice began to melt.

Mizraith turned to One-Thumb and Amoli. "You weaken us with your presence." A bar of gold floated over to the woman. "That will compensate you. Lastel, you will have the *krrf*, once I take care of this. Be careful for the next few hours. Go."

As they backed out, other figures began to gather in the room. One-Thumb recognized the outline of Markmor flickering.

In the foyer, Amoli handed the gold to her eunuch. "Let's get back to the Maze," she said. "This place is dangerous."

One-Thumb sent the pirate cook home and spent the rest of the night in the familiar business of dispensing drink and *krrf* and haggling over rates of exchange. He took a judicious amount of *krrf* himself—the domestic kind—to keep alert. But nothing supernatural happened, and nothing more exciting than a routine eye-gouging over a dice dispute. He did have to step over a deceased ex-patron when he went to lock up at dawn. At least he'd had the decency to die outside, so no report had to be made.

One reason he liked to take the death shift was the interesting ambience of Sanctuary in the early morning. The sunlight was hard, revealing rather than cleansing. Litter and excrement in the gutters. A few exhausted revelers, staggering in small groups or sitting half-awake, blade out, waiting for a bunk to clear at first bell. Dogs nosing the evening's remains. Decadent, stale, worn, mortal. He took dark pleasure in it. Double pleasure this morning, a slight *krrf* overdose singing deathsong in his brain.

He almost went east, to check on Mizraith. "Be careful for the next few hours"—that must have meant his bond to Mizraith made him somehow vulnerable in the weird struggle with Markmor over Marype. But he had to go back to the estate and dispose of the bones in the dogs' troughs, and then be Lastel for a noon meeting.

There was one drab whore in the waiting room of the Lily Garden, who gave him a thick smile and then recognized him and slumped back to doze. He went through the velvet curtain to where the eunuch sat with his back against the wall, glaive across his lap.

He didn't stand. "Any trouble, One-Thumb?"

"No trouble. No *krrf*, either." He heaved aside the bolt on the massive door to the tunnel. "For all I know, it's still going on. If Mizraith had lost, I'd know by now, I think."

"Or if he'd won," the eunuch said.

"Possibly. I'll be in touch with your mistress if I have anything for her." One-Thumb lit the waiting lamp and swung the door closed behind him.

Before he'd reached the bottom of the stairs, he knew something was wrong. Too much light. He turned the wick all the way down; the air was slightly glowing. At the foot of the stairs, he set down the lamp, drew his rapier, and waited.

The glow coalesced into a fuzzy image of Mizraith. It whispered, "You are finally in the dark, Lastel. One-Thumb. Listen: I may die soon. Your charm, I've transferred to Stefab, and it holds. Pay him as you've paid me. . . ." He wavered, disappeared, came back. "Your *krrf* is in this tunnel. It cost more than you can know." Darkness again.

One-Thumb waited a few minutes more in the darkness and silence (fifty steps from the light above) before relighting the lamp. The block of *krrf* was at his feet. He tucked it under his left arm and proceeded down the tunnel, rapier in hand. Not that steel would be much use against sorcery, if that was to be the end of this. But an empty hand was less.

The tunnel kinked every fifty steps or so, to restrict line-of-sight. One-Thumb went through three corners and thought he saw light at the fourth. He stopped, doused the lamp again, and listened. No footfalls. He set down the *krrf* and lamp and filled his left hand with a dagger, then headed for the light. It didn't have to be magic; three times he had surprised interlopers in the tunnel. Their husks were secreted here and there, adding to the musty odor.

But no stranger this time. He peered around the corner and saw Lastel, himself, waiting with sword out.

"Don't hold back there," his alter ego said. "Only one of us leaves this tunnel."

One-Thumb raised his rapier slowly. "Wait . . . if you kill me, you die forever. If I kill you, the same. This is a sorcerer's trap."

"No, Mizraith's dead."

"His son is holding the spell."

Lastel advanced, crabwise dueler's gait. "Then how am I here?"

One-Thumb struggled with his limited knowledge of the logic of sorcery. Instinct moved him forward, point in line, left-hand weapon ready for side parry or high block. He kept his eye on Lastel's point, *krrf*-steady as his own. The *krrf* sang doom, and lifted his spirit.

It was like fencing with a mirror. Every attack drew instant parry, remise, parry, remise, parry, re-remise, break to counter. For several minutes, a swift yet careful ballet, large twins mincing, the tunnel echoing clash.

One-Thumb knew he had to do something random, unpredictable; he lunged with a cutover, impressing to the right.

Lastel knew he had to do something random, unpredictable; he lunged with a double-disengage, impressing to the right

They missed each other's blades

Slammed home.

One-Thumb saw his red blade emerge from the rich brocade over Lastel's back, tried to shout and coughed blood over his killer's shoulder. Lastel's rapier had cracked breastbone and heart and slit a lung as well.

They clung to each other. One-Thumb watched bright blood spurt from the other's back and heard his own blood falling, as the pain grew. The dagger still in his left hand, he stabbed, almost idly. Again he stabbed. It seemed to take a long time. The pain grew. The other man was doing the same. A third stab, he watched the blade rise and slowly fall, and inching slide back out of the flesh. With every second, the pain seemed to double; with every second, the flow of time slowed by half. Even the splash of blood was slowed, like a viscous oil falling through water as it sprayed away. And now it stopped completely, a thick scarlet web frozen there between his dagger and Lastel's back—his own back— and as the pain spread and grew, marrow itself on fire, he knew he would look at that forever. For a flickering moment he saw the image of two sorcerers, smiling.

Myrtis

Christine Dewees

"I feel as young as I look. I could satisfy every man in this house if I took the notion to, or if any one of them had half the magnificence of Lythande."

So speaking, Myrtis, proprietor of the Aphrodisia House, leaned over the banister outside her private parlor and cast judgment on the activity of her establishment below.

"Certainly, madame."

Her companion on the narrow balcony was a well-dressed young man lately arrived with his parents from the imperial capital. He eased as far from her as possible when she turned to smile at him.

"Do you doubt me, young man?"

The words rolled off Myrtis' tongue with an ease and inflection of majesty. To many of the longtime residents of Sanctuary, Myrtis was the city's unofficial royalty. On the Street of Red Lanterns she reigned supreme.

"Certainly not, madame."

"You have seen the girls now. Did you have a particular lady in mind, or would you prefer to explore my establishment further?"

Myrtis guided him back into her parlor with a slight pressure against his arm. She wore a high-necked dark gown that only hinted at the legendary figure beneath. The madam of the Aphrodisia House was beautiful, more beautiful than any of the girls working for her; fathers told this to their sons, who were, in turn, passing this indisputable fact along to their sons. But a ravishing beauty that endured unchanging for three generations was awesome rather than desirable. Myrtis did not compete with the girls who worked for her.

The young man cleared his throat. It was clearly his first visit to any brothel. He fingered the tassels on the side of an immense wine-colored velvet love seat before speaking. "I think I'll go a round with the violet-silks."

Myrtis stared at him until he fidgeted one of the tassels loose and his face flushed a deep crimson.

"Call Cylene. Tell her the Lavender Room."

A girl too young to be working jumped up from a cushion where she had waited in silence for such a command. The youth turned to follow her.

"Four pieces of silver—Cylene is very talented. And a name—I think that you should be known as Terapis." Myrtis smiled to reveal her even white teeth.

The youth, who would henceforth be known as Terapis within the walls of the Aphrodisia House, searched his purse to find a single gold piece. He stood arrogant and obviously well-rehearsed while Myrtis counted out his change. The young girl took his hand to lead him to Cylene for two hours of unimaginable bliss.

"Children!" Myrtis mumbled to herself when she was alone in her parlor again.

Four of the nine knobs on the night candle had melted away. She opened a great leather-bound ledger and entered the youth's true name as well as the one she had just given him, his choice for the evening, and that he had paid in gold. It had been fifteen years or more since she had given the nom-de-guerre of Terapis to one of the house's gentlemen. She had a good memory for all those who lingered in the sybaritic luxury of the Aphrodisia House.

A gentle knocking on the parlor door awoke Myrtis late the next morning.

"Your breakfast is ready, madame."

"Thank you, child. I'll be down for it."

She lay still for a few moments in the semidarkness. Lythande had used careful spells to preserve her beauty and give her the longevity of a magician, but there were no spells to numb the memory. The girls, their gentlemen, all passed through Myrtis' mind in a blurred unchanging parade that trapped her beneath the silken bedclothes.

"Flowers for you, madame."

The young girl who had sat quietly on the cushion the previous evening walked nonchalantly into the boudoir bearing a large bouquet of white flowers, which she began arranging in a crystal vase.

"A slave from the palace brought them. He said they were from Terapis."

A surprise. There were always still surprises, and renewed by that comforting knowledge Myrtis threw back the bedcovers. The girl set down the flowers and held an embroidered day-robe of emerald satin for Myrtis to wrap around herself.

Five girls in their linen shifts busied themselves with restoring the studied disorder of the lower rooms as Myrtis passed through them on her way to the kitchen. Five cleaning, one too pregnant to be of any use, another off nursing a newborn; that meant twenty girls were still in the upper rooms. Twenty girls whose time was fully accounted for; in all, a very good night for the Aphrodisia House. Others might be suffering with the new regime, but the foreigners expected a certain style and discretion which in Sanctuary could be found only at the Aphrodisia.

"Madame, Dindan ordered five bottles of our best Aurveshan wine last night. We have only a dozen bottles left. . . ." A balding man stepped in front of her with a shopping list.

"Then buy more."

"But, madame, since the prince arrived it is almost impossible to buy Aurveshan wines!"

"Buy them! But first sell the old bottles to Dindan at the new prices."

"Yes, madame."

The kitchen was a large, brightly lit room hidden away at the back of the house. Her cooks and an assortment of tradesmen haggled loudly at the back door while the half-dozen or so young children of her working girls raced around the massive center table. Everyone grew quiet as Myrtis took her seat in a sunlit alcove that faced a tiny garden.

Despite the chaos the children caused, she always let the girls keep them if they wanted to. With the girl-children there was no problem with their earning their keep; no virgin was ever too ugly. But the boy-children were apprenticed off at the earliest possible age. Their wages were garnished to support the ongoing concern that was the Aphrodisia House.

"There is a soldier at the front door, madame," one of the girls who had been cleaning the lower rooms interrupted as Myrtis spread a thick blue-veined cheese over her bread. "He demands to see you, madame."

"Demands to see me?" Myrtis laid down the cheese knife. "A soldier has nothing that 'demands' to see me at the front door. At this hour, soldiers are less use than tradesmen. Send him around to the back."

The girl ran back up the stairs. Myrtis finished spreading her cheese on the bread. She had eaten half of it when a tall man cast a shadow over her private dining alcove.

"You are blocking my sunlight, young man," she said without looking up.

"You are Madame Myrtis, proprietress of this . . . brothel?" he demanded without moving.

"You are blocking my sunlight and my view of the garden."

He stepped to one side.

"The girls are not available during the day. Come back this evening."

"Madame Myrtis, I am Zalbar, captain of Prince Kadakithis' personal guard. I have not come to inquire after the services of your girls."

"Then what have you come for?" she asked, looking up for the first time.

"By order of Prince Kadakithis, a tax of ten gold pieces for every woman living on the Street of Red Lanterns is to be levied and collected at once if they are to be allowed to continue to practice their trade without incurring official displeasure."

Only the slight tensing of Myrtis' hands betrayed her indignation at Zalbar's statement. Her voice and face remained dispassionately calm.

"The royal concubines are no longer pleasing?" she replied with a sneering smile. "You cannot expect every woman on the Street of Red Lanterns to have ten gold pieces. How do you expect them to earn the money for your taxes?"

"We do not expect them to be able to pay the tax, madame. We expect to close your brothel and every other house like it on the Street. The women, including yourself, will be sent elsewhere to lead more productive lives."

Myrtis stared at the soldier with a practiced contempt that ended their conversation. The soldier fingered the hilt of his sword.

"The tax will be collected, madame. You will have a reasonable amount of time to get the money for yourself and the others. Let us say, three days? I'll return in the evening."

He turned about without waiting for a reply and left through the back door in complete silence. Myrtis went back to her interrupted breakfast while the staff and the girls were hysterical with questions and the seeds of rumor. She let them babble in this manner while she ate; then she strode to the head of the common table.

"Everything shall continue as usual. If it comes to paying their tax, arrangements will be made. You older girls already have ample gold set aside. I will make the necessary adjustments for the newer girls. Unless you doubt me—in which case, I'll arrange a severance for you."

"But madame, if we pay once, they will levy the tax again and again until we can't pay it. Those Hell Hounds . . ." A girl favored more by intelligence than beauty spoke up.

"That is certainly their desire. The Street of Red Lanterns is as old as the walls of Sanctuary itself. I can assure you that we have survived much worse than the Hell Hounds." Myrtis smiled slightly to herself, remembering the others who had tried and failed to shut down the Street. "Cylene, the others will be coming to see me. Send them up to the parlor. I'll wait for them there."

The emerald day-robe billowed out from behind her as Myrtis ascended the staircase to the lower rooms and up again to her parlor. In the privacy of her rooms, she allowed her anger to surface as she paced.

"Ambutta!" she shouted, and the young girl who attended her appeared.

"Yes, madame?"

"I have a message for you to carry." She sat at the writing table composing the message as she spoke to the still-out-of-breath girl. "It is to be delivered in the special way as before. No one must see you leave it. Do you understand that? If you cannot leave it without being seen, come back here. Don't let yourself become suspicious."

The girl nodded. She tucked the freshly folded and sealed message into the bodice other ragged cast-off dress and ran from the room. In time, Myrtis expected her to be a beauty, but she was still very much a

child. The message itself was to Lythande, who preferred not to be con-
tacted directly. She would not rely on the magician to solve the Street's
problems with the Hell Hounds, but no one else would understand her
anger or alleviate it.

The Aphrodisia House dominated the Street. The Hell Hounds would
come to her first, then visit the other establishments. As word of the tax
spread, the other madams would begin a furtive pilgrimage to the back
entrance of the Aphrodisia. They looked to Myrtis for guidance, and she
looked out the window for inspiration. She had not found one by the
time her guests began to appear.

"It's an outrage. They're trying to put us on the streets like common
whores!" Dylan of the artificially flaming red hair exclaimed before sitting in the chair Myrtis indicated to her.

"Nonsense, dear," Myrtis explained calmly. "They wish to make us
slaves and send us to Ranke. In a way, it is a compliment to Sanctuary."

"They can't do such a thing!"

"No, but it will be up to us to explain that to them."

"How?"

"First we'll wait until the others arrive. I hear Amoli in the hall; the
others won't be long in coming."

It was a blatant stall for time on Myrtis' part. Other than her convic-
tion that the Hell Hounds and their prince would not succeed where others had failed in the past, Myrtis had no idea how to approach the utterly
incorruptible elite soldiers. The other madams of the Street talked
among themselves, exchanging the insight Myrtis had revealed to Dylan,
and reacting poorly to it. Myrtis watched their reflections in the rough-
cut glass.

They were all old. More than half of them had once worked for her.
She had watched them age in the unkind manner that often overtakes
youthful beauty and transforms it into grotesquerie. Myrtis might have
been the youngest of them—young enough to be working in the houses
instead of running one of them. But when she turned from the window to
face them, there was the unmistakable glint of experience and wisdom in
her eyes.

"Well, it wasn't really a surprise," she began. "It was rumored before
Kittycat got here, and we've seen what has happened to the others the
Hell Hounds have been turned loose on. I admit I'd hoped that some of

the others would have held their ground better and given us a bit more time."

"Time wouldn't help. I don't have a hundred gold pieces to give them!" a woman whose white-paste makeup cracked around her eyes as she spoke interrupted Myrtis.

"You don't need a hundred gold pieces!" a similarly made-up woman snarled back.

"The gold is unimportant." Myrtis' voice rose above the bickering. "If they can break one of us, they can drive us all out."

"We could close our doors; then they'd suffer. Half of my men are from Ranke."

"Half of all our men are, Gelicia. They won the war and they've got the money," Myrtis countered. "But they'll kowtow to the Hell Hounds, Kittycat, and their wives. The men of Ranke are very ambitious. They'll give up much to preserve their wealth and positions. If the prince is officially frowning on the Street, their loyalties will be less strained if we have closed our doors without putting up a fight."

Grudgingly the women agreed.

"Then what will we do?"

"Conduct your affairs as always. They'll come to the Aphrodisia first to collect the taxes, just as they came here first to announce it. Keep the back doors open and I'll send word. If they can't collect from me, they won't bother you."

There was mumbled disagreement, but no one dared to look straight at Myrtis and argue the point of her power on the Street. Seated in her high-backed chair, Myrtis smiled contentedly. She had yet to determine the precise solution but the house madams of the Street of Red Lanterns controlled much of the gold within Sanctuary and she had just confirmed her control of them.

They left her parlor quickly after the decision was rendered. If the Street was to function as usual, they all had work to do. She had work to do.

The Hell Hounds would not return for three days. In that time, the Aphrodisia House would earn far more than those three hundred gold pieces the empire wanted, and would spend only slightly less than that amount to maintain itself. Myrtis opened the ledger, making new notations in a clear, educated hand. The household sensed that order had been restored at least temporarily, and one by one they filed into the parlor to report their earnings or debts.

It was well into afternoon and Ambutta had not returned from placing her message behind a loose stone in the wall behind the altar at the temple of Ils. For a moment, Myrtis worried about the girl. The streets of Sanctuary were never truly safe, and perhaps Ambutta no longer seemed as childlike to all eyes. There was always an element of risk. Twice before girls had been lost in the streets, and not even Lythande's magic could find them again.

Myrtis put such thoughts aside and ate dinner alone in her parlor. She had thought a bribe or offer of free privileges might still be the way out of her problem with the taxes. Prince Kadakithis was probably sincere, though, in his determination to make Sanctuary the ideal city of his advisers' philosophies, though the capital city of the empire displayed many of the same excesses that Sanctuary did. The young prince had a wife and concubines with whom he was supposedly well pleased. There had never been any suspicion that he might partake of the delights of the Street himself. And as for the Hell Hounds, their first visit had been to announce the taxes.

The elite guard were men made of a finer fiber than most of the soldiers or fighters Sanctuary had known. On reflection, Myrtis doubted that they could be bought or bribed, and knew for certain that they would never relent in their persecution of the Street if the first offer did not succeed in converting them.

It was gathering dusk. The girls could be heard throughout the house, giggling as they prepared for the evening. Myrtis kept no one who showed no aptitude or enjoyment of the profession. Let the other houses bind their girls with poverty or drugs; the Aphrodisia House was the pinnacle of ambition for the working girls of the Street.

"I got your message," a soft voice called from the drapery-hung doorway near her bed.

"I was beginning to get worried. My girl has not returned."

Lythande walked to her side, draping an arm about her shoulders and taking hold of her hand.

"I've heard the rumors in the streets. The new regime has chosen its next enemy, it would seem. What is the truth of their demands?"

"They intend to levy a tax of ten gold pieces on every woman living on the Street."

Lythande's habitual smile faded, and the blue-star-tattooed forehead wrinkled into a frown. "Will you be able to pay that?"

"The intent is not that we pay, but that the Street be closed and that we be sent up to the empire. If I pay it once, they'll keep on levying it until I can't pay."

"You could close the house. . . ."

"Never!" Myrtis pulled her hands away. "The Aphrodisia House is mine. I was running this house when the Rankan Empire was a collection of half-naked barbaric tribes!"

"But they aren't any longer," Lythande reminded her gently. "And the Hell Hounds—if not the prince—are making substantial changes in all our lives."

"They won't interfere with magic, will they?"

Myrtis' concern for Lythande briefly overshadowed her fears for the Aphrodisia House. The magician's thin-lipped smile returned.

"For now it is doubtful. There are men in Ranke who have the ability to affect us directly, but they have not followed the prince to Sanctuary, and I do not know if he could command their loyalty."

Myrtis stood up. She walked to the leaded-glass window, with its thick, obscuring panes that revealed movement on the Street but very little else.

"I'll need your help, if it's available," she said without facing Lythande.

"What can I do?"

"In the past you've prepared a drug for me from a qualis-berry extract. I recall you said it was quite difficult to mix—but I should like enough for two people when it's mixed with pure qualis liqueur."

"Delicate and precise, but not particularly difficult. It is very subtle. Are you sure you will only need enough to serve two?"

"Yes, Zalbar and myself. I agree; the drug must be subtle."

"You must be very certain of your methods, then."

"Of some things, at least. The Street of Red Lanterns does not lie outside the walls of Sanctuary by accident—you know that. The Hell Hounds and their prince have much more to lose by hindering us than by letting the Street exist in peace. If our past purpose were not enough to convince them, then surely the fact that much of the city's gold passes through my hands every year will matter.

"I will use the qualis-berry love potion to open Zalbar's eyes to reality, not to close them."

"I can have it for you perhaps by tomorrow evening, but more likely the day after. Many of the traders and smugglers of the bazaar are no longer well supplied with the ingredients I will need, but I can investigate other sources. When the Hell Hounds drove the smugglers into the Swamp of Night Secrets, many honest men suffered."

Myrtis' eyes narrowed; she released the drapery she had clutched.

"And if the Street of Red Lanterns wasn't here . . . The mongers and merchants, and even the smugglers, might not want to admit it, but without us to provide them with their gold while 'respectable' people offer promises, they would suffer even more than they do now."

There was a gentle knocking on the door. Lythande stepped back into the shadows of the room. Ambutta entered, a large bruise visible on the side of her face.

"The men have begun to arrive, Madame Myrtis. Will you collect their money, or shall I take the ledger downstairs?"

"I shall attend to them. Send them up to me and, Ambutta—" She stopped the girl as she headed out of the parlor. "Go to the kitchen and find out how many days we could go without buying anything from any of the tradesmen."

"Yes, madame."

The room was suddenly empty, except for Myrtis. Only a slight rippling of the wall tapestries showed where Lythande had opened a concealed panel and disappeared into the secret passages of the Aphrodisia House. Myrtis had not expected the magician to stay, but despite all their years together, the magician's sudden comings and goings still unsettled her. Standing in front of a full-length mirror, Myrtis rearranged the pearl-and-gold pins in her hair, rubbed scented oils into her skin, and greeted the first gentleman caller as if the day had been no different from any other.

Word of the taxation campaign against the Street had spread through the city much as Lythande had observed. The result was that many of their infrequent guests and visitors came to the house to pay their last respects to an entertainment that they openly expected would be gone in a very short time. Myrtis smiled at each of them as they arrived, accepted their money, and asked their second choice of the girls before assuring them that the Aphrodisia House would never close its doors.

"Madame?"

Ambutta peered around the doorway when the flow of gentlemen had abated slightly.

"The kitchen says that we have enough food for ten days, but less of ordinary wine and like."

Myrtis touched the feather of her pen against her temple.

"Ten days? Someone has grown lax. Our storerooms can hold enough for many months. But ten days is all we will have, and it will have to be enough. Tell the kitchen to place no orders with the tradesmen tomorrow or the next day, and send word to the other back doors.

"And, Ambutta, Irda will carry my messages in the future. It is time that you were taught more important and useful things."

A steady stream of merchants and tradesmen made their way through the Aphrodisia House to Myrtis' parlor late the next morning as the effects of her orders began to be felt in the town.

"But Madame Myrtis, the tax isn't due yet, and surely the Aphrodisia House has the resources. . . ." The puffy-faced gentleman who sent meat to half the houses on the Street was alternately irate and wheedling.

"In such unsettled times as these, good Mikkun, I cannot look to luxuries like expensive meats. I sincerely wish that this were not true. The taste of salted meat has always reminded me of poverty. But the Governor's Palace does not care about the poverty of those who live outside its walls, though it sends its forces to tax us," Myrtis said in feigned helplessness.

In deference to the sad occasion she had not put on one of the brightly embroidered day-robes as was her custom but wore a soberly cut dress of a fashion outdated in Sanctuary at least twenty years before. She had taken off her jewelry, knowing that its absence would cause more rumors than if she had indeed sold a part of it to the gem cutters. An atmosphere of austerity enveloped the house and every other on the Street, as Mikkun could attest, for he'd visited most of them.

"But madame, I have already slaughtered two cows! For three years I have slaughtered the cows first to assure you the freshest meat early in the day. Today, for no reason, you say you do not want my meat! Madame, you already have a debt to me for those two cows!"

"Mikkun! You have never, in all the years I've known you, extended

credit to any house on the Street and now . . . now you're asking me to
consider my daily purchases a debt to you!" She smiled disarmingly to
calm him, knowing full well that the butcher and the others depended on
the hard gold from the Street to pay their own debts.

"There will be credit in the future!"

"But we will not be here to use it!"

Myrtis let her face take on a mournful pout. Let the butcher and his
friends start dunning the "respectable" side of Sanctuary, and word
would spread quickly to the palace that something was amiss. A "something" that she would explain to the Hell Hound captain, Zalbar, when
he arrived to collect the tax. The tradesman left her parlor muttering
prophecies of doom she hoped would eventually be heard by those in a
position to worry about them.

"Madame?"

Ambutta's child-serious face appeared in the doorway moments after
the butcher had left. Her ragged dress had already been replaced with
one of a more mature cut, brighter color, and new cloth.

"Amoli waits to speak with you. She is in the kitchen now. Shall I send
her up?"

"Yes, bring her up."

Myrtis sighed after Ambutta left. Amoli was her only rival on the
Street. She was a woman who had not learned her trade in the upper
rooms of the Aphrodisia, and also one who kept her girls working for
her through their addiction to *krrf*, which she supplied to them. If anyone on the Street was nervous about the tax, though, it was Amoli; she
had very little gold to spare. The smugglers had recently been forced by
the same Hell Hounds to raise the price of a well-refined brick of the
drug to maintain their own profits.

"Amoli, good woman, you look exhausted."

Myrtis assisted a woman less than a third her age to the love seat.

"May I get you something to drink?"

"Qualis, if you have any." Amoli paused while Myrtis passed the
request along to Ambutta. "I can't do it, Myrtis—this whole scheme of
yours is impossible. It will ruin me!"

The liqueur arrived. Ambutta carried a finely wrought silver tray with
one glass of the deep red liquid. Amoli's hands shook violently as she
grasped the glass and emptied it in one gulp. Ambutta looked sagely to

her mistress; the other madam was, perhaps, victim of the same addiction as her girls?

"I've been approached by Jubal. For a small fee, he will send his men up here tomorrow night to ambush the Hell Hounds. He has been looking for an opportunity to eliminate them. With them gone, Kittycat won't be able to make trouble for us."

"So Jubal is supplying the *krrf* now?" Myrtis replied without sympathy.

"They all have to pay to land their shipments in the Night Secrets, or Jubal will reveal their activities to the Hell Hounds. His plan is fair. I can deal with him directly. So can anyone else—he trades in anything. But you and Lythande will have to unseal the tunnels so his men face no undue risk tomorrow night."

The remnants of Myrtis' cordiality disappeared. The Lily Garden had been isolated from the rat's nest of passages on the Street when Myrtis realized the extent of *krrf* addiction within it. Unkind experience warned her against mixing drugs and courtesans. There were always men like Jubal waiting for the first sign of weakness, and soon the houses were nothing more than slavers' dens, the madams forgotten. Jubal feared magic, so she had asked Lythande to seal the tunnels with eerily visible wards. So long as she—Myrtis—lived, the Street would be hers, and not Jubal's, nor the city's.

"There are other suppliers whose prices are not so high. Or perhaps Jubal has promised you a place in his mansion? I have heard he learned things besides fighting in the pits of Ranke. Of course, his home is hardly the place for sensitive people to live."

Myrtis wrinkled her nose in the accepted way to indicate someone who lived Downwind. Amoli replied with an equally understandable gesture of insult and derision, but she left the parlor without looking back.

The problems with Jubal and the smugglers were only just beginning. Myrtis pondered them after Ambutta removed the tray and glass from the room. Jubal's ruthless ambition was potentially more dangerous than any threat radiating directly from the Hell Hounds. But they were completely distinct from the matters at hand, so Myrtis put them out of her mind.

The second evening was not as lucrative as the first, nor the third day as frantic as the second. Lythande's aphrodisiac potion appeared in the hands of a dazed street urchin. The geas the magician had placed on the young beggar dissipated as soon as the vial left his hands. He had glanced around him in confusion and disappeared at a run before the day steward could hand him a copper coin for his inconvenience.

Myrtis poured the vial into a small bottle of qualis, which she then placed between two glasses on the silver tray. The decor of the parlor had been changed subtly during the day. The red liqueur replaced the black-bound ledger, which had been banished to the night steward's cubicle in the lower rooms. The draperies around her bed were tied back, and a padded silk coverlet was creased to show the plump pillows. Musky incense crept into the room from burners hidden in the corners. Beside her bed, a large box containing the three hundred gold pieces sat on a table.

Myrtis hadn't put on any other jewelry. It would only have detracted from the ebony low-cut, side-slit gown she wore. The image was perfect. No one but Zalbar would see her until the dawn, and she was determined that her efforts and planning would not be in vain.

She waited alone, remembering her first days as a courtesan in Ilsig, when Lythande was a magician's raw apprentice and her own experiences a nightmare adventure. At that time she had lived to fall wildly in love with any young lordling who could offer her the dazzling splendor of privilege. But no man came forward to rescue her from the ethereal, but doomed, world of the courtesan. Before her beauty faded, she had made her pact with Lythande. The magician visited her infrequently, and for all her boasting, there was no passionate love between them. The spells had let Myrtis win for herself the permanent splendor she had wanted as a young girl; a splendor no high-handed barbarian from Ranke was going to strip away.

"Madame Myrtis?"

A peremptory knock on the door forced her from her thoughts. She had impressed the voice in her memory and recognized it though she had only heard it once before.

"Do come in."

She opened the door for him, pleased to see by the hesitation in his step that he was unaware that he would be entering her parlor and boudoir.

"I have come to collect the taxes!" he said quickly. His military precision did not completely conceal his awe and vague embarrassment at viewing the royal and erotic scene displayed before him.

He did not turn as Myrtis shut the door behind him and quietly slid a concealed bolt into place.

"You have very nearly undone me, Captain," she said with downcast eyes and a light touch on his arm. "It is not so easy as you might think to raise such a large sum of money."

She lifted the ebony box inlaid with pearl from the table beside her bed and carried it slowly to him. He hesitated before taking it from her arms.

"I must count it, madame," he said almost apologetically.

"I understand. You will find that it is all there. My word is good."

"You . . . you are much different now from how you seemed two days ago."

"It is the difference between night and day."

He began assembling piles of gold on her ledger table in front of the silver tray with the qualis.

"We have been forced to cut back our orders to the town's merchants in order to pay you."

From the surprised yet thoughtful look he gave her, Myrtis guessed that the Hell Hounds had begun to hear complaints and anxious whining from the respectable parts of town as Mikkun and his friends called back their loans and credit.

"Still," she continued, "I realize that you are doing only what you have been told to do. It's not you personally who is to blame if any of the merchants and purveyors suffer because the Street no longer functions as it once did."

Zalbar continued shuffling his piles of coins around, only half-listening to Myrtis. He had half the gold in the box neatly arranged when Myrtis slipped the glass stopper out of the qualis decanter.

"Will you join me in a glass of qualis, since it is not your fault and we still have a few luxuries in our larder. They tell me a damp fog lies heavy on the streets."

He looked up from his counting and his eyes brightened at the sight of the deep red liqueur. The common variety of qualis, though still expensive, had a duller color and was inclined to visible sediment. A man of his position might live a full life and never glimpse a fine, pure qualis, much less be offered a glass of it. Clearly the Hell Hound was tempted.

"A small glass, perhaps."

She poured two equally full glasses and set them both on the table in front of him while she replaced the stopper and took the bottle to the table by her bed. An undetectable glance in a side mirror confirmed that Zalbar lifted the glass farthest from him. Calmly she returned and raised the other.

"A toast then. To the future of your prince and to the Aphrodisia House!"

The glasses clinked.

The potion Lythande had made was brewed in part from the same berries as the qualis itself. The fine liqueur made a perfect concealing dilutant. Myrtis could taste the subtle difference the charm itself made in the normal flavor of the intoxicant, but Zalbar, who had never tasted even the common qualis, assumed that the extra warmth was only a part of the legendary mystique of the liqueur. When he had finished his drink, Myrtis swallowed the last of hers and waited patiently for the faint flush which would confirm that the potion was working.

It appeared in Zalbar first. He became bored with his counting, fondling one coin while his eyes drifted off toward nothingness. Myrtis took the coin from his fingers. The potion took longer to affect her, and its action when it did was lessened by the number of times she had taken it before and by the age-inhibiting spells Lythande wove about her. She had not needed the potion, however, to summon an attraction toward the handsome soldier or to coax him to his feet and then to her bed.

Zalbar protested that he was not himself and did not understand what was happening to him. Myrtis did not trouble herself to argue with him. Lythande's potion was not one to rouse a wild, blind lust, but one that endowed a lifelong affection in the drinker. The pure qualis played a part in weakening his resistance. She held him behind the curtains of her bed until he had no doubt of his love for her. Then she helped him dress again.

"I'll show you the secrets of the Aphrodisia House," she whispered in his ear.

"I believe I have already found them."

"There are more."

Myrtis took him by the hand, leading him to one of the drapery-covered walls. She pushed aside the fabric; released a well-oiled catch; took a sconce from the wall; then led him into a dark, but airy, passageway.

"Walk carefully in my footsteps, Zalbar—I would not want to lose

you to the oubliettes. Perhaps you have wondered why the Street is outside the walls and its buildings are so old and well built? Perhaps you
think Sanctuary's founders wished to keep us outside their fair city?
What you do not know is that these houses—especially the older ones
like the Aphrodisia—are not really outside the walls at all. My house is
built of stone four feet thick. The shutters on our windows are aged
wood from the mountains. We have our own wells and storerooms
which can supply us—and the city—for weeks, if necessary. Other passages lead away from here toward the Swamp of Night Secrets, or into
Sanctuary and the Governor's Palace itself. Whoever has ruled in Sanctuary has always sought our cooperation in moving men and arms if a siege
is laid."

She showed the speechless captain catacombs where a sizable garrison
could wait in complete concealment. He drank water from a deep well
whose water had none of the brackish taste so common in the seacoast
town. Above he could hear the sounds of parties at the Aphrodisia and
the other houses. Zalbar's military eye took all this in, but his mind saw
Myrtis, candlelit in the black gown, as a man's dream come true, and the
underground fortress she was revealing to him as a soldier's dream come
true. The potion worked its way with him. He wanted both Myrtis and
the fortress for his own to protect and control.

"There is so much about Sanctuary that you Rankans know nothing
about. You tax the Street and cause havoc with trade in the city. You
wish to close the Street and send all of us, including myself, to the slave
pens or worse. Your walls will be breachable then. There are men in
Sanctuary who would stop at nothing to control these passages, and they
know the swamp and the palace better than you or your children could
ever hope to."

She showed him a wall flickering with runes and magic signs. Zalbar
went to touch it and found his fingers singed for his curiosity.

"These warding walls keep us safe now, but they will fade if we are
not here to renew them properly. Smugglers and thieves will find the
entrance we have kept invulnerable for generations. And you, Zalbar,
who wish that Sanctuary will become a place of justice and order, will
know in your heart that you are responsible, because you knew what was
here and let the others destroy it."

"No, Myrtis. So long as I live, none of this shall be harmed."

"There is no other way. Do you not already have your orders to levy a second tax?"

He nodded.

"We have already begun to use the food stored in these basements. The girls are not happy; the merchants are not happy. The Street will die. The merchants will charge higher prices, and the girls will make their way to the streets. There is nowhere else for them to go. Perhaps Jubal will take—"

"I do not think that the Street will suffer such a fate. Once the prince understands the true part you and the others play, he will agree to a nominal tax which would be applied to maintaining the defense of Sanctuary and therefore be returned to you."

Myrtis smiled to herself. The battle was won. She held his arm tightly and no longer fought the effect of the adulterated qualis in her own emotions. They found an abandoned officer's quarters and made love on its bare wooden-slats bed, and again when they returned to the parlor of the Aphrodisia House.

The night candle had burned down to its last knob by the time Myrtis released the hidden bolt and let the Hell Hound captain rejoin his men. Lythande was in the room behind her as soon as she shut the door.

"Are you safe now?" the magician asked with a laugh.

"I believe so."

"The potion?"

"A success, as always. I have not been in love like this for a long time. It is pleasant. I almost do not mind knowing how empty and hurt I will feel as I watch him grow old."

"Then why use something like the potion? Surely the catacombs themselves would have been enough to convince a Hell Hound?"

"Convince him of what? That the defenses of Sanctuary should not be entrusted to whores and courtesans? Except for your potion, there is nothing else to bind him to the idea that we—that I should remain here as I always have. There was no other way!"

"You're right," Lythande said, nodding. "Will he return to visit you?"

"He will care, but I do not think he will return. That was not the purpose of the drug."

She opened the narrow glass-paned doors to the balcony overlooking the emptying lower rooms. The soldiers were gone. She looked back into the room. The three hundred gold pieces still lay half-counted on the table next to the empty decanter. He might return.

"I feel as young as I look," she whispered to the unnoticing rooms. "I could satisfy every man in this house if I took the notion to, or if any one of them had half the magnificence of my Zalbar."

Myrtis turned back to an empty room and went to sleep alone.

The Secret of the Blue Star

Marion Zimmer Bradley

On a night in Sanctuary, when the streets bore a false glamour in the silver glow of a full moon, so that every ruin seemed an enchanted tower and every dark street and square an island of mystery, the mercenary-magician Lythande sallied forth to seek adventure.

Lythande had but recently returned—if the mysterious comings and goings of a magician can be called by so prosaic a name—from guarding a caravan across the Grey Wastes to Twand. Somewhere in the wastes, a gaggle of desert rats—two-legged rats with poisoned steel teeth—had set upon the caravan, not knowing it was guarded by magic, and had found themselves fighting skeletons that bowled and fought with eyes of flame; and at their center a tall magician with a blue star between blazing eyes, a star that shot lightnings of a cold and paralyzing flame. So the desert rats ran, and never stopped running until they reached Aurvesh, and the tales they told did Lythande no harm except in the ears of the pious.

And so there was gold in the pockets of the long, dark magician's robe, or perhaps concealed in whatever dwelling sheltered Lythande. For at the end, the caravan master had been almost more afraid of Lythande than he was of the bandits, a situation that added to the generosity with which he rewarded the magician. According to custom, Lythande neither smiled nor frowned, but remarked, days later, to Myrtis, the proprietor of the Aphrodisia House in the Street of Red Lanterns, that sorcery, while a useful skill and filled with many aesthetic delights for the contemplation of the philosopher, in itself put no beans on the table.

A curious remark, that, Myrtis pondered, putting away the ounce of gold Lythande had bestowed upon her in consideration of a secret which lay many years behind them both. Curious that Lythande should speak of beans on the table, when no one but herself had ever seen a bite of food or a drop of drink pass the magician's lips since the blue star had adorned that high and narrow brow. Nor had any woman in the quarter even been able to boast that a great magician had paid for her favors, or been able to imagine how such a magician behaved in that situation when all men were alike reduced to flesh and blood.

Perhaps Myrtis could have told if she would; some other girls thought so, when, as sometimes happened, Lythande came to the Aphrodisia House and was closeted long with its owner; even, on rare intervals, for an entire night. It was said, of Lythande, that the Aphrodisia House itself had been the magician's gift to Myrtis, after a famous adventure still whispered in the bazaar, involving an evil wizard, two horse traders, a caravan master, and a few assorted toughs who had prided themselves upon never giving gold for any woman and thought it funny to cheat an honest working woman. None of them had ever showed their faces— what was left of them—in Sanctuary again, and Myrtis boasted that she need never again sweat to earn her living, and never again entertain a man, but would claim her madam's privilege of a solitary bed.

And then, too, the girls thought, a magician of Lythande's stature could have claimed the most beautiful women from Sanctuary to the mountains beyond Ilsig; not courtesans alone, but princesses and noblewomen and priestesses would have been for Lythande's taking. Myrtis had doubtless been beautiful in her youth, and certainly she boasted enough of the princes and wizards and travelers who had paid great sums for her love. She was beautiful still (and of course there were those who said that Lythande did not pay her, but that, on the contrary, Myrtis paid the magician great sums to maintain her aging beauty with strong magic) but her hair had gone grey and she no longer troubled to dye it with henna or goldenwash from Tyrisis-beyond-the-sea.

But if Myrtis were not the woman who knew how Lythande behaved in that most elemental of situations, then there was no woman in Sanctuary who could say. Rumor said also that Lythande called up female demons from the Grey Wastes, to couple in lechery, and certainly Lythande was neither the first nor the last magician of whom that could be said.

But on this night Lythande sought neither food nor drink nor the delights of amorous entertainment; although Lythande was a great frequenter of taverns, no man had ever yet seen a drop of ale or mead or fire-drink pass the barrier of the magician's lips. Lythande walked along the far edge of the bazaar, skirting the old rim of the Governor's Palace, keeping to the shadows in defiance of footpads and cutpurses. She possessed a love for shadows which made the folk of the city say that Lythande could appear and disappear into thin air.

Tall and thin, Lythande, above the height of a tall man, lean to emaciation, with the blue-star-shaped tattoo of the magician-adept above thin, arching eyebrows; wearing a long, hooded robe which melted into the shadows. Clean-shaven, the face of Lythande, or beardless—none had come close enough, in living memory, to say whether this was the whim of an effeminate or the hairlessness of a freak. The hair beneath the hood was as long and luxuriant as a woman's, but greying, as no woman in this city of harlots would have allowed it to do.

Striding quickly along a shadowed wall, Lythande stepped through an open door, over which the sandal of Thufir, god of pilgrims, had been nailed up for luck; but the footsteps were so soft, and the hooded robe blended so well into the shadows, that eyewitnesses would later swear, truthfully, that they had seen Lythande appear from the air, protected by sorceries, or by a cloak of invisibility.

Around the hearth fire, a group of men were banging their mugs together noisily to the sound of a rowdy drinking song, strummed on a worn and tinny lute—Lythande knew it belonged to the tavernkeeper, and could be borrowed—by a young man, dressed in fragments of foppish finery, torn and slashed by the chances of the road. He was sitting lazily, with one knee crossed over the other; and when the rowdy song died away, the young man drifted into another, a quiet love song from another time and another country. Lythande had known the song, more years ago than bore remembering, and in those days Lythande the magi-

cian had borne another name and had known little of sorcery. When the
song died, Lythande had stepped from the shadows, visible, and the fire-
light glinted on the blue star, mocking at the center of the high forehead.

There was a little muttering in the tavern, but they were not unaccus-
tomed to Lythande's invisible comings and goings. The young man raised
eyes which were surprisingly blue beneath the black hair elaborately
curled above his brow. He was slender and agile, and Lythande marked
the rapier at his side, which looked well handled, and the amulet, in the
form of a coiled snake, at his throat. The young man said, "Who are you,
who has the habit of coming and going into thin air like that?"

"One who compliments your skill at song." Lythande flung a coin to
the tapster's boy. "Will you drink?"

"A minstrel never refuses such an invitation. Singing is dry work."
But when the drink was brought, he said, "Not drinking with me, then?"

"No man has ever seen Lythande eat or drink," muttered one of the
men in the circle round them.

"Why, then, I hold that unfriendly," cried the young minstrel. "A
friendly drink between comrades shared is one thing; but I am no servant
to sing for pay or to drink except as a friendly gesture!"

Lythande shrugged, and the blue star above the high brow began to
glimmer and give forth blue light. The onlookers slowly edged backward,
for when a wizard who wore the blue star was angered, bystanders did
well to be out of the way. The minstrel set down the lute, so it would be
well out of range if he must leap to his feet. Lythande knew, by the excru-
ciating slowness of his movements and great care, that he had already
shared a good many drinks with chance-met comrades. But the minstrel's
hand did not go to his sword hilt but instead closed like a fist over the
amulet in the form of a snake.

"You are like no man I have ever met before," he observed mildly, and
Lythande, feeling inside the little ripple, nerve-long, that told a magician
he was in the presence of spellcasting, hazarded quickly that the amulet
was one of those which would not protect its master unless the wearer
first stated a set number of truths—usually three or five—about the owner's attacker or foe. Wary, but amused, Lythande said, "A true word. Nor
am I like any man you will ever meet, live you never so long, minstrel."

The minstrel saw, beyond the angry blue glare of the star, a curl of
friendly mockery in Lythande's mouth. He said, letting the amulet go,

"And I wish you no ill; and you wish me none, and those are true sayings too, wizard, hey? And there's an end of that. But although perhaps you are like to no other, you are not the only wizard I have seen in Sanctuary who bears a blue star about his forehead."

Now the blue star blazed rage, but not for the minstrel. They both knew it. The crowd around them had all mysteriously discovered that they had business elsewhere. The minstrel looked at the empty benches.

"I must go elsewhere to sing for my supper, it seems."

"I meant you no offense when I refused to share a drink," said Lythande. "A magician's vow is not as lightly overset as a lute. Yet I may guest-gift you with dinner and drink in plenty without loss of dignity, and in return ask a service of a friend, may I not?"

"Such is the custom of my country. Cappen Varra thanks you, magician."

"Tapster! Your best dinner for my guest, and all he can drink tonight!"

"For such liberal guesting I'll not haggle about the service," Cappen Varra said, and set to the smoking dishes brought before him. As he ate, Lythande drew from the folds of his robe a small pouch containing a quantity of sweet-smelling herbs, rolled them into a blue-grey leaf, and touched his ring to spark the roll alight. He drew on the smoke, which drifted up sweet and greyish.

"As for the service, it is nothing so great; tell me all you know of this other wizard who wears the blue star. I know of none other of my order south of Azehur, and I would be certain you did not see me, nor my wraith."

Cappen Varra sucked at a marrowbone and wiped his fingers fastidiously on the tray-cloth beneath the meats. He bit into a ginger-fruit before replying.

"Not you, wizard, nor your fetch or doppelgänger; this one had shoulders brawnier by half, and he wore no sword, but two daggers cross-girt astride his hips. His beard was black; and his left hand missing three fingers."

"Ils of the Thousand Eyes! Rabben the Half-handed, here in Sanctuary! Where did you see him, minstrel?"

"I saw him crossing the bazaar; but he bought nothing that I saw. And I saw him in the Street of Red Lanterns, talking to a woman. What service am I to do for you, magician?"

"You have done it." Lythande gave silver to the tavernkeeper—so much that the surly man bade Shalpa's cloak cover him as he went—and laid another coin, gold this time, beside the borrowed lute.

"Redeem your harp; that one will do your voice no boon." But when the minstrel raised his head in thanks, the magician had gone unseen into the shadows.

Pocketing the gold, the minstrel asked, "How did he know that? And how did he go out?"

"Shalpa the swift alone knows," the tapster said. "Flew out by the smoke hole in the chimney for all I ken! That one needs not the night-dark cloak of Shalpa to cover him, for he has one of his own. He paid for your drinks, good sir, what will you have?" And Cappen Varra proceeded to get very drunk, that being the wisest thing to do when entangled unawares in the private affairs of a wizard.

Outside in the street, Lythande paused to consider. Rabben the Half-handed was no friend; yet there was no reason his presence in Sanctuary must deal with Lythande, or personal revenge. If it were business concerned with the Order of the Blue Star, if Lythande must lend Rabben aid, or if the Half-handed had been sent to summon all the members of the order, the star they both wore would have given warning.

Yet it would do no harm to make certain. Walking swiftly, the magician had reached a line of old stables behind the Governor's Palace. There silence and secrecy for magic. Lythande stepped into one of the little side alleys, drawing up the magician's cloak until no light remained, slowly withdrawing farther and farther into the silence until nothing remained anywhere in the world—anywhere in the universe but the light of the blue star ever glowing in front. Lythande remembered how it had been set there, and at what cost—the price an adept paid for power.

The blue glow gathered, fulminated in many-colored patterns, pulsing and glowing, until Lythande stood *within* the light; and there, in the Place That Is Not, seated upon a throne carved apparently from sapphire, was the Master of the Star.

"Greetings to you, fellow star, star-born, *shyryu*." The terms of endearment could mean fellow, companion, brother, sister, beloved, equal, pilgrim; its literal meaning was *sharer of starlight*. "What brings you into the Pilgrim Place this night from afar?"

"The need for knowledge, star-sharer. Have you sent one to seek me out in Sanctuary?"

"Not so, *shyryu*. All is well in the Temple of the Star-sharers; you have not yet been summoned; the hour is not yet come."

For every Adept of the Blue Star knows; it is one of the prices of power. At the world's end, when all the doings of mankind and mortals are done, the last to fall under the assault of Chaos will be the Temple of the Star; and then, in the Place That Is Not, the Master of the Star will summon all of the Pilgrim Adepts from the farthest corners of the world, to fight with all their magic against Chaos; but until that day, they have such freedom as will best strengthen their powers. The Master of the Star repeated, reassuringly, "The hour has not come. You are free to walk as you will in the world."

The blue glow faded, and Lythande stood shivering. So Rabben had not been sent in that final summoning. Yet the end and Chaos might well be at hand for Lythande before the hour appointed, if Rabben the Half-handed had his way.

It was a fair test of strength, ordained by our masters. Rabben should bear me no ill will. . . .

Rabben's presence in Sanctuary need not have to do with Lythande. He might be here upon his lawful occasions—if anything of Rabben's could be said to be lawful; for it was only upon the last day of all that the Pilgrim Adepts were pledged to fight upon the side of Law against Chaos. And Rabben had not chosen to do so before then.

Caution would be needed, and yet Lythande knew that Rabben was near. . . .

South and east of the Governor's Palace, there is a little triangular park, across from the Avenue of Temples. By day the graveled walks and turns of shrubbery are given over to predicants and priests who find not enough worship or offerings for their liking; by night the place is the haunt of women who worship no goddess except She of the filled purse and the empty womb. And for both reasons the place is called, in irony, the Promise of Heaven; in Sanctuary, as elsewhere, it is well known that those who promise do not always perform.

Lythande, who frequented neither women nor priests as a usual thing, did not often walk here. The park seemed deserted; the evil winds had begun to blow, whipping bushes and shrubbery into the shapes of strange beasts performing unnatural acts; and moaning weirdly around the walls and eaves of the temples across the street, the wind that was said in Sanctuary to be the moaning of Azyuna in Vashanka's bed. Lythande moved swiftly, skirting the darkness of the paths. And then a woman's scream rent the air.

From the shadows Lythande could see the frail form of a young girl in a torn and ragged dress; she was barefoot and her ear was bleeding where one jeweled earring had been torn from the lobe. She was struggling in the iron grip of a huge burly black-bearded man, and the first thing Lythande saw was the hand gripped around the girl's thin, bony wrist, dragging her; two fingers missing and the other cut away to the first joint. Only then—when it was no longer needed—did Lythande see the blue star between the black bristling brows, the cat-yellow eyes of Rabben the Half-handed!

Lythande knew him of old, from the Temple of the Star. Even then Rabben had been a vicious man, his lecheries notorious. Why, Lythande wondered, had the Masters not demanded that he renounce them as the price of his power? Lythande's lips tightened in a mirthless grimace; so notorious had been Rabben's lecheries that if he renounced them, everyone would know the Secret of his Power.

For the powers of an Adept of the Blue Star depended upon a secret. As in the old legend of the giant who kept his heart in a secret place outside his body, and with it his immortality, so the Adept of the Blue Star poured all his psychic force into a single Secret; and the one who discovered the Secret would acquire all of that adept's power. So Rabben's Secret must be something else. . . . Lythande did not speculate on it.

The girl cried out pitifully as Rabben jerked at her wrist; as the burly magician's star began to glow, she thrust her free hand over her eyes to shield them from it. Without fully intending to intervene, Lythande stepped from the shadows, and the rich voice that had made the prentice magicians in the outer court of the Blue Star call Lythande "minstrel" rather than "magician" rang out:

"By Shipri the All-Mother, release that woman!"

Rabben whirled. "By the nine-hundred-and-ninety-ninth eye of lls! Lythande!"

"Are there not enough women in the Street of Red Lanterns, that you must mishandle girl-children in the Street of Temples?" For Lythande could see how young she was, the thin arms and childish legs and ankles, the breasts not yet full-formed beneath the dirty, torn tunic.

Rabben turned on Lythande and sneered, "You were always squeamish, *shyryu*. No woman walks here unless she is for sale. Do you want her for yourself? Have you tired of your fat madam in the Aphrodisia House?"

"You will not take her name into your mouth, *shyryu*!"

"So tender for the honor of a harlot?"

Lythande ignored that. "Let that girl go, or stand to my challenge."

Rabben's star shot lightnings; he shoved the girl to one side. She fell nerveless to the pavement and lay without moving. "She'll stay there until we've done. Did you think she could run away while we fought? Come to think of it, I never did see you with a woman, Lythande—is that your Secret, Lythande, that you've no use for women?"

Lythande maintained an impassive face; but whatever came, Rabben must not be allowed to pursue *that* line. "You may couple like an animal in the streets of Sanctuary, Rabben, but I do not. Will you yield her up, or fight?"

"Perhaps I should yield her to you; this is unheard of, that Lythande should fight in the streets over a woman! You see, I know your habits well, Lythande!"

Damnation of Vashanka! Now indeed I shall have to fight for the girl!

Lythande's rapier snicked from its scabbard and thrust at Rabben as if of its own will.

"Ha! Do you think Rabben fights street brawls with the sword like any mercenary?" Lythande's sword tip exploded in the blue starglow, and became a shimmering snake, twisting back on itself to climb past the hilt, fangs dripping venom as it sought to coil around Lythande's fist. Lythande's own star blazed. The sword was metal again but twisted and useless, in the shape of the snake it had been, coiling back toward the scabbard. Enraged, Lythande jerked free of the twisted metal, sent a spitting rain of fire in Rabben's direction. Quickly the huge adept covered himself in fog, and the fire-spray extinguished itself. Somewhere outside consciousness Lythande was aware of a crowd gathering; not twice in a lifetime did two Adepts of the Blue Star battle by sorcery in the streets of Sanctuary. The blaze of the stars, blazing from each magician's brow, raged lightnings in the square.

On a howling wind came little torches ravening, that flickered and whipped at Lythande; they touched the tall form of the magician and vanished. Then a wild whirlwind sent trees lashing, leaves swirling bare from branches, and battered Rabben to his knees. Lythande was bored; this must be finished quickly. Not one of the goggling onlookers in the crowd knew afterward what had been done, but Rabben bent, slowly, slowly, forced inch by inch down and down, to his knees, to all fours, prone, pressing and grinding his face farther and farther into the dust, rocking back and forth, pressing harder and harder into the sand . . .

Lythande turned and lifted the girl. She stared in disbelief at the burly sorcerer grinding his black beard frantically into the dirt.

"What did you—"

"Never mind—let's get out of here. The spell will not hold him long, and when he wakes from it he will be angry." Neutral mockery edged Lythande's voice, and the girl could see it, too, Rabben with beard and eyes and blue star covered with the dirt and dust—

She scurried along in the wake of the magician's robe; when they were well away from the Promise of Heaven, Lythande halted, so abruptly that the girl stumbled.

"Who are you, girl?"

"My name is Bercy. And yours?"

"A magician's name is not lightly given. In Sanctuary they call me Lythande." Looking down at the girl, the magician noted, with a pang, that beneath the dirt and dishevelment she was very beautiful and very young.

"You can go, Bercy. He will not touch you again; I have bested him fairly upon challenge."

She flung herself onto Lythande's shoulder, clinging. "Don't send me away!" she begged, clutching, eyes filled with adoration. Lythande scowled.

Predictable, of course. Bercy believed, and who in Sanctuary would have disbelieved, that the duel had been fought for the girl as prize, and she was ready to give herself to the winner. Lythande made a gesture of protest.

"No—"

The girl narrowed her eyes in pity. "Is it then with you as Rabben said—that your secret is that you have been deprived of manhood?" But beyond the pity was a delicious flicker of amusement—what a tidbit of gossip! A juicy bit for the Streets of Women.

"Silence!" Lythande's glance was imperative. "Come."

She followed, along the twisting streets that led into the Street of Red Lanterns. Lythande strode with confidence, now, past the House of Mermaids, where, it was said, delights as exotic as the name promised were to be found; past the House of Whips, shunned by all except those who refused to go elsewhere; and at last, beneath the face of the Green Lady as she was worshiped far away and beyond Ranke, the Aphrodisia House.

Bercy looked around, eyes wide, at the pillared lobby, the brilliance of a hundred lanterns, the exquisitely dressed women lounging on cushions till they were summoned. They were finely dressed and bejeweled—Myrtis knew her trade, and how to present her wares—and Lythande guessed that the ragged Bercy's glance was one of envy; she had probably sold herself in the bazaars for a few coppers or for a loaf of bread, since she was old enough. Yet somehow, like flowers covering a dungheap, she had kept an exquisite fresh beauty, all gold and white, flowerlike. Even ragged and half-starved, she touched Lythande's heart.

"Bercy, have you eaten today?"

"No, master."

Lythande summoned the huge eunuch Jiro, whose business it was to conduct the favored customers to the chambers of their chosen women, and throw out the drunks and abusive customers into the street. He came, huge-bellied, naked except for a skimpy loincloth and a dozen rings in his ear—he had once had a lover who was an earring-seller and had used him to display her wares.

"How may we serve the magician Lythande?"

The women on the couches and cushions were twittering at one another in surprise and dismay, and Lythande could almost hear their thoughts:

None of us has been able to attract or seduce the great magician, and this ragged street wench has caught his eyes? And, being women, Lythande knew, they could see the unclouded beauty that shone through the girl's rags.

"Is Madame Myrtis available, Jiro?"

"She's sleeping, O great wizard, but for you she's given orders she's to be waked at any hour. Is this"—no one alive can be quite so supercilious as the chief eunuch of a fashionable brothel—"*yours*, Lythande, or a gift for my madame?"

"Both, perhaps. Give her something to eat and find her a place to spend the night."

"And a bath, magician? She has fleas enough to louse a floorful of cushions!"

"A bath, certainly, and a bath woman with scents and oils," Lythande said, "and something in the nature of a whole garment."

"Leave it to me," said Jiro expansively, and Bercy looked at Lythande in dread, but went when the magician gestured to her to go. As Jiro took her away, Lythande saw Myrtis standing in the doorway; a heavy woman, no longer young, but with the frozen beauty of a spell. Through the perfect spelled features, her eyes were warm and welcoming as she smiled at Lythande.

"My dear, I had not expected to see you here. Is that yours?" She moved her head toward the door through which Jiro had conducted the frightened Bercy. "She'll probably run away, you know, once you take your eyes off her."

"I wish I thought so, Myrtis. But no such luck, I fear."

"You had better tell me the whole story," Myrtis said, and listened to Lythande's brief, succinct account of the affair.

"And if you laugh, Myrtis, I take back my spell and leave your grey hairs and wrinkles open to the mockery of everyone in Sanctuary!"

But Myrtis had known Lythande too long to take that threat very seriously. "So the maiden you rescued is all maddened with desire for the love of Lythande!" She chuckled. "It is like an old ballad, indeed!"

"But what am I to do, Myrtis? By the paps of Shipri the All-Mother, this is a dilemma!"

"Take her into your confidence and tell her why your love cannot be hers," Myrtis said.

Lythande frowned. "You hold my Secret, since I had no choice; you knew me before I was made magician, or bore the blue star—"

"And before I was a harlot," Myrtis agreed.

"But if I make this girl feel like a fool for loving me, she will hate me as much as she loves; and I cannot confide in anyone I cannot trust with my life and my power. All I have is yours, Myrtis, because of that past we shared. And that includes my power, if you ever should need it. But I cannot entrust it to this girl."

"Still she owes you something, for delivering her out of the hands of Rabben."

Lythande said, "I will think about it; and now make haste to bring me food, for I am hungry and athirst." Taken to a private room, Lythande ate and drank, served by Myrtis's own hands. And Myrtis said, "I could never have sworn your vow—to eat and drink in the sight of no man!"

"If you sought the power of a magician, you would keep it well enough," said Lythande. "I am seldom tempted now to break it; I fear only lest I break it unawares; I cannot drink in a tavern lest among the women there might be some one of those strange men who find diversion in putting on the garments of a female; even here I will not eat or drink among your women, for that reason. All power depends on the vows and the secret."

"Then I cannot aid you," Myrtis said, "but you are not bound to speak truth to her; tell her you have vowed to live without women."

"I may do that," Lythande said, and finished the food, scowling.

Later Bercy was brought in, wide-eyed, enthralled by her fine gown and her freshly washed hair, that softly curled about her pink-and-white face. The sweet scent of bath oils and perfumes hung about her.

"The girls here wear such pretty clothes, and one of them told me they could eat twice a day if they wished! Am I pretty enough, do you think, that Madame Myrtis would have me here?"

"If that is what you wish. You are more than beautiful."

Bercy said boldly, "I would rather belong to *you,* magician," and flung herself again on Lythande, her hands clutching and clinging, dragging the lean face down to hers. Lythande, who rarely touched anything living, held her gently, trying not to reveal consternation.

"Bercy, child, this is only a fancy. It will pass."

"No," she wept. "I love you, I want only you!"

And then, unmistakably, along the magician's nerves, Lythande felt that little ripple, that warning thrill of tension which said: *spellcasting is in use.* Not against Lythande. That could have been countered. But somewhere within the room.

Here, in the Aphrodisia House? Myrtis, Lythande knew, could be trusted with life, reputation, fortune, the magical power of the Blue

Star itself; she had been tested before this. Had she altered enough to turn betrayer, it would have been apparent in her aura when Lythande came near.

That left only the girl, who was clinging and whimpering, "I will die if you do not love me! I will die! Tell me it is not true, Lythande, that you are unable to love! Tell me it is an evil lie that magicians are emasculated, incapable of loving women. . . ."

"That is certainly an evil lie," Lythande agreed gravely. "I give you my solemn assurance that I have never been emasculated." But Lythande's nerves tingled as the words were spoken. A magician might lie, and most of them did. Lythande would lie as readily as any other, in a good cause. But the law of the Blue Star was this: when questioned directly on a matter bearing directly on the Secret, the Adept might not tell a direct lie. And Bercy, unknowing, was only one question away from the fatal one hiding the Secret.

With a mighty effort, Lythande's magic wrenched at the very fabric of Time itself; the girl stood motionless, aware of no lapse, as Lythande stepped away far enough to read her aura. And yes, there within the traces of that vibrating field was the shadow of the Blue Star. Rabben's; overpowering her will.

Rabben. Rabben the Half-handed, who had set his will on the girl, who had staged and contrived the whole thing, including the encounter where the girl had needed rescue; put the girl under a spell to attract and bespell Lythande.

The law of the Blue Star forbade one Adept of the Star to kill another; for all would be needed to fight side by side, on the last day, against Chaos. Yet if one adept could prise forth the secret of another's power . . . then the powerless one was not needed against Chaos and could be killed.

What could be done now? Kill the girl? Rabben would take that, too, as an answer; Bercy had been so bespelled as to be irresistible to any man; if Lythande sent her away untouched, Rabben would know that Lythande's Secret lay in that area and would never rest in his attempts to uncover it. For if Lythande was untouched by this sex spell to make Bercy irresistible, then Lythande was a eunuch, or a homosexual, or . . . sweating, Lythande dared not even think beyond that. The Secret was safe only if never questioned. It would not be read in the aura; but one simple question, and all was ended.

I should kill her, Lythande thought. *For now I am fighting not for my magic alone, but for my Secret and for my life. For surely, with my power gone, Rabben would lose no time in making an end of me, in revenge for the loss of half a hand.*

The girl was still motionless, entranced. How easily she could be killed! Then Lythande recalled an old fairy tale, which might be used to save the Secret of the Star.

The light flickered as Time returned to the chamber. Bercy was still clinging and weeping, unaware of the lapse; Lythande had resolved what to do, and the girl felt Lythande's arms enfolding her, and the magician's kiss on her welcoming mouth.

"You must love me or I shall die!" Bercy wept.

Lythande said, "You shall be mine." The soft neutral voice was very gentle. "But even a magician is vulnerable in love, and I must protect myself. A place shall be made ready for us without light or sound save for what I provide with my magic; and you must swear that you will not seek to see or to touch me except by that magical light. Will you swear it by the All-Mother, Bercy? For if you swear this, I shall love you as no woman has ever been loved before."

Trembling, she whispered, "I swear." And Lythande's heart went out in pity, for Rabben had used her ruthlessly; so that she burned alive with her unslaked and bewitched love for the magician, that she was all caught up in her passion for Lythande. Painfully, Lythande thought: *If she had only loved me, without the spell; then I could have loved . . .*

Would that I could trust her with my Secret! But she is only Rabben's tool; her love for me is his doing, and none of her own will . . . and not real . . . And so everything which would pass between them now must be only a drama staged for Rabben.

"I shall make all ready for you with my magic."

Lythande went and confided to Myrtis what was needed; the woman began to laugh, but a single glance at Lythande's bleak face stopped her cold. She had known Lythande since long before the Blue Star was set between those eyes; and she kept the Secret for love of Lythande. It wrung her heart to see one she loved in the grip of such suffering. So she said, "All will be prepared. Shall I give her a drug in her wine to weaken her will, that you may the more readily throw a glamour upon her?"

Lythande's voice held a terrible bitterness. "Rabben has done that already for us, when he put a spell upon her to love me."

"You would have it otherwise?" Myrtis asked, hesitating.

"All the gods of Sanctuary—they laugh at me! All-Mother, help me! But I would have it otherwise; I could love her, if she were not Rabben's tool."

When all was prepared, Lythande entered the darkened room. There was no light but the light of the Blue Star. The girl lay on a bed, stretching up her arms to the magician with exalted abandon.

"Come to me, come to me, my love!"

"Soon," said Lythande, sitting beside her, stroking her hair with a tenderness even Myrtis would never have guessed. "I will sing to you a love song of my people, far away."

She writhed in erotic ecstasy. "All you do is good to me, my love, my magician!"

Lythande felt the blankness of utter despair. She was beautiful, and she was in love. She lay in a bed spread for the two of them, and they were separated by the breadth of the world. The magician could not endure it.

Lythande sang, in that rich and beautiful voice, a voice lovelier than any spell:

> *Half the night is spent; and the crown of moonlight*
> *Fades, and now the crown of the stars is paling;*
> *Yields the sky reluctant to coming morning;*
> *Still I lie lonely.*
> *I will love you as no woman has ever been loved.*

Lythande could see tears on Bercy's cheeks.

Between the girl on the bed, and the motionless form of the magician, as the magician's robe fell heavily to the floor, a wraith-form grew, the very wraith and fetch, at first, of Lythande, tall and lean, with blazing eyes and a star between its brows and a body white and unscarred; the form of the magician, but this one triumphant in virility, advancing on the motionless woman, waiting. Her mind fluttered away in arousal, was caught, captured, bespelled. Lythande let her see the image for a moment; she could not see the true Lythande behind; then, as her eyes closed in ecstatic awareness of the touch, Lythande smoothed light fingers over her closed eyes.

"See—what I bid you to see!

"Hear—what I bid you hear!

"Feel—only what I bid you feel, Bercy!"

And now she was wholly under the spell of the wraith. Unmoving, stony-eyed, Lythande watched as her lips closed on emptiness and she kissed invisible lips; and moment by moment Lythande knew what touched her, what caressed her. Rapt and ravished by illusion, that brought her again and again to the heights of ecstasy, till she cried out in abandonment. Only to Lythande that cry was bitter; for she cried out not to Lythande but to the man-wraith who possessed her.

At last she lay all but unconscious, satiated; and Lythande watched in agony. When she opened her eyes again, Lythande was looking down at her, sorrowfully.

Bercy stretched up languid arms. "Truly, my beloved, you have loved me as no woman has ever been loved before."

For the first and last time, Lythande bent over her and pressed her lips in a long, infinitely tender kiss. "Sleep, my darling." And as she sank into ecstatic, exhausted sleep, Lythande wept.

Long before she woke, Lythande stood, girt for travel, in the little room belonging to Myrtis. "The spell will hold. She will make all haste to carry her tale to Rabben—the tale of Lythande, the incomparable lover! Of Lythande, of untiring virility, who can love a maiden into exhaustion!" The rich voice of Lythande was harsh with bitterness.

"And long before you return to Sanctuary, once freed of the spell, she will have forgotten you in many other lovers," Myrtis agreed. "It is better and safer that it should be so."

"True." But Lythande's voice broke. "Take care of her, Myrtis. Be kind to her."

"I swear it, Lythande."

"If only she could have loved *me*"—the magician broke and sobbed again for a moment; Myrtis looked away, wrung with pain, knowing not what comfort to offer.

"If only she could have loved me as I am, freed of Rabben's spell! Loved me without pretense! But I feared I could not master the spell Rabben had put on her . . . nor trust her not to betray me, knowing . . ."

Myrtis put her plump arms around Lythande, tenderly.

"Do you regret?"

The question was ambiguous. It might have meant: Do you regret that *you did not kill the girl?* Or even: *Do you regret your oath and the secret you must bear to the last day?* Lythande chose to answer the last.

"Regret? How can I regret? One day I shall fight against Chaos with all of my order; even at the side of Rabben, if he lives unmurdered as long as that. And that alone must justify my existence and my Secret. But now I must leave Sanctuary, and who knows when the chances of the world will bring me this way again? Kiss me farewell, my sister."

Myrtis stood on tiptoe. Her lips met the lips of the magician.

"Until we meet again, Lythande. May She attend and guard you forever. Farewell, my beloved, my sister."

Then the magician Lythande girded on her sword, and went silently and by unseen ways out of the city of Sanctuary, just as the dawn was breaking. And on her forehead the glow of the Blue Star was dimmed by the rising sun. Never once did she look back.

The Making of
Thieves' World

Robert Lynn Asprin

It was a dark and stormy night . . .

Actually, that Thursday night before Boskone '78 was a very pleasant night. Lynn Abbey, Gordy Dickson, and I were enjoying a quiet dinner in the Boston Sheraton's Mermaid Restaurant prior to the chaos which inevitably surrounds a major science fiction convention.

As so often happens when several authors gather socially, the conversation turned to the subject of writing in general and specifically to problems encountered and pet peeves. Not to be outdone by my dinner companions, I voiced one of my long-standing gripes: that whenever one set out to write heroic fantasy, it was first necessary to reinvent the universe from scratch regardless of what had gone before. Despite the carefully crafted Hyborean world of Howard or even the delightfully complex town of Lankhmar which Leiber created, every author was expected to beat his head against the writing table and devise a world of his own. Imagine, I proposed, if our favorite sword-and-sorcery characters shared the same settings and time frames, imagine the story potentials. Imagine the tie-ins. What if . . .

What if Fafhrd and Mouser had just finished a successful heist. With an angry crowd on their heels, they pull one of their notorious double-back escapes and elude the pursuing throng. Now suppose this angry, torch-waving pack runs headlong into Conan, hot and tired from the trail, his dead horse a day's walk behind him. All he wants is a jug of wine and a wench. Instead, he's confronted with a lynch mob. What if his saddlebags are full of loot from one of his own ventures, yet undiscovered?

Or what if Kane and Elric took jobs marshaling opposite armies in the same war?

Why, I proclaimed, the possibilities are endless. Pouring a little more wine, I admitted that one of my pet projects under consideration was to do a collection of fantasy stories featuring not one, but an array of central characters. They would all share the same terrain and be peripherally aware of each other's existence as their paths crossed. The only problem: my writing schedule was filling up so fast I wasn't sure when or if I'd ever get a chance to write it.

More wine flowed.

Gordy sympathized eloquently, pointing out that this was a problem all writers encountered as they grew more and more successful. Time! Time to fulfill your commitments and still be able to write the fun things you really want to write. As an example, he pointed out that there were countless story potentials in his Dorsai universe, but that he was barely able to find the time to complete the Childe Cycle novels, much less pursue all the spinoffs.

More wine flowed.

The ideal thing, Lynn suggested, was to be able to franchise one's ideas and worlds out to other authors. The danger there, Gordy pointed out, was the danger of losing control. None of us were particularly wild about letting any Tom, Dick, or Harry play around with our pet ideas.

More wine flowed.

Anthologies! If we went to an anthology format, we could invite authors to participate, as well as having final say as to the acceptability of the stories submitted.

Gordy ordered a bottle of champagne.

Of course, he observed, you'll be able to get some topflight authors for this because it'll be fun. They'll do it more for the love of the idea than for the money.

I remarked on the ease with which "*our*" idea had become "*my*" anthology. As the weight of the project had suddenly come to rest on my shoulders, I asked whether he intended to assist or at least contribute to the anthology. His reply set the classic pattern for nearly all the contributors to *Thieves' World*:

I'd love to, but I don't have the time. It's a lovely idea, though.

(Five minutes later) I just thought of a character who would fit into this perfectly.

(Fifteen minutes later . . . thoughtful stare into nothingness converting into a smug grin) I've got my story!

During this last exchange, Lynn was saying very little. Unbeknownst to me, she had mentally dealt herself out of the project when Gordy proposed "established writers only." At that point in time, she had in her suitcase the manuscript for *Daughter of the Bright Moon*, hoping to find an interested editor at Boskone. She was far from being "established." It is to her credit, however, that she successfully hid her disappointment at being excluded, and accompanied Gordy and me as we finished the last of the champagne and went "trolling for editors."

It may seem to you that it was rather early to try to find a publisher for such a nebulous work. That's how it struck me at the time. Gordy pointed out, however, that if we could find an editor and nudge him into an appraisal of the dollar value of the idea, I would have a better feel for what my budget would be when I went to line up my authors. (The fact that this made sense to me at the time will serve as an indication of the lateness of the hour and the amount of wine we had consumed.)

To this end, we devised a subtle tactic. We would try to find an author and an editor in the same room, preferably in the same conversation. We would then pitch the idea to the author as a potential contributor and see if the editor showed interest.

We found such a duo and launched into our song and dance. The editor yawned, but the author thought it was a great idea. Of course, he didn't have the time to write anything . . . Then he thought of a character! That's how John Brunner came on board.

The next morning, the effects of our dinner wine dissipated and I began to realize what I had let myself in for. A brand-new author, barely published, and I was going to try to edit an anthology? Soliciting contributions from the best in the field, yet! That revelation sobered me up faster than a bucket of ice water and a five-day hotel bill.

Still, the ball was already rolling, and I had story commitments from Gordy and John. I might as well see how far things could go.

FRIDAY: I ambushed Joe Haldeman over a glass of lunch. He thought it was a terrific idea, but he didn't have any time. Besides, he pointed out, he had never written heroic fantasy. I countered by reminding him of his stay in Viet Nam, courtesy of the U.S. Army. Surely, I pressed, there must be one or two characters he had encountered who would fit into a sword-and-sorcery setting with minimal rewriting. His eyes cleared. He had his character.

SATURDAY: I finally found out what was bothering Lynn and assured her of a place on the *Thieves' World* roster. I was confident she would be "established" before the anthology came out, and even if she wasn't, I knew she could produce a solid story. No, I don't have a crystal ball. Lynn and I both live in Ann Arbor and share workspace when we're writing. As such, I had been reading the manuscript of *Daughter of the Bright Moon* as she was writing it, and knew her writing style even before the editors saw it. [My prophecy proved correct. Ace/Sunridge bought her manuscript, and a major promo campaign is currently under way. The book should be on the stands when you see this anthology.]

SUNDAY: Wonder of wonders. Over cognac at the Ace dead-dog party, Jim Baen expresses a solid interest in the anthology . . . if I succeed in filling the remaining slots with authors of an equal quality as those already committed. Leaving the party, I encounter Jim Odbert in the hall and do a little bragging. He brings me down to earth by asking about the street map. I hadn't even thought about it, but he was right! It would be absolutely necessary for internal continuity. Thinking fast, I commission him on the spot and retire, harboring a nagging hunch that this project might be a bit more involved than I had imagined.

Back in Ann Arbor, I face the task of filling the remaining openings for the anthology. My magic wand for this feat is a telephone. Having been a fan for many years, I have had passing contact with several prominent authors, many of whom don't know that I'm writing now. I figure it will be easier to jog their memories over the phone than trying to do the same thing by letter.

The problem now is . . . who? Solid authors . . . that's a must. Authors who know me well enough that they won't hang up when I call. Authors who *don't* know me so well that they'll hang up when I call.

Andy! Andy Offutt. Our paths had crossed several times at cons, and I know we share a mutual admiration of Genghis Khan.

Andy doesn't have any time, but is superenthusiastic over the idea and has his character. Yes, that's all one sentence. If anything, I've condensed it. If you've ever talked to Andy on the phone, you'll understand.

Next will be Poul Anderson. Poul and I know each other mostly by reputation through Gordy and through a medieval reenactment organization known as the Society for Creative Anachronism, Inc. Sir Bela of Eastmarch and Yang the Nauseating. Hooboy, do we know each other. In spite of that, Poul agrees to do a story for me . . . if he gets the time . . . in fact, he has a character in mind.

The list is growing. Confident now that the impressive array of authors submitting stories will offset my own relative obscurity, I go for a few who may not remember me.

Roger Zelazny was Pro Guest of Honor at a convention in Little Rock, Arkansas, where I was Fan Guest of Honor. He remembers and listens to my pitch.

I spoke briefly with Marion Zimmer Bradley about the swordwork in *Hunter of the Red Moon*—when we passed in the hall at a Westercon in Los Angeles—two years ago. She remembers me and listens to my pitch.

Philip José Farmer and I have seen each other twice: once in Milwaukee and once in Minneapolis. Both times we were at opposite ends of a table with half a dozen people crowded between us. He acknowledges the memory, then listens in silence for fifteen minutes while I do my spiel. When I finally grind to a halt, he says okay and hangs up. I find out later that this is his way of expressing enthusiasm. If he hadn't been enthusiastic, he would have said no and hung up.

By this time it's Minicon. Jim Odbert passes me a set of maps. Then he, Gordy, Joe, Lynn, and I sit around half the night discussing the history of the city and the surrounding continent. A set of house rules is devised and agreed upon: (1) Each contributor is to send me a brief description of the main character of his/her story. (2) These descriptions will be copied and distributed to the other contributors. (3) Any author can use these characters in his/her story, providing they're not killed off or noticeably reformed.

I run all this through a typewriter and mail it out to all the contributors. It occurs to me that this isn't nearly as difficult as I had feared. My only worry is that the mails might slow communication with John Brunner in England, causing him to be late with his submission. Except for that, everything was going fine.

Then the fun began. . . .

Andy, Poul, and John all send me notes in varying degrees of gentleness correcting my grammar and/or word usage in the flier. They are willing to accept without confirmation that my spelling was intended as a joke. These are the people I'm supposed to be editing! Riiiiight!

Poul sends me a copy of his essay "On Thud and Blunder," to ensure the realism of the setting, particularly the economic structure of the town. He also wants to know about the judicial system in Sanctuary.

Andy wants to know about the deities worshiped, preferably broken down by nationality and economic class of worshipers. Fortunately, he includes a proposed set of gods, which I gleefully copy and send to the other contributors. He heads his ten-page letters with "To Colossus: The Asprin Project." It occurs to me that with his own insight as an anthology editor, this could be more truth than humor.

To make my job a little easier, some of the authors start playing poker with their character sketches: "I won't show you mine till you show me yours." They delay submitting their sketches until they see what the other authors turn in. One of these is Gordy. Remember him? He's the one who got me into this in the first place. He's the one who "had his character" before there was an anthology! Terrific! John Brunner submits his story—a full year before the stated deadline. So much for transatlantic delays. I haven't gotten all the character descriptions yet. More important, I haven't gotten the advance money yet! His agent begins to prod gently for payment.

Roger reappraises his time commitments and withdraws from the project. Oh, well. You can't win them all.

Poul wants to know about the architectural style of Sanctuary.

Andy and Poul want to know about the structure and nationality of names.

A call comes in from Ace. Jim Baen wants the manuscript a full three months ahead of the contracted deadline. I point out that this is impossible—the new deadline would give me only two weeks between receiving the stories from the authors and submitting the complete manuscript to New York. If I encountered difficulties with any of the stories or if any of the submissions came in late, it would disrupt the schedule completely. They point out that if I can meet the new schedule, they'll make it their lead book for the month it's released. The avaricious side of me is screaming, but I stick to my guns and repeat that it's impossible to guarantee. They offer a contract for a second *Thieves' World* anthology, suggesting that if a couple stories are late, I can include them in the next book. Under attack now both from my publisher and my own greedy nature, I roll my eyes heavenward, swallow hard, and agree.

A new note is rapidly dispatched to the contributors, politely reminding them of the approaching deadline. Also included is Gordy's character sketch for Jamie the Red, which he had finally submitted under mild duress (his arm will heal eventually).

Andy calls and wants to know the prince's name. I haven't given it any thought, but am willing to negotiate. An hour later, I hang up. It occurs to me that I haven't written my story yet.

Gordy notifies me that he can't get his story done in time for the first book. Terrific! With Gordy and Roger both out of the first volume, it's starting to look a little short.

Andy's story comes in, as do Joe's and Poul's.

Andy's story includes a discussion with Joe's One-Thumb character. Joe has killed One-Thumb off in his story. A minor sequencing problem.

Poul's story has Cappen Varra going off on an adventure with Gordy's Jamie the Red. Gordy's Jamie the Red story won't be in the first book! A major sequencing problem! Oh, well. I owe Gordy one for talking me into editing this monster.

I look at the stories already in the bin and decide that the first draft of my story needs some drastic rewriting.

A note arrives from Phil Farmer. He had sent me a letter months ago, which apparently never arrived, withdrawing from the project. Realizing that withdrawing at this late date would leave me in a bad spot, he is now rearranging his writing schedule in order to send me "something." Of course, it will be a little late. I am grateful, but panicky.

Lynn finishes her story and starts to gloat. I threaten to beat her head in with my Selectric.

Ace calls again. They want additional information for the cover copy. They also want a word count. I explain the situation as calmly as I can. Halfway through my explanation, the phone melts.

Ma Bell fixes my phone in record time (I am rapidly becoming their favorite customer), and I hurriedly call Marion to ask for a rough word count on her unsubmitted story. She tells me she sent me a letter which must not have arrived. (It didn't.) She tells me she'll have to withdraw from the project because of time pressures in her other writing commitments. She tells me to stop gibbering and say something. I calm myself and explain I'd *really* like to have a story from her. I explain I really *need* her story. I mention that her character is on the cover of the book. She observes that the water gushing from the phone is threatening to flood her living room and agrees to try to squeeze the story into her writing schedule . . . before she flies to London in two weeks.

With steady hand but trembling mind, I call Ace and ask for Jim Baen. I explain the situation: I have six stories in hand (yes, I finally finished mine) and two more on the way . . . a little late . . . maybe. He informs me that with just six stories the book will be too short. He wants at least one more story and an essay from me about how much fun it was to edit the anthology. To calm my hysterics, he suggests I commission a backup story in case the two en route don't arrive in time. I point out that there are only two weeks remaining before the deadline. He concedes that with such a limited time frame, I probably won't be able to get a story from a "name" author. He'll let me work with an "unknown," but the story had better be good!

Christine Dewees is a kindly, white-haired grandmother who rides a Harley and wants to be a writer. Lynn and I have been criticizing her efforts for some time and have repeatedly encouraged her to submit something to an editor. So far, she has resisted our proddings, insisting that she would be embarrassed to show her work to a professional editor. I decide to kill two birds with one stone.

In my most disarming "nothing can go wrong" tones, I give my spiel to Christine and pass her a *Thieves' World* package. Three hours later, my phone rings. Christine loves the character of Myrtis, the madam of the Aphrodisia House, and is ready to do a story centering around her. I stammer politely and point out that Myrtis is one of Marion's characters and that she might object to someone else writing her characters. Christine cackles and tells me she's already cleared it with Marion (don't ask me how she got the phone number!), and everything is effervescent. Two days later, she hands me the story, and I still haven't gotten around to looking up "effervescent" in the dictionary. With seven stories now in hand, I declare *Thieves' World I* to be complete and begin writing my "fun fun" essay. The stories from Marion and Phil can wait until the second book.

Then Marion's story arrives.

Marion's story interfaces so nicely with Christine's that I decide to use them both in the first book. Rather than cut one of the other stories, the volume is assembled with intros, maps, eight stories, and essay, crated, and shipped off to New York.

Endo volume one! Print it!

The whole whirlwind process of editing this monster child was only vaguely as I had imagined it would be. Still, in hindsight, I loved it. With all the worries and panics, the sky-high phone bills and the higher bar bills, I loved every minute. I find myself actually looking forward to the next volume . . . and that's what worries me!

Tales from the Vulgar Unicorn

*Not included in the original *Tales from the Vulgar Unicorn*

Introduction

Robert Asprin

Moving his head with minute care to avoid notice, Hakiem the Story-teller studied the room over the untouched rim of his wine cup. This was, of course, done through slitted eyes. It would not do to have anyone suspect he was not truly asleep. What he saw only confirmed his growing feelings of disgust.

The Vulgar Unicorn was definitely going downhill. A drunk was snoring on the floor against the wall, passed out in a puddle of his own vomit, while several beggars made their way from table to table, interrupting the undertoned negotiations and haggling of the tavern's normal clientele.

Though his features never moved, Hakiem grimaced inside. Such goings-on were never tolerated when One-Thumb was around. The bartender/owner of the Vulgar Unicorn had always been quick to evict such riffraff as fast as they appeared. While the tavern had always been shunned by the more law-abiding citizens of Sanctuary, one of the main reasons it was favored by the rougher element was that here a man could partake of a drink or perhaps a little larcenous conversation uninterrupted. This tradition was rapidly coming to an end.

The fact that he would not be allowed to linger for hours over a cup of the tavern's cheapest wine if One-Thumb were here never entered Hakiem's mind. He had a skill. He was a storyteller, a tale-spinner, a weaver of dreams and nightmares. As such, he considered himself on a measurably better plane than the derelicts who had taken to frequenting the place.

One-Thumb had been missing for a long time now, longer than any of his previous mysterious disappearances. Fear of his return kept the tavern open and the employees honest, but the place was degenerating in his absence. The only way it could sink any lower would be if a Hell Hound took to drinking here.

Despite his guise of slumber, Hakiem found himself smiling at that thought. A Hell Hound in the Vulgar Unicorn? Unlikely at best. Sanctuary still chafed at the occupying force from the Rankan Empire, and the five Hell Hounds were hated second only to the military governor, Prince Kadakithis, whom they guarded. Though it was a close choice between Prince Kittycat with his naive lawmaking and the elite soldiers who enforced his words, the citizens of Sanctuary generally felt the military governor's quest to clean up the worst hellhole in the empire was stupid, while the Hell Hounds were simply devilishly efficient. In a town where one was forced to live by wit as often as skill, efficiency could be grudgingly admired, while stupidity, particularly stupidity with power, could only be despised.

No, the Hell Hounds weren't stupid. Tough, excellent swordsmen and seasoned veterans, they seldom set foot in the Maze, and never entered the Vulgar Unicorn. On the west side of town, it was said that one came here only if he was seeking death . . . or selling it. While the statement was somewhat exaggerated, it was true that most of the people who frequented the Maze either had nothing to lose or were willing to risk everything for what they might gain there. As rational men, the Hell Hounds were unlikely to put in an appearance at the Maze's most notorious tavern.

Still, the point remained that the Vulgar Unicorn sorely needed One-Thumb's presence and that his return was long overdue. In part, that was why Hakiem was spending so much time here of late: hope of acquiring the story of One-Thumb's return and possibly the story of his absence. That alone would be enough to keep the storyteller haunting the tavern, but the stories he gained during his wait were a prize in themselves. Hakiem was a compulsive collector of stories, from habit as well as by profession, and many stories had their beginnings, middle, or ends within these walls. He collected them all, though he knew that most of them could not be repeated, for he knew the value of a story is in its merit, not in its salability.

Spiders of the Purple Mage

Philip José Farmer

1

This was the week of the great rat hunt in Sanctuary.

The next week, all the cats that could be caught were killed and degutted.

The third week, all dogs were run down and disemboweled.

Masha zil-Ineel was one of the very few people in the city who didn't take part in the rat hunt. She just couldn't believe that any rat, no matter how big, and there were some huge ones in Sanctuary, could swallow a jewel so large.

But when a rumor spread that someone had seen a cat eat a dead rat and that the cat had acted strangely afterward, she thought it wise to pretend to chase cats. If she hadn't, people might wonder why not. They might think that she knew something they didn't. And then she might be the one run down.

Unlike the animals, however, she'd be tortured until she told where the jewel was.

She didn't know where it was. She wasn't even sure that there *was* an emerald.

But everybody knew that she'd been told about the jewel by Benna nus-Katarz. Thanks to Masha's blabbermouth drunken husband, Eevroen.

Three weeks ago, on a dark night, Masha had returned late from mid-wifing in the rich merchants' eastern quarter. It was well past midnight, but she wasn't sure of the hour because of the cloud-covered sky. The second wife of Shoozh the spice importer had borne her fourth infant. Masha had attended to the delivery personally while Doctor Nadeesh had sat in the next room, the door only half-closed, and listened to her reports. Nadeesh was forbidden to see any part of a female client except for those normally exposed and especially forbidden to see the breasts and genitals. If there was any trouble with the birthing, Masha would inform him, and he would give her instructions.

This angered Masha, since the doctors collected half of the fee, yet were seldom of any use. In fact, they were usually a hindrance.

Still, half a fee was better than none. What if the wives and concubines of the wealthy were as nonchalant and hardy as the poor women, who just squatted down wherever they happened to be when the pangs started and gave birth unassisted? Masha could not have supported herself, her two daughters, her invalid mother, or her lazy alcoholic husband. The money she made from doing the more affluent women's hair and from her tooth-pulling and manufacturing false teeth in the marketplace wasn't enough. But midwifery added the income that kept her and her family just outside hunger's door.

She would have liked to pick up more money by cutting men's hair in the marketplace, but both law and ancient custom forbade that.

Shortly after she had burned the umbilical cord of the newborn to insure that demons didn't steal it and had ritualistically washed her hands, she left Shoozh's house. His guards, knowing her, let her through the gate without challenge, and the guards of the gate to the eastern quarters also allowed her to pass. Not however without offers from a few to share their beds with her that night.

"I can do much better than that sot of a husband of yours," one said.

Masha was glad that her hood and the darkness prevented the guards from seeing her burning face by the torchlight. However, if they could have seen that she was blushing with shame, they might have been embarrassed. They would know then that they weren't dealing with a brazen slut of the Maze but with a woman who had known better days and a higher position in society than she now held. The blush alone would have told them that.

What they didn't know and what she couldn't forget was that she had once lived in this walled area and her father had been an affluent, if not wealthy, merchant.

She passed on silently. It would have made her feel good to have told them her past and then ripped them with the invective she'd learned in the Maze. But to do that would lower her estimate of herself.

Though she had her own torch and the means for lighting it in the cylindrical leather case on her back, she did not use them. It was better to walk unlit and hence unseen into the streets. Though many of the lurkers in the shadows would let her pass unmolested, since they had known her when she was a child, others would not be so kind. They would rob her for the tools of her trade and the clothes she wore and some would rape her. Or try to.

Through the darkness she went swiftly, her steps sure because of long experience. The adobe buildings of the city were a dim whitish bulk ahead. Then the path took a turn, and she saw some small flickers of light here and there. Torches. A little farther, and a light became a square. The window of a tavern.

She entered a narrow winding street and strode down its center. Turning a corner, she saw a torch in a bracket on the wall of a house and two men standing near it. Immediately she crossed to the far side and, hugging the walls, passed the two. Their pipes glowed redly; she caught a whiff of the pungent and sickly smoke of *kleetel*, the drug used by the poor when they didn't have money for the more expensive *krrf*. Which was most of the time.

After two or three pipefuls, the smokers would be vomiting. But they would claim that the euphoria would make the upchucking worth it.

There were other odors: garbage piled by the walls, slop jars of excrement, and puke from *kleetel* smokers and drunks. The garbage would be shoveled into goat-drawn carts by Downwinders whose families had long held this right. The slop jars would be emptied by a Downwinder family that had delivered the contents to farmers for a century and had fought fiercely to keep this right. The farmers would use the excrement to feed their soil; the urine would be emptied into the mouth of the White Foal River and carried out to sea.

She also heard the rustling and squealing of rats as they searched for edible portions and dogs growling or snarling as they chased the rats or fought one another. And she glimpsed the swift shadows of running cats.

Like a rat, she sped down the street in a half-run, stopping at corners to look around them before venturing farther. When she was about a half-mile from her place, she heard the pounding of feet ahead. She froze and tried to make herself look like part of the wall.

2

At that moment the moon broke through the clouds.

It was almost a full moon. The light revealed her to any but a blind person. She darted across the street to the dark side and played wall again.

The slap of feet on the hard-packed dirt of the street came closer. Somewhere above her, a baby began crying.

She pulled a long knife from a scabbard under her cloak and held the blade behind her. Doubtless, the one running was a thief or else someone trying to outrun a thief or mugger or perhaps a throat-slitter. If it was a thief who was getting away from the site of the crime, she would be safe. He'd be in no position to stop to see what he could get from her. If he was being pursued, the pursuers might shift their attention to her.

If they saw her.

Suddenly, the pound of feet became louder. Around the corner came a tall youth dressed in a ragged tunic and breeches and shod with buskins. He stopped and clutched the corner and looked behind him. His breath rasped like a rusty gate swung back and forth by gusts of wind.

Somebody was after him. Should she wait here? He hadn't seen her, and perhaps whoever was chasing him would be so intent he or they wouldn't detect her either.

The youth turned his face, and she gasped. His face was so swollen that she almost didn't recognize him. But he was Benna nus-Katarz, who had come here from Ilsig two years ago. No one knew why he'd immigrated, and no one, in keeping with the unwritten code of Sanctuary, had asked him why.

Even in the moonlight and across the street, she could see the swellings and dark spots, looking like bruises, on his face. And on his hands. The fingers were rotting bananas.

He turned back to peer around the corner. His breathing became less heavy. Now she could hear the faint slap of feet down the street. His chasers would be here soon.

Benna gave a soft ululation of despair. He staggered down the street toward a mound of garbage and stopped before it. A rat scuttled out but stopped a few feet from him and chittered at him. Bold beasts, the rats of Sanctuary.

Now Masha could hear the loudness of approaching runners and worried that it sounded like sheets being ripped apart.

Benna moaned. He reached under his tunic with clumsy fingers and drew something out. Masha couldn't see what it was, though she strained. She inched with her back to the wall toward a doorway. Its darkness would make her even more undetectable.

Benna looked at the thing in his hand. He said something that sounded to Masha like a curse. She couldn't be sure; he spoke in the Ilsig dialect.

The baby above had ceased crying; its mother must have given it the nipple, or perhaps she'd made it drink water tinctured with a drug.

Now Benna was pulling something else from inside his tunic. Whatever it was, he molded it around the other thing, and now he had cast it in front of the rat.

The big gray beast ran away as the object arced toward him. A moment later, it approached the little ball, sniffing. Then it darted forward, still smelling it, touched it with its nose, perhaps tasted it, and was gone with it in its mouth.

Masha watched it squeeze into a crack in the old adobe building at the next corner. No one lived there. It had been crumbling, falling down for years, unrepaired and avoided even by the most desperate of transients and bums. It was said that the ghost of old Lahboo the Tight-Fisted haunted the place since his murder, and no one cared to test the truth of the stories told about the building.

Benna, still breathing somewhat heavily, trotted after the rat. Masha, hearing that the footsteps were louder, went alongside the wall, still in the shadows. She was curious about what Benna had gotten rid of, but she didn't want to be associated with him in any way when his hunters caught up with him.

At the corner, the youth stopped and looked around him. He didn't seem able to make up his mind which route to take. He stood, swaying, and then fell to his knees. He groaned, and pitched forward, softening his fall with outstretched arms.

Masha meant to leave him to his fate; it was the only sensible thing to do. But as she rounded the corner, she heard him moaning. And then she thought she heard him say something about a jewel.

She stopped. Was that what he had put in something, perhaps a bit of cheese, and thrown to the rat? It would be worth more money than she'd earn in a lifetime, and if she could, somehow, get her hands on it . . . Her thoughts raced as swiftly as her heart, and now she was breathing heavily. A jewel! A jewel? It would mean release from this terrible place, a good home for her mother and her children. And for herself.

And it might mean release from Eevroen.

But there was also a terrible danger very close. She couldn't hear the sounds of the pursuers now, but that didn't mean they'd left the neighborhood. They were prowling around, looking into each doorway. Or perhaps one had looked around the corner and seen Benna. He had motioned to the others, and they were just behind the corner, getting ready to make a sudden rush.

She could visualize the knives in their hands.

If she took a chance and lost, she'd die, and her mother and daughters would be without support. They'd have to beg; Eevroen certainly would be of no help. And Handoo and Kheem, three and five years old, would grow up, if they didn't die first, to be child whores. It was almost inevitable.

While she stood undecided, knowing that she had only a few seconds to act and perhaps not that, the clouds slid below the moon again. That made the difference in what she'd do. She ran across the street toward Benna. He was still lying in the dirt of the street, his head only a few inches from some stinking dog turds. She scabbarded her dagger, got down on her knees, and rolled him over. He gasped with terror when he felt her hands upon him.

"It's all right!" she said softly. "Listen! Can you get up if I help you? I'll get you away!"

Sweat poured into her eyes as she looked toward the far corner. She could see nothing, but if the hunters wore black, they wouldn't be visible at this distance.

Benna moaned and then said, "I'm dying, Masha."

Masha gritted her teeth. She had hoped that he'd not recognize her voice, not at lest until she'd gotten him to safety. Now, if the hunters found him alive and got her name from him, they'd come after her. They'd think she had the jewel or whatever it was they wanted.

"Here. Get up," she said, and struggled to help him. She was small, about five feet tall and weighing eighty-two pounds. But she had the muscles of a cat, and fear was pumping strength into her. She managed to get Benna to his feet. Staggering under his weight, she supported him toward the open doorway of the building on the corner.

Benna reeked of something strange, an odor of rotting meat but unlike any she'd ever smelled. It rode over the stale sweat and urine of his body and clothes.

"No use," Benna mumbled through greatly swollen lips. "I'm dying. The pain is terrible, Masha."

"Keep going!" she said fiercely. "We're almost there!"

Benna raised his head. His eyes were surrounded with puffed-out flesh. Masha had never seen such edema; the blackness and the swelling looked like those of a corpse five days dead in the heat of summer.

"No!" he mumbled. "Not old Lahboo's building!"

3

Under other circumstances, Masha would have laughed. Here was a dying man or a man who thought he was dying. And he'd be dead soon if his pursuers caught up with him. (Me, too, she thought.) Yet he was afraid to take the only refuge available because of a ghost.

"You look bad enough to scare even the Tight-Fisted One," she said. "Keep going or I'll drop you right now!"

She got him inside the doorway, though it wasn't easy what with the boards still attached to the lower half of the entrance. The top planks had fallen inside. It was a tribute to the fear people felt for this place that no one had stolen the wood, an expensive item in the desert town.

Just after they'd climbed over, Benna almost falling, she heard a man utter something in the raspy tearing language. He was nearby, but he must have just arrived. Otherwise, he would have heard the two.

Masha had thought she'd reached the limits of terror, but she found that she hadn't. The speaker was a Raggah!

Though she couldn't understand the speech—no one in Sanctuary could—she'd heard Raggah a number of times. Every thirty days or so five or six of the cloaked, robed, hooded, and veiled desert men came to the bazaar and the farmers' market. They could speak only their own language, but they used signs and a plentitude of coins to obtain what they wanted. Then they departed on their horses, their mules loaded down with food, wine, *vuksibah* (the very expensive malt whiskey imported from a far north land), goods of various kinds: clothing, bowls, braziers, ropes, camel and horse hides. Their camels bore huge panniers of feed for chickens, ducks, camels, horses, and hogs. They also purchased steel tools: shovels, picks, drills, hammers, wedges.

They were tall, and though they were very dark, most had blue or green eyes. These looked cold and hard and piercing, and few looked directly into them. It was said that they had the gift, or the curse, of the evil eye.

They were enough, in this dark night, to have made Masha marble with terror. But what was worse, and this galvanized the marble, they were the servants of the purple mage!

Masha guessed at once what had happened. Benna had had the guts—and the complete stupidity—to sneak into the underground maze of the mage on the river isle of Shugthee and to steal a jewel. It was amazing that he'd had the courage, astounding that he could get undetected into the caves, an absolute wonder that he'd penetrated the treasure hold, and fantastic that he'd managed to get out. What weird tales he could tell if he survived! Masha could think of no similar event, no analogue, to the adventures he must have had.

"*Mofandsf!*" she thought. In the thieves' argot of Sanctuary, "Mindboggling!"

At that moment Benna's knees gave, and it was all she could do to hold him up. Somehow, she got him to the door to the next room and into a closet. If the Raggah came in, they would look here, of course, but she could get him no further.

Benna's odor was even more sickening in the hot confines of the closet, though its door was almost completely open. She eased him down. He mumbled, "Spiders . . . spiders."

She put her mouth close to his ear. "Don't talk loudly, Benna. The Raggah are close by. Benna, what did you say about the spiders?"

"Bites . . . bites," he murmured. "Hurt . . . the . . . the emerald . . . rich . . . !"

"How'd you get in?" she said. She put her hand close to his mouth to clamp down on it if he should start to talk loudly.

"Wha . . . ? Camel's eye . . . bu . . ."

He stiffened, the heels of his feet striking the bottom of the closet door. Masha pressed her hand down on his mouth. She was afraid that he might cry out in his death agony. If this were it. And it was. He groaned, and then relaxed. Masha took her hand away. A long sigh came from his open mouth.

She looked around the edge of the closet. Though it was dark outside, it was brighter than the darkness in the house. She should be able to make out anyone standing in the doorway. The noise the heels made could have attracted the hunters. She saw no one, though it was possible that someone had already come in and was against a wall. Listening for more noise.

She felt Benna's pulse. He was dead or so close to it that it didn't matter anymore. She rose and slowly pulled her dagger from the scabbard. Then she stepped out, crouching, sure that the thudding of her heart could be heard in this still room.

So unexpectedly and suddenly that a soft cry was forced from her, a whistle sounded outside. Feet pounded in the room—there *was* someone here!—and the dim rectangle of the doorway showed a bulk plunging through it. But it was going out, not in. The Raggah had heard the whistle of the garrison soldiers—half the city must have heard it—and he was leaving with his fellows.

She turned and bent down and searched under Benna's tunic and in his loincloth. She found nothing except slowly cooling lumpy flesh. Within ten seconds, she was out on the street. Down a block was the advancing light of torches, their holders not yet visible. In the din of shouts and whistles, she fled hoping that she wouldn't run into any laggard Raggah or another body of soldiers.

Later, she found out that she'd been saved because the soldiers were looking for a prisoner who'd escaped from the dungeon. His name was Badniss, but that's another tale.

4

Masha's two-room apartment was on the third floor of a large adobe building which, with two others, occupied an entire block. She entered it on the side of the Street of the Dry Well, but first she had to wake up old Shmurt, the caretaker, by beating on the thick oaken door. Grumbling at the late hour, he unshot the bolt and let her in. She gave him a *padpool*, a tiny copper coin, for his trouble and to shut him up. He handed her her oil lamp, she lit it, and she went up the three flights of stone steps.

She had to wake up her mother to get in. Wallu, blinking and yawning in the light of an oil lamp in the corner, shot the bolt. Masha entered and at once extinguished her lamp. Oil cost money, and there had been many nights when she had had to do without it.

Wallu, a tall skinny sagging-breasted woman of fifty, with gaunt deeply lined features, kissed her daughter on the cheek. Her breath was sour with sleep and goat's cheese. But Masha appreciated the peck; her life had few expressions of love in it. And yet she was full of it; she was a bottle close to bursting with pressure.

The light on the rickety table in the corner showed a blank-walled room without rugs. In a far corner the two infants slept on a pile of tattered but clean blankets. Beside them was a small chamber pot of baked clay painted with the black and scarlet rings-within-rings of the Darmek guild.

In another corner was her false-teeth-making equipment, wax, molds, tiny chisels, saws, and expensive wire, hardwood, iron, a block of ivory. She had only recently repaid the money she'd borrowed to purchase these. In the opposite corner was another pile of cloth, Wallu's bed, and beside it another thundermug with the same design. An ancient and wobbly spinning wheel was near it; Wallu made some money with it, though not much. Her hands were gnarled with arthritis, one eye had a cataract, and the other was beginning to lose its sight for some unknown reason.

Along the adobe wall was a brass charcoal brazier and above it a wooden vent. A bin held charcoal. A big cabinet beside it held grain and some dried meat and plates and knives. Near it was a baked clay vase for water. Next to it was a pile of cloths.

Wallu pointed at the curtain in the doorway to the other room.

"He came home early. I suppose he couldn't cadge drinks enough from his friends. But he's drunk enough to suit a dozen sailors."

Grimacing, Masha strode to the curtain and pulled it aside.

"*Shewaw!*" (A combination of "Whew!," "Ugh," and "Yech!")

The stink was that which greeted her nostrils when she opened the door to the Vulgar Unicorn tavern. A blend of wine and beer, stale and fresh, sweat, stale and fresh, vomit, urine, frying blood sausages, *krrf*, and *kleetel*.

Eevroen lay on his back, his mouth open, his arms spread out as if he were being crucified. Once, he had been a tall muscular youth, very broad-shouldered, slim-waisted, and long-legged. Now he was fat, fat, fat, double-chinned, huge-paunched with rings of sagging fat around his waist. The once bright eyes were red and dark-bagged, and the once-sweet breath was a hell pit of stenches. He'd fallen asleep without changing into nightclothes; his tunic was ripped, dirty, and stained with various things, including puke. He wore cast-off sandals, or perhaps he'd stolen them.

Masha was long past weeping over him. She kicked him in the ribs, causing him to grunt and to open one eye. But it closed and he was quickly snoring like a pig again. That, at least, was a blessing. How many nights had she spent in screaming at him while he bellowed at her or in fighting him off when he staggered home and insisted she lie with him? She didn't want to count them.

Masha would have gotten rid of him long ago if she had been able to. But the law of the empire was that only the man could divorce unless the woman could prove her spouse was too diseased to have children or was impotent.

She whirled and walked toward the washbasin. As she passed her mother, a hand stopped her.

Wallu, peering at her with one half-good eye, said, "Child! Something has happened to you! What was it?"

"Tell you in a moment," Masha said, and she washed her face and hands and armpits. Later, she regretted very much that she hadn't told Wallu a lie. But how was she to know that Eevroen had come out of his stupor enough to hear what she said? If only she hadn't been so furious that she'd kicked him . . . but regrets were a waste of time, though there wasn't a human alive who didn't indulge in them.

She had no sooner finished telling her mother what had happened with Benna when she heard a grunt behind her. She turned to see Eevroen swaying in front of the curtains, a stupid grin on his fat face. The face once so beloved.

Eevroen reeled toward her, his hands out as if he intended to grab her. He spoke thickly but intelligibly enough.

"Why'n't you go after the rat? If you caught it, we coulda been rich?"

"Go back to sleep," Masha said. "This has nothing to do with you."

"Nothin' do wi' me?" Eevroen bellowed. "Wha' you mean? I'm your husband! Wha'ss yoursh ish mine. I wan' tha' jewel!"

"You damned fool," Masha said, trying to keep from screaming so that the children wouldn't wake and the neighbors wouldn't hear, "I don't have the jewel. There was no way I could get it—if there ever was any."

Eevroen put a finger alongside his nose and winked the left eye. "If there wa' ever any, heh? Masha, you tryna hoi' ou' on me? You go' the jewel, and you lyin' to you' mo . . . mo . . . mama."

"No, I'm not lying!" she screamed, all reason for caution having deserted her quite unreasonably. "You fat stinking pig! I've had a terrible time, I almost got killed, and all you can think about is the jewel! Which probably doesn't exist! Benna was dying! He didn't know what he was talking about! I never saw the jewel! And . . ."

Eevroen snarled, "You tryn'a keep i' from me!" and he charged her.

She could easily have evaded him, but something swelled up in her and took over, and she seized a baked-clay water jug from a shelf and brought it down hard over his head. The jug didn't break, but Eevroen did. He fell face-forward. Blood welled from his scalp; he snored.

By then the children were awake, sitting up, wide-eyed, but silent. Maze children learned at an early age not to cry easily.

Shaking, Masha got down on her knees and examined the wound. Then she rose and went to the rag rack and returned with some dirty ones, no use wasting clean ones on him, and stanched the wound. She felt his pulse; it was beating steadily enough for a drunkard who'd just been knocked out with a severe blow.

Wallu said, "Is he dead?"

She wasn't concerned about him. She was worrying about herself, the children, and Masha. If her daughter should be executed for killing her husband, however justified she was, then she and the girls would be without support.

"He'll have a hell of a headache in the morning," Masha said. With some difficulty, she rolled Eevroen over so that he would be facedown, and she turned his head sideways and then put some rags under the side of his head: Now, if he should vomit during the night, he wouldn't choke to death. For a moment she was tempted to put him back as he had fallen. But the judge might think that she was responsible for his death.

"Let him lie there," she said. "I'm not going to break my back dragging him to our bed. Besides, I wouldn't be able to sleep, he snores so loudly and he stinks so badly."

She should have been frightened of what he'd do in the morning. But, strangely, she felt exuberant. She'd done what she'd wanted to do for several years now, and the deed had discharged much of her anger—for the time being, anyway.

She went to her room and tossed and turned for a while, thinking of how much better life would be if she could get rid of Eevroen.

Her last thoughts were of what life could be if she'd gotten the jewel that Benna had thrown to the rat.

5

She awoke an hour or so past dawn, a very late time for her, and smelled bread baking. After she'd sat on the chamber pot she rose and pushed the curtain aside. She was curious about the lack of noise in the next room. Eevroen was gone. So were the children. Wallu, hearing the little bells on the curtain, turned.

"I sent the children out to play," she said. "Eevroen woke up about dawn. He pretended he didn't know what had happened, but I could tell that he did. He groaned now and then—his head I suppose. He ate some breakfast, and then he got out fast."

Wallu smiled. "I think he's afraid of you."

"Good!" Masha said. "I hope he keeps on being afraid."

She sat down while Wallu, hobbling around, served her a half loaf of bread, a hunk of goat cheese, and an orange. Masha wondered if her husband also remembered what she'd said to her mother about Benna and the jewel.

He had.

When she went to the bazaar, carrying the folding chair in which she put her dental patients, she was immediately surrounded by hundreds of men and women. All wanted to know about the jewel.

Masha thought, The damn fool!

Eevroen, it seemed, had procured free drinks with his tale. He'd staggered around everywhere, the taverns, the bazaar, the farmers' market, the waterfront, and he'd spread the news. Apparently, he didn't say anything about Masha's knocking him out. That tale would have earned him only derision, and he still had enough manhood left not to reveal that. At first, Masha was going to deny the story. But it seemed to her that most people would think she was lying, and they would be sure that she had kept the jewel. Her life would be miserable from then on. Or ended. There were plenty who wouldn't hesitate to drag her off to some secluded place and torture her until she told where the jewel was.

So she described exactly what had happened, omitting how she had tried to brain Eevroen. There was no sense in pushing him too hard. If he was humiliated publicly, he might get desperate enough to try to beat her up.

She got only one patient that day. As fast as those who'd heard her tale ran off to look for rats, others took their place. And then, inevitably, the governor's soldiers came. She was surprised they hadn't appeared sooner. Surely one of their informants had sped to the palace as soon as he had heard her story, and that would have been shortly after she'd come to the bazaar.

The sergeant of the soldiers questioned her first, and then she was marched to the garrison, where a captain interrogated her. Afterward, a colonel came in, and she had to repeat her tale. And then, after sitting in a room for at least two hours, she was taken to the governor himself. The handsome youth, surprisingly, didn't detain her long. He seemed to have checked out her movements, starting with Doctor Nadeesh. He'd worked out a timetable between the moment she left Shoozh's house and the moment she came home. So, her mother had also been questioned.

A soldier had seen two of the Raggah running away; their presence was verified.

"Well, Masha," the governor said, "you've stirred up a rat's nest," and he smiled at his own joke while the soldiers and courtiers laughed.

"There is no evidence that there was any jewel," he said, "aside from the story this Benna told, and he was dying from venom and in great pain. My doctor has examined his body, and he assures me that the swellings were spider bites. Of course, he doesn't know everything. He's been wrong before.

"But people are going to believe that there was indeed a jewel of great value, and nothing anyone says, including myself, will convince them otherwise.

"However, all their frantic activity will result in one great benefit. We'll be rid of the rats for a while."

He paused, frowning, then said, "It would seem, however, that this fellow Benna might have been foolish enough to steal something from the purple mage. I would think that that is the only reason he'd be pursued by the Raggah. But then there might be another reason. In any event, if there is a jewel, then the finder is going to be in great peril. The mage isn't going to let whoever finds it keep it.

"Or at least I believe so. Actually, I know very little about the mage, and from what I've heard about him, I have no desire to meet him."

Masha thought of asking him why he didn't send his soldiers out to the isle and summon the mage. But she kept silent. The reason was obvious. No one, not even the governor, wanted to provoke the wrath of a mage. And as long as the mage did nothing to force the governor into action, he would be left strictly alone to conduct his business—whatever that was.

At the end of the questioning, the governor told his treasurer to give a gold *sheboozh* to Masha.

"That should more than take care of any business you've lost by being here," the governor said.

Thanking him profusely, Masha bowed as she stepped back, and then walked swiftly homeward.

The following week was the great cat hunt. It was also featured, for Masha anyway, by a break-in to her apartment. While she was off helping deliver a baby at the home of the merchant Ahloo shik-Mhanukhee, three masked men knocked old Shmurt the doorkeeper out and broke down the door to her rooms. While the girls and her mother cowered in a corner, the three ransacked the place, even emptying the chamber pots on the floor to determine that nothing was hidden there.

They didn't find what they were looking for, and one of the frustrated interlopers knocked out two of Wallu's teeth in a rage. Masha was thankful, however, that they did not beat or rape the little girls. That may have been not so much because of their mercifulness as that the door-keeper woke up sooner than they had expected. He began yelling for help, and the three thugs ran away before the neighbors could gather or the soldiers come.

Eevroen continued to come in drunk late at night. But he spoke very little, just using the place to eat and sleep. In fact he seemed to be doing his best to avoid her. That was fine with her.

6

Several times, both by day and night, Masha felt someone was following her. She did her best to detect the shadower, but whether she got the feeling by day or night, she failed to do it. She decided that her nervous state was responsible.

Then the great dog hunt began. Masha thought this was the apex of hysteria and silliness. But it worried her. After all the poor dogs were gone what would next be run down and killed and gutted? To be more precise, who? She hoped that the who wouldn't be she.

In the middle of the week of the dog hunt, little Kheem became sick. Masha had to go to work, but when she came home after sundown, she found that Kheem was suffering from a high fever. According to her mother, Kheem had also had convulsions. Alarmed, Masha set out at once for Doctor Nadeesh's house in the eastern quarter. He admitted her and listened to her describe Kheem's symptoms. But he refused to accompany her to her house.

"It's too dangerous to go into the Maze at night," he said. "And I wouldn't go there in the day unless I had several bodyguards. Besides I am having company tonight. You should have brought the child here."

"She's too sick to be moved," Masha said. "I beg you to come."

Nadeesh was adamant, but he did give her some powders which she could use to cool the child's fever.

She thanked him audibly and cursed him silently. On the way back, while only a block from her apartment, she heard a sudden thud of foot-steps behind her. She jumped to one side and whirled, drawing her dag-ger at the same time. There was no moon, and the nearest light was from oil lamps shining through some iron-barred windows in the second story above her.

By its faintness she saw a dark bulk. It was robed and hooded, a man by its tallness. Then she heard a low hoarse curse and knew it was a man. He had thought to grab or strike her from behind, but Masha's unexpected leap had saved her. Momentarily, at least. Now the man rushed her, and she glimpsed something long and dark in his uplifted hand. A club.

Instead of standing there frozen with fear or trying to run away, she crouched low and charged him. That took him by surprise. Before he could recover, he was struck in the throat with her blade.

Still, his body knocked her down, and he fell hard upon her. For a moment, the breath was knocked out of her. She was helpless, and when another bulk loomed above her, she knew that she had no chance.

The second man, also robed and hooded, lifted a club to bring it down on her exposed head.

Writhing, pinned down by the corpse, Masha could do nothing but await the blow. She thought briefly of little Kheem, and then she saw the man drop the club. And he was down on his knees, still gripping whatever it was that had closed off his breath.

A moment later, he was facedown in the dry dirt, dead or unconscious.

The man standing over the second attacker was short and broad and also robed and hooded. He put something in his pocket, probably the cord he'd used to strangle her attacker, and he approached her cautiously. His hands seemed to be empty, however.

"Masha?" he said softly.

By then she'd recovered her wind. She wriggled out from under the dead man, jerked the dagger from the windpipe, and started to get up.

The man said, in a foreign accent, "You can put your knife away, my dear. I didn't save you just to kill you."

"I thank you, stranger," she said, "but keep your distance anyway."

Despite the warning, he took two steps toward her. Then she knew who he was. No one else in Sanctuary stank so of rancid butter.

"Smhee," she said, equally softly.

He chuckled. "I know you can't see my face. So, though it's against my religious convictions, I will have to take a bath and quit smearing my body and hair with butter. I am as silent as a shadow, but what good is that talent when anyone can smell me a block away?"

Keeping her eyes on him, she stopped and cleaned her dagger on the dead man's robe.

"Are you the one who's been following me?" she said. She straightened up.

He hissed with surprise, then said, "You saw me?"

"No. But I knew someone was dogging me."

"Ah! You have a sixth sense. Or a guilty conscience. Come! Let's get away before someone comes along."

"I'd like to know who these men are . . . were."

"They're Raggah," Smhee said. "There are two others fifty yards from here, lookouts, I suppose. They'll be coming soon to find out why these two haven't shown up with you."

That shocked her even more than the attack.

"You mean the purple mage wants me? Why?"

"I do not know. Perhaps he thinks as so many others do. That is, that Benna told you more than you have said he did. But come! Quickly!"

"Where?"

"To your place. We can talk there, can't we?"

They walked swiftly toward her building. Smhee kept looking back, but the place where they had killed the two men was no longer visible. When they got to the door, however, she stopped.

"If I knock on the door for the keeper, the Raggah might hear it," she whispered. "But I have to get in. My daughter is very sick. She needs the medicine I got from Doctor Nadeesh."

"So that's why you were at his home," Smhee said. "Very well. You bang on the door. I'll be the rear guard."

He was suddenly gone, moving astonishingly swift and silently for such a fat man. But his aroma lingered.

She did as he suggested, and presently Shmurt came grumbling to the door and unbolted it. Just as she stepped in she smelled the butter more strongly, and Smhee was inside and pushing the door shut before the startled doorkeeper could protest.

"He's all right," Masha said.

Old Shmurt peered with runny eyes at Smhee by the light of his oil lamp. Even with good vision, however, Shmurt couldn't see Smhee's face. It was covered with a green mask.

Shmurt looked disgusted.

"I know your husband isn't much," he croaked. "But taking up with this foreigner, this tub of rotten butter . . . *shewaw*!"

"It's not what you think," she said indignantly.

Smhee said, "I *must* take a bath. Everyone knows me at once."

"Is Eevroen home?" Masha said. Shmurt snorted and said, "At this early hour? No, you and your stinking lover will be safe."

"Dammit!" Masha said. "He's here on business!"

"Some business!"

"Mind your tongue, you old fart!" Masha said. "Or I'll cut it out!"

Shmurt slammed the door to his room behind him. He called, "Whore! Slut! Adulteress!"

Masha shrugged, lit her lamp, and went up the steps with Smhee close behind her. Wallu looked very surprised when the fat man came in with her daughter.

"Who is this?"

"Someone *can't* identify me?" Smhee said. "Does she have a dead nose?"

He removed his mask.

"She doesn't get out much," Masha said. She hurried to Kheem, who lay sleeping on her rag pile. Smhee took off his cloak, revealing thin arms and legs and a body like a ball of cheese. His shirt and vest, made of some velvety material speckled with glittering sequins, clung tightly to his trunk. A broad leather belt encircled his paunch, and attached to it were two scabbards containing knives, a third from which poked the end of a bamboo pipe, and a leather bag about the size of Masha's head. Over one shoulder and the side of his neck was coiled a thin rope.

"Tools of the trade," he said in answer to Masha's look.

Masha wondered what the trade was, but she didn't have time for him. She felt Kheem's forehead and pulse, then went to the water pitcher on the ledge in the corner.

After mixing the powder with the water as Nadeesh had instructed and pouring out some into a large spoon, she turned. Smhee was on his knees by the child and reaching into the bag on his belt.

"I have some talent for doctoring," he said as she came to his side. "Here. Put that quack's medicine away and use this."

He stood up and held out a small leather envelope. She just looked at him.

"Yes, I know you don't want to take a chance with a stranger. But please believe me. This green powder is a thousand times better than that placebo Nadeesh gave you. If it doesn't cure the child, I'll cut my throat. I promise you."

"Much good that'd do the baby," Wallu said.

"Is it a magical potion?" Masha said.

"No. Magic might relieve the symptoms, but the disease would still be there, and when the magic wore off, the sickness would return. Here. Take it! I don't want you two to say a word about it, ever, but I was once trained in the art of medicine. And where I come from, a doctor is twenty times superior to any you'll find in Sanctuary."

Masha studied his dark shiny face. He looked as if he might be about forty years old. The high broad forehead, the long straight nose, the well-shaped mouth would have made him handsome if his cheeks weren't so thick and his jowls so baggy. Despite his fatness, he looked intelligent; the black eyes below the thick bushy eyebrows were keen and lively.

"I can't afford to experiment with Kheem," she said.

He smiled, perhaps an acknowledgment that he detected the uncertainty in her voice. "You can't afford not to," he said. "If you don't use this, your child will die. And the longer you hesitate, the closer she gets to death. Every second counts."

Masha took the envelope and returned to the water pitcher. She set the spoon down without spilling its contents and began working as Smhee called out to her his instructions. He stayed with Kheem, one hand on her forehead, the other on her chest. Kheem breathed rapidly and shallowly.

Wallu protested. Masha told her to shut up more harshly than she'd intended. Wallu bit her lip and glared at Smhee.

Kheem was propped up by Smhee, and Masha got her to swallow the greenish water. Ten minutes or so later, the fever began to go down. An hour later, according to the sandglass, she was given another spoonful. By dawn, she seemed to be rid of it, and she was sleeping peacefully.

7

Meantime, Masha and Smhee talked in low tones. Wallu had gone to bed, but not to sleep, shortly before sunrise. Eevroen had not appeared. Probably he was sleeping off his liquor in an empty crate on the wharf or in some doorway. Masha was glad. She had been prepared to break another basin over his head if he made a fuss and disturbed Kheem.

Though she had seen the fat little man a number of times, she did not know much about him. Nobody else did either. It was certain that he had first appeared in Sanctuary six weeks (sixty days) ago. A merchant ship of the Banmalts people had brought him, but this indicated little about his origin since the ship ported at many lands and islands.

Smhee had quickly taken a room on the second floor of a building, the first of which was occupied by the Khabeeber or "Diving Bird" Tavern. (The proprietor had jocularly named it thus because he claimed that his customers dived as deeply into alcohol for surcease as the *khabeeber* did into the ocean for fish.) He did no work nor was he known to thieve or mug. He seemed to have enough money for his purposes, whatever they were, but then he lived frugally. Because he smeared his body and hair with rancid butter, he was called "the Stinking Butterball" or "Old Rotten," though not to his face. He spent time in all the taverns and also was often seen in the farmers' market and the bazaar. As far as was known, he had shown no sexual interest in men or women or children. Or, as one wag put it, "not even in goats."

His religion was unknown though it was rumored that he kept an idol in a small wooden case in his room.

Now, sitting on the floor by Kheem, making the child drink water every half-hour, Masha questioned Smhee. And he in turn questioned her.

"You've been following me around," Masha said. "Why?"

"I've also investigated other women."

"You didn't say why."

"One answer at a time. I have something to do here, and I need a woman to help me. She has to be quick and strong and very brave and intelligent. And desperate."

He looked around the room as if anybody who lived in it had to be desperate indeed.

"I know your history," he said. "You came from a fairly well-to-do family, and as a child you lived in the eastern quarter. You were not born and bred in the Maze, and you want to get out of it. You've worked hard, but you just are not going to succeed in your ambition. Not unless something unusual comes your way and you have the courage to seize it, no matter what the consequences might be."

"This has to do with Benna and the jewel, doesn't it?" she said.

He studied her face by the flickering light of the lamp.

"Yes."

He paused.

"And the purple mage."

Masha sucked in a deep breath. Her heart thudded far more swiftly than her fatigue could account for. A coldness spread from her toes to the top of her head, a not unpleasant coldness.

"I've watched in the shadows near your building," he said. "Many a night. And two nights ago I saw the Raggah steal into other shadows and watch the same window. Fortunately, you did not go out during that time to midwife. But tonight . . ."

"Why would the Raggah be interested in me?"

He smiled slowly.

"You're smart enough to guess why. The mage thinks you know more than you let on about the jewel. Or perhaps he thinks Benna told you more than you've repeated."

He paused again, then said, "Did he?"

"Why should I tell you if he did?"

"You owe me for your life. If that isn't enough to make you confide in me, consider this. I have a plan whereby you cannot only be free of the Maze, you can be richer than any merchant, perhaps richer than the governor himself. You will even be able to leave Sanctuary, to go to the capital city itself. Or anywhere in the world."

She thought, If Benna could do it, we can.

But then Benna had not gotten away.

She said, "Why do you need a woman? Why not another man?"

Smhee was silent for a long time. Evidently, he was wondering just how much he should tell her. Suddenly, he smiled, and something invisible, an unseen weight seemed to fall from him. Somehow, he even looked thinner.

"I've gone this far," he said. "So I must go all the way. No backing out now. The reason I must have a woman is that the mage's sorcery has a weakness. His magical defenses will be set up to repel men. He will not have prepared them against women. It would not occur to him that a woman would try to steal his treasure. Or . . . kill him."

"How do you know that?"

"I don't think it would be wise to tell you that now. You must take my word for it. I do know far more about the purple mage than anyone else in Sanctuary."

"You might, and that still wouldn't be much," she said.

"Let me put it another way. I do know much about him. More than enough to make me a great danger to him."

"Does he know much about you?"

Smhee smiled again. "He doesn't know I'm here. If he did, I'd be dead by now."

They talked until dawn, and by then Masha was deeply committed. If she failed, then her fate would be horrible. And the lives of her daughters and her mother would become even worse. Far worse. But if she continued as she had, she would be dooming them anyway. She might die of a fever or be killed, and then they would have no supporter and defender.

Anyway, as Smhee pointed out, though he didn't need to, the mage was after her. Her only defense was a quick offense. She had no other choice except to wait like a dumb sheep and be slaughtered. Except that, in this situation, the sheep would be tortured before being killed.

Smhee knew what he was saying when he had said that she was desperate.

8

When the wolf's tail, the false dawn, came, she rose stiffly and went through to her room and looked out the window. Not surprisingly, the corpses of the Raggah were gone.

Shortly thereafter, Kheem awoke, bright-eyed, and asked for food. Masha covered her with kisses, and, weeping joyfully, prepared breakfast. Smhee left. He would be back before noon. But he gave her five *shaboozh* and some lesser coin. Masha wakened her mother, gave her the money, and told her that she would be gone for a few days. Wallu wanted to question her, but Masha told her sternly that she would be better off if she knew no more than she did now.

"If Eevroen wants to know where I am, tell him that I have been called to help deliver a rich farmer's baby. If he asks for the man's name, tell him it is Shkeedur sha-Mizl. He lives far out and only comes into town twice a year except on special business. It doesn't matter that it's a lie. By the time I get back—it'll be soon—we'll be leaving at once. Have everything we'll need for a long journey packed into that bag. Just clothes and eating utensils and the medicine. If Kheem has a relapse, give her Smhee's powders."

Wallu wailed then, and Masha had to quiet her down.

"Hide the money. No! Leave one *shaboozh* where Eevroen will find it when he looks for money. Conceal the rest where he can't find it. He'll take the *shaboozh* and go out to drink, and you won't be bothered with him or his questions."

When the flaming brass bowl of the noon sun had reached its apex, Smhee came. His eyes looked very red, but he didn't act fatigued. He carried a carpet bag from which he produced two dark cloaks, two robes, and the masks which the priests of Shalpa wore in public.

He said, "How did you get rid of your mother and the children?"

"A neighbor is keeping the children until Mother gets back from shopping," she said. "Eevroen still hasn't shown up."

"Nor will he for a long time," Smhee said. "I dropped a coin as I passed him staggering this way. He snatched it, of course, and ran off to a tavern.

"The *Sailfish* will be leaving port in three days. I've arranged for passage on her and also to be hidden aboard her if her departure is delayed. I've been very busy all morning."

"Including taking a bath," she said.

"You don't smell too good yourself," he said. "But you can bathe when we get to the river. Put these on."

She went into her room, removed her clothes, and donned the priest's garb. When she came out, Smhee was fully dressed. The bag attached to his belt bulged beneath his cloak.

"Give me your old clothes," he said. "We'll cache them outside the city, though I don't think we'll be needing them."

She did so, and he stuffed them into the belt bag.

"Let's go," he said.

She didn't follow him to the door. He turned and said, "What's the matter? Your liver getting cold?"

"No," she said. "Only . . . Mother's very shortsighted. I'm afraid she'll be cheated when she buys the food."

He laughed and said something in a foreign tongue.

"For the sake of Igil! When we return, we'll have enough to buy out the farmers' market a thousand times over!"

"If we get back . . ." she murmured. She wanted to go to Looza's room and kiss the children goodbye. But that was not wise. Besides, she might lose her determination if she saw them now.

They walked out while old Shmurt stared. He was the weakest point in their alibi, but they hoped they wouldn't need any. At the moment, he was too dumbfounded at seeing them to say anything. And he would be afraid to go to the soldiers about this. He probably was thinking that two priests had magically entered the house, and it would be indiscreet to interfere in their business.

Thirty minutes later, they mounted the two horses which Smhee had arranged to be tied to a tree outside city limits.

"Weren't you afraid they'd be stolen?" she said.

"There are two stout fellows hidden in the grass near the river," he said. He waved toward it, and she saw two men came from it. They waved back and started to walk back to the city.

There was a rough road along the White Foal River, sometimes coming near the stream, sometimes bending far away. They rode over it for three hours, and then Smhee said, "There's an old adobe building a quarter-mile inland. We'll sleep there for a while. I don't know about you, but I'm weary."

She was glad to rest. After hobbling the horses near a stand of the tall brown desert grass, they lay down in the midst of the ruins. Smhee went to sleep at once. She worried about her family for a while, and suddenly she was being shaken by Smhee. Dawn was coming up.

They ate some dried meat and bread and fruit and then mounted again. After watering the horses and themselves at the river, they rode at a canter for three more hours. And then Smhee pulled up on the reins. He pointed at the trees a quarter-mile inland. Beyond, rearing high, were the towering cliffs on the other side of the river. The trees on this side, however, prevented them from seeing the White Foal.

"The boat's hidden in there," he said. "Unless someone's stolen it. That's not likely, though. Very few people have the courage to go near the Isle of Shugthee."

"What about the hunters who bring down the furs from the north?"

"They hug the eastern shore, and they only go by in daylight. Fast."

They crossed the rocky ground, passing some low-growing purplish bushes and some irontrees with grotesquely twisted branches. A rabbit with long ears dashed by them, causing her horse to rear up. She controlled it, though she had not been on a horse since she was eleven. Smhee said that he was glad that it hadn't been his beast. All he knew about riding was the few lessons he'd taken from a farmer after coming to Sanctuary. He'd be happy if he never had to get on another one.

The trees were perhaps fifteen or twenty deep from the river's edge.

They dismounted, removed the saddles, and hobbled the beasts again. Then they walked through the tall canelike plants, brushing away the flies and other pestiferous insects, until they got to the stream itself. Here grew stands of high reeds, and on a hummock of spongy earth was Smhee's boat. It was a dugout which could hold only two.

"Stole it," Smhee said without offering any details.

She looked through the reeds down the river. About a quarter of a mile away, the river broadened to become a lake about two and a half miles across. In its center was the Isle of Shugthee, a purplish mass of rock. From this distance, she could not make out its details.

Seeing it, she felt coldness ripple over her.

"I'd like to take a whole day and a night to scout it," he said. "So you could become familiar with it, too. But we don't have time. However, I can tell you everything I know. I wish I knew more."

She doffed her clothes and bathed in the river while Smhee unhobbled the horses and took them some distance up, to let them drink. When she came back, she found him just returning with them.

"Before dusk comes, we'll have to move them down to a point opposite the isle," he said. "And we'll saddle them, too."

They left the horses to go to a big boulder outside the trees but distant from the road. At its base was a hollow large enough for them to lie down in. Here they slept, waking now and then to talk softly or to eat a bite or to go behind the rock and urinate. The insects weren't so numerous here as in the trees, but they were bad enough.

Not once, as far as they knew, did anyone pass on the road.

When they walked the horses down the road, Smhee said, "You've been very good about not asking questions, but I can see you're about to explode with curiosity. You have no idea who the purple mage really is. Not unless you know more than the other Sancturites."

"All I know," she said, "is that they say that the mage came here about ten years ago. He came with some hired servants, and many boxes, some small, some large. No one knew what his native land was, and he didn't stay long in town. One day he disappeared with the servants and the boxes. It was some time before people found out that he'd moved into the caves of the Isle of Shugthee. Nobody had ever gone there because it was said that it was haunted by the ghosts of the Shugthee. They were a little hairy people who inhabited this land long before the first city of the ancients was built here."

"How do you know he's a mage?" Smhee said.

"I don't, but everybody says he is. Isn't he?"

"He is," Smhee said, looking grim.

"Anyway. He sent his servants in now and then to buy cattle, goats, pigs, chickens, horses, vegetables, and animal feed and fruit. These were men and women from some distant land. Not from his, though. And then one day they ceased coming in. Instead, the Raggah came. From that day on, no one has seen the servants who came with the mage."

"He probably got rid of them," Smhee said. "He may have found some reason to distrust them. Or no reason at all."

"The fur trappers and hunters who've gone by the isle say they've seen some strange things. Hairy beast-faced dwarfs. Giant spiders."

She shuddered.

"Benna died of spider bites," Smhee said.

The fat little man reached into his belt bag and brought out a metal jar. He said, "Before we leave in the boat tonight we'll rub the ointment in this on us. It will repel some of the spiders but not, unfortunately, all."

"How do you know that?"

"I know."

They walked silently for a while. Then he sighed, and said, "We'll get bitten. That is certain. Only . . . all the spiders that will bite us—I hope so, anyway—won't be real spiders. They'll be products of the mage's magic. Apparitions. But apparitions that can kill you just as quickly or as slowly and usually as painfully as the real spiders."

He paused, then said, "Benna probably died from their bites."

Masha felt as if she were turning white under her dark skin. She put her hands on his arm.

"But . . . but . . . !"

"Yes, I know. If the spiders were not real, then why should they harm him? That is because he thought they were real. His mind did the rest to him."

She didn't like that she couldn't keep her voice from shaking, but she couldn't help it.

"How can you tell which is real and which magical?"

"In the daylight the unreal spiders look a little transparent. By that I mean that if they stand still, you can see dimly through them. But then they don't stand still much. And we'll be in the dark of night. So . . .

"Look here, Masha. You have to be strong stuff to go there. You have to overcome your fear. A person who lets fear conquer him or her is going to die even if he knows that the spider is unreal. He'll make the sting of the bite himself and the effects of the venom. And he'll kill himself. I've seen it happen in my native land."

"But you say that we might get bitten by a real spider. How can I tell which is which in the dark?"

"It's a problem."

He added after a few seconds, "The ointment should repulse most of the real spiders. Maybe, if we're lucky. You see, we have an advantage that Benna didn't have. I know what faces us because I come from the mage's land. His true name is Kemren, and he brought with him the real spiders and some other equally dangerous creatures. They would have been in some of the boxes. I am prepared for them, and so will you be. Benna wasn't, and any of these Sanctuary thieves will get the same fate."

Masha asked why Kemren had come here. Smhee chewed on his lower lip for a while before answering.

"You may as well know it all. Kemren was a priest of the goddess Weda Krizhtawn of the island of Sherranpip. That is far east and south of here, though you may have heard of it. We are a people of the water, of lakes, rivers, and the sea. Weda Krizhtawn is the chief goddess of water, and she has a mighty temple with many treasures near the sea.

"Kemren was one of the higher priests, and he served her well for years. In return, he was admitted into the inner circle of mages and taught both black and white magic. Though, actually, there is little difference between the two branches, the main distinction being whether the magician uses his powers for good or evil.

"And it isn't always easy to tell what is good and what is evil. If a mage makes a mistake, and his use turns out to be for evil, even if he sincerely thought it was for good, then there is a . . . backlash. And the mage's character becomes changed for the worse in proportion to the amount of magical energy used."

He stopped walking.

"We're opposite the isle now."

It wasn't visible from the road. The plain sloped upward from the road, becoming a high ridge near the river, where tall spreading blackish *hukharran* bush grew on top of it. They walked the horses up the ridge, where they hobbled them near a pool of rainwater. The beasts began cropping the long brownish grass that grew among the bushes.

The isle was in the center of the lake and seemed to be composed mostly of a purplish rock. It sloped gently from the shore until near the middle, where a series of peculiar formations formed a spine. The highest prominence was a monolith perforated near its top as if a tunnel had been carved through it.

"The camel's eye Benna spoke of," Smhee said.

"Over there is the formation known as the ape's head, and at the other end is that which the natives call the dragon's tail."

On the edge of the isle grew some trees, and in the waters by it were the ubiquitous tall reeds.

There was no sight or sound of life on it. Even the birds seemed to shun it.

"But I floated down past it at night several times," he said, "and I could hear the lowing of some cattle and the braying of a donkey. Also, I heard a weird call, but I don't know if it was from a bird or an animal. Also, I heard a peculiar grunting sound, but it wasn't from pigs."

"That camel's eye looks like a good place for a sentry," she said. "I got the impression from Benna that that is where he entered the caves. It must've been a very dangerous climb, especially during the dark."

"Benna was a good man," Smhee said. "But he wasn't prepared enough. There are eyes watching now. Probably through holes in the rocks. From what I heard, the mage had his servants buy a number of excavating tools. He would have used them to enlarge the caves and to make tunnels to connect the caves."

She took a final look in the sunlight at the sinister purple mass and turned away.

9

Night had come. The winds had died down. The sky was cloudy, but the covering was thin. The full moon glowed through some of these, and now and then broke through. The night birds made crazy startling sounds. The mosquitoes hummed around them in dense masses, and if it hadn't been for Smhee's ointment it would have driven them out of the trees within a few minutes. Frogs croaked in vast chorus; things plopped into the water.

They shoved the boat out to the edge of the reeds and climbed in. They wore their cloaks now but would take them off when they got to the isle. Masha's weapons were a dagger and a short thin sword used for thrusting only.

They paddled silently as possible, the current helping their rate of speed, and presently the isle loomed darkly to their right. They landed halfway down the eastern shore and dragged the dugout slowly to the nearest tree.

They put their cloaks in the boat, and Masha placed a coil of rope over her shoulder and neck.

The isle was quiet. Not a sound. Then came a strange grunting cry followed by a half-moaning, half-squalling sound. Her neck iced.

"Whatever that is," Smhee said, "it's no spider."

He chuckled as if he were making a joke.

They'd decided—what else could they do?—that the camel's eye would be too heavily guarded after Benna's entrance through it. But there had to be more accessible places to get in. These would be guarded, too, especially since they must have been made more security-conscious by the young thief.

"What I'd like to find is a secret exit," Smhee said. "Kemren must have one, perhaps more. He knows that there might come a time when he'll be sorely in need of it. He's a crafty bastard."

Before they'd taken the boat, Smhee had revealed that Kemren had fled Sherranpip with many of the temple's treasures. He had also taken along spiders' eggs and some of the temple's animal guardians.

"If he was a high priest," Masha had said, "why would he do that? Didn't he have power and wealth enough?"

"You don't understand our religion," the fat thief had said. "The priests are surrounded by treasures that would pop your eyes out of their sockets if you saw them. But the priests themselves are bound by vows to extreme poverty, to chastity, to a harsh bare life. Their reward is the satisfaction of serving Weda Krizhtawn and her people. It wasn't enough for Kemren. He must have become evil while performing some magic that went wrong. He is the first priest ever to commit such a blasphemy.

"And I, a minor priest, was selected to track him down and to make him pay for his crime. I've been looking for him for thirteen years. During that time, to effect the vengeance of Weda Krizhtawn, I have had to break some of my own vows and to commit crimes which I must pay for when I return to my land."

"Won't she pardon you for these because you have done them in her name?" Masha had said.

"No. She accepts no excuses. She will thank me for completing my mission, but I must still pay. Look at me. When I left Sherranpip, I was as skinny as you. I led a very exemplary life. I ate little, I slept in the cold and rain, I begged for my food, I prayed much. But during the years of my crimes and the crimes of my years, I have eaten too well so that Kemren, hearing of the fat fellow, would not recognize me. I have been reeling drunk, I have gambled—a terrible sin—I have fought with fists and blade, I have taken human lives, I . . ."

He looked as if he were going to weep.

Masha said, "But you didn't quit smearing yourself with butter?"

"I should have, I should have!" he cried. "But, apart from lying with women, that is the one thing I could not bring myself to do, though it was the first I should have done! And I'll pay for that when I get home, even though that is the hardest thing for a priest to do! Even Kemren, I have heard, though he no longer worships Weda Krizhtawn, still butters himself!

"And the only reason I quit doing that is that I'm sure that he's conditioned his real spiders, and his guardian animals, to attack anyone who's covered with butter. That way he can make sure, or thinks he can make sure, that no hunter of him will ever be able to get close. That is why, though it almost killed me with shame and guilt, I bathed this morning!"

Masha would have laughed if she hadn't felt so sorry for him. That was why his eyes had looked so red when he'd shown up at her apartment after bathing. It hadn't been fatigue but tears that had done it.

They drew their weapons, Masha a short sword and Smhee a long dagger. They set out for the base of the ridge of formations that ran down the center of the isle like serrations on a dragon's back. Before they'd gone far, Smhee put a restraining hand on her arm.

"There's a spider's web just ahead. Between those two bushes. Be eyeful of it. But look out for other dangers, since one will be obvious enough to distract your attention from others. And don't forget that the thorns of these bushes are probably poisonous."

In the dim moonlight she saw the web. It was huge, as wide as the stretch of her arms. She thought, If it's so big, what about its spinner?

It seemed empty though. She turned to her left and walked slowly, her head turned to watch it.

Then something big scuttled out from under the bush at her. She stifled her scream and leaped toward the thing instead of following her desire to run away from it. Her sword leaped out as the thing sprang, and it spitted itself. Something soft touched the back of her hand. The end of a waving leg.

Smhee came up behind it as she stood there holding the sword out as far as she could to keep the arachnid away. Her arm got heavy with its weight, and slowly the blade sank toward the ground. The fat man slashed the thing's back open with his dagger. A foul odor vented from it. He brought his foot down on a leg and whispered, "Pull your sword out! I'll keep it pinned!"

She did so and then backed away. She was breathing very hard.

He jumped up and came down with both feet on the creature. Its legs waved for a while longer, but it was dying if not already dead.

"That was a real spider," he said, "although I suppose you know that. I suspect that the false spiders will be much smaller."

"Why?" she said. She wished her heart would quit trying to leap up through her throat.

"Because making them requires energy, and it's more effective to make a lot of little spiders and costs less energy than to make a few big ones. There are other reasons which I won't explain just now."

"Look out!" she cried, far louder than she should have. But it had been so sudden and had taken her off guard.

Smhee whirled and slashed out, though he hadn't seen the thing. It bounded over the web, its limbs spread out against the dimness, its great round ears profiled. It came down growling, and it fell upon Smhee's blade. This was no man's-head-sized spider but a thing as big as a large dog and furry and stinking of something—monkey?—and much more vital than the arachnid. It bore Smhee backward with his weight; he fell on the earth.

Snarling, it tried to bury its fangs in Smhee's throat. Masha broke from her paralysis and thrust with a fury and strength that only fear could provide. The blade went through its body. She leaped back, drawing it out, and then lunged again. This time the point entered its neck.

Smhee, gasping, rolled it off him and stood up. He said, "By Wishu's whiskers I've got blood all over me. A fine mess! Now the others will smell me!"

"What is it?" Masha said shakily.

"A temple guardian ape. Actually, it's not an ape but a very large tailless monkey. Kemren must have brought some cubs with him."

Masha got close to the dead beast, which was lying on its back. The open mouth showed teeth like a leopard's.

"They eat meat," he said. "Unlike other monkeys, however, they're not gregarious. Our word for them, translated, would be the solitary ape."

Masha wondered if one of Smhee's duties had been teaching. Even under these circumstances, he had to be pedantic.

He looked around. "Solitary or not, there are probably a number on this isle."

After dragging the two carcasses into the river, they proceeded cautiously. Smhee looked mostly ahead; Masha, behind. Both looked to both sides of them. They came to the base of the ridges of rock. Smhee said, "The animal pens are north. That's where I heard them as I went by in the boat. I think we should stay away from them. If they scent us and start an uproar, we'll have the Raggah out and on our asses very quickly."

Smhee stopped suddenly, and said, "Hold it!"

Masha looked around quickly. What had he seen or heard?

The fat man got down on his knees and pushed against the earth just in front of him.

He rose and said, "There's a pit under that firm-looking earth. I felt it give way as I put my foot on it. That's why it pays not to walk swiftly here."

They circled it, Smhee testing each step before taking another. Masha thought that if they had to go this slowly, they would take all night before they got to the ridge. But then he led her to a rocky place, and she breathed easier. However, he said. "They could carve a pit in the stone and put a pivoting lid over it."

She said, "Why are we going this way? You said the entrances are on the north end."

"I said that I only observed people entering on the north end. But I also observed something very interesting near here. I want to check it out. It may be nothing for us, but again . . ."

Still moving slowly but faster than on the earth, they came to a little pool. It was about ten feet in diameter, a dark sheet of water on which bubbles appeared and popped. Smhee crouched down and stared at its sinister-looking surface.

She started to whisper a question, but he said, "Shh!"

Presently, something scuttled with a clatter across the solid rock from the shore. She jumped but uttered no exclamation. The thing looked like a spider in the dark, an enormous one, larger than the one they'd killed. It paid no attention to them or perhaps it wasn't at all aware of them. It leaped into the pool and disappeared. Smhee said, "Let's get behind that boulder."

When they were in back of it, she said, "What's going on?"

"When I was spying, I saw some things going into and coming out of this hole. It was too far away to see what they were, though I suspected they were giant spiders or perhaps crabs."

"So?"

His hand gripped her wrist.

"Wait!"

The minutes oozed by like snails. Mosquitoes hummed around them, birds across the river called, and once she heard, or thought she heard, that peculiar half-grunt, half-squall. And once she started when something splashed in the river. A fish. She hoped that was all it was.

Smhee said softly, "Ah!"

He pointed at the pool. She strained her eyes and then saw what looked like a swelling of the water in its center. The mound moved toward the edge of the pool, and then it left the water. It clacked as it shot toward the river. Soon another thing came and then another, and all of a sudden at least twenty popped up and clattered across the rocks.

Smhee finally relieved her bursting question.

"They look like the *bengil* crab of Sherranpip. They live in that hole but they must catch fish in the river."

"What is that to us?"

"I think the pool must be an entrance to a cave. Or caves. The crabs are not water-breathers."

"Are they dangerous?"

"Only when in water. On land they'll either run or, if cornered, try to defend themselves. They aren't poisonous, but their claws are very powerful."

He was silent for a moment, then said, "The mage is using them to defend the entrance to a cave. I'm sure. An entrance which is also an exit. For him as for the crabs. That pool has to be one of his secret escape routes."

Masha thought, Oh, no, and she rolled her eyes. Was this fat fool really thinking about trying to get inside through the pool?

"How could the mage get out this way if the crabs would attack him?"

"He would throw poisoned meat to them. He could do any number of things. What matters just now is that he wouldn't have bothered to bring their eggs along from Sherranpip unless he had a use for them. Nor would he have planted them here unless he needed them to guard this pool. Their flesh is poisonous to all living things except the *ghoondah* fish."

He chuckled. "But the mage has outsmarted himself. If I hadn't noticed the *bengil*, I would never have considered that pool as an entrance."

While he had been whispering, another group had emerged and run for the river. He counted them, thirty in all.

"Now is the time to go in," he said. "They'll all be feeding. That crab you first saw was their scout. It found a good place for catching fish, determined that there wasn't any enemy around, and returned with the good news. In some ways, they're more ant than crab. Fortunately, their nests aren't as heavily populated as an ant hole."

He said, however, that they should wait a few minutes to make sure that all had left. "By all, I mean all but a few. There are always a few who stay behind to guard the eggs."

"Smhee, we'll drown!"

"If other people can get out through the pool, then we can get in."

"You don't know for sure that the pool is an escape route! What if the mage put the crabs there for some other reason?"

"What if? What if? I told you this would be very dangerous. But the rewards are worth the risk."

She stiffened. That strange cry had come again. And it was definitely nearer.

"It may be hunting us," Smhee said. "It could have smelled the blood of the ape."

"What is it?" she said, trying to keep her teeth from chattering.

"I don't know. We're downwind from it, but it sounds as if it'll soon be here. Good! That will put some stiffening in our backbone, heat our livers. Let's go now!"

So, he was scared, too. Somehow, that made her feel a little better.

They stuck their legs down into the chilly water. They found no bottom. Then Smhee ran around to the inland side and bent down. He probed with his hand around the edge.

"The rock goes about a foot down, then curves inward," he said. "I'll wager that this was once a pothole of some sort. When Kemren came here, he carved out tunnels to the cave it led to and then somehow filled it with river water."

He stood up. The low strange cry was definitely closer now. She thought she saw something huge in the darkness to the north, but it could be her imagination.

"Oh, Igil!" she said. "I have to urinate!"

"Do it in the water. If it smells your urine on the land, it'll know a human's been here. And it might call others of its kind. Or make such an uproar the Raggah will come."

He let himself down into the water and clung to the stony edge.

"Get in! It's cold, but not as cold as death!"

She let herself down to his side. She had to bite her lip to keep it from gasping with shock.

He gave her a few hurried instructions and said, "May Weda Krizhtawn smile upon us!"

And he was gone.

10

She took a deep breath while she was considering getting out of the pool and running like a lizard chased by a fox to the river and swimming across it. But instead she dived, and as Smhee had told her to do, swam close to the ceiling of rock. She was blind here even with her eyes open, and, though she thought mostly about drowning, she had room to think about the crabs.

Presently, when her lungs were about to burst and her head rang and the violent urge to get air was about to make her breathe, her flailing hand was grasped by something. The next instant, she was pulled into air.

There was darkness all about. Her gasping mingled with Smhee's.

He said, between the wheezing, "There's plenty of air space between the water and the ceiling. I dived down and came up as fast as I could out of the water, and I couldn't touch the rock above."

After they'd recovered their wind, he said, "You tread water while I go back. I want to see how far back this space goes."

She didn't have to wait long. She heard his swimming—she hoped it was his and not something else—and she called out softly when he was near. He stopped and said, "There's plenty of air until just before the tunnel or cave reaches the pool. Then you have to dive under a downthrust ledge of rock. I didn't go back out, of course, not with that creature out there. But I'm sure my estimate of distance is right."

She followed him in the darkness until he said, "Here's another downthrust."

She felt where he indicated. The stone did not go more than six inches before ceasing.

"Does the rope or your boots bother you any?" he said. "If they're too heavy, get rid of them."

"I'm all right."

"Good. I'll be back soon—if things are as I think they are."

She started to call to him to wait for her, but it was too late. She clung to the rough stone with her fingertips, moving her legs now and then. The silence was oppressive; it rang in her ears. And once she gasped when something touched her thigh.

The rope and boots did drag her down, and she was thinking of at least getting rid of the rope when something struck her belly. She grabbed it with one hand to keep it from biting her and with the other reached for her dagger. She went under water, of course, and then she realized that she wasn't being attacked. Smhee, diving back, had run into her.

Their heads cleared the surface. Smhee laughed.

"Were you as frightened as I? I thought sure a *bengil* had me!"

Gasping, she said, "Never mind. What's over there?"

"More of the same. Another air space for perhaps a hundred feet. Then another downcropping."

He clung to the stone for a moment. Then he said, "Have you noticed how fresh the air is? There's a very slight movement of it, too."

She had noticed but hadn't thought about it. Her experience with watery caves was nil until now.

"I'm sure that each of these caves is connected to a hole which brings in fresh air from above," he said. "Would the mage have gone to all this trouble unless he meant to use this for escape?"

He did something. She heard him breathing heavily, and then there was a splash.

"I pulled myself up the rock and felt around," he said. "There is a hole up there to let air from the next cave into this one. And I'll wager that there is a hole in the ceiling. But it must curve so that light doesn't come in. Or maybe it doesn't curve. If it were day above, we might see the hole."

He dived; Masha followed him. They swam ahead then, their right hands out from side to side to feel the wall. When they came to the next downcropping, they went through beneath it at once.

At the end of this cave they felt a rock ledge that sloped gently upward. They crawled out onto it. She heard him fumbling around and then he said, "Don't cry out. I'm lighting a torch."

The light nevertheless startled her. It came from the tip of a slender stick of wood in his hand. By its illumination she saw him apply it to the end of a small pine torch. This caught fire, giving them more area of vision. The fire on the stick went out. He put the stick back into the opened belt bag.

"We don't want to leave any evidence we've been here," he said softly. "I didn't mention that this bag contains many things, including another waterproof bag. But we must hurry. The torch won't last long, and I've got just one more."

They stood up and moved ahead. A few feet beyond the original area first illuminated by the torch were some dark bulks. Boats. Twelve of them, with light wood frameworks and skin coverings. Each could hold three people. By them were paddles.

Smhee took out a dagger and began ripping the skins. Masha helped him until only one boat was left undamaged.

He said, "There must be entrances cut into the stone sections dividing the caves we just came through. I'll wager they're on the left-hand side as you come in. Anyone swimming in would naturally keep to the right wall and so wouldn't see the archways. The ledges where the crabs nest must also be on the left. Remember that when we come back. But I'd better find out for sure. We want to know exactly how to get out when the time comes."

He set his torch in a socket in the front of the boat and pushed the boat down the slope and into the water. While Masha held the narrow craft steady, he got into it. She stood on the shore, feeling lonely with all that darkness behind her while she watched him by the light of the brand. Within a few minutes he came back, grinning.

"I was right! There's an opening cut into the stone division. It's just high enough for a boat to pass through if you duck down."

They dragged the boat back up onto the ledge.

The cave ended about a hundred feet from the water. To the right was a U-shaped entrance. By its side were piles of torches and flint and steel and punk boxes. Smhee lit two, gave one to Masha, and then returned to the edge of the ledge to extinguish his little one.

"I think the mage has put all his magic spiders inside the caves," he said. "They'd require too much energy to maintain on the outside. The further away they are from him, the more energy he has to use to maintain them. The energy required increases according to the square of the distance."

Masha didn't ask him what he meant by "square."

"Stick close to me. Not just for your sake. For mine also. As I said, the mage will not have considered women trying to get into his place, so his powers are directed against men only. At least, I hope they are. That way he doesn't have to use as much energy on his magic."

"Do you want me to lead?" she said, hoping he wouldn't say yes.

"If you had as much experience as I, I wouldn't hesitate a moment. But you're still an apprentice. If we get out of here alive, you will be on your way to being a master."

They went up the steps cutout of the stone. At the top was another archway. Smhee stopped before it and held his torch high to look within it. But he kept his head outside it.

"Ha!"

11

He motioned her to come to his side. She saw that the interior of the deep doorway was grooved. Above the grooves was the bottom of a slab of stone.

"If the mechanism is triggered, that slab will crash down and block off anyone chasing the mage," he said. "And it'd crush anyone in the portal. Maybe . . ."

He looked at the wall surrounding the archway but could find nothing.
"The release mechanism must be in the other room. A time-delay device."

He got as near to the entrance as he could without going into it, and he stuck his torch through the opening.

"I can't see it. It must be just around the corner. But I do see what looks like webs."

Masha breathed deeply.

"If they're real spiders, they'll be intimidated by the torches," he said. "Unless the mage has conditioned them not to be or uses magic to overcome their natural fear. The magic spiders won't pay any attention to the flame."

She thought that it was all very uncertain, but she did not comment.

He bent down and peered at the stone floor just beyond the doorway. He turned. "Here. Your young eyes are better than my old ones. Can you see a thread or anything like it raised above the floor just beyond the door?"

She said, "No, I can't."

"Nevertheless."

He threw his torch through the doorway. At his order, she got down with her cheek against the stone and looked against the flame.

She rose, saying, "I can see a very thin line about an inch above the floor. It could be a cord."

"Just as I thought. An old Sherranpip trick."

He stepped back after asking her to get out of the way. And he leaped through the doorway and came down past the cord. She followed. As they picked up their torches, he said pointing, "There are the mechanisms. One is the time-delay. The other releases the door so it'll fall behind the first who enters and trap him. Anyone following will be crushed by the slab."

After telling her to keep an eye on the rest of the room, he examined the array of wheels, gears, and counterweights and the rope that ran from one device through a hole in the ceiling.

"The rope is probably attached to an alarm system above," he said. "Very well. I know how to actuate both of these. If you should by any foul chance come back alone, all you have to do is to jump through and then throw a torch or something on that cord. The door will come down and block off your pursuers. But get outside as fast as you can because . . ."

Masha said, "I know why."

"Good woman. Now, the spiders."

The things came before the webs were clearly visible in the light. She had expected to see the light reflected redly in their eyes, but it wasn't. Their many eyes were huge and purplish and cold. They scuttled forward, waving the foremost pair of legs, then backed away as Smhee waved his torch at them. Masha walked half-turned away from him so that she could use the brand to scare away any attack from the rear or side.

Suddenly, something leaped from the edge of the darkness and soared toward her. She thrust the brand at it. But the creature seemed to go through the torch.

It landed on her arm and seized the hand that held the torch. She had clenched her teeth to keep from screaming, if something like this happened. But she didn't even think of voicing her terror and disgust. She closed her hand on the body of the thing to crush it, and the fingers felt nothing.

The next moment, the spider disappeared.

She told Smhee what had happened.

"Thanks be to Klooshna!" he said. "You are invulnerable to them. If you weren't, you'd be swelling up now!"

"But what if if'd been a real spider?" she said as she kept waving her torch at the monsters that circled them. "I didn't know until my hand closed on it that it was not real."

"Then you'd be dying. But the fact that it ignored the brand showed you what it really was. You realized that even if you didn't think consciously about it."

They came to another archway. While she threw her torch through it and got down to look for another thread, Smhee held off the spiders.

"There doesn't seem to be any," she said.

"*Seem* isn't good enough," he said. "Hah, back, you creatures of evil! Look closely! Can you see any thin lines in the floor itself? Minute cracks?"

After a few seconds, she said, "Yes. They form a square."

"A trapdoor to drop us into a pit," he said. "You jump past it. And let's hope there isn't another trap just beyond it."

She said that she'd need a little run to clear the line. He chased the spiders, waving his torch furiously, and they backed away. When she called to him that she was safe, he turned and ran and leaped. A hairy, many-legged thing dashed through the entrance after him. Masha stepped up to the line and thrust her brand at it. It stopped. Behind it were masses that moved, shadows of solidity.

Smhee leaped toward the foremost one and jammed the burning red of his brand into the head. The stink of charred flesh assailed their nostrils. It ran backward but was stopped by those behind it. Then they retreated, and the thing, its eyes burned out, began running around and around, finally disappearing into the darkness. The others were now just beyond the doorway in the other cave. Smhee threw his torch into it.

"That'll keep them from coming through!" he said, panting. "I should have brought some extra torches, but even the greatest mind sometimes slips. Notice how the weight of those spiders didn't make the trapdoor drop? It must have a minimum limit. You only weigh eighty-five pounds. Maybe . . . ?"

"Forget it," she said.

"Right you are," he said, grinning. "But Masha if you are to be a master thief, you must think of everything."

She thought of reminding him about the extra torches he'd forgotten but decided not to. They went on ahead through an enormous cavern and came to a tunnel. From its dark mouth streamed a stink like a newly opened tomb. And they heard the cry that was half-grunt, half-squall.

Smhee halted. "I hate to go into that tunnel. But we must. You look upward for holes in the ceiling, and I'll look everywhere else."

The stone, however, looked solid. When they were halfway down the bore, they were blasted with a tremendous growling and roaring.

"Lions?" Masha said.

"No. Bears."

12

At the opposite end were two gigantic animals, their eyes gleaming redly in the light, their fangs a dull white.

The two intruders advanced after waiting for the bears to charge. But these stayed by the doorway, though they did not cease their thunderous roaring nor their slashes at the air with their paws.

"The bears were making the strange cry," she said. "I've seen dancing bears in the bazaars, but I never heard them make a noise like that. Nor were they near as large."

He said, "They've got chains around their necks. Come on."

When they were within a few feet of the beasts, they stopped. The stench was almost overpowering now, and they were deafened by the uproar in the narrowness of the tunnel.

Smhee told her to hold her torch steady. He opened his belt bag and pulled out two lengths of bamboo pipe and joined them. Then, from a small wooden case, he cautiously extracted a feathered dart. He inserted it in one end and raised the blowpipe almost to his lips.

"There's enough poison on the tip of the dart to kill a dozen men," he said. "However, I doubt that it would do much harm, if any, if the dart sticks in their thick fat. So . . ."

He waited a long time, the pipe now at his lips. Then his cheeks swelled, and the dart shot out. The bear to the right, roaring even louder, grabbed at the missile stuck in its left eye. Smhee fitted another dart into the pipe and took a step closer. The monster on the left lunged against the restraining collar and chain. Smhee shot the second dart into its tongue.

The first beast struck fell to one side, its paws waving, and its roars subsided. The other took longer to become quiet, but presently both were snoring away.

"Let's hope they die," Smhee said. "I doubt we'll have time to shoot them again when we come back."

Masha thought that a more immediate concern was that the roaring might have alarmed the mage's servants.

They went through a large cavern, the floor of which was littered with human, cattle, and goat skeletons and bear dung. They breathed through their mouths until they got to an exit. This was a doorway which led to a flight of steps. At the top of the steps was another entrance with a closed massive wooden door. Affixed to one side was a great wooden bar.

"Another hindrance to pursuers," Smhee said. "Which will, in our case, be the Raggah."

After a careful inspection of the door, he gripped its handle and slowly opened it. Freshly oiled, it swung noiselessly. They went out into a very large room illuminated by six great torches at one end. Here streams of water ran out from holes in the ceiling and down wooden troughs and onto many wooden wheels set between metal uprights.

Against the right-hand side of the far wall was another closed door as massive as the first. It, too, could be barred shut.

Unlike the bare walls of the other caves, these ware painted with many strange symbols.

"There's magic here," Smhee said. "I smell it."

He strode to the pool in which were set the wheels. The wheels went around and around impelled by the down-pouring water. Masha counted aloud. Twelve.

"A magical number," Smhee said.

They were set in rows of threes. At one end of the axle of each were attached some gears which in turn were fixed to a shaft that ran into a box under the wheel. Smhee reached out to the nearest wheel from the pool edge and stopped it. Then he released it and opened the lid of the box beneath the wheel. Masha looked past him into the interior of the box. She saw a bewildering army of tiny gears and shafts. The shafts were connected to more gears at the axle end of tiny wheels on uprights.

Smhee stopped the wheel again and spun it against the force of the waterfall. The mechanism inside started working backward.

Smhee smiled. He closed the box and went to the door and barred it. He walked swiftly to the other side of the pool. There was a large box on the floor by it. He opened it and removed some metal pliers and wrenches.

"Help me get those wheels off their stands," he said.

"Why?"

"I'll explain while we work." He looked around. "Kemren would have done better to have set human guards here. But I suppose he thought that no one would ever get this far. Or, if they did, they'd not have the slightest idea what the wheels are for."

He told her what she was to do with the wheels, and they waded into the pool. The water came only to their ankles; a wide drain in the center ensured against overflow.

Masha didn't like being drenched, but she was sure that it would be worthwhile.

"These boxes contain devices which convert the mechanical power of the water-driven wheels to magical power," he said. "There are said to be some in the temple of Weda Krizhtawn, but I was too lowly to be allowed near them. However, I heard the high priests talking about them. They sometimes got careless in the presence of us lowly ones. Anyway, we were bound by vows to keep silent.

"I don't know exactly what these particular wheels are for. But they must be providing energy for whatever magic he's using. Part of the energy, anyway."

She didn't really understand what he was talking about, though she had an inkling. She worked steadily, ignoring the wetting, and removed a wheel. Then she turned it around and reattached it.

The wheel bore symbols on each of the paddles set along its rims. There were also symbols painted on its side.

Each wheel seemed to have the same symbols but in a different sequence.

When their work was done, Smhee said, "I don't know what their reversal will do. But I'll wager that it won't be for Kemren's good. We must hurry now. If he's sensitive to the inflow-outflow of his magic, he'll know something's wrong."

She thought that it would be better not to have aroused the mage. However, Smhee was the master; she, the apprentice.

Smhee started to turn away from the wheels but stopped.

"Look!"

His finger pointed at the wheels.

"Well?"

"Don't you see something strange?"

It was a moment before she saw what had made her uneasy without realizing why. No water was spilling from the paddles down to the pool. The water just seemed to disappear after striking them.

She looked wonderingly from them to him. "I see what you mean."

He spread out his hands. "I don't know what's happening . . . but that water has to be going someplace."

They put their boots back on, and he unshot the bar of the door. It led to another flight of steps, ending in another door. They went down a corridor the walls of which were bare stone. But there were also lit torches set in brackets on them.

At the end of the corridor they came to a round room. Light came down from torches; the room was actually a tall shaft. Looking up from the bottom, they could see a black square outlined narrowly by bright light at its top.

13

Voices came from above.

"It has to be a lift," Smhee whispered. He said something in his native tongue that sounded like a curse.

"We're stuck here until the lift comes down."

He'd no sooner spoken than they heard a squeal as of metal, and the square began descending slowly.

"We're in luck!" Smhee said. "Unless they're sending down men to see what's happened to the wheels."

They retreated, through the door at the other end. Here they waited with their blades ready. Smhee kept the door open a crack.

"There are only two. Both are carrying bags and one has a haunch of meat. They're going to feed the bears and the spiders!"

Masha wondered how the men intended to get past the bears to the arachnids. But maybe the bears attacked only strangers.

"One man has a torch," he said.

The door swung open, and a Raggah wearing a red-and-black-striped robe stepped through. Smhee drove his dagger into the man's throat. Masha came out from behind the door and thrust her sword through the other man's neck.

After dragging the bodies into the room, they took off the robes and put them on.

"It's too big for me," she said. "I look ridiculous."

"Cut off the bottom," he said, but she had already started doing that. "What about the blood on the robes?"

"We could wash it out, but then we'd look strange with dripping robes. We'll just have to take a chance."

They left the bodies lying on the floor and went back to the lift. This was an open-sided cage built of light (and expensive) imported bamboo. The top was closed, but it had a trapdoor. A rope descended through it.

They looked up but could see no one looking down.

Smhee pulled on the rope, and a bell clanged. No one was summoned by it, though.

"Whoever pulls this up is gone. No doubt he, or they, are not expecting the two to return so early. Well, we must climb up the pull-ropes. I hope you're up to it."

"Better than you, fat one," Masha said.

He smiled. "We'll see."

Masha, however, pulled herself up faster than he. She had to climb up onto the beam to which the wheel was attached and then crawl along it and swing herself down into the entrance. Smhee caught her as she landed on the edge, though she didn't need his help.

They were in a hallway the walls of which were hung with costly rugs and along which was expensive furniture. Oil lamps gave an adequate illumination.

"Now comes the hard part," he said between deep breaths. "There is a staircase at each end of this hall. Which leads to the mage?"

"I'd take that one," she said, pointing.

"Why?"

"I don't exactly know why. I just feel that it's the right one."

He smiled, saying, "That's as good a reason as any for me. Let's go."

Their hands against each other inside their voluminous sleeves, but holding daggers, the hoods pulled out to shadow their faces, they walked up the stairs. These curved to end in another hall, even more luxuriously furnished. There were closed doors along it, but Smhee wouldn't open them.

"You can wager that the mage will have a guard or guards outside his apartment."

They went up another flight of steps in time to see the back of a Raggah going down the hall. At the corner, Masha looked around it. No one in sight. She stepped out, and just then a Raggah came around the corner at the right-hand end of the hall. She slowed, imperceptibly, she hoped, then resumed her stride. She heard Smhee behind her saying, "When you get close, within ten feet of her, move quickly to one side."

She did so just as the Raggah, a woman, noticed the blood on the front of her robe. The woman opened her mouth, and Smhee's thrown knife plunged into her belly. She fell forward with a thump. The fat man withdrew his knife, wiped it on the robe, and they dragged her through a doorway. The room was unlit. They dropped her near the door and went out, closing it behind them.

They went down to the end of the hall from which the woman had come and looked around the corner. There was a very wide and high-ceilinged corridor there, and from a great doorway halfway down it came much light, many voices, and the odor of cooking. Masha hadn't realized until then how hungry she was; saliva ran in her mouth.

"The other way," Smhee said, and he trotted toward the staircase. At its top, Masha looked around the corner. Halfway down the length of this hall a man holding a spear stood before a door. By his side crouched a huge black wolfish dog on a leash.

She told Smhee what she'd seen.

As excited as she'd ever seen him, he said, "He must be guarding the mage's rooms!"

Then, in a calmer tone, "He isn't aware of what we've done. He must be with a woman or a man. Sexual intercourse, you know, drains more out of a person than just physical energy. Kemren won't be sensitive to the wheels just now."

Masha didn't see any reason to comment on that. She said, "The dog didn't notice me, but we can't get close before he alerts the guard."

Masha looked behind her. The hall was still empty. But what if the mage had ordered a meal to be delivered soon?

She told Smhee what she'd just thought. After a brief consultation, they went back down the stairs to the hall. There they got an exquisitely silver-chased tray and put some small painted dishes and gold pitchers on it. These they covered with a golden cloth, the worth of which was a thousand times more than Masha could make if she worked as dentist and midwife until she was a hundred years old.

With this assemblage, which they hoped would look like a late supper tray, they went to the hall. Masha had said that if the mage was with a sexual partner, it would look more authentic if they carried two trays. But even before Smhee voiced his objections, she had thought that he had to have his hands free. Besides, the tray clattering on the floor was bad enough, though its impact would be softened by the thick rug.

The guard seemed half-asleep, but the dog, rising to its feet and growling, fully awakened him. He turned toward them, though not without a glance at the other end of the hall first. Masha, in front of Smhee, walked as if she had a right to be there. The guard held the spear pointing at them in one hand and said something in his harsh back-of-the-throat speech.

Smhee uttered a string of nonsense syllables in a low but equally harsh voice. The guard said something. And then Masha stepped to one side, dropping the tray. She bent over, muttering something guttural, as if she were apologizing for her clumsiness.

She couldn't see Smhee, but she knew that he was snatching the blow-pipe from his sleeve and applying it to his lips. She came up from her bent position, her sword leaping out of her scabbard, and she ran toward the dog. It bounded toward her, the guard having released the leash. She got the blade out from the leather just in time and rammed it into the dog's open mouth as it sprang soundlessly toward her throat. The blade drove deep into its throat, but she went backward from its weight and fell onto the floor.

The sword had been torn from her grip, but the dog was heavy and unmoving on her chest. She pushed him off though he must have weighed as much as she. She rolled over and got quickly, but trembling, to her feet. The guard was sitting down, his back against the wall. One hand clutched the dart stuck in his cheek. His eyes were open but glazing. In a few seconds the hand fell away. He slumped to one side, and his bowels moved noisily.

The dog lay with the upper length of the sword sticking from its mouth. His tongue extended from the jaws, bloody, seeming almost an independent entity, a stricken worm.

Smhee grabbed the bronze handle of the door.

"Pray for us, Masha! If he's barred the door on the inside . . . !"

The door swung open.

Smhee bounded in, the dead man's spear in his hands. Masha, following, saw a large room the air of which was green and reeking of incense. The walls were covered with tapestries, and the heavy dark furniture was ornately carved with demons' heads. They paused to listen and heard nothing except a faint burbling noise.

"Get the bodies in quickly!" Smhee said, and they dragged the corpses inside. They expected the dreaded mage to walk in at any time, but he still had not appeared when they shut the door.

Smhee whispered, "Anyone coming by will notice that there is no guard."

They entered the next room cautiously. This was even larger and was obviously the bedroom. The bed was huge and round and on a platform with three steps. It was covered with a rich scarlet material brocaded in gold.

"He must be working in his laboratory," Smhee whispered.

They slowly opened the door to the next room.

The burbling became louder then. Masha saw that it proceeded from a great glass vessel shaped like an upside-down cone. A black-green liquid simmered in it, and large bubbles rose from it and passed out the open end. Beneath it was a brazier filled with glowing coals. From the ceiling above a metal vent admitted the fumes.

The floor was mosaic marble in which were set pentagrams and nonagrams. From the center of one rose a wisp of evil-smelling smoke. A few seconds later, the smoke ceased.

There were many tables holding other mysterious equipment and racks holding long thick rolls of parchment and papyrus. In the middle of the room was a very large desk of some shiny reddish wood. Before it was a chair of the same wood, its arms and back carved with human-headed dragons.

The mage, clad in a purple silk robe which was embroidered with golden centaurs and gryphons, was in the chair. His face was on the desk, and his arms were spread out on it. He stank of rancid butter.

Smhee approached him slowly, then grabbed the thin curly hair of the mage's topknot and raised the head.

There was water on the desk, and water ran from the dead man's nose and mouth.

"What happened to him?" she whispered.

Smhee did not reply at once. He lifted the body from the chair and placed it on the floor. Then he knelt and thumped the mage's chest.

The fat man rose smiling.

"What happened is that the reversal of the wheels' motion caused the water which should have fallen off the paddles to go instead to the mage. The conversion of physical energy to magical energy was reversed."

He paused.

"The water went into the mage's body. He *drowned*!"

He raised his eyes and said, "Blessed is Weda Krizhtawn, the goddess of water! She has her revenge through her faithful servant, Rhandhee Ghee!"

He looked at Masha. "That is my true name, Rhandhee Ghee. And I have revenged the goddess and her worshipers. The defiler and thief is dead, and I can go home now. Perhaps she will forgive some of my sins because I have fulfilled her intent, I won't go to hell, surely. I will suffer in a purgatory for a while and then, cleansed with pain, will go to the lowest heaven. And then, perhaps . . ."

"You forget that I am to be paid," she said.

"No, I didn't. Look. He wears golden rings set with jewels of immense value. Take them, and let's be off."

She shuddered and said, "No. They would bring misfortune."

"Very well. The next room should be his treasure chamber."

It was. There were chests and boxes filled with emeralds, diamonds, turquoises, rubies, and many other jewels. There were golden and silver idols and statuettes. There was enough wealth to purchase a dozen of the lesser cities of the empire and all their citizens.

But she could only take what she could carry and not be hampered in the leaving.

Exclaiming ecstatics, she reached toward a coffer sparkling with diamonds.

At her touch, the jewels faded and were gone.

14

She cried out in anguish.

"They're products of his magic!" Smhee said. "Set here to fool thieves. Benna must have taken one of these, though how he got here and then away I've no idea! The jewel did not disappear because the mage was alive and his powers were strong. But I'll wager that not long after the rat carried the jewel off, it disappeared. That's why the searchers found no jewel though they turned the city upside down and inside out!"

"There's plenty of other stuff to take!" she said.

"No, too heavy. But he must have put his real jewels somewhere. The next room!"

But there were no other rooms.

"Don't you believe it," Smhee said. He tore down the tapestries and began tapping on the walls, which were of a dense-grained purplish wood erected over the stone. Presently, he said, "Ah!" and he moved his hands swiftly over the area. "Here's a hole in the wood just big enough to admit my little finger. I put my finger in thus, and I pull thus, and thus . . . !"

A section of the wood swung out. Masha got a burning lamp and thrust it into the room beyond. The light fell on ten open chests and twenty open coffers. Jewels sparkled.

They entered.

"Take two handsful," Smhee said. "That's all. We aren't out of here yet."

Masha untied the little bag attached to her belt, hesitated, then scooped out enough to fill the bag. It almost tore her heart apart to leave the rest, but she knew that Smhee's advice was wisdom. Perhaps, someday, she could come back for more. No. That would be stupid. She had far more than enough.

On the way out, Smhee stopped. He opened the mage's robe and revealed a smooth-shaven chest on which was tattooed a representation of a fearful six-armed four-legged being with a glaring long-tusked face. He cut around this and peeled the skin off and put it rolled and folded into a small jar of ointment. Replacing the jar in his bag, he rose, saying, "The goddess knows that I would not lie about his death. But this will be the proof if any is demanded."

"Maybe we should look for the mage's secret exit," she said. "That way, we won't run into the Raggah."

"No. At any moment someone may see that the guard is missing. Besides, the mage will have put traps in his escape route, and we might not elude those."

They made their way back to the corridor of the lift shaft without being observed. But two men stood in front of the entrance to the lift. They were talking excitedly and looking down the shaft. Then one ran down the corridor, away from the corner behind which the two intruders watched.

"Going to get help before they venture down to find out why the two feeders haven't come back," Smhee muttered.

The man who'd stayed was looking down the shaft. Masha and Smhee took him from behind, one cutting the throat, the other stabbing him in the back. They let themselves down on the ropes and then cut them before going down through the open trapdoor. But as they left the cage, a spear shot through the trapdoor and thudded point-first into the floor. Men shouted above.

"They'll bring ropes and come down on those," Smhee said. "And they'll send others outside to catch us when we come out of the pool. Run, but remember the traps!"

And the spiders, she thought. And the crabs. I hope the bears are dead.

They were. The spiders, all real now that the mage was dead, were alive. These were driven back by the torches the two had paused to light, and they got to the skin boat. They pushed this out and began paddling with desperation. The craft went through the first arch and then through the second. To their right now were some ledges on which were masses of pale-white things with stalked eyes and clacking pincers. The crabs. The two directed their boat away from these, but the writhing masses suddenly became individual figures leaping outward and splashing into the dark water. Very quickly, the ledges were bare. There was no sign of the monsters, but the two knew that these were swimming toward them.

They paddled even faster, though it had not seemed possible until then. And then the prow of the boat bumped into the wall.

"Swim for it!" Smhee bellowed, his voice rebounding from the far walls and high ceilings of the cave.

Masha feared entering the waters; she expected to be seized by those huge claws. But she went over, the boat tipping, and dived. Something did touch her leg as she went under the stone downcropping. Then her head was above the surface of the pool and Smhee's was beside her.

They scrambled out onto the hard stone. Behind them came the clacking, but none of the crabs tried to leave the pool.

The sky was black; thunder bellowed in the north; lightning traced white veins. A wind blew, chilling them in their wet clothes.

They ran toward the dugout but not in a straight line since they had to avoid the bushes with the poisonous thorns. Before they reached it, rain fell. They dragged the craft into the river and got aboard. Above them lightning cracked across the sky. Another bolt struck shortly thereafter, revealing two bears and a number of men behind them.

"They can't catch us now!" Smhee yelled. "But they'll be going back to put their horses on rafts. They'll go all the way into Sanctuary itself to get us!"

Save your breath, Masha thought. I know all that.

The wind-struck river was rough now, but they got through the waves to the opposite shore. They climbed panting up the ridge and found their horses, whinnying from fear of the lightning. When they got to the bottom of the ridge, they sped away, their passage fitfully lit by the dreadful whiteness that seemed to smash all around them. They kept their horses at a gallop for a mile, then eased them up.

"There's no way they can catch us!" Smhee shouted through the thunder. "We've got too much of a head start!"

Dawn came. The rain stopped. The clouds cleared away; the hot winter sun of the desert rose. They stopped at the hut where they had slept, and the horses rested, and they ate bread and cheese.

"Three more hours will bring us within sight of Sanctuary," the fat man said. "We'll get your family aboard the *Sailfish*, and the Raggah can search for us in vain."

He paused, then said, "What do you intend to do about Eevroen?"

"Nothing," she said. "If he gets in my way I'll brain him again."

He laughed so much he choked on his bread. When he'd cleared his throat, he said, "You are some woman! Brave as the goddess makes them! And supple in mind, too. If I were not vowed to chastity, I would woo you! I maybe forty-five and fat, but . . ."

He stopped to stare down at his hand. His face froze into an expression of horror.

Masha became equally paralyzed.

A small purple spider was on Smhee's hand.

"Move slowly," he said softly through rigid lips. "I dare not move. Slap it when you've got your hand within a few inches of it."

She got up and took a step toward him. Where had the creature come from? There were no webs in the hut. Had it come from outside and crawled upon him?

She took another step, leaned over, and brought her hand slowly down at an angle toward the thing. Its eyes were black and motionless, seemingly unaware of her presence.

Maybe it's not poisonous, she thought.

Suddenly, Smhee screamed, and he crushed the spider with his other hand. He leaped up then, brushing off the tiny body.

"It bit me! It bit me!"

The dark swelling had started.

"It's not one of the mage's creatures," she said. "Its venom may not be deadly."

"It's the mage's," he said. His face was white under the heavy pigment.

"It must have crawled into my bag. It couldn't have done it when we were on the way to the mage's rooms. It must have gotten in when I opened the bag to skin off the tattoo."

He howled. "The mage has gotten his revenge!"

"You don't know that," she said, but she was certain that it was as Smhee had said. She removed her small belt bag and carefully poured out the jewels. But that was all it contained.

"It's beginning to hurt," Smhee said. "I can make it back to the city. Benna did, and he was bitten many times. But I know these spiders. I will die as surely as he did, though I will take longer. There is no antidote."

He sat down, and for a while he rocked back and forth, eyes closed, moaning. Then he said, "Masha, there is no sense in my going on with you. But, since I have made it possible for you to be as wealthy as a queen, I beg you to do one favor for me. If it is not too much to ask."

"What is that?" she said.

"Take the jar containing the tattooed skin to Sherranpip. And there tell our story to the highest priest of Weda Krizhtawn. He will pray for me to her, and a great tombstone will be erected for me in the courtyard of the peacocks, and pilgrims will come from all over Sherranpip and the islands around and will pray for me. But if you don't want . . ."

Masha knelt and kissed him on the mouth. He felt cold.

She stood up and said, "I promise you that I will do that. That, as you said, is the least I can do."

He smiled, though it cost him to do it.

"Good. Then I can die in peace. Go. May Weda Krizhtawn bless you."

"But the Raggah . . . they will torture you!"

"No. This bag contains a small vial of poison. They will find only a corpse. If they find me at all."

Masha burst into tears, but she took the jar, and after kissing Smhee again, she rode off, his horse trotting behind hers.

At the top of the hill she stopped to look behind at the hut.

Far off, coming swiftly, was a dark mass. The Raggah.

She turned away and urged her horse into a gallop.

Goddess

David Drake

"By Savankala and the Son!" Regli swore. "Why can't she bear land be done with it? And why does she demand to see her brother but won't see me?" The young lord's sweat-stained tunic looked as if it had been slept in. Indeed, Regli would have slept in it if he had slept any during the two days he had paced outside the bedroom, now couching room, of his wife. Regli's hands repeatedly flexed the shank of his riding crop. There were those—and not all of them women—who would have said that agitation heightened Regli's already notably good looks, but he had no mind for such nonsense now. Not with his heir at risk!

"Now, now," said Doctor Mernorad, patting the silver-worked lapels of his robe. The older man prided himself as much on his ability to see both sides of a question as he did on his skill at physic—though neither ability seemed much valued today in Regli's town house. "One can't hurry the gods, you know. The child will be born when Sabellia says it should be. Any attempt to hasten matters would be sacrilege as well as foolishness. Why, you know there are some . . . I don't know what word to use, *practitioners*, who use forceps in a delivery? Forceps of *metal*! It's disgusting. I tell you Prince Kadakithis makes a great noise about smugglers and thieves; but if he wanted to clean up a *real* evil in Sanctuary, he'd start with the so-called doctors who don't have proper connections with established temples."

"Well, damn it!" Regli snapped. "You've got a 'proper connection' to the temple of Sabellia in Ranke itself, and you can't tell me why my wife's been two days in labor. And if any of those bitch-midwives who've stood shift in there know"—he gestured toward the closed door—"they sure aren't telling anybody." Regli knuckled the fringe of blond whiskers sprouting on his jawbone. His wealth and breeding had made him a person of some importance even in Ranke. Here in Sanctuary, where he served as master of the scrolls for the prince governor, he was even less accustomed to being balked. The fact that Fate, in the form of his wife's abnormally prolonged labor, was balking him infuriated Regli to the point that he needed to lash out at something. "I can't imagine why Samlane insists on seeing no one but midwives from the temple of Heqt," he continued, snapping his riding crop at specks on the mosaic walls. "That place has no very good reputation I'm told. Not at all."

"Well, you have to remember that your wife is from Cirdon," said Mernorad reasonably, keeping a wary eye on his patron's lash. "Though they've been forty years under the empire, worship of the Trinity hasn't really caught on there. I've investigated the matter, and these women do have proper midwives' licenses. There's altogether too much loose talk among laymen about 'this priesthood' or 'that particular healer' not being competent. I assure you that the medical profession keeps very close watch on itself. The worst to be said on, the record—the only place it counts—about the temple of Heqt here in Sanctuary is that thirty years ago the chief priest disappeared. Unfortunate, of course, but nothing to discredit the temple."

The doctor paused, absently puffing out one cheek, then the other, so that his curly white sideburns flared. "Though I do think," he added, "that since you have engaged me anyway, their midwives might consult with one of my, well, stature."

The door between the morning room and the hall was ajar. A page in Regli's livery of red and gold tapped the jamb deferentially. The two Rankans looked up, past the servant to the heavier man beyond in the hall. "My lord," said the page, bowing, "Samlor hil Samt."

Samlor reached past the servant to swing the door fully open before

Regli nodded entry. He had unpinned his dull traveling cloak and draped it over his left arm, close to his body where it almost hid the sheathed fighting knife. Northern fashion, Samlor wore boots and breeches with a long-sleeved overtunic gathered at the wrists. The garments were plain and would have been a nondescript brown had they not been covered with white road dust. His sole jewelry was a neck-thonged silver medallion stamped with the toad face of the goddess Heqt. Samlor's broad face was deep red, the complexion of a man who will never tan but who is rarely out of the sun. He cleared his throat, rubbed his mouth with the back of his big fist, and said, "My sister sent for me. She's in there, the servant says?" He gestured.

"Why yes," said Regli, looking a little puzzled to find the quirt in his hands. The doctor was getting up from his chair. "Why, you're much older, aren't you?" the lord continued inanely.

"Fourteen years," Samlor agreed sourly, stepping past the two Rankans to the bedroom door. He tossed his cloak over one of the ivory-inlaid tables along the wall. "You'd have thought the folks would have guessed something when the five between us were stillborn, but no, hell, no. . . . And much luck the bitch ever brought them."

"I say!" Regli gasped at the stocky man's back. "You're speaking of my wife!"

Samlor turned, his knuckles already poised to rap on the door panel. "You had a choice," he said. "I'm the one who was running caravans through the mountains trying to keep the Noble House of Kodrix afloat long enough to marry its daughter well—and her slutting about so that the folks had to go to Ranke to get offers from anybody but a brothel-keeper. No wonder they drink." He hammered on the door.

Mernorad tugged the white-faced Regli back. "Master Samlor," the physician said sharply.

"It's Samlor, dammit!" The Cirdonian wasn't shouting in response to a question from within the bedroom. "I didn't ride five hundred miles to stand at a damned doorway either." He turned to Mernorad. "Yes?" he asked.

The physician pointed. "Your weapon," he said. "The Lady Samlane has been distraught. Not an uncommon thing for women in her condition, of course. She, ah, attempted to have her condition, ah, terminated some months ago. . . . Fortunately, we got word before. . . . And even though she has since been watched at all times, she, ah, with a spoon . . .

Well. I'd simply rather that—things like your knife—not be where the lady could snatch them, lest something untoward occur. . . ."

Within the bedroom, a bronze bar creaked as it was lifted from the door slots. Samlor drew his long dagger and laid it on an intaglio table. Only the edge of the steel winked. The hilt was of a hard, pale wood, smooth but wrapped with a webbing of silver wire for a sure grip. The morning room had been decorated by a former occupant. In its mosaic battle scenes and the weapons crossed on its walls, the room suited Samlor's appearance far better than it did that of the young Rankan lord who now owned it. The door was opened inward by a sour, grey-haired woman in temple garb. The air that puffed from the bedroom was warm and cloying like the smell of an overripe peach. Two branches of the sextuple oil lamp within had been lighted, adding to the sunlight seeping through the stained glass separating the room from the inner court.

If the midwife looked harsh, then Samlane herself on the bed looked like Death. All the flesh of her face and her long, white hands seemed to have been drawn into the belly that now mounded her linen wrapper. A silk coverlet lay rumpled at the foot of the bed. "Come in, brother dear." A spasm rippled the wrapper. Samlane's face froze her mouth half-open. The spasm passed. "I won't keep you long, Samlor," she added through a false smile. "Leah, wait outside."

Midwife, husband, and doctor all began to protest. "Heqt's face, get out, get out!" Samlane shrieked, her voice rising even higher as a new series of contractions racked her. Her piercing fury cut through all objection. Samlor closed the door behind the midwife. Those in the morning room heard the door latched but not barred. Regli's house had been built for room-by-room defense in the days when bandits or a mob would burst into a dwelling and strip it, in despite of anything the government might attempt.

The midwife stood, stiff and dour, with her back to the door. Regli ignored her and slashed at the wall again. "In the year I've known her, Samlane hasn't mentioned her brother a dozen times—and each of those was a curse!" he said.

"You must remember, this is a trying time for the lady, too," Mernorad said. "With her parents, ah, unable to travel, it's natural that she wants her brother—"

"Natural?" Regli shouted. "It's *my* child she's bearing! My *son*, perhaps. What am I doing out here?"

"What would you be doing in there?" the doctor observed, tart himself in response to his patron's anger.

Before either could say more, the door swung open, bumping the midwife. Samlor gestured with his thumb. "She wants you to fix her pillows," he said curtly. He picked up his knife and began walking across the morning room toward the hall. The midwife eeled back into the bedroom, hiding all but a glimpse of Samlane's face. The lampstand beside the bed gave her flesh a yellow cast. The bar thudded back in place almost as soon as the door closed.

Regli grabbed Samlor's arm. "But what did she want?" he demanded.

Samlor shook his arm free. "Ask her, if you think it's any of your business," he said. "I'm in no humor to chatter." Then he was out of the room and already past the servant who should have escorted him down the staircase to the front door.

Mernorad blinked. "Certainly a surly brute," he said. "Not at all fit for polite company."

For once it was Regli who was reasonable. "Oh, that's to be expected," he said. "In Cirdon, the nobility always prided itself on being useless—which is why Cirdon is part of the Rankan Empire and not the reverse. It must have bothered him very much when he had to go into trade himself or starve with the rest of his family." Regli cleared his throat, then patted his left palm with the quirt. "That of course explains his hostility toward Samlane and the absurd—"

"Yes, quite absurd," Mernorad agreed hastily.

"—absurd charges he leveled at her," the young noble continued. "Just bitterness, even though he himself had preserved her from the, oh, as he saw it, lowering to which he had been subjected. Actually, I have considerable mining and trading interests myself, besides my—very real—duties here to the State."

The diversion had settled Regli's mind only briefly. He resumed his pacing, the shuffle of his slippers and his occasional snappish comments being almost the only sounds in the morning room for an hour. "Do you hear something?" Mernorad said suddenly.

Regli froze, then ran to the bedroom door. "Samlane!" he shouted. "*Samlane!*" He gripped the bronze latch and screamed as his palm seared.

Acting with dreadful realization and more strength than was to be expected of a man of his age, Mernorad ripped a battle-ax from the staples holding it to the wall. He swung it against the door panel. The oak had charred to wafer thinness. The heavy blade splintered through, emitting a jet of oxygen into the superheated bedroom.

The room exploded, blasting the door away in a gout of fire and splinters. The flames buried Mernorad against the far wall as a blazing husk before they curled up to shatter the plastered ceiling.

The flame sucked back, giving Regli a momentary glimpse into the fully-involved room. The midwife had crawled from the bed almost back to the door before she died. The fire had arched her back so that the knife wound in her throat gaped huge and red.

Samlane may have cut her own jugular as well, but too little remained of her to tell. She had apparently soaked the bedding in lamp oil and then clutched the open flame to her. All Regli really had to see, however, to drive him screaming from his house, was the boot knife. The wooden hilt was burned off, and the bare tang poked upright from Samlane's distended belly.

Samlor had asked a street boy where the temple of Heqt was. The child had blinked, then brightened and said, "Oh—the Black Spire!" Sitting on a bench outside a tavern across from the temple, Samlor thought he understood why. The temple had been built of gray limestone, its walls set in a square but roofed with the usual hemispherical dome. The obelisk crowning the dome had originally commemorated the victories of Alar hil Aspar, a mercenary general of Cirdonian birth. Alar had done very well by his adopted city—and well enough for himself in the process to be able to endow public buildings as one form of conspicuous consumption. None of Alar's boasts remained visible through the coating three decades of wood and dung smoke had deposited on the spire. Still, to look at it, the worst that could be said about the temple of Heqt was that it was ugly, filthy, and in a bad district—all of which were true of most other buildings in Sanctuary, so far as Samlor could tell.

As the caravan master swigged his mug of blue john, an acolyte emerged from the main doorway of the temple. She waved her censer three times and chanted an evening prayer to the disinterested street before retreating back inside.

The tavern's doorway brightened as the tapster stepped out carrying a lantern. "Move, buddy, these're for customers," he said to the classically handsome young man sitting on the other bench. The youth stood but did not leave. The tapster tugged the bench a foot into the doorway, stepped onto it, and hung the lantern from a hook beneath the tavern's sign. The angle of the lantern limned in shadow a rampant unicorn, its penis engorged and as large as the horn on its head.

Instead of returning to the bench on which he had been sitting, the young man sat down beside Samlor. "Not much to look at, is it?" he said to the Cirdonian, nodding toward the temple.

"Nor popular, it seems," Samlor agreed. He eyed the local man carefully, wondering how much information he could get from him. "Nobody's gone in there for an hour."

"Not surprising," the other man said with a nod. "They come mostly after dark, you know. And you wouldn't be able to see them from here anyway."

"No?" said Samlor, sipping a little more of his clabbered milk. "There's a back entrance?"

"Not just that," said the local man. "There's a network of tunnels beneath the whole area. They—the worshipers—enter from inns or shops or tenements from blocks away. In Sanctuary, those who come to Heqt come secretly."

Samlor's left hand toyed with his religious medallion. "I'd heard that before," he said, "and I don't figure it. Heqt brings the spring rains . . . she's the genetrix, not only in Cirdon but everywhere she's worshiped at all—except Sanctuary. What happened here?"

"You're devout, I suppose?" asked the younger man, eyeing the disk with the face of Heqt.

"Devout, devout," said Samlor with a grimace. "I run caravans. I'm not a priest. Sure, maybe I spill a little drink to Heqt at meals . . . without her, there'd be no world but desert, and I see enough desert already."

The stranger's skin was so pale that it looked yellow now that most of the light was from the lamp above. "Well, they say there was a shrine to Dyareela here before Alar tore it down to build his temple. There wouldn't be anything of course, except perhaps the tunnels, and they may have been old when the city was built on top of them. Have you heard there's supposed to be a demon kept in the lower crypts?"

Samlor nodded curtly. "I heard that."

"A hairy, long-tailed, fang-snapping demon," said the younger man with a bright smile. "Pretty much of a joke nowadays, of course. People don't really believe in that sort of thing. Still, the first priest of Heqt here disappeared. . . . And last year Alciros Foin went into the temple with ten hired bravos to find his wife. Nobody saw the bullies again, but Foin was out on the street the next morning. He was alive, even though every inch of skin had been flayed off him."

Samlor finished his mug of blue john. "Men could have done that," he said.

"Would you prefer to meet men like that rather than . . . a demon?" asked the local, smiling.

The two men stared in silence at the temple. "Do you want a drink?" Samlor asked abruptly.

"Not I," said the other.

"You say that fellow was looking for his wife?" the Cirdonian pressed, his eyes on the shadow-hidden temple and not on his companion.

"That's right. Women often go through the tunnels, they say. Fertility rites. Some say the priests themselves have more to do with any increase in conceptions than the rites do—but what man can say what women are about?"

"And the demon?"

"Aiding the conceptions?" said the local. Samlor had kept his face turned from the other so that he would not have to see his smile, but the smile freighted the words themselves stickily. "Perhaps, but some people will say anything. That would be a night for the . . . suppliant, wouldn't it?"

Samlor turned and smiled back, baring his teeth like a cat eyeing a throat vein. "Oh, quite a night indeed," he said. "Are there any places known to have entrances to—that?" He gestured across the dark street. "Or is it just rumor? Perhaps this inn itself?"

"There's a hostel west of here a furlong," said the youth. "Near the beef market—the Man in Motley. They say there's a network beneath like worm tunnels, not really connected to each other. A man could enter one and walk for days without ever seeing another soul."

Samlor shrugged. He stood and whistled for attention, then tossed his empty mug to the tapster behind the bar. "Just curiosity," he said to his companion. "I've never been in Sanctuary before." Samlor stepped into the street, over a drain that held something long dead. When he glanced back, he saw the local man still seated empty-handed on the bench. In profile against the light, his face had the perfection of an ancient cameo.

Samlor wore boots and he was long familiar with dark nights and bad footing, so he did not bother to hire a linkman. When he passed a detachment of the watch, the imperial officer in command stared at the dagger the Cirdonian now carried bare in his hand. Still, Samlor looked to be no more than he was, a sturdy man who would rather warn off robbers than kill them, but who was willing and able to do either. I'll have to buy another boot knife, Samlor thought; but for the time he'd make do, make do. . . .

The Man in Motley was a floor lower than the four-story tenements around it. The ground level was well lighted. Across the street behind a row of palings, a slave gang worked under lamps scraping dung from the cobbles of the beef market. Tomorrow their load would be dried in the sun for fuel. The public room of the inn was occupied by a score of men, mostly drovers in leather and homespun. A barmaid in her fifties was serving a corner booth. As Samlor entered, the host thrust through the hangings behind the bar with a cask on his shoulder.

Samlor had sheathed his knife. He nodded to the brawny innkeeper and ducked beneath the bar himself. "Hey!" cried the host.

"It's all right," Samlor muttered. He slipped behind the hangings.

A stone staircase, lighted halfway by an oil lamp, led down into the cellars. Samlor followed it, taking the lamp with him. The floor beneath the public room was of dirt. A large trap, now closed and bolted, gave access to deliveries from the street fronting the inn. The walls were lined with racked bottles, small casks, and great forty-gallon fooders set on end. One of the fooders was of wood so time-blackened as to look charred. Samlor rapped it with his knife hilt, then compared the sound to the duller note of the tun beside it.

The stairs wreaked as the host descended. He held a bung-starter in one heavy fist. "Didn't they tell you to go by the side?" he rasped. "D'ye think I want the name of running a devil's brothel?" He took another step. "By Ils and his sisters, you'll remember the next time!"

Samlor's fingers moved on his knife hilt. He still held the point away from the innkeeper. "We don't have a quarrel," he said. "Let's leave it at that."

The host spat as he reached the bottom of the stairs. "Sure, I know you hot-pants folderols. Well, when I'm done with you, you take my greetings to your pandering psalm-singers and tell them there'll be no more customers through here!"

"The priests share their privileges for a price?" Samlor said in sudden enlightenment. "But I don't come for sex, friend."

Whatever the tavernkeeper thought he understood, it frightened him as sight of the dagger had not. He paused with the bung-starter half-raised. First he swallowed. Then, with a guttural sound of pure terror, he flung the mallet into the shadows and fled back up the stairs. Samlor frowned, shrugged, and turned again to the fooder.

There was a catch disguised as a knot, obvious enough if one knew something of the sort had to be there. Pressed, the side of the cask swung out to reveal a dry, dark tunnel sloping gently downward. Samlor's tongue touched his lips. It was, after all, what he had been looking for. He picked up the lamp, now burned well down. He stepped into the tunnel, closing the door behind him.

The passage twisted but did not branch. It was carved through dense, yellow clay, shored at intervals with timbers too blackened for Samlor to identify the wood. There were tiny skitterings that seemed to come from just beyond the light. Samlor walked slowly enough not to lose the lamp flame, steadily enough not to lose his nerve. Despite the disgrace of his vocation, Samlor was a noble of Cirdon; and there was no one else in his family to whom he could entrust this responsibility.

There was a sound behind him. Without turning, Samlor lashed out with a boot. His hobnails ground into something warm and squealing where his eyes saw nothing at all. He paused for a moment to finger his medallion of Heqt, then continued. The skittering preceded him at a greater distance.

When the tunnel entered a shelf of rock it broadened suddenly into a low-ceilinged, circular room. Samlor paused. He held his lamp out at arm's length and a little back of his line of sight so that the glare would not blind him. The room was huge and empty, pierced by a score of doorways. Each but the one at which Samlor stood and one other was closed by an iron grate.

Samlor touched but did not draw his double-edged dagger. "I'll play your silly game," he whispered. Taking short steps, he walked around the circumference of the room and out the other open door. Another empty passage stretched beyond it. Licking his lips again, Samlor followed the new tunnel.

The double clang of gratings behind him was not really unexpected. Samlor waited, poised behind his knife point, but no one came down the stone boring from either direction. No one and no thing. Samlor resumed walking, the tunnel curving and perhaps descending slightly with each step. The stone was beginning to vibrate, a tremor that was too faint to be music.

The passage broadened again. This time the room so formed was not empty. Samlor spun to face what first seemed a man standing beside the doorway. The figure's only movement was the flicker of the lamp flame over its metallic luster. The Cirdonian moved closer and prodded the empty torso. It was a racked suit of mail, topped by a slot-fronted helmet.

Samlor scratched at a link of the armor, urged by a suspicion that he did not consciously credit even as he attempted to prove it. The tightly woven rings appeared to be of verdigrised copper, but the edge of Samlor's knife could not even mar the apparent corrosion. "Blood and balls," the caravan master swore under his breath.

He was touching one of the two famed suits of armor forged by the sorcerer Hast-ra-kodi in the fire of a burning diamond. Forged with the help of two demons, legend had it; and if that was open to doubt by a modern rationalist, there could be no doubt at all that the indestructible armor had clothed heroes for three of the five ages of the world.

Then, twelve hundred years ago, the twin brothers Harash and Hakkad had donned the mail and marched against the wizard-prince Sterl. A storm overtook the expedition in the mountains; and in the clear light of dawn, all had disappeared—armor, brothers, and the three thousand men of their armament. Some said the earth had gaped; others, that everything had been swallowed by the still-wider jaws of airy monsters whose teeth flashed in the lightning and whose backs arched high as the thunderheads. Whatever the cause, the armor had vanished that night. The reappearance of one of the suits in this underground room gave Samlor his first tangible proof of the power that slunk through the skittering passages.

From the opening across the room came the sound of metal scraping stone, scraping and jingling. Samlor backed against the wall, sucking his cheeks hollow.

Into the chamber of living rock stepped the other suit of Hast-ra-kodi's armor. This one fitted snugly about a man whom it utterly covered, creating a figure that had nothing human in it but its shape. The unknown metal glowed green, and the sword the figure bore free in one gauntleted hand blazed like a green torch.

"Do you come to worship Dyareela?" the figure asked in a voice rusty with disuse.

Samlor set his lamp carefully on the flooring and sidled a pace away from it. "I worship Heqt," he said, fingering his medallion with his left hand. "And some others, perhaps. But not Dyareela."

The figure laughed as it took a step forward. "I worshiped Heqt, too. I was her priest—until I came down into the tunnels to purge them of the evil they held." The tittering laughter ricocheted about the stone walls like the sound caged weasels make. "Dyareela put a penance on me in return for my life, my life, my life. . . . I wear this armor. That will be your penance too, Cirdonian: put on the other suit."

"Let me pass, priest," Samlor said. His hands were trembling. He clutched them together on his bosom. His fighting knife was sheathed.

"No priest," the figure rasped, advancing.

"Man! Let me pass!"

"No man, not man," said the thing, its blade rising and a flame that dimmed the oil lamp. "They say you keep your knife sharp, *suppliant*— but did gods forge it? Can it shear the mesh of Hast-ra-kodi?"

Samlor palmed the bodkin-pointed push dagger from his wrist sheath and lunged, his left foot thrusting against the wall of the chamber. Armor or no armor, the priest was not a man of war. Samlor's left hand blocked the sword arm while his right slammed the edgeless dagger into the figure's chest. The bodkin slipped through the rings like thread through a needle's eye. The figure's mailed fist caught the Cirdonian and tore the skin over his cheek. Samlor had already twisted his steel clear. He punched it home again through armor, ribs, and the spongy lungs within.

The figure staggered back. The sword clanged to the stone flooring. "What—?" it began. Something slopped and gurgled within the indestructible helmet. The dagger hilt was a dark tumor against the glowing mail. The figure groped vainly at the knob hilt with both hands. "What are you?" it asked in a whisper. "You're not a man, not . . ." Muscles and sinews loosened as the brain controlling them starved for lack of oxygen. One knee buckled and the figure sprawled headlong on the stone. The green glow seeped out of it like blood from a rag, staining the flooring and dripping through it in turn.

"If you'd been a man in your time," Samlor said harshly, "I wouldn't have had to be here now."

He rolled the figure over to retrieve his bodkin from the bone in which it had lodged. Hemorrhages from mouth and nose had smeared the front of the helmet. To Samlor's surprise, the suit of mail now gaped open down the front. It was ready to be stripped off and worn by another. The body within was shriveled, its skin as white as that of the grubs that burrow beneath tree bark.

Samlor wiped his edgeless blade with thumb and forefinger. A tiny streak of blood was the only sign that it had slipped between metal lines to do murder. The Cirdonian left both suits of armor in the room. They had not preserved other wearers. Wizard mail and its tricks were for those who could control it, and Samlor was all too conscious of his own humanity.

The passageway bent, then formed a tee with a narrow corridor a hundred paces long. The corridor was closed at either end by living rock. Its far wall was, by contrast, artificial—basalt hexagons a little more than a foot in diameter across the flats. There was no sign of a doorway. Samlor remembered the iron grates clanging behind him what seemed a lifetime ago. He wiped his right palm absently on his thigh.

The caravan master walked slowly down and back the length of the corridor, from end to end. The basalt plaques were indistinguishable one from another. They rose ten feet to a bare ceiling that still bore the tool marks of its cutting. Samlor stared at the basalt from the head of the tee, aware that the oil in his lamp was low and that he had no way of replenishing it.

After a moment he looked down at the floor. Struck by a sudden notion, he opened his fly and urinated at the base of the wall. The stream splashed, then rolled steadily to the right down the invisible trench worn by decades of footsteps. Thirty feet down the corridor the liquid stopped and pooled, slimed with patches of dust that broke up the reflected lamplight.

Samlor examined with particular care the plaques just beyond the pool of urine. The seeming music was louder here. He set his knife point against one of the hexagons and touched his forehead to the butt cap. Clearly and triumphantly rolled the notes of a hydraulic organ, played somewhere in the complex of tunnels. Samlor sheathed the knife again

and sighted along the stones themselves, holding the light above his
head. The polished surface of one waist-high plaque had been dulled by
sweat and wear. Samlor pressed it and the next hexagon over hinged out
of the wall.

The plaque that had lifted was only a hand's breadth thick, but what
the lamp showed beyond it was a tunnel rather than a room: the remain-
der of the wall was of natural basalt columns, twenty feet long and lying
on their sides. To go further, Samlor would have to crawl along a hole
barely wide enough to pass his shoulders; and the other end was capped
as well.

Samlor had spent his working life under an open sky. He had thus far
borne the realization of the tons of rock above his head only by res-
olutely not thinking about it. This rathole left him no choice . . . but he
would go through it anyway. A man had to be able to control his mind,
or he wasn't a man. . . .

The Cirdonian set the lamp on the floor. It would gutter out in a few
minutes anyway. If he had tried to take it into the tunnel with him, it
would almost immediately have sucked all the life from the narrow column of air among the hexagons. He drew his fighting knife and, holding
both arms out in front of him, wormed through the opening. His body
blocked all but the least glimmer of the light behind him, and the black
basalt drank even that.

Progress was a matter of groping with boot toes and left palm,
fighting the friction of his shoulders and pelvis scraping the rock. Samlor took shallow breaths, but even so before he had crawled his own
length the air became stale. It hugged him like a flabby blanket as he
inched forward in the darkness. The music of the water organ was all
about him.

The knife point clinked on the far capstone. Samlor squirmed a little
nearer, prayed to Heqt, and thrust outward with his left hand. The stone
swung aside. Breathable air flooded the Cirdonian with the rush of organ
music.

Too relieved to be concerned at what besides air might wait beyond
the opening, Samlor struggled out. He caught himself on his knuckles
and left palm, then scrabbled to get his legs back under him. He had
crawled through the straight side of a semicircular room. Panels in the
arched ceiling fifty feet above his head lighted the room ocher. It was

surely not dawn yet. Samlor realized he had no idea of what might be the ultimate source of the clear, rich light.

The hydraulic organ must still be at a distance from this vaulted chamber, but the music made the walls vibrate with its intensity. There was erotic love in the higher notes, and from the lower register came fear as deep and black as that which had settled in Samlor's belly hours before. Lust and mindless hatred lilted, rippling and bubbling through the sanctuary. Samlor's fist squeezed his dagger hilt in frustration. He was only the thickness of the edge short of running amok in this empty room. Then he caught himself, breathed deeply, and sheathed the weapon until he had a use for it.

An archway in the far wall suggested a door. Samlor began walking toward it, aware of the scrapes the basalt had given him and the groin muscle he had pulled while wrestling with the figure in armor. *I'm not as young as I was*, he thought. Then he smiled in a way that meshed all too well with the pattern of the music: after all, he was likely through with the problems of aging very soon.

The sanctuary was strewn with pillows and thick brocades. There was more substantial furniture also. Its patterns were unusual but their function was obvious in context. Samlor had crossed enough of the world to have seen most things, but his personal tastes remained simple. He thought of Samlane; fury lashed him again. This time instead of gripping the knife, he touched the medallion of Heqt. He kicked at a rack of switches. They clattered into a construct of ebony with silken tie-downs. Its three hollow levels could be adjusted toward one another by the pulleys and levers at one end of it.

Well, it wasn't for her, Samlor thought savagely. It was for the house, the honor of the Lords Kodrix of Cirdon. And perhaps—perhaps for Heqt. He'd never been a religious man, always figured it'd be best if the gods settled things among themselves . . . but there were some things that *any* man—

Well, that was a lie. Not any man, just Samlor hil Samt for sure and probably no other fool so damned on the whole continent. Well, so be it then; he was a fool and a fanatic, and before the night finished he'd have spilled the blood of a so-called demon or died trying.

Because the illumination was from above, Samlor had noticed the bas reliefs only as patterns of shadows along the walls. The detail struck him as he approached the archway. He stopped and looked carefully.

The carvings formed a series of panels running in bands across the polished stone. The faces in each tableau were modeled with a precise detail that made it likely they were portraits, though none of the personages were recognizable to Samlor. He peered up the curving walls and saw the bands continuing to the roof vaults. How and when they had been carved was beyond estimation; the caravan master was not even sure he could identify the stone, creamy and mottled but seemingly much harder than marble.

Time was of indeterminable importance. Knowing that he might have only minutes to live, Samlor began following some of the series of reliefs. One group of carvings made clear the unguessed unity between the "sorcerer" Hast-ra-kodi and the "goddess" Dyareela. Samlor stared at the conclusion of the pattern, swallowing hard but not speaking. He was unutterably glad he had not donned either suit of mail when he might have done so.

The panels reeked of bloodshed and repression. Kings and priests had stamped out the worship of Dyareela a hundred times in a hundred places. The rites had festered in the darkness, then burst out again—cancers metastasizing from the black lump here in the vaults beneath Sanctuary. A shrine in the wasteland before it was a city; and even as a city, a brawling, stinking, leaderless hive where no one looked too hard for Evil's heart since Evil's limbs enveloped all.

Alar hil Aspar—a brash outsider, a reformer flushed with his triumph over brigandage—had at last razed the fane of Dyareela here. Instead of salt, he had sown the ruins with a temple to Heqt, the goddess of his upbringing. Fool that he was, Alar had thought that ended it.

Just above the archway, set off from the courses around it by a border of ivy leaves, was a cameo that caught Samlor's eye as he returned sick and exhausted by what he had been looking at. A file of women led by a piper cavorted through the halls of a palace. The women carried small animals and icons of obviously more than symbolic significance, but it was to the piper's features that Samlor's gaze was drawn. The Cirdonian swore mildly and reached up to touch the stone. It was smooth and cold to his fingertips.

So much fit. Enough, perhaps.

Samlor stepped through the double-hung doors closing the archway.

The crossbowman waiting beyond with his eyes on the staircase screamed and spun around. The patterned screen that would have concealed the ambush from someone descending the stairs was open to the archway—but judging from the bowman's panic, the mere sight of something approaching from the sanctuary would probably have flushed him anyway.

Samlor had survived too many attacks ever to be wholly unprepared for another. He lunged forward, shouting to further disconcert the bowman. The screen was toppling as the bowman jerked back from the fingers of Samlor's left hand thrusting for his eyes. The bowstring slapped and the quarrel spilled chips from the archway before ricocheting sideways through a swinging door panel. Samlor, sprawled across his attacker's lower legs, slashed at the other's face with the knife he had finally cleared. The bowman cried out again and parried with the stock of his own weapon. Samlor's edge thudded into the wood like an ax in a fire log. Three of the bowman's fingers flew out into the room.

Unaware of his maiming, the bowman tried to club Samlor with his weapon. It slipped away from him. He saw the blood-spouting stumps of his left hand, the index finger itself half severed. Fright had made the bowman scream; mutilation now choked his voice with a rush of vomit.

Samlor squirmed forward, pinning his attacker's torso with his own. He wrestled the crossbow out of the unresisting right hand. There was a pouch of iron quarrels at the bowman's belt, but Samlor ignored them: they were on the left side and no longer a threat. The gagging man wore the scarlet and gold livery of Regli's household.

The Cirdonian glanced quickly around the room, seeing nothing but a helical staircase reaching toward more lighted panels a hundred feet above. He waggled his knife a foot from his captive's eyes, then brought the point of it down on the other's nose. "You tried to kill me," he said softly. "Tell me why or you're missing more than some fingers only."

"Sabellia, Sabellia," the maimed retainer moaned. "You've ruined me now, you bastard."

Samlor flicked his blade sideways, knowing that the droplet of blood that sprang out would force the other's eyes to cross on it. They would fill with its red proximity. "Talk to me, little man," the caravan master said. "Why are you here?"

The injured man swallowed bile. "My lord Regli," he said, closing his eyes to avoid the blood and the dagger point, "he said you'd killed his wife. He sent us all after you."

Samlor laid the dagger point on the other's left eye socket. "How many?" he demanded.

"A dozen," gabbled the other. "All the guards and us coachmen besides."

"The watch?"

"Oh, gods, get that away from my eye," the retainer moaned. "I almost shook—" Samlor raised the blade an inch. "Not the watch," the other went on. "My lord wants to handle this himself for the, the scandal."

"And where are the others?" The point dipped, brushed an eyelash, and rose again harmlessly.

The wounded man was rigid. He breathed trough his mouth, quick gasps as if a lungful of air would preserve him in the moment the knife edge sawed through his windpipe. "They all thought you'd run for Cirdon," he whispered. "You'd left your cloak behind. I slipped it away, took it to a S'danzo I know. She's a liar like all of them, but sometimes not. . . . I told her I'd pay her for the truth of where I'd find you, and I'd pay her for nothing; but I'd take a lie out of her hide if six of my friends had to hold down her blacksmith buddy. She, she described where I'd meet you. I recognized it, I'd taken the Lady Samlane—"

"Here?" Samlor's voice and his knife both trembled. Death slid closer to the room than it had been since the first slash and scramble of the fight.

"Lord, lord," the captive pleaded. "Only this far. I swear by my mother's bones!"

"Go on, then." The knife did not move.

The other man swallowed. "That's all. I waited here—I didn't tell anybody, Lord Regli put a thousand royals on your head . . . and . . . and the S'danzo said I'd live through the meeting. Oh gods, the slut, the slut."

Samlor smiled. "She hasn't lied to you yet," he said. The smile was gone, replaced with a bleakness as cruel as the face of a glacier. "Listen," he went on, rising to one knee and pinning his prisoner by psychological dominance in the stead of his body weight. "My sister asked me for a knife. I told her I'd leave her one if she gave me a reason to."

A spasm racked the Cirdonian's face. His prisoner winced at the trembling of the dagger point. "She said the child wasn't Regli's," Samlor went on. "Well, whoever thought it would be, the way she sniffed around? But she said a demon had got it on her . . . and that bothered even her at the last. Being used, she said. Being used. She'd tried to have it aborted after she thought about things for a while, but a priest of Heqt was waiting with Regli in the shop where she'd gone to buy the drugs. After that, she wasn't without somebody watching her, asleep or awake. The temple of Heqt wanted the child born. Samlane said she'd use the knife to end the child when they pulled it from her . . . and I believed that, though I knew she'd be in no shape for knifings just after she'd whelped.

"Seems she knew that too, but she was more determined than even I'd have given her credit for being. She could give a lot of folks points for stubborn, my sister."

Samlor shook himself, then gripped a handful of the captive's tunic. He ripped the garment with his knife. "What are you doing?" the retainer asked in concern.

"Tying you up. Somebody'll find you here in time. I'm going to do what I came here for, and when it's done I'll leave Sanctuary. If I've got that option still."

Sweat was washing streaks in the blood flecks on the captive's face. "Sweet goddess, don't do that," he begged. "Not tied, not—that. You haven't been here when . . . others were here. You—" The injured man wiped his lips with his tongue. He closed his eyes. "Kill me yourself, if you must," he said so softly it was almost a matter for lip-reading to understand him. "Don't leave me here."

Samlor stood. His left hand was clenched, his right holding the dagger pointed down at a slight angle. "Stand up," he ordered. Regli's man obeyed, wide-eyed. He braced his back against the wall, holding his left hand at shoulder height but refusing to look at its ruin. The severed arteries had pinched off. Movement had dislodged some of the scabs, but the blood only oozed instead of spurting as it had initially. "Tell Regli that I'm mending my family's honor in my way, as my sister seems to have done in hers," Samlor said. "But don't tell him where you found me—or how. If you want to leave here now, you'll swear that."

"I swear!" the other babbled. "By anything you please!"

The caravan master's smile flickered again. "Did you ever kill anyone, boy?" he asked conversationally.

"I was a coachman," the other said with a nervous frown. "I—I mean . . . no."

"Once I pulled a man apart with hot pincers," Samlor continued quietly. "He was headman of a tribe that had taken our toll payment but still tried to cut out a couple horses from the back of our train. I slipped into the village that night, jerked the chief out of his bed, and brought him back to the laager. In the morning I fixed him as a display for the rest." The Cirdonian reached forward and wiped his dagger clean on the sleeve of the other man's tunic. "Don't go back on your word to me, friend," he said.

Regli's man edged to the helical staircase. As he mounted each of the first dozen steps, he looked back over his shoulder at the Cirdonian. When the pursuit or thrown knife did not come as he had feared or expected, the retainer ran up the next twenty steps without pausing. He looked down from that elevation and said, "One thing, master."

"Say it," responded Samlor.

"They opened the Lady Samlane to give the child separate burial."

"Yes?"

"And it didn't look to be demon spawn, as you say," Regli's man called. "It was a perfect little boy. Except that your knife was through its skull."

Samlor began to climb the steps, ignoring the scrabbling slippers of the man above him on the twisting staircase. The door at the top thudded, leaving nothing of the hapless ambusher but splotches of his blood on the railing. Should have stuck to his horses, Samlor thought. He laughed aloud, well aware that the epitaph probably applied to himself as well. Still, he had a better notion than that poor fool of a coachman of what he was getting into . . . though the gods all knew how slight were his chances of getting out of it alive. If the fellow he was looking for was a real magician, rather than someone like Samlor himself who had learned a few spells while knocking around the world, it was over for sure.

The door at the top of the stairs pivoted outward. Samlor tested it with a fingertip, then paused to steady his heart and breathing. As he stood there, his left hand sought the toad-faced medallion. The dagger in his right hand pointed down, threatening nothing at the moment but ready.

He pushed the door open.

On the other side, the secret opening was only a wall panel. Its frescoes were geometric and in no way different from those of the rest of the temple hallway. To the left, the hall led to an outside door heavily banded with iron. From his livery and the mutilation of his outflung left hand, the coachman could be recognized where he lay. The rest of the retainer appeared to have been razored into gobbets of flesh and bone, no other one of them as large as what remained of the left hand. Under the circumstances, Samlor had no sympathy to waste on the corpse.

The Cirdonian sighed and turned to the right, stepping through the hangings of brass beads into the sanctuary of Heqt. The figure he expected was waiting for him.

Soft, gray dawnlight crept through hidden slits in the dome. Mirrors had been designed to light the grinning, gilded toad face of Heqt at the top of the dome beneath the spire. Instead, the light was directed downward onto the figure on the floral mosaic in the center of the great room. The hair of the waiting man glowed like burning wire. "Did the night keep you well, friend?" Samlor called as he stepped forward.

"Well," agreed the other with a nod. There was no sign of the regular priests and acolytes of Heqt. The room brightened as if the light fed on the beauty of the waiting man. "As I see she kept you, Champion of Heqt."

"No champion," Samlor said, taking another step as casual as the long knife dangling from his right hand. "Just a man looking for the demon who caused his sister's death. I didn't have to look any farther than the bench across the street last night, did I?"

The other's voice was a rich tenor. It had a vibrancy that had been missing when he and Samlor had talked of Heqt and Dyareela the night before. "Heqt keeps sending her champions, and I . . . I deal with them. You met the first of them, the priest?"

"I came looking for a demon," the Cirdonian said, walking very slowly, "and all it was, was a poor madman who had convinced himself that he was a god."

"I am Dyareela."

"You're a man who saw an old carving down below that looked like him," Samlor said. "That worked on your mind, and you worked on other people's minds. . . . My sister, now, she was convinced her child would look like a man but be a demon. She killed it in her womb. The only way that she'd have been able to kill it, because they'd never have let her near it, Regli's heir, and her having tried abortion. But such a waste, because it was just a child, only a madman's child."

The sun-crowned man gripped the throat of his white tunic and ripped downward with unexpected strength. "I am Dyareela," it said. Its right breast was pendulous, noticeably larger than the left. The male genitals were of normal size, flaccid, hiding the vulva that must lie behind them. "The one there," it said, gesturing toward the wall beyond which the coachman lay, "came to my fane to shed blood without my leave." The naked figure giggled. "Perhaps I'll have you wash in his blood, Champion," it said. "Perhaps that will be the start of your penance."

"A mad little hermaphrodite who knows a spell or two," Samlor said. "But there'll be no penance for any again from you, little one. You're fey, and I know a spell for your sort. She wasn't much, but I'll have your heart for what you led my sister to."

"Will you conjure me by Heqt, then, Champion?" asked the other with its arms spread in welcome and laughter in its liquid voice. "Her temple is my temple, her servants are my servants . . . the blood of her champions is mine for a sacrifice!"

Samlor was twenty feet away, a full turn and a half. He clutched his medallion left-handed, hoping it would give him enough time to complete his spell. "Do I look like a priest to talk about gods?" he said. "Watch my dagger, madman."

The other smiled, waiting as Samlor cocked the heavy blade. It caught a stray beam of sunlight. The double edge flashed back dawn.

"By the Earth that bore this," Samlor cried, "and the Mind that gave it shape;

"By the rown of this hilt and the silver wire that laps it;

"By the cold iron of this blade and by the white-hot flames it flowed from;

"By the blood it has drunk and the souls it has eaten—*know thy hour!*"

Samlor hurled the dagger. It glinted as it rotated. The blade was point-first and a hand's breadth from the smiling face when it exploded in a flash and a thunderclap that shook the city. The concussion hurled Samlor backward, bleeding from the nose and ears. The air was dense with flecks of paint and plaster from the frescoed ceiling.

Dyareela stood with the same smile, arms lifting in triumph, lips opening further in throaty laughter. *"Mine for a sacrifice!"*

A webbing of tiny cracks was spreading from the center of the dome high above. Samlor staggered to his feet, choking on dust and knowing that if he was lucky he was about to die.

Heqt's gilded bronze head, backed by the limestone spire, plunged down from the ceiling. It struck Dyareela's upturned face like a two-hundred-ton crossbow bolt. The floor beneath disintegrated. The limestone column scarcely slowed, hurtling out of sight as the earth itself shuddered to the impact.

Samlor lost his footing in the remains of Regli's coachman. An earth-shock pitched him forward against the door panel. It was unlocked. The Cirdonian lunged out into the street as the shattered dome followed its pinnacle into a cavern that gaped with a sound like the lowest note of an organ played by gods.

Samlor sprawled in the muddy street. All around him men were shouting and pointing. The Cirdonian rolled onto his back and looked at the collapsing temple.

Above the ruins rose a pall of shining dust. More than imagination shaped the cloud into the head of a toad.

The Fruit of Enlibar

Lynn Abbey

The hillside groves of orange trees were all that remained of the legendary glory of Enlibar. Humbled descendants of the rulers of an empire dwarfing Ilsig or Ranke eked out their livings among the gnarled, ancient trees. They wrapped each unripe fruit in leaves for the long caravan journey and wrapped each harvest in a fresh retelling of their legends. By shrewd storytelling these once proud families survived, second only to the S'danzo in their ability to create mystery, but like the S'danzo crones they flavored their legends with truth and kept the skeptics at bay.

The oranges of Enlibar made their way to Sanctuary once a year. When the fist-sized fruits were nearly ripe, Haakon, the sweetmeat vendor of the bazaar, would fill his cart and hawk oranges in the town as well as in the stalls of the bazaar. During those few days he would make enough money to buy expensive trinkets for his wife and children, another year's lodgings for his mistress, and have enough gold left to take to Gonfred, the only honest goldsmith in town.

The value of each orange was such that Haakon would ignore the unwritten code of the bazaar and reserve the best of his limited supply for his patrons at the Governor's Palace. It had happened, however, that

two of the precious fruits had been bruised. Haakon decided not to sell
that pair at all but to share them with his friends the bazaar smith,
Dubro, and his young wife, the half-S'danzo Illyra.

He scored the peel deftly with an inlaid silver tool meant especially for
this one purpose. When his fingers moved away the pebbly rind fell back
from the deep-colored pulp and Illyra gasped with delight. She took one
of the pulp sections and drizzled the juice onto the back of her hand,
then lapped it up with the tip of her tongue: the mannerly way to savor
the delicate flavor of the bloodred juice.

"These are the best; better than last year's," she exclaimed with a
smile.

"You say that every year, Illyra. Time dulls your memory; the taste
brings it back." Haakon sucked the juice off his hand with less delicacy:
his lips showed the Stain of Enlibar. "And, speaking of time dulling your
memory—Dubro, do you recall, about fifteen years back, a death-pale
boy with straw hair and wild eyes running about the town?"

Haakon watched as Dubro closed his eyes and sank back in thought.
The smith would have been a raw youth then himself, but he had
always been slow, deliberate, and utterly reliable in his judgments.
Illyra would have been a skirt-clinging toddler that long ago so
Haakon did not think to ask her, nor to glance her way while he
awaited Dubro's reply. Had he done so he would have seen her tremble
and a bloodred drop of juice disappear into the fine dust beneath her
chair.

"Yes," Dubro said without opening his eyes, "I remember one as that:
quiet, pale . . . nasty. Lived a few years with the garrison, then disappeared."

"Would you know him again after all this time?"

"Nay. He was that sort of lad who looks childish until he becomes a
man, then one never sees the child in his face again."

"Would you reckon 'Walegrin' to be his name?"

Ignored, beside them, Illyra bit down on her tongue and stifled sudden
panic before it became apparent.

"It might be . . . nay, I could not be sure. I doubt as I ever spoke to the
lad by name."

Haakon shrugged as if the questions had been idle conversation. Illyra
ate her remaining share of the oranges, then went into the ramshackle

stall, where she lit three cones of incense before returning to the men with a ewer of water.

"Illyra, I've just asked your husband if he'd come with me to the palace. I've got two sacks of oranges to deliver for the prince and another set of arms would make the work easier. But he says he won't leave you here alone."

Illyra hesitated. The memories Haakon had aroused were still fresh in her mind, but all that had been fifteen years ago, as he had said. She stared at the clouded-over sky.

"No, there'll be no problem. It may rain today and, anyway, you've taken everyone's money this week with your oranges," she said with forced brightness.

"Well then, you see Dubro—there's no problem. Bank the fires and we'll be off. I'll have you back sweating again before the first raindrops fall."

Illyra watched them leave. Fear filled the forge, fear left over from a dimly remembered childhood. Visions she had shared with no one, not even Dubro. Visions not even the S'danzo gifts could resolve into truth or illusion. She caught up her curly black hair with a set of combs and went back inside.

When the bed was concealed under layers of gaudy, bright cloth and her youth under layers of kohl, Illyra was ready to greet the townsfolk. She had not exaggerated her complaints about the oranges. It was just as well that Haakon's supply was diminishing. For two days now she had had no querents until late in the day. Lonely and bored she watched the incense smoke curl into the darkness of the room, losing herself in its endless variations.

"Illyra?"

A man drew back the heavy cloth curtain. Illyra did not recognize his voice. His silhouette revealed only that he was as tall as Dubro, though not as broad.

"Illyra? I was told I'd find Illyra, the crone, here."

She froze. Any querent might have cause to resent a S'danzo prophecy, regardless of its truth, and plot revenge against the seeress. Only recently she had been threatened by a man in the red-and-gold livery of a Rankan lord. Her hand slid under the folds of the tablecloth and eased a tiny dagger loose from a sheath nailed to the table leg.

"What do you want?" She held her voice steady; greeting a paying querent rather than a thug.

"To talk with you. May I come in?" He paused, waiting for a reply, and when there was none continued, "You seem unduly suspicious, S'danzo. Do you have many enemies here, little sister?"

He stepped into the room and let the cloth fall behind him. Illyra's dagger slid silently from her hand into the folds of her skirts.

"Walegrin."

"You remember so quickly? Then you did inherit *her* gift?"

"Yes, I inherited it, but this morning I learned that you had returned to Sanctuary."

"Three weeks past. It has not changed at all except, perhaps, for the worse. I had hoped to complete my business without disturbing you but I have encountered complications, and I doubt any of the other S'danzo would help me."

"The S'danzo will never forget."

Walegrin eased his bulk into one of Dubro's chairs. Light from the candelabra fell on his face. He endured the exposure, though—as Dubro had guessed—there was no trace of youth left in his features. He was tall and pale, lean in the way of powerful men whose gentler tissues have boiled away. His hair was sun-bleached to brittle straw, confined by four thick braids and a bronze circlet. Even for Sanctuary he cut an exotic, barbarian figure.

"Are you satisfied?" he asked when her gaze returned to the velvet in front of her.

"You have become very much like him," she answered slowly.

"I think not, 'Lyra. My tastes, anyway, do not run as our father's did—so put aside your fears on that account. I've come for your help. True S'danzo help, as your mother could have given me. I could pay you in gold, but I have other items which might tempt you more."

He reached under his bronze-studded leather kilt to produce a suede pouch of some weight, which he set, unopened, on the table. She began to open it when he leaned forward and grasped her wrist tightly.

"It wasn't me, 'Lyra. I wasn't there that night. I ran away, just like you did."

His voice carried Illyra back those fifteen years, sweeping the doubts from her memories. "I was a child then, Walegrin. A little child, no more than four. Where could I have run to?"

He released her wrist and sat back in the chair. Illyra emptied the pouch onto her table. She recognized only a few of the beads and bracelets, but enough to realize that she gazed upon all of her mother's jewelry. She picked up a string of blue glass beads strung on a creamy braided silk.

"These have been restrung," she said simply.

Walegrin nodded. "Blood rots the silk and stinks to the gods. I had no choice. All the others are as they were."

Illyra let the beads fall back into the pile. He had known how to tempt her. The entire heap was not worth a single gold piece, but no storehouse of gold could have been more valuable to her.

"Well, then, what do you want from me?"

He pushed the trinkets aside and from another pouch produced a palm-sized pottery shard, which he placed gently on the velvet.

"Tell me everything about that: where the rest of the tablet is; how it came to be broken; what the symbols mean—everything!"

There was nothing in the jagged fragment that justified the change that came over Walegrin as he spoke of it. Illyra saw a piece of common orange pottery with a crowded black design set under the glaze; the sort of ware that could be found in any household of the empire. Even with her S'danzo gifts focused on the shard it remained stubbornly common. Illyra looked at Walegrin's icy green eyes, his thought-protruded brows, the set of his chin atop the studded vambrace on his forearm, and thought better of telling him what she actually saw.

"Its secrets are locked deeply within it. To a casual glance its disguises are perfect. Only prolonged examination will draw its secrets out." She placed the shard back on the table.

"How long?"

"It would be hard to say. The gift is strengthened by symbolic cycles. It may take until the cycle of the shard coincides. . . ."

"I know the S'danzo! I was there with you and your mother—don't play bazaar games with me, little sister. I know too much."

Illyra sat back on her bench. The dagger in her skirts clunked to the floor. Walegrin bent over to pick it up. He turned it over in his hands and without warning thrust it through the velvet into the table. Then, with his palm against the smooth of the blade, he bent it back until the hilt touched the table. When he removed his hand the knife remained bent.

"Cheap steel. Modern stuff, death to the one who relies on it," he explained, drawing a sleek knife from within the vambrace. He placed the dark, steel blade with the beads and bracelets. "Now, tell me about my pottery."

"No bazaar games. If I didn't know from looking at you, I'd say it was a broken piece of 'cotta. You've had it a long time. It shows nothing but its associations with you. I believe it is more than that, or you wouldn't be here. You know about the S'danzo and what you call 'bazaar games,' but it's true—right now I see nothing; later I might. There are ways to strengthen the vision—I'll try them."

He flipped a gold coin onto the table. "Get what you'll need."

"Only my cards," she answered, flustered by his gesture.

"Get them!" he ordered without picking up the coin.

She removed the worn deck from the depths of her blouse and set the shard atop them while she lit more candles and incense. She allowed Walegrin to cut the pack into three piles, then turned over the topmost card of each pile.

Three of Flames: a tunnel running from light to darkness with three candle sconces along the way.

The Forest: primeval, gnarled trunks; green canopy; living twilight.

Seven of Ore: red clay; the potter with his wheel and kiln.

Illyra stared at the images, losing herself in them without finding harmony or direction. The Flame card was pivotal, but the array would not yield its perspective to her; the Forest, symbolic of the wisdom of the ages, seemed unlikely as either her brother's goal or origin; and the Seven must mean more than was obvious. But, was the Ore card appearing in its creativity aspect? Or was red clay the omen of bloodletting, as was so often true when the card appeared in a Sanctuary-cast array?

"I still do not see enough. Bazaar games or not, this is not the time to scry this thing."

"I'll come again after sundown—that would be a better time, wouldn't it? I've no garrison duties until after sunrise tomorrow."

"For the cards, yes, of course, but Dubro will have banked the forge for the night by then, and I do not want to involve him in this."

Walegrin nodded without argument. "I understand. I'll come by at midnight. He should be long asleep by then, unless you keep him awake."

Illyra sensed it would be useless to argue. She watched silently as he swept the pile of baubles, the knife, and the shard into one pouch, wincing slightly as he dribbled the last beads from her sight.

"As is your custom, payment will not be made until the question is answered."

Illyra nodded. Walegrin had spent many years around her mother learning many of the S'danzo disciplines and rousing his father's explosive jealousy. The leather webbing of his kilt creaked as he stood up. The moment for farewell came and passed. He left the stall in silence.

A path cleared when Walegrin strode through a crowd. He noticed it here, in this bazaar where his memories were of scrambling through the aisles, taunted, cursed, fighting, and thieving. In any other place he accepted the deference except here, which had once been his home for a while.

One of the few men in the throng who could match his height, a dark man in a smith's apron, blocked his way a moment. Walegrin studied him obliquely and guessed he was Dubro. He had seen the smith's short aquiline companion several times in other roles about the town without learning the man's true name or calling; they each glanced to one side to avoid a chance meeting.

At the entrance to the bazaar, near a tumbledown set of columns still showing traces of the Ilsigi kings who had them built, a man crept out of the shadows and fell in step beside Walegrin. Though this second had the manner and dress of the cityborn, his face was like Walegrin's: lean, hard, and parched.

"What have you learned, Thrusher?" Walegrin began, without looking down.

"That man Downwind who claimed to read such things . . ."

"Yes?"

"Runo went down to meet with him, as you were told. When he did not return for duty this morning Malm and I went to look for him. We found them both . . . and these." He handed his captain two small copper coins.

Walegrin turned them over in his palm, then threw them far into the harbor. "I'll take care of this myself. Tell the others we will have a visitor at the garrison this evening—a woman."

"Yes, Captain," Thrusher responded, a surprised grin making its way across his jaw. "Shall I send the men away?"

"No, set them as guards. Nothing is going well. Each time we have set a rendezvous something has gone wrong. At first it was petty nuisance, now Runo is dead. I will not take chances in this city above all others. And, Thrusher . . ." Walegrin caught his man by the elbow. "Thrusher, this woman is S'danzo, my half-sister. See that the men understand this."

"They will understand, we all have families somewhere."

Walegrin grimaced and Thrusher understood that his commander had not suddenly weakened to admit family concerns.

"We have need of the S'danzo? Surely there are more reliable seers in Sanctuary than scrounging the aisles of the bazaar. Our gold is good and nearly limitless." Thrusher, like many men in the Rankan Empire, considered the S'danzo best suited to resolving love triangles among house servants.

"We have need of this one."

Thrusher nodded and oozed back into the shadows as deftly as he had emerged. Walegrin waited until he was alone on the filthy streets before changing direction and striding, shoulders set and fists balled, into the tangled streets of the Maze.

The whores of the Maze were a special breed unwelcomed in the great pleasure houses beyond the city walls. Their embrace included a poison dagger and their nightly fee was all the wealth that could be removed from a man's person. A knot of these women clung to the doorway of the Vulgar Unicorn, the Maze's approximation of a town hall, but they stepped aside meekly when Walegrin approached. Survival in the Maze depended upon careful selection of the target.

An aura of dark foul air enveloped Walegrin as he stepped down into the sunken room. A moment's quiet passed over the other guests, as it always did when someone entered. A Hell Hound, personal puritan of the prince, could shut down conversation for the duration of his visit, but a garrison officer, even Walegrin, was assumed to have legitimate business and was ignored with the same slit-eyed wariness the regulars accorded one another.

The itinerant storyteller Hakiem occupied the bench Walegrin preferred. The heavy-lidded little man was wilier than most suspected. Clutching his leather mug of small ale tenderly, he had selected one of the few locations in the room that provided a good view of all the exits, public and private. Walegrin stepped forward, intending to intimidate the

weasel from his perch, but thought better of the move. His affairs in the
Maze demanded discretion, not reckless bullying.

From a lesser location he signaled the bartender. No honest wench
would work the Unicorn so Buboe himself brought the foaming mug,
then returned a moment later with one of the Enlibar oranges he had
arranged behind the counter. Walegrin broke the peel with his thumbnail; the red juice ran through the ridges of the peel, forming patterns not
unlike those on his pottery shard.

A one-armed beggar with a scarred face and a pendulous, cloudy eye
sidled into the Unicorn, careful to avoid the disapproving glance of
Buboe. As the ragged creature moved from table to table collecting copper pittance from the disturbed patrons, Walegrin noted the tightly
wound tunic under his rags and knew the left arm was as good as the one
that was snapping up the coins. Likewise, the scar was a self-induced dis-
figurement and the yellow rheum running down his cheek the result of
seeds placed under his eyelids. The beggar announced his arrival at Walegrin's table with a tortured wheeze. Without looking up Walegrin tossed
him a silver coin. He had run with the beggars himself and seen their
cunning deceit become crippling reality many times too often.

Buboe split the last accessible louse in his copious beard between his
grimy fingernails, looked up, and noticed the beggar, whom he threw
into the street. He shuffled a few more mugs of beer to his patrons, then
returned to the never-ending task of chasing lice.

The door opened again, admitting another who, like Walegrin, was in
the Maze on business. Walegrin drew a small circle in the air with a finger and the newcomer hastened to his table.

"My man was slain last night by following your suggestions." Walegrin stared directly into the newcomer's eyes as he spoke.

"So I've heard, and the Enlibrite potter as well. I've rushed over here
to assure you that it was not my doing (though I knew you would suspect
me). Why, Walegrin, even if I did want to double-cross you (and I doubly
assure you that such thoughts never go through my mind) I'd hardly have
killed the Enlibrite as well, would I?"

Walegrin grunted. Who was to say what a man of Sanctuary might do
to achieve his goals? But the information broker was likely to be telling
the truth. He had an air of distracted indignation about him that a liar
would not think to affect.

And if he were truthful then, like as not, Runo had been the victim of coincidental outrage. The coins showed that robbery was not the motive. Perhaps the potter had enemies. Walegrin reminded himself to enter the double slaying in the garrison roster where, in due course, it might be investigated when the dozens preceding it had been disposed of. "Still, once again, I have received no information. I will still make no payment." Walegrin casually spun the beer mug from one hand to the other as he spoke, concealing the import of his conversation from prying eyes.

"There're others who can bait your bear: Markmor, Enas Yorl, even Lythande, if the price is right. Think of this only as a delay, my friend, not failure."

"No! The omens here grow bad. Three times you've tried and failed to get me what I require. I conclude my business with you."

The information broker survived by knowing when to cut his losses. Nodding politely, he left Walegrin without a word and left the Unicorn before Buboe had thought to get his order.

Walegrin leaned back on his stool, hands clenched behind his head, his eyes alert for movement but his thoughts wandering. The death of Runo had affected him deeply, not because the man was a good soldier and longtime companion, though he had been both, but because the death had demonstrated the enduring power of the S'danzo curse on his family. Fifteen years before, the S'danzo community had decreed that all things meaningful to his father should be taken away or destroyed while the man looked helplessly on. For good measure the crones had extended the curse for five generations. Walegrin was the first. He dreaded that day when his path crossed with some forgotten child of his own who would bear him no better will than he bore his own ignominious sire.

It had been sheer madness to return to Sanctuary, to the origin of the curse, despite the assurances of the purple mage's protection. Madness! The S'danzo felt him coming. The purple mage, the one person Walegrin trusted to unravel the spell, had disappeared long before he and his men arrived in town. And now the Enlibrite potter and Runo were dead by some unknown hand. How much longer could he afford to stay? True, there were many magicians here, and any could be bought, but they all had their petty loyalties. If they could reconstruct the shard's inscription, they certainly could not be trusted to keep quiet about it. If Illyra did not provide the answers at midnight, Walegrin resolved to take his men somewhere far from this accursed town.

He would have continued his litany of dislike had he not been brought to alertness by the distress call of a mountain hawk: a bird never seen or heard within the walls of Sanctuary. The call was the alarm signal amongst his men. He left a few coins on the table and departed the Unicorn without undue notice.

A second call led him down a passageway too narrow to be called an alley, much less a street. Moving with stealth and caution, Walegrin eased around forgotten doorways, suspecting ambush with every step. Only a third call and the appearance of a familiar face in the shadows quickened his pace.

"Malm, what is it?" he asked, stepping over some soft, stinking mass without looking down.

"See for yourself."

A weak shaft of light made its way through the jutting roofs of a half-dozen buildings to illuminate a pair of corpses. One was the information broker who had just left Walegrin's company, a makeshift knife still protruding from his neck. The other was the beggar to whom he'd given the silver coin. The latter bore the cleaner mark of the accomplished killer.

"I see," Walegrin replied dully.

"The ragged one, he followed the other away from the Unicorn. I'd been following the broker since we found out about Runo, so I began to follow them both. When the broker caught on that he was being followed, he lit up this cul-de-sac—by mistake, I'd guess—and the beggar followed him. I found the broker like this and killed the beggar myself."

Two more deaths for the curse. Walegrin stared at the bodies, then praised Malm's diligence and sent him back to the garrison barracks to prepare for Illyra's visit. He left the corpses in the cul-de-sac where they might never be found. This pair he would not enter into the garrison roster.

Walegrin paced the length of the town, providing the inhibiting impression of a garrison officer actually on duty, though if a murder had occurred at his feet he would not have noticed. Twice he passed the entrance of the bazaar, twice hesitated, and twice continued on his way. Sunset found him by the Promise of Heaven as the priests withdrew into their temples and the Red Lanterns women made their first promenade. By full darkness he was on the Wideway, hungry and close in spirit to the fifteen-year-old who had swum the harbor and stowed away in the hold of an outbound ship one horrible night many years ago.

In the moonless night that memory returned to him with palpable force. In the grip of his depravities and obsessed by the imagined infidelity of his mistress, his father had tortured and killed her. Walegrin could recall that much. After the murder he had run from the barracks to the harbor. He knew the end of the story from campfire tales after he'd joined the army himself. Unsatisfied with murder, his father had dismembered her body, throwing the head and organs into the palace sewer-stream and the rest into the garrison stewpot.

Sanctuary boasted no criers to shout out the hours of the night. When there was a moon its progress gave approximate time, but in its absence night was an eternity, and midnight that moment when your joints grew stiff from sitting on the damp stone pilings of the Wideway and dark memories threatened the periphery of your vision. Walegrin bought a torch from the cadaverous watchman at the charnel house and entered the quiet bazaar.

Illyra emerged from the blacksmith's stall the second time Walegrin used the mountain hawk cry. She had concealed herself in a dark cloak, which she held tightly around herself. Her movements betrayed her fears. Walegrin led the way in hurried silence. He took her arm at the elbow when they came into sight of the barracks. She hesitated, then continued without his urging.

Walegrin's men were nowhere to be seen in the common room that separated the men's and offices' quarters. Illyra paced the room like a caged animal, remembering.

"You'll need a table, candles, and what else?" he asked, eager to be on with the night's activity and suddenly mindful that he had brought her back to this place.

"It's so much smaller than I remember it," she said, then added, "Just the table and candles, I've brought the rest myself."

Walegrin pulled a table closer to the hearth. While he gathered up candles she unfastened her cloak and placed it over the table. She wore somber woolens appropriate for a modest woman from the better part of town instead of the gaudy layers of the S'danzo costume. Walegrin wondered from whom she had borrowed them and if she had told her husband after all. It mattered little so long as she could pierce the spell over his shard.

"Shall I leave you alone?" Walegrin asked after removing the pottery fragment from the pouch and placing it on the table.

"No, I don't want to be alone in here." Illyra shuffled her fortune cards, dropping several in her nervousness, then set the deck back on the table and asked, "Is it too much to ask for some wine and information about what I'm supposed to be looking for?" A trace of the bazaar scrappiness returned to her voice and she was less lost within the room.

"My man Thrusher wanted to lay in an orgy feast when I told him I'd require the common room tonight. Then I told him I only wanted the men out—but it's a poor barracks without a flask in it, poorer than Sanctuary." He found a half-filled wineskin behind a sideboard, squirted some into his mouth, and swallowed with a rare smile. "Not the best vintage, but passable. You'll have to drink from the skin. . . ." He handed it to her.

"I drank from a skin before I'd seen a cup. It's a trick you never forget." Illyra took the wineskin from him and caught a mouthful of wine without splattering a drop. "Now, Walegrin," she began, emboldened by the musty wine, "Walegrin, I can't get either your pottery nor Haakon's oranges out of my mind. What is the connection?"

"If this Haakon peddles Enlibar oranges, then it's simple. I got the shard in Enlibar, in the ruins of the armory there. We searched three days and found only this. But, if anyone's got a greater piece, he knows not what he has, else there'd be an army massing somewhere that'd have the empire quaking."

Illyra's eyes widened. "All from a piece of cheap red clay?"

"Not the pottery, my dear sister. The armorer put the formula for Enlibar steel on a clay tablet and had a wizard spell the glaze to conceal it. I sensed the spell, but I cannot break it."

"But this might only be a small piece." Illyra ran her finger along the fragment's worn edges. "Maybe not even a vital part."

"Your S'danzo gifts are heedless of time, are they not?"

"Well, yes—the past and future are clear to us."

"Then you should be able to scry back to when the glaze was applied and glimpse the entire tablet."

Illyra shifted uneasily. "Yes, perhaps, I could glimpse it but, Walegrin, I don't 'read.' " She shrugged and grinned with the wine.

Walegrin frowned, considering the near-perfect irony of the curse's functioning. No doubt Illyra could, would, see the complete tablet and be unable to tell him what was on it.

"Your cards, they have writing on them."

She shrugged again. "I use the pictures and my gifts. My cards are not

S'danzo work." She seemed to apologize for the deck's origin, turning the pile facedown to hide the offensive ink trails. "S'danzo are artists. We paint pictures in fate." She squirted herself another mouthful of wine.

"Pictures?" Walegrin asked. "Would you see a clear enough image of the tablet to draw its double here on the table?"

"I could try. I've never done anything like that before."

"Then try now," Walegrin suggested, taking the wineskin away from her.

Illyra placed the shard atop the deck, then brought both to her forehead. Exhaling until she felt the world grow dim, the wine-euphoria left her and she became S'danzo exercising that capricious gift the primordial gods had settled upon her kind. She exhaled again and forgot that she was in her mother's death chamber. Eyes closed she lowered the deck and pottery to the table and drew three cards, faceup.

Seven of Ore: again, red clay; the potter with his wheel and kiln.

Quicksilver: a molten waterfall; the alchemic ancestor of all ores: the ace card of the suit of Ores.

Two of Ore: steel; war card; death card with masked men fighting. She spread her fingers to touch each card and lost herself in search of the Enlibrite forge.

The armorer was old, his hand shook as he moved the brush over the unfired tablet. An equally ancient wizard fretted beside him, glancing fearfully over her shoulder beyond the limits of Illyra's S'danzo gifts. Their clothing was like nothing Illyra had seen in Sanctuary. The vision wavered when she thought of the present and she dutifully returned to the armory. Illyra mimicked the armorer's motions as he covered the tablet with rows of dense, incomprehensible symbols. The wizard took the tablet and sprinkled fine sand over it. He chanted a singsong language as meaningless as the ink marks. Illyra sensed the beginnings of the spell and withdrew across time to the barracks in Sanctuary.

Walegrin had removed the cloth from the table and placed a charcoal stylus in her hand without her sensing it. For a fleeting moment she compared her copying to the images still in her mind. Then the image was gone and she was fully back in the room, quietly watching Walegrin as he stared at the table.

"Is it what you wanted?" she asked softly.

Walegrin did not answer, but threw back his head in cynical laughter.

"Ah, my sister! Your mother's people are clever. Their curse reaches back to the dawn of time. Look at this!"

He pointed at the copied lines and obediently Illyra examined them closely.

"They are not what you wanted?"

Walegrin took the card of Quicksilver and pointed to the lines of script that delineated the waterfall. "These are the runes that have been used since Ilsig attained her height, but this—" He traced a squiggle on the table. "This is older than Ilsig. By Calisard, Vortheld, and a thousand gods of long-dead soldiers, how foolish I've been! For years I've chased the secret of Enlibar steel and never realized that the formula would be as old as the ruins we found it in."

Illyra reached across the table and held his clenched fists between her palms. "Surely there are those who can read this? How different can one sort of writing be from another?" she asked with an illiterate's innocence.

"As different as the speech of the Raggah is from yours."

Illyra nodded. It was not the time to tell him that when the Raggah came to trade they bargained with hand signals so none could hear their speech. "You could go to a scriptorium along Governor's Walk. They sell letters like Blind Jakob sells fruit—it won't matter what the letter says as long as you pay the price," she suggested.

"You don't understand, 'Lyra. If the formula becomes known again, ambition will seek it out. Rulers will arm their men with Enlibar steel and set out to conquer their neighbors. Wars will ruin the land and the men who live on it." Walegrin had calmed himself and begun to trace the charcoal scratches onto a piece of translucent parchment.

"But, you wish to have it." Illyra's tone became accusing.

"For ten years I've campaigned for Ranke. I've taken my men far north, beyond the plains. In those lands there're nomads with no cause to fear us. Swift and outnumbering us by thousands they cut through our ranks like a knife through soft cheese. We fell back and the emperor had our commanders hanged as cowards. We went forward again, with new officers, and were thrown back again with the same results. I was commissioned myself and feared we'd be sent forward a third time, but Ranke has discovered easier gold to conquer in the east and the army left its dead in the field to chase some other imperial ambition.

"I remembered the stories of Enlibar. I hid there when I first escaped this town. With Enlibar steel my men's swords would reap nomad blood and I would not be deemed a coward.

"I found men in the capital who listened to my plans. They knew the army and knew the battlefield. They're no friends of a hidebound emperor who sees no more of war than a parade ground, but they became my friends. They gave me leave to search the ruins with my men and arranged for the garrison posts here when all omens said the answer lay in Sanctuary. If I can return to them with the formula the army won't be the whipping boy of lazy emperors. Men who understand steel and blood will rule . . . but, I've failed them. The damned S'danzo curse has preceded me! The purple mage was gone when I got here and my dreams have receded further with each step I decided to take."

"Walegrin," Illyra began, "the S'danzo are not that powerful. Look at the cards. I cannot read your writing, but I can read them and there are no curses in your fate. You've found what you came for. Red clay yields steel through the Ore-ruler, Quicksilver. True, Quicksilver is a deceiver, but only because its depths are concealed. Quicksilver will let you change this scribbling into something more to your liking." She was S'danzo again, dispensing wisdom amid her candles, but without the bright colors and heavy kohl her words had a new urgent sincerity.

"You are touched by the same curse! You lie with your husband yet have no children."

Illyra shrank back ashamed. "I . . . I use the S'danzo gifts; I must believe in their powers. But you seek the power of steel and war. You need not believe in S'danzo; you need not fear them. You ran away— you escaped! The only curse upon you is that of your own guilt."

She averted her eyes from his face and collected her cards carefully lest her trembling fingers send the deck flying across the rough-hewn floors. She shook out her cloak, getting relief from her anger in the whiplike snap of the heavy material.

"I've answered your questions. I'll take my payment, if you please." She extended her hand, still not looking at his face.

Walegrin unfastened the suede pouch from his belt and placed it on the table. "I'll get the torch and we can leave for the bazaar."

"No, I'll take the torch and go alone."

"The streets are no place for a woman after dark."

"I'll get by—I did before."

"I'll have one of my men accompany you."

"All right," Illyra agreed, inwardly relieved by the compromise.

From the speed with which the soldier appeared Illyra guessed he had been right outside all along and party to everything that had passed. Regardless, the man took the torch and walked slightly ahead of her, attentive to duty but without any attempt at conversation until they reached the bazaar gates, where Illyra had to step forward to guide them both through the maze of stalls.

She took her leave of the man without farewell and slipped into the darkness of her home. Familiarity obviated need for light. She moved quickly and quietly, folding the clothes into a neat bundle and storing the precious pouch with her few other valuables before easing into the warm bed.

"You've returned safely. I was ready to pull on my trousers and come looking for you. Did he give you all that he promised?" Dubro whispered, settling his arms around her.

"Yes, and I answered all his questions. He has the formula now for Enlibar steel, whatever that is, and if his purposes are true he'll make much of it." Her body released its tension in a series of small spasms and Dubro held her tighter.

"Enlibar steel," he mused softly. "The swords of legend were of Enlibar steel. The man who possesses such steel now would be a man to be reckoned with . . . even if he were a blacksmith."

Illyra pulled the linen over her ears and pretended not to hear.

"Sweetmeats! Sweetmeats! Always the best in the bazaar! Always the best in Sanctuary!"

Mornings were normal again with Haakon wheeling his cart past the blacksmith's stall before the crowds disrupted the community. Illyra, one eye ringed with kohl and the other still pristine, raced out to purchase their breakfast treats.

"There's news in the town," the vendor said as he dropped three of the pastries onto Illyra's plate. "Twice news in fact. All of last night's watch from the garrison took its leave of the town during the night and the crippled scribe who lived in the Street of Armorers was carried off amid much screaming and commotion. Of course, there was no watch to answer the call. The Hell Hounds consider it beneath them to patrol the law-abiding parts of town." Haakon's ire was explained, in part, by his own residence in the upper floors of a house on the Street of Armorers.

Illyra looked at Dubro, who nodded slowly in return.

"Might they be connected?" she asked.

"Pah! What would fleeing garrison troops want with a man who reads fifteen dead languages but can't pass water without someone to guide his hands?"

What indeed?

Dubro went back to his forge and Illyra stared over the bazaar walls to the palace, which marked the northern extent of the town. Haakon, who had expected a less mysterious reaction to his news, muttered farewell and wheeled his cart to another stall for a more sympathetic audience.

The first of the day's townsfolk could be heard arguing with other vendors. Illyra hurried back into the shelter of the stall to complete her daily transformation into a S'danzo crone. She pulled Walegrin's three Ore cards from her deck and placed them in the pouch with her mother's jewelry, lit the incense of gentle-forgetting, and greeted the first querent of the day.

The Dream of the Sorceress

A. E. van Vogt

The scream brought Stulwig awake in pitch darkness. He lay for a long moment stiff with fear. Like any resident of old, decadent Sanctuary his first fleeting thought was that the ancient city, with its night prowlers, had produced another victim's cry of terror. This one was almost as close to his second-floor greenhouse residence as—

His mind paused. Realization came, then, in a flickering self-condemnation.

Did it again!

His special nightmare. It had come out of that shaded part of his brain where he kept his one dark memory. Never a clear recall. Perhaps not even real. But it was all he had from the night three years and four moons ago when his father's death cry had come to him in his sleep.

He was sitting up, now, balancing himself on the side of the couch. And thinking once more, guiltily: If only that first time I had gone to his room to find out.

Instead, it was morning before he had discovered the dead body with its slit throat and its horrifying grimace. Yet there was no sign of a struggle. Which was odd. Because his father at fifty was physically a good example of the healer's art he and Alten both practiced. Lying there in the light of day after his death, his sprawled body looked as powerful and strong as that of his son at thirty.

The vivid images of that past disaster faded. Stulwig sank back and down onto the sheep fur. Covered himself. Listened in the continuing dark to the sound of wind against a corner of his greenhouse. It was a strong wind; he could feel the bedroom tremble. Moments later, he was still awake when he heard a faraway muffled cry—someone being murdered out there in the Maze?

Oddly, that was the final steadying thought. It brought his inner world into balance with the outer reality. After all, this was Sanctuary where, every hour of each night, a life ended violently like a candle snuffed out.

At this time of early, early morning he could think of no purpose that he could have about anything. Not with those dark, dirty, dusty, wind-blown streets. Nor in relation to the sad dream that had brought him to shocked awareness. Nothing for him to do, actually, but turn over, and—

He woke with a start. It was daylight. And someone was knocking at his outer door two rooms away.

"One moment!" he called out.

Naturally, it required several moments. A few to tumble out of his night-robe. And even more to slip into the tunic, healer's gown, and slippers. Then he was hurrying through the bright sunlight of the greenhouse. And on into the dimness of the hallway beyond, with its solid door. Solid, that was, except for the vent at mouth level.

Stulwig placed his lips at his end, of the slanted vent, and asked, "Who is it?"

The answering voice was that of a woman. "It's me. Illyra. Alone."

The seeress! Stulwig's heart quickened. His instant hope: another chance for her favors. And alone—that was a strange admission this early in the morning.

Hastily, he unblocked the door. Swung it open, past his own gaunt form. And there she stood in the dimness, at the top of his stairway. She was arrayed as he remembered her, in her numerous skirts and S'danzo scarfs. But the beautiful face above all those cloth frills was already shaded with creams and powders.

She said, "Alten, I dreamed of you."

There was something in her tone: an implication of darkness. Stulwig felt an instant chill. She was giving him a sorceress's signal.

Her presence, alone, began to make sense. What she had to offer him transcended a man's itching for a woman. And she expected him to realize it.

Standing there, just inside his door, Stulwig grew aware that he was trembling. A dream. The dream of a sorceress.

He swallowed. And found his voice. It was located deep in his throat, for when he spoke it was a husky sound: "What do you want?"

"I need three of your herbs." She named them: stypia, gernay, dalin.

This was the bargaining moment. And in the world of Sanctuary there were few victims at such a time. From his already long experience, Stulwig made his offer: "The stypia and the gernay for the dream. For the dalin one hour in my bed tonight for an assignation."

Silence. The bright eyes seemed to shrink.

"What's this?" asked Stulwig. "Is it possible that with your seeress's sight you believe that this time there will be no evasion?"

Twice before, she had made reluctant assignation agreements. On each occasion, a series of happenings brought about a circumstance whereby he needed her assistance. And for that, release from the assignation was her price.

Stulwig's voice softened to a gentler tone: "Surely, it's time, my beautiful, that you discover how much greater pleasure it is for a woman to have lying on her the weight of a normal man rather than that monstrous mass of blacksmith's muscles, the possessor of which by some mysterious power captured you when you were still too young to know any better. Is it a bargain?"

She hesitated a moment longer. And then, as he had expected after hearing the name of the third drug, she nodded.

A business transaction. And that required the goods to be on hand. Stulwig didn't argue. "Wait!" he admonished.

Himself, he did not wait. Instead, he backed quickly out of the hallway and into the greenhouse. He presumed that, with her seeress's sight, she knew that he knew about the very special person who wanted the dalin. He felt tolerant. That prince—he thought. In spite of all the advice the women receive as to when they are, and are not, capable of accepting the male seed, the youthful governor evidently possessed his concubines so often that they were unable to divert his favors away from the one who—by sorceresses' wisdom—was most likely in the time of pregnancy capability.

328 THIEVES' WORLD: FIRST BLOOD

And so—a miscarriage was needed. An herb to bring it on.

Suppressing excitement, the dream almost forgotten in his state of overstimulation, the healer located all three herbs, in turn. The stypia came from a flowering plant that spread itself over one entire end of his big, bright room. Someone would be using it soon for a persistent headache. The gernay was a mixture of two roots, a flower, and a leaf, all ground together, to be made into a tea with boiling water, steeped, and drunk throughout the day. It was for constipation.

While he worked swiftly, deftly, putting each separately into a small pouch, Stulwig pictured Illyra leaving her little stall. At the opportune moment she had pushed aside the black curtains that blocked her away from the sight of curious passersby. His mental image was of a one-room dwelling place in a dreary part of the bazaar. Coming out of that flimsy shelter at this hour of the morning was not the wisest act even for a seeress. But, of course, she would have some knowing to guide her. So that she could dart from one concealment to another at exactly the right moments, avoiding danger. And then, naturally, once she got to the narrow stairway leading up to his roof abode, there would be only the need to verify that no one was lurking on the staircase itself.

He brought the three bags back to the hallway, and placed two of them into her slender hands. And with that, there it was again, the reason for her visit. The special dream. For him.

He waited, not daring to say anything for, suddenly, there was that tenseness again.

She seemed not to need prompting. She said simply, "In my dream, Ils came to me in the form of an angry young man and spoke to me about you. His manner was ferocious throughout; and my impression is that he is displeased with you." She finished, "In his human form he had jet black hair that came down to his shoulders."

There was silence. Inside Stulwig, a blankness spread from some inner center of fear. A numbness seemed to be in all locations.

Finally: "Ils!" he croaked.

The impossible!

There were tales that reported the chief god of old Ilsig occasionally interfering directly in human affairs. But that he had done so in connection with Alten Stulwig brought a sense of imminent disaster.

Illyra seemed to know what he was feeling. "Something about your father," she said, softly, "is the problem."

Her hand and arm reached out. Gently, she took hold of the third pouch; tugged at it. Stulwig let go. He watched numbly, then as she turned and went rapidly down the stairway. Moments later there was a flare of light as the bottom door opened—and shut. Just before it closed he had a glimpse of the alley that was there, and of her turning to go left.

Ils!

All that morning, after the sick people started to arrive, Stulwig tried to put the thought of the god out of his mind. There were several persons who talked excessively about their ailments; and for a change he let them ramble on. The sound of each person's voice, in turn, distracted him for a precious time from his inner feeling of imminent disaster. He was accustomed to pay attention, to compare, and decide. And, somehow, through all the numbness he managed to hold on to that ability.

A persistent stomachache—"What have you been eating?" The flower of the agris plant was exchanged for a silver coin.

A pain in the chest. "How long? Where, exactly?" The root of the dark melles was eaten and swallowed while he watched, in exchange for one small, broken Rankan gold piece.

Persistently bleeding gums. The flower and seeds of a rose, and the light brown grindings from the husk of grain, were handed over, with the instruction: "Take a spoonful of each morning and night."

There were a dozen like that. All were anxious and disturbed. And they took up his time until the morning was almost over. Suddenly, the visitors ceased to come. At once, there was the awful thought of Ils the Mighty, angry with him.

"What could he want of me?"

That was the persistent question. Not, what purpose could Alten Stulwig have in this awful predicament? But what intention did the superbeing have in relation to him? Or what did he require of him?

It was almost the noon hour before the second possibility finally penetrated the madness of merely waiting for further signals. And the more personal thought took form.

"It's up to me. I should ask certain people for advice, or even"—sudden hope—"information."

Just like that he had something he could do.

At that moment there was one more patient. And then, as the rather stocky woman departed with her little leather bag clutched in one greasy hand, Stulwig hastily put on his street boots. Grabbed his staff. And, moments later, was heading down the stairs two at a time.

Arrived at the bottom; naturally, he paused. And peered forth cautiously. The narrow street, as he now saw it, pointed both left and right. The nearest crossing was an alleyway to the left. And Stulwig presumed, as his gaze flicked back and forth, Illyra, on her leave-taking that morning, had turned up that alley.

Though it was still not clear why she had gone left when her stall was to the right. Going by the alley was, for her, a long, devious route home. . . .

His own destination, already decided, required Stulwig to pass her stall. And so, his stave at the ready, he walked rightward. A few dozen steps brought him to a crowded thoroughfare. Again, a pause. And, once more, his gaze flicking back and forth. Not that he felt in danger here, at this hour. What he saw was a typical throng. There were the short people who wore the sheeny satinish cloth of west Caronne. They mingled casually with the taller folk in dark tunics from the far south of the Empire. Equally at ease were red-garbed sailors on shore leave from a Cleean vessel. Here and there a S'danzo woman in her rich attire reminded him of Illyra. There were other races, and other dress, of course. But these were more of a kind. The shabby poor. The thieves. The beggars. All too similar, one to the other, to be readily identified.

For a few moments, as he stood there, Stulwig's own problem faded from the forefront of his mind. In its place came a feeling he had had before: a sense of wonder.

Me! Here in this fantastic world.

All these people. This city, with its ancient buildings, its towers, and its minarets. And the meaning of it all going back and back into the dim reaches of a fabulous history.

Almost—standing there—Stulwig forgot where he was heading. And when the memory came again it seemed to have a different form.

A more practical form. As if what he had in mind was a first step of several that would presently lead him to—what?

Mental pause.

It was, he realized, the first dim notion of having a goal beyond mere information. First, of course, the facts; those he had to have.

Somehow, everything was suddenly clearer. As he started forward it was almost as if he had a purpose with a solution implicit in it.

Illyra's stall he passed a short time later. Vague disappointment, then, as he saw that the black curtains were drawn.

Stulwig stalked on, heading west out of town across the bridge that spanned the White Foal River. He ignored the hollow-eyed stares of the Downwinders as he passed their hovels, and only slowed his pace when he reached his destination, a large estate lorded over by a walled mansion. A sell-sword stood guard just inside the large, spreading yard. Theirs was a language Stulwig understood. He took out two coppers and held them forth.

"Tell Jubal that Alten Stulwig wishes to see him."

The coppers were skillfully palmed, and transferred to a slitted pocket in the tight-fitting toga. In a baritone voice the sell-sword called out the message—

Stulwig entered the throne room, and saw that gleaming-skinned black man sitting on the throne chair. He bowed courteously toward the throne. Whereupon Jubal waved one large arm, beckoning his visitor. And then he sat scowling as Stulwig told his story.

Despite the scowl, there was no resistance, or antagonism, in the bright, wicked eyes; only interest. Finally, as Stulwig fell silent, the merchant said, "You believe, as I understand you, that one or another of my numerous paid informants may have heard something at the time of your father's death that would provide a clue: information, in short, that is not even available from a sorceress."

"I so believe," acknowledged Stulwig.

"And how much will you pay if I can correctly recall something that was said to me in passing more than three long years ago?"

Stulwig hesitated, and hoped that his desperation did not show on that sunburned face of his; it was the one thing the chapped skin was good for: sometimes it enabled him to conceal his feelings. What he sensed now was a high cost; and the best outward show for that was to act as if this was a matter about which he was merely curious. "Perhaps," he said, in his best practical tone, "your next two visits for healing free—"

"For what I remember," said the big black, "the price is the medium Rankan gold piece *and* the two visits."

Long, unhappy pause. All this trouble and cost for an innocent man who, himself, had done nothing. It seemed unfair. "Perhaps," ventured

Stulwig, "if you were to give me the information I could decide if the price is merited."

He was slightly surprised when Jubal nodded. "That seems reasonable. We're both men of our word."

The big man twisted his lips, as if he were considering. Then: "The morning after your father died, a night prowler who watches the dark hours for me saw Vashanka come through your door—not out of it, through it. He was briefly a figure of dazzling light as he moved down the street. Then he vanished in a blinding puff of brightness akin to lightning. The flare-up, since it lit up the entire street, was seen by several other persons, who did not know its origin."

Jubal continued, "I should tell you that there is an old story that a god can go through a wall or a door only if a second god is nearby on the other side. So we may reason that for Vashanka to be able to emerge in the fashion described there was another god outside. However, my informants did not see this second mighty being."

"Bu-u-t-t!" Stulwig heard a stuttering voice. And only when the mad sound collapsed into silence did he realize that it was his own mouth that had tried to speak.

What he wanted to say, what was trying to form in his mind and in his tongue, was that, for Vashanka to have penetrated into the barricaded greenhouse in the first place, then there must already have been a god inside; who had somehow inveigled his way past his father's cautious resistance to nighttime visitors.

The words, the meaning, wouldn't come. The logic of it was too improbable for Stulwig to pursue the matter.

Gulping, he fumbled in his pocket. Identified the desired coin with his fingers. Brought it out. And laid it into the outstretched palm. The price was cheap—it was as if a voice inside him spoke his acceptance of that truth.

For a while after Stulwig left Jubal's grounds, his feeling was that he had now done what there was to do. He had the information he had craved. So what else was there? Go home and—and—

Back to normalcy.

It was an unfortunate way of describing the reality to himself. It brought a mental picture of a return to his daily routine as if no warning had been given. His deep, awful feeling was that something more was expected of him. What could it be?

It was noon. The glowing orb in the sky burned down upon Stulwig. His already miserably sunburned face itched abominably, and he kept scratching at the scabs; and hating himself because his sun-sensitive skin was his one disaster that no herb or ointment seemed to help. And here he was stumbling in the direct rays, making it worse.

He was walking unsteadily, half-blinded by his own inner turmoil and physical discomfort, essentially not heeding the crowds around him when . . . the part of him that was guiding him, holding him away from collisions, helping him find a pathway through an ever-changing river of people—that part, still somehow observant, saw a familiar man's face.

Stulwig stopped short. But already the man was gone by; his feet scraping at the same dusty street as were the feet of a dozen other passers of the moment; scraping dust and breathing it in.

Normally, Stulwig would have let him go. But this was not a normal time. He spun around. He jammed his stave against the ground as a brace. And took four long, swift steps. He reached.

Almost gently, then, his fingers touched the sleeve and, through it, the arm of the man. "Cappen Varra," Stulwig said.

The young man with the long black hair that rested on his shoulders turned his head. The tone of Stulwig's voice was evidently not threatening; for Cappen merely paused without tensing. Nor did he make a quick reach of the hand toward the blade at his side.

But it took several moments before he seemed to realize who his interceptor was. Then: "Oh! the healer?" He spoke questioningly.

Stulwig was apologetic. "I would like to speak to you, sir. Though, as I recall it you only sought my services on one occasion. And I think somebody told me that you had recently departed from Sanctuary for a visit to your distant home."

The minstrel did not reply immediately. He was backing off, away from the main stream of that endlessly moving crowd; backing toward a small space between a fruit stand and a table on which stood a dozen small crates, each containing a half dozen or so small, live, edible, noisy birds.

Since Stulwig had shuffled after him, Cappen was able to say in a low voice, "It was a very decisive time for me. The herbs you gave me produced a series of regurgitations which probably saved my life. I still believe I was served poisoned food."

"I need advice," said Alten Stulwig.

"We can talk here," said Cappen.

It was not an easy story to tell. There was a rise and fall of street sounds. Several times he coughed from an intake of dust thrown at him by the heel of a passerby. But in the end he had completed his account. And it was then, suddenly, that the other man's eyes widened, as if a startling thought had come to him.

"Are you telling me that you are seriously pursuing the murderer of your father, despite that you have now discovered that the killer may well be the second-most-powerful Rankan god?"

It was the first time that meaning had been spoken so exactly. Stulwig found himself suddenly as startled as his questioner. Before he could say anything, the lean-faced, good-looking wandering singer spoke again: "What—what happens if he ever lets you catch up with him?"

The way the question was worded somehow steadied the healer. He said, "As we know, Vashanka can come to me any time he wishes. My problem is that I do not know why he came to my father, nor why he would come to me. If I could find that out, then perhaps I could go to the temple of Ils and ask the priests for help."

Cappen frowned, and said, "Since you seem to have these powerful purposes, perhaps I should remind you of the myth." He went on: "You know the story. Vashanka is the god of warriors and weapons, the wielder of lightning, and other powerful forces. You know of this?"

"What I don't understand," Stulwig replied helplessly, "is why would such a being kill my father?"

"Perhaps"—a shrug—"they were rivals for the affection of the same woman." He went on, "It is well known that the gods frequently assume human form in order to have concourse with human females." The beautiful male face twisted. The bright eyes gazed into Stulwig's. "I have heard stories," Cappen said, "that you, as your father before you, often accept a woman's favors in exchange for your services as a healer; the woman having nothing else to give pays the price in the time-honored way of male-female. As a consequence you actually have many half-brothers out there in the streets, and you yourself—so it has been said—have sired a dozen sons and daughters, unacknowledged because of course no one can ever be sure who is the father of these numerous waifs, unless there is unmistakable facial resemblance."

Another shrug. "I'm not blaming you. These are the truths of our world. But—"

He stopped. His hand extended gingerly, and touched Stulwig's stave. "It's tough wood."

Stulwig was uneasy. "Awkward to handle in close quarters, and scarcely a weapon to ward off the god of lightning."

"Nevertheless," said Cappen, "it's your best defense. Use it firmly. Keep it between you and any attacker. Yield ground and flee only when there's a good moment."

"But," protested Stulwig, "suppose Vashanka seeks me out? Shall I pit my staff against the Rankan god of war?" When Cappen merely stood there, looking indifferent now, the healer continued in a desperate tone, "There are stories of how Ils helped individuals in battle in the old days. But I grew up after the Rankan conquest and"—he was gloomy—"somehow the powers of the defeated god of old Ilsig didn't seem worth inquiring about. So I'm ignorant of what he did, or how."

Abruptly, Cappen Varra was impatient. "You asked for my advice," he said curtly. "I have given it to you. Goodbye."

He walked off into the crowd.

They brought Stulwig before the prince, who recognized him. "Why, it's the healer," he said. Whereupon he glanced questioningly at Molin Torchholder.

The Hall of Justice was all too brightly lit by the midafternoon sunlight. The sun was at that location in the sky whereby its rays shone directly through the slanting vents that were designed to catch, and siphon off, rainwater . . . as the high priest said accusingly, "Your Most Gracious Excellency, we found this follower of Ils in the temple of Vashanka."

With the brilliant light pouring down upon him, Stulwig started toward the dais—and the two Hell Hounds, who had been holding him, let him go.

He stopped only when he came to the long wooden barrier that separated the accused criminals from the high seat, where the prince sat in judgment. From that fence, Stulwig spoke his protest. "I did no harm, Your Highness. And I meant no harm. Tell His Excellency"—he addressed Torchholder—"that your assistants found me on my knees before the—" He hesitated; he had been about to say "the idol." Uneasily, his mind moved over to the word "statue." But he rejected that also, shuddering. After a long moment he finished lamely—"before Vashanka himself, praying for his assistance."

"Yes, but a follower of Ils praying to a son of Savankala"—Torch-holder was grim—"absolutely forbidden by the doctrines of our religion."

There seemed to be no answer that he could make. Feeling helpless, Stulwig waited. It was a year since he had last seen the youthful governor, who would now decide his fate. Standing there, Stulwig couldn't help but notice that there were changes in the young ruler's appearance—for the better, it seemed to him. The prince, as all knew, was at this time twenty years old. He had been representative in Sanctuary for his older half-brother, the emperor, for only one of those years, but that year had brought a certain maturity where once there had been softness. It was still a boyish face, but a year of power had marked it with an appearance of confidence.

The young governor seemed undecided, as he said, "Well—it does not look like a serious crime. I should think we would encourage converts rather than punishing them." He hesitated, then followed the amenities. "What penalty do you recommend?" He addressed the high priest of Rankan deities courteously.

There was a surprisingly long pause. Almost, it was as if the older man was having second thoughts. Torchholder said finally, "Perhaps, we should inquire what he was praying for. And then decide."

"An excellent idea," the prince agreed heartily.

Once more, then, Stulwig told his story, ending in a humble tone, "Therefore, sir, as soon as I discovered that, apparently, the great gods themselves were involved in some disagreement, I decided to pray to Vashanka, to ask what he wanted me to do; asked him what amends I could make for whatever my sin might be."

He was surprised as he completed his account to see that the prince was frowning. And, in fact, moments later, the young governor bent down toward one of the men at a table below him to one side, and said something in a low voice. The aide's reply was equally inaudible.

The youngest ruler Sanctuary had ever had thereupon faced forward. His gaze fixed on Stulwig's face. "There are several people in these parts," he said in an alarmingly severe voice, "of whose whereabouts we maintain a continuing awareness. Cappen Varra, for several reasons, is one of these. And so, Mr. Healer, I have to inform you that Cappen left Sanctuary half a moon ago, and is not expected back for at least two more moons."

"B-b-bu-ut—" Stulwig began. And stopped. Then in a high-pitched voice: "That man in the seeress's dream !" he stuttered. "Long black hair to the shoulders. Ils in human form!"

There was silence after he had spoken there in that great Hall of Justice, where a youthful Rankan prince sat in judgment, looking down from his high bench. Other offenders were waiting in the back of the room. They were guarded by slaves, with the two Hell Hounds that had brought Stulwig acting as overseers.

So there would be witnesses to this judgment. The wisdom of it, whatever course it might take, would be debated when the news of it got out.

Standing there, Stulwig suppressed an impulse to remind His Highness of a certain night thirteen moons ago. In the wee hours he had been called out of his bed, and escorted to the palace.

On that occasion he had been taken directly into the prince's bedroom. There he found a frightened young man, who had awakened in the darkness with an extremely fast heartbeat—more than double normal, Stulwig discovered when he counted the pulse. The attending court healer had not been able, by his arts, to slow the madly beating organ. Stulwig had braced himself, and had taken the time to ask the usual questions, which produced the information that His Highness had imbibed excessively all evening.

A minor heart condition was thus revealed. The cure: primarily time for the body to dispose of the alcohol through normal channels. But Stulwig asked, and was given, permission to return to his greenhouse. He raced there accompanied by a Hell Hound. Arrived at his quarters, he procured the mixture of roots, nettles, and a large red flower which, when steeped in boiling water, and swallowed in mouthfuls every few minutes, within an hour had the heartbeat down, not to normal, but sufficiently to be reassuring.

He thereupon informed the young man that, according to his father, persons that he had attended when they were young, who had the same reaction, were still alive two decades later. The prince was greatly relieved, and promised to limit himself to no more than one drink of an evening.

Remained, then, the task of saving face for the court healer. Which Stulwig did by thanking that disgraced individual for calling him for consultation; and, within the hearing of the prince, adding that it took many individuals to accumulate experience of all the ills that men were heir to. "And one of these days I shall be asking your help."

. . . Would the youthful governor remember that night, and decide—hopeful thought—that Alten Stulwig was too valuable to penalize?

What the prince did, first, was ask one more question. He said, "During the time you were with the person who seemed to be Cappen Varra, did he break into song, or recite a verse?"

The significance of the question was instantly apparent. The minstrel was known for his gaiety, and his free and easy renditions under all circumstances. Stulwig made haste to say, "No, Highness, not a sound, or a poetic phrase. Contrariwise, he seemed very serious."

A few moments later, the prince rendered his judgment. He said, "Since mighty Vashanka himself seems to be acting directly in this matter, it would be presumptuous of us to interfere."

The lean-faced young man glanced at Molin. The high priest hesitated, then nodded. Whereupon the prince turned once more to Stulwig.

"Most worthy healer," he said, "you are released to whatever the future holds for you. May the gods dispense justice upon you, balancing your virtues against your sins."

—*So he does remember!* thought Stulwig, gratefully.

Surprisingly, after he had been escorted outside, Stulwig knew at once which was the proper place for him to go. Many times he had been confronted by grief or guilt, or the hopelessness of a slighted lover, or a betrayed wife. For none of these had his herbs ever accomplished more than a passing moment of sleep or unconsciousness.

So now, as he entered the Vulgar Unicorn, he muttered under his breath the bitter advice he had given on those special occasions for what his father had called ailments of the spirit. The words, heard only by himself, were: "What you need, Alten, is a good stiff drink."

It was the ancient prescription for calming the overwrought or the overemotional. In its fashion, however, liquor in fact was a concoction of brewed herbs, and so within his purview.

The smell of the inn was already in his nostrils. The dimly lit interior blanked his vision. But Stulwig could see sufficiently well so that he was aware of vague figures sitting at tables, and of the gleam of polished wood. He sniffed of the mingling odors of hot food cooking. And already felt better.

And he knew this interior sufficiently well. So he strode forward confidently toward the dividing barrier where the brew was normally dispensed. And he had his lips parted to give his order when his eyes, more accustomed to the light, saw who it was that was taking the orders.

"*One-Thumb!*" The name was almost torn out of his lips; so great was his surprise and delight.

Eagerly, he reached forward and grasped the other's thick hand. "My friend, you had us all worried. You have been absent—" He stopped, confused. Because the time involved even for a long journey was long. Much more than a year. He finished his greeting with a gulp, "You are right welcome, sir."

The owner of the Vulgar Unicorn had become more visible with each passing moment. So that when he gestured with one of his big hands at a helper, Stulwig perceived the entire action; even saw the youth turn and come over.

The roly-poly but rugged One-Thumb indicated a table in one corner. "Bring two cups of brew thither for my friend and myself," he said. To Alten he added, "I would have words with you, sir."

So there they sat presently. And, after several sips, One-Thumb said, "I shall say quickly what need be said. Alten, I must confess that I am not the real One-Thumb. I came because, with my sorcerer's seeing, when this past noon hour my body took on the form at which you are gazing, I had a visitor who informed me that the transformation to a known person related to you."

It was a long explanation. Long enough for Stulwig to have a variety of reactions. First, amazement. Then, progressively, various puzzlements. And, finally, tentative comprehension, and acceptance.

And since he held a drink in his hand, he raised it, and said, "To the real One-Thumb, wherever he may be."

With that, still thinking hard as to what he could gain from this meeting, he sipped from his cup, took a goodly quaff from it, and set it down. All the while noticing that the other did not drink to the toast.

The false One-Thumb said unhappily, "My seeing tells me that the real One-Thumb is in some strange location. It is not quite clear that he is still dead; but he was killed."

Up came Stulwig's glass. "Very well, then, to Enas Yorl, the sorcerer, who in whatever shape seems to be willing to be my friend."

This time the other man's cup came up slowly. He sipped. "I suppose," he said, "no one can refuse to drink to himself; since my motives are worthy I shall do so."

Stulwig's mind was flickering again with the meanings of what had been said in that long explanation. So, now, he asked the basic question: "Enas," he mumbled, "in what way does your being in One-Thumb's body shape relate to me?"

The fleshy head nodded. "Pay careful heed," said the voice of One-Thumb. "The goddess Azyuna appeared to me as I was experiencing the anguish of changing form, and asked me to give you this message. You must go home before dark. But do not this night admit to your quarters any person who has the outward appearance of a man. Do this no matter how pitifully he begs for a healer's assistance, or how many pieces of gold he is prepared to pay. Tonight, direct all male visitors to other healers."

It took a while to drink to that, and to wonder about it aloud. And, of course, as Sanctuarites, they discussed once more the story of Azyuna. How Vashanka had discovered that she (his sister) and his ten brothers had plotted to murder the father-god of Ranke, Savankala. Whereupon, Vashanka in his rage slew all ten of the brothers; but his sister he reserved for a worse fate. She became his unwilling mistress. And at time when the winds moaned and sobbed, it was said that Azyuna was again being forced to pay the price of her intended betrayal of her parents.

And now she had come down from heaven to warn a mere human being against the brother who exacted that shame from her.

"How," asked Stulwig, after he had quaffed most of a second cup and had accordingly reached a philosophical state of mind, "would you, old wise Enas Yorl, explain why a goddess would take the trouble to warn a human being against some scheme of her god-brother-lover?"

"Because," was the reply, "she may be a goddess but she is also a woman. And as all men know, women get even in strange ways."

At that, Stulwig, remembering certain experiences of his own, shuddered a little, nodded agreement, and said, "I estimate that we have been imbibing for a goodly time, and so perhaps I had better take heed of your warning, and depart. Perhaps, there is something I can do for you. A fee, perhaps."

"Make it one free visit when one of my changing shapes becometh ill."

"But not this night." Stulwig stood up, somewhat lightheaded, and was even able to smile at his small jest.

"No, not this night," agreed One-Thumb, also standing up. The big man added quickly, "I shall appear to accompany you to the door as if to bid you goodbye. But in fact I shall go out with you. And so One-Thumb will vanish once more, perhaps this time forever."

"He has done nobly this day," said Stulwig. Whereupon he raised the almost empty third cup, and said, "To the spirit of One-Thumb, wherever it may be, my good wishes."

As it developed, Enas Yorl's plan of escape was made easy. Because as they emerged from the inn there, coming up, was a small company of Rankan military led by a Hell Hound. The latter, a man named Quag, middle-aged, but with a prideful bearing, said to Stulwig, "Word came to His Highness that you were imbibing heavily; and so he has sent me and this company to escort you to your residence."

Stulwig turned to bid farewell to the false One-Thumb. And at once observed that no such person was in sight. Quag seemed to feel that he was surprised. "He went around that corner." He indicated with his thumb. "Shall we pursue him?"

"No, no."

It was no problem at all for a man with three cups of brew in him to step forward, and walk beside a Hell Hound like an equal.

And to say, "I'm somewhat surprised at His Highness taking all this trouble for a person not of Ranke birth, or"—daringly—"religion."

Quag was calm, seemingly unoffended. "These are not matters about which I am qualified to have an opinion."

"Of course," Stulwig continued with a frown, "getting me back to my quarters could place me in a location where the mighty Vashanka could most easily find me."

They were walking along a side street in the Maze. But a goodly crowd pressed by at that moment. So if Quag were contemplating a reply it was interrupted by the passing of so great a number of individuals.

When they had wended through the mob, Stulwig continued, "After all, we have to remember that it is Ils that is the god of a thousand eyes. Which, presumably, means that he can see simultaneously where everybody in the world of Ilsig is at any one moment. No such claim—of many eyes—is made for either Savankala or his son, Vashanka. And so we may guess that Vashanka does not know that—"

He stopped, appalled. He had almost let slip that the goddess Azyuna had come to Enas Yorl with a warning. And, of course, her brother-lover, with his limited vision, would not know that she had done so.

"These are all fine points," Stulwig finished lamely, "and of concern only to an individual like myself who seems to have earned the displeasure of one of these mighty beings."

Quag was calm. "Having lived many years," he said, "it could be that I have some clarifying information for you, whereby you may judge the seriousness of your situation." He continued, after a moment of silence, "In Sanctuary, the reason for the gods interfering in human affairs can have only one underlying motive. Someone has got above himself. What would be above a healer? A woman of noble family taken advantage of. An insult to a priest or god. Was your father guilty of either sin?"

"Hmm!" Stulwig did not resist the analysis. He nodded thoughtfully in the Sanctuary way of agreement, shaking his head from side to side. "No question," he said, "it was not a chance killing. The assassin by some means penetrated a barricaded residence, committed the murder, and departed without stealing any valuables. In a city where people are daily killed most casually for their possessions, when—as in this instance of my father's assassination—the possessions are untouched, we are entitled to guess a more personal motive."

He added unhappily, "I have to confess that the reason I did not run to his rescue when I heard his cry, was that he had established an agreement with me that neither of us would intrude upon the other during the night hours. So it could have been a lady of quality being avenged."

For a small time they walked silently. Then: "I advise you to abandon this search." Quag spoke earnestly. "Go back to your healing profession, and leave murderers to the authorities."

This time Stulwig did the up-and-down headshake, meaning no. He said unhappily, "When Ils himself manifests in a dream, which unmistakably commands me to track down the killer, I have no choice."

The Hell Hound's craggy face was visibly unimpressed. "After all," he said dismissingly, "your Ils failed all his people in Sanctuary when he allowed the city to be overrun by armies that worshiped another god."

"The city is being punished for its sinfulness." Stulwig automatically spoke the standard explanation given by the priests of Ils. "When we have learned our lesson, and paid our penalty, the invader will be impelled to depart."

"When I left the palace," said Quag, "there was no sign of the prince's slaves packing his goods." Shrugging. "Such a departure for such a reason is difficult for me to envision, and I suggest you build no hopes on it."

He broke off. "Ah, here we are. As soon as you are safely inside—and of course we'll search the place and make sure there is no one lurking in a dark corner—"

It was a few periods later. "Thank you," said a grateful Stulwig. He watched them, then, go down the stairs. When Quag paused at the bottom, and looked back questioningly, Stulwig dutifully closed and barricaded the door.

And there he was.

It was a quiet evening. Two men patients and one woman patient knocked on the door. Each, through the vent, requested healing service. Stulwig sent the men down the street to Kurd; and they departed in their considerably separated times, silently accepting.

Stulwig hesitated when he heard the woman's voice. She was a long-time patient, and would pay in gold. Nevertheless, he finally directed her to a healer named Nemis. When the woman objected, he gave as his excuse that he had eaten bad food, and was not well. She seemed to accept that; for she went off, also.

Shortly after midnight there was a fourth hesitant knock. It was Illyra. As he heard her whisper, something inside Stulwig leaped with excitement. She had come, she said, as they had agreed upon that morning.

An exultant Stulwig unlocked the door. Admitted her. Motioned her toward his bedroom. And, as she went with a heavy rustling of her numerous skirts, he barricaded the door again.

Moments later, he was snuffing out the candles, and flinging off his clothes. And then in pitch darkness he joined her in the bed. As he located her naked body, he had no sense of guilt; no feeling of being wrong.

In Sanctuary everybody knew the game. There were no prissies. Every woman was someone's mistress whether she liked it or not. Every man was out for himself, and took advantage where he could. There were, true, codes of honor and religion. But they did not apply to love, liquor, or making a living. You drove the hardest bargain right now.

The opportunity seen. Instantly, the mind wildly scanned the possibilities. Then came the initial outrageous demand, thereupon negotiated downward by the equally determined defenses of the second party to the transaction.

And that was what had brought the beautiful Illyra into his embrace. Her own agreement that, unless something happened to interfere, she would be available for him in the man-woman relation.

Apparently, once she realized that the bargain was binding, she did not resist its meaning. In the darkness Stulwig found her naked body fully acceptant of him. Complete with many small motions and excitements. Most of the women who paid in kind for his services lay like frozen statues, occasionally vibrating a little in the final moments of the act. After which they hastily slipped out of bed. Dressed. And raced off down the stairs and out into the Maze.

With Illyra so different, even to the point of sliding her palms over his skin, Stulwig found himself thinking once more of the huge blacksmith who was her established lover. It was hard to visualize this female, even though she seemed somewhat larger than he would have guessed, with such a massive male on top of her. Although—

A sudden realization: there were surprisingly strong muscles that lay under him. . . . This woman is no weakling. In fact—

Presently, as he proceeded with the lovemaking, Stulwig found himself mentally shaking his head. . . . Those voluminous S'danzo skirts, he thought, conceal more than slender flesh—his sudden impression was that, in fact, Illyra was on the plump side. And that obviously she wore the skirts to hide a considerably heavier body than she wanted onlookers to know about. Not hard to do, with her face so thin and youthful.

No mind. She was a woman who had not been easy to capture. And here she was, actually responding. Interesting, also, that her skin felt unusually warm, almost as if she had a temperature.

He was coming to the climax. And so the size of her was temporarily blanked out. Thus, the awareness of a transformation of her plump body into that of an Amazon was like coming out of a glorious dream into a nightmare.

His sudden impossible impression: he was lying on top of a woman over six feet tall, with hips that spread out beneath him at least a foot wider than he was.

His stunned thought, immediately spoken: "Illyra. What is this? Some sorceress's trick?"

In a single, sliding motion he disengaged from that massive female body. Slid off onto the floor. And scrambled to his feet.

As he did so there was a flash of incredible brightness. It lit up the entire room, revealing an oversized, strange, naked woman in his couch, sitting up now.

And revealing, also, a man's huge lighted figure coming through a door that, before his father's death, had been a private entrance to Alten's bedroom. It was an entrance that he had, long ago now, sealed up. . . . Through it came the shining figure into the bedroom.

One incredulous look was all Stulwig had time for. And many, many desperate awarenesses: the glowing one, the being who shone with a fiery body brightness—was Vashanka.

By the time he had that thought, he had numbly grasped his staff. And, moments later, was backing naked through the doorway that led out to the greenhouse.

Inside the bedroom a god was yelling in a deep, baritone voice at the nude Amazon, who was still sitting on the edge of the bed. And the Amazon was yelling back in a voice that was like that of a male tenor. They spoke in a language that was not Ilsigi.

In his time Stulwig had learned several hundred basic medically useful words in half a dozen dialects of the Rankan Empire. So now, after a few familiar words had come through to him—suddenly, the truth.

The woman was Azyuna. And Vashanka was berating her for her infidelity. And she was yelling back, accusing him of similar infidelities with human women.

The revelation dazzled Stulwig. So the gods, as had so often been suggested in vague tales about them, were like humans in their physical needs. Fleshly contacts. Angry arguments. Perhaps even intake of food with the consequent digestion and elimination by stool and urination.

But much more important for this situation was the intimate act she had sought with a human male. . . . Trust a woman! thought Stulwig. Hating her incestuous relationship. Degraded. Sad. Hopeless. But nevertheless jealous when her god-husband-brother went off to earth, and, as gods have done since the beginning of time, lay with a human woman. Or two. Or a hundred.

So she had got even. Had taken the form of a human woman. And had cunningly enticed a male—this time, himself; three and a half years ago, his father—to lie with her. Not too difficult to do in lustful Sanctuary.

And thus, Ten-Slayer, in his jealous rage, had become Eleven-Slayer—if humans like the elder Stulwig counted in the arithmetic of the divine ones.

Standing, now, in the center of the greenhouse, with no way at all that he could use as a quick escape (it always required a fair time to unbarricade his door), Stulwig braced himself. Clutched his staff. And waited for he knew not what.

He grew aware, then, that the word battle in the bedroom had come to an ending. The woman was standing now, hastily wrapping the S'danzo skirts around her huge waist. That was a momentary revelation. So such skirts could fit all female sizes without alteration.

Moments later, the woman came out. She had three of the filmy scarfs wrapped around her upper body. Her eyes avoided looking at Stulwig as she thudded past him on bare feet. And then he heard her at the door, removing the barricade.

That brought a sudden, wild hope to the man. Perhaps, if he backed in that direction, he also might make it through the doorway, once it was unblocked.

But his belief was: he dared not move. Dared not turn his head.

As Stulwig had that tense realization, the brightness—which had been slightly out of his line of vision—moved. There was an awesome sound of heavy, heavy footsteps. And then—

Vashanka strode into view.

There was no question in Stulwig's numbed mind. What he was seeing, suddenly, was clearly a sight not given to many men to observe so close up. The Rankan god Vashanka. Maker of lightning in the sky. Master of weaponry. Killer of ten god-brothers. Murderer of Jutu Stulwig (father of Alten).

The mighty being stood now, poised in the doorway leading from the bedroom. And he literally had to stoop down so that his head did not strike the top of the doorjamb.

He was a massive figure whose every stretch and fold of skin was lit up like a fire. The light that enveloped him from head to foot actually seemed to flicker, as if tiny tongues of white heat were burning there.

Those innumerable fires suffused the greenhouse with a brightness greater than daylight.

Clearly, a human confronted by a god should not rely on force alone. At no time was that realization a coherent thought in Stulwig's mind. But the awful truth of it was there in his muscles and bones. Every movement he made reflected the reality of a man confronting an overwhelming power.

Most desperately, he wanted to be somewhere, far away.

Which was impossible. And so—

Stulwig heard his voice stuttering out the first meaning of those defensive thought-feelings: "I'm innocent. I didn't know who she was."

It was purpose of a desperate sort. Avoid this incredible situation by explaining. Arguing. Proving.

The baleful eyes stared at him after he had spoken. If the being behind those eyes understood the words, there was no clear sign.

The man stammered on: "She came as a sorceress with whom I had arranged a rendezvous for this night. How could I know that it was a disguise?"

The Ilsig language, suddenly, did not seem to be a sufficient means of communication. Stulwig had heard that its verbal structure was despised by Rankans who had learned the speech of the conquered race. The verbs—it was said—were regarded by Rankans as lacking force. Whereas the conqueror's tongue was alive with verbs that expressed intense feeling, absolute purpose, uttermost determination.

Stulwig, fleetingly remembering those comparisons, had the thought: To Vashanka it will seem as if I'm begging for mercy, whereas all I want is understanding.

Feeling hopeless, the man clung to his staff. It was all he had. So he held it up between himself and the great fire god. But each passing instant he was recalling what Quag, the Hell Hound, had said—about Ils having failed his people of Sanctuary.

Suddenly, it was hard to believe that the minor magic of a failed god, as projected into a wooden stick—however tough the wood—could withstand even one blow from the mighty Vashanka.

As he had that cringing thought, Stulwig grew aware that the god had extended one hand. Instantly, the flame of the arm-hand grew brighter. Abruptly, it leaped. And struck the staff.

Utter confusion of brightness.

And confusion in his dazzled eyes as to what was happening, or what had happened.

Only one thing was clear: the attack of the god against the man had begun.

. . . He was still alive; that was Stulwig's first awareness. Alive with, now, a vague memory of having seen the lightning strike the staff. And of hearing a bass-voiced braying sound. But of what exactly had happened at the moment of the fire interacting with the staff there was no afterimage in his eyes.

Uncertain, still somehow clinging miraculously to the staff, Stulwig took several steps backward before the awful brightness let go of his vision centers. And there, striding toward him, was the fire god.

Up came the staff, defensively. But even as he was remembering the words of Cappen Varra, about holding the staff in front of him, Stulwig—the staff fighter—instinctively swung the staff in a hitting motion.

Swung it at the great being less than five feet away. And felt a momentary savage surge of hope, as mighty Vashanka actually ducked to avoid the blow.

Staff fighting! He had done a lot of it out there in the wilderness, where he either tended wild herbs, or gathered herbs for his greenhouse. Amazing how often a wandering nomad or two, seeing him alone, instantly unsheathed swords and came in for the kill.

In such a battle it would be deathly dangerous merely to prod with the staff. Used as a prod, the staff could be snatched. At which, it was merely a tussle of two men tugging for possession. And virtual certainty that some wild giant of a man would swiftly wrestle it away from the unwise person who had mistakenly tried to use it as if it also were a sword.

By Ils—thought a jubilant Stulwig—there is power in this staff. And he, the lightning god, perceives it as dangerous.

With that realization, he began to swing with all the force he could muster: whack, whack, whack! Forgotten was Cappen Varra's admonishment to use the staff only as a barrier.

It was fascinating—and exciting—to Stulwig to notice that Vashanka jumped back from the staff whenever it swung toward him. Once, the god actually leaped way up to avoid being hit. The staff went by almost two foot-lengths beneath his lowest extremity.

—But why is he staying? Why isn't he trying to get away if the staff is dangerous to him . . . ? That thought came suddenly, and at once brought a great diminishment to Stulwig's battle impulse.

The fear that hit the man abruptly was that there had to be a reason why Vashanka continued to fight by avoidance. Could it be that he expected the power in the staff to wear off?

The awful possibility brought back the memory of what Ils—Cappen Varra had said. The instant shock of what must already have happened to the staff's defense power sent Stulwig backing at top speed toward the hallway leading to the stairs. He gulped with joy, then, as he glanced back for just an instant, and saw that the normally barricaded door had been left wide open by Azyuna.

With that, he spun on his heels, and almost literally flung himself down the stairs, taking four, and once five, steps at a time. He came to the bottom. And, mercifully, that door also was open. It had been hard to see as he made his wild escape effort.

At that ultimate last moment, the entire stairwell suddenly lit up like day. And there was instantly no question but that the demon-god had belatedly arrived, and was in hot pursuit.

Out in that night, so dark near his entrance, Stulwig ran madly to the nearest corner. Darted around it. And then ran along the street until he came to a main thoroughfare. There he stopped, took up position with his back against a closed stall, and his staff in front of him.

Belated realization came that he was still stark naked.

There were people here even at this late hour. Some of them looked at Stulwig. But almost everybody stopped and stared in the direction from which Stulwig had come—where a great brightness shone into the sky, visible above a long, low building with a dozen projecting towers.

Everywhere, now, voices were expressing amazement. And then, even as Stulwig wondered if Vashanka would actually continue his pursuit—abruptly, the brilliant light winked out.

It took a while, then, to gather his courage. But the feeling was: Even though I made the mistake of fighting, I won—

Returning took a while longer. Also, the streets were darker again; and so his nakedness was not so obvious. Passersby had to come close before, in a city where so many were skimpily dressed, they could see a naked man at night. Thus he was able to act cautiously, without shame.

Finally, then, holding his staff in front of him, Stulwig climbed the stairs up to his darkened quarters. Found the candle that was always lit (and replaced, of course, at proper intervals) at the bottom of a long tube in his office. And then, when he had made certain that the place was, indeed, free of intruders, he hastily replaced the barricade.

A little later.

Stulwig lay sprawled on his bed, unable to sleep. He considered taking one of the herbs he normally prescribed for light sleepers. But that might send him off into a drugged unconsciousness. And for this night that seemed a last resort. Not to be done casually.

Lying there, tossing, he grew aware that there were sounds coming to him out of the night. Voices. Many voices. A crowd of voices.

Huh?

Up and over into the greenhouse. First, removing a shutter. And then, looking out and down.

The streets that he could see from his second floor were alive with torchlights. And, everywhere, people. Several times, as passersby went beneath his window, Stulwig leaned out and called stentoriously: "What is it? What's happening?"

From the replies that were yelled back, totaling at least as many as he could count on the fingers of both hands, he was able to piece together the reason for the celebration—for that was what it was.

The people of Sanctuary celebrating a victory.

What had occurred: beginning shortly after the brilliance of Vashanka had dwindled to darkness in a puff of vanishment, messengers began to run along the streets of the Maze and through all the lesser sections of the city.

The messengers were Jubal's spies and informants. And as a result of the message they spread—

Myrtis' women whispered into the ears of males, as each in turn received that for which he had paid. An electrifying piece of information it was, for the men flung on their clothes, grabbed their weapons, and charged off into the night distances of the Maze.

The worshipers at the bar of the Vulgar Unicorn suddenly drained their cups. And they, also, took to their heels—that was the appearance. An astonished barkeep ventured to the door. Peered out. And, hearing the pad of feet and the rustle of clothing, and seeing the torches, hastily locked up and joined the throngs that were streaming in one direction: toward the temple of Ils.

From his open shutter Stulwig could see the temple with its gilded dome. All the portions that he could see were lit up, and the light was visible through numerous glass reflectors. A thousand candles must be burning inside for there to be so many shining surfaces.

And inside the temple the priests were in a state of excitement. For the message that Jubal's informants carried to all Sanctuary was that Ils had engaged in battle with the lightning god of the Rankans, and had won.

There would be exultant worshiping until the hour of dawn: that was the meaning that Stulwig had had shouted up to him.

As the meaning finally came to him, Stulwig hastily closed the shutter. And stood there, shivering. It was an inner cold, not an outer one. Was this wise?—he wondered. Suppose the people in the palace came out to learn what all the uproar was? Suppose Vashanka, in his rage at being made to appear a loser, sent his lightning bolts down upon the city. Come to think of it, the sky above had already started to look very cloudy and threatening.

His entire body throbbing with anxiety, Stulwig nonetheless found himself accepting the celebration as justified. It was true. Ils was the victor. And he had deliberately sought the opportunity. So it could be that the ancient god of Ilsig was at long last ready for—what?

What could happen? How could the forces of the Rankan Empire be persuaded to depart from Sanctuary?

Stulwig was back in bed, the wonder and the mystery of it still seething inside him.

And he was still awake, later, when there came a gentle knock on his outer door.

Instant shock. Fear. Doubt. And then, trembling, he was at the vent asking the question: "Who is it?"

The voice of Illyra answered softly, "I am here, Alten, as we agreed this morning, to pay my debt in kind."

Long pause. Because the doubt and shock, and the beginning of disappointment, were absolutely intense. So long a pause that the woman spoke again: "My blacksmith, as you call him, has gone to the temple of Ils and will not be back until morning."

On one level—the level of his desire—it had the ring of truth. But the denying thought was stronger. Suppose this was Azyuna, forced by her shamed brother-lover to make one more entrance into the home of the healer; so that the brother could use some mysterious connection with her to penetrate hard walls. Then, when death had been dealt, Ils would again be disgraced.

Thinking thus, a reluctant Stulwig said, "You are freed of your promise, Illyra. Fate has worked once more to deny me one of the great joys of life. And once more enabled you to remain faithful to that hulking monster."

The healer uttered a long sigh; finished: "Perhaps, I shall have better fortune next time."

As he returned to his sheepskin he did have the male thought that a night when a man made love to a goddess could surely not be considered a total loss.

In fact—

Remembering, suddenly, that the affair had also included embracing, in its early stages, an Illyra look-alike, Stulwig began to relax.

It was then that sweet sleep came.

Vashanka's Minion

Janet Morris

1

The storm swept down on Sanctuary in unnatural fury, as if to punish the thieves for their misdeeds. Its hailstones were large as fists. They pummeled Wideway and broke windows on the Street of Red Lanterns and collapsed the temple of Ils, most powerful of the conquered Ilsigi gods.

The lightning it brought snapped up from the hills and down from the devilish skies and wherever it spat the world shuddered and rolled. It licked round the dome of Prince Kadakithis' palace and when it was gone, the storm god Vashanka's name was seared into the stone in huge, hieratic letters visible from the harbor. It slithered in the window of Jubal's walled estate and circled round the slave trader's chair while he sat in it, turning his black face blue with terror.

It danced on a high hill between the slaver's estate and the cowering town, where a mercenary named Tempus schooled his new Syrese horse in the art of death. He had bought the tarnished silver beast sight unseen, sending to a man whose father's life he had once saved.

"Easy," he advised the horse, who slipped in a sharp turn, throwing mud up into his rider's face. Tempus cursed the mud and the rain and the hours he would need to spend on his tack when the lesson was done. As for the screaming, stumbling hawk-masked man who fled iron-shod hooves in ever-shortening circles, he had no gods to invoke—he just howled.

The horse wheeled and hopped; its rider clung tightly, reins flapping loose, using only his knees to guide his mount. If the slaver who kept a private army must flaunt the fact, then the mercenary-cum-guardsman would reduce its ranks. He would teach Jubal the overweening flesh merchant that he who is too arrogant is lost. He saw it as part of his duty to the Rankan prince governor he was sworn to protect. Tempus had taken down a dozen hawk-masks. This one, stumbling, gibbering, would make thirteen.

"Kill," suggested the mercenary, tiring of his sport in the face of the storm.

The flattened ears of the misty horse flickered, came forward. It lunged, neck out. Teeth and hooves thunked into flesh. Screaming. Then the screaming stopped.

Tempus let the horse pummel the corpse awhile, stroking the beast's neck and cooing soft praise. When bones showed in a lightning flash, he backed the horse off and set it at a walk toward the walled city.

It was then that the lightning came circling round man and mount.

"Stand, stand." The horse, though he shook like a newborn foal, stood. The searing red light violated Tempus' tight-shut lids and made his eyes tear. An awful voice rang inside his head, deep and thunderous: *"You are mine."*

"I have never doubted it," grated the mercenary.

"You have doubted it repeatedly," growled the voice querulously, if thunder can be said to carp. *"You have been unruly, faithless though you pledged me your troth. You have been, since you renounced your inheritance, a mage, a philosopher, an auditing Adept of the Order of the Blue Star, a—"*

"Look here, God. I have also been a cuckold, a foot soldier in the ranks, a general at the end of that. I have bedded more iron in flesh than any ten other men who have lived as long as I. Now You ring me round with thunder and compass me with lightning though I am here to expand Your worship among these infidels. I am building Your accursed temple as fast as I can. I am no priest, to be terrified by loud words and bright manifestations. Get Thee hence, and leave this slum unenlightened. They do not deserve me, and they do not deserve You!"

A gust sighed fiercely, flapping Tempus' woolens against his mail beneath.

"I have sent you hither to build me a temple among the heathens, O sleepless one! A temple you will build!"

"A temple I will build. Yes, sir, Vashanka, lord of the Edge and the Point. If You leave me alone to do it." Damn pushy tutelary god. "You blind my horse, O God, and I will put him under Your threshold instead of the enemies slain in battle Your ritual demands. Then we will see who comes to worship there."

"Do not trifle with me, Man."

"Then let me be. I am doing the best I can. There is no room for foreign gods in the hearts of these Sanctuarites. The Ilsig gods they were born under have seen to that. Do something amazing: strike the fear of You into them."

"I cannot even make you cower, O impudent human!"

"Even Your visitations get old, after three hundred fifty years. Go scare the locals. This horse will founder, standing hot in the rain."

The thunder changed its tune, becoming canny. *"Go you to the harbor, My son, and look upon what My Majesty hath wrought! And into the Maze, where I am making My power known!"*

With that, the corral of lightning vanished, the thunder ceased, and the clouds blew away on a west wind, so that the full moon shone upon the land.

"Too much *krrf*," the mercenary, who had sold himself for a Hell Hound, sighed. "Hell Hound" was what the citizenry called the prince's guard; as far as Tempus was concerned, Sanctuary was Hell. The only thing that made it bearable was *krrf*, his drug of choice. Rubbing a clammy palm across his mouth, he dug in his human-hide belt until searching fingers found a little silver box he always carried. Flipping it open, he took a pinch of black Caronne *krrf* and, clenching his fist, piled the dust into the hollow between his first thumb joint and the fleshy muscle leading to his knuckle. He sniffed deeply, sighed, and repeated the process, inundating his other nostril.

"Too much damn *krrf*," he chuckled, for the *krrf* had never been stepped on—he did not buy adulterated drugs—and all six and a half feet of him tingled from its kiss. One of these days he would have to stop using it—the same day he lay down his sword.

He felt for its hilt, patted it. He had taken to calling it his "Wriggle-be-good," since he had come to this godforsaken warren of magicians and changelings and thieves. Then, the initial euphoria of the drug past, he kneed his horse homeward.

It was the *krrf*, not the instructions of the lightning or any fear of Vashanka, that made him go by way of the harbor. He was walking out his horse before taking it to the stable the Hell Hounds shared with the barracks personnel. What had ever possessed him to come down-country among the Ilsigi? It was not for his fee, which was exorbitant, that he had come, for the sake of those interests in the Rankan capital who underwrote him—those who hated the emperor so much that they were willing to back such a loser as Kadakithis, if they could do it without becoming the brunt of too many jokes. It was not for the temple, though he was pleased to build it. It was some old, residual empathy in Tempus for a prince so inept as to be known far and wide as "Kitty" which had made him come. Tempus had walked away from his primogeniture in Azehur, a long time ago, leaving the throne to his brother, who was not compromised by palace politics. He had deposited a treatise on the nature of being in the temple of a favored goddess, and he had left. Had he ever, really, been that young? Young as Prince Kadakithis, whom even the Wrigglies disparaged?

Tempus had been around in the days when the Ilsigi had been the Enemy: the Wrigglies. He had been on every battlefield in the Rankan/Ilsigi conflict. He had spitted more Ilsigi than most men, watched them writhe soundlessly until they died. Some said he had coined their derogatory nick-name, but he had not, though he had doubtless helped spread it.

He rode down Wideway, and he rode past the docks. A ship was being made fast, and a crowd had gathered round it. He squeezed the horse's barrel, urging it into the press. With only four of his fellow Hell Hounds in Sanctuary, and a local garrison whose personnel never ventured out in groups of less than six, it was incumbent upon him to take a look.

He did not like what he saw of the man who was being helped from the storm-wracked ship that had come miraculously to port with no sail intact, who murmured through pale cruel lips to the surrounding Ilsigi, then climbed into a Rankan litter bound for the palace.

He spurred the horse. "Who?" he demanded of the eunuch master whose path he suddenly barred.

"Aspect, the archmage," lisped the palace lackey, "if it's any business of yours."

Behind the lackey and the quartet of ebony slaves the shoulder-borne litter trembled. The view curtain with Kitty's device on it was drawn back, fell loose again.

"Out of my way, Hound," squeaked the enraged little pastry of a eunuch master.

"Don't get flapped, Eunice," said Tempus, wishing he were in Caronne, wishing he had never met a god, wishing he were anywhere else. *Oh, Kitty, you have done it this time.* Alain Aspect, yet! Alchemist extraordinaire, assassin among magicians, dispeller of enchantments, in a town that ran on contract sorcery?

"Back, back, back," he counseled the horse who twitched its ears and turned its head around reproachfully, but obeyed him.

He heard titters among the eunuchs, another behind in the crowd. He swung round in his saddle. "Hakiem, if I hear any stories about me I do not like, I will know whose tongue to hand on my belt."

The bent, news-nosed storyteller, standing amid the children who always clustered round him, stopped laughing. His rheumy eyes met Tempus's. "I have a story I would like to tell you, Hell Hound. One you would like to hear, I humbly imagine."

"What is it, then, old man?"

"Come to closer, Hell Hound, and say what you will pay."

"How can I tell you how much it's worth until I hear?" The horse snorted, raised his head, sniffed a rank, evil breeze come suddenly from the stinking Downwind beach.

"We must haggle."

"Somebody else, then, old man. I have a long night ahead." He patted the horse, watching the crowd of Ilsigi surging round, their heads level with his hips.

"That is the first time I have seen him backed off!": a stage whisper reached Tempus through the buzz of the crowd. He looked for the source of it, could not find one culprit more likely than the rest. There would be a lot more of that sort of talk, when word spread. But he did not interfere with sorcerers. Never again. He had done it once, thinking his tutelary god could protect him. His hand went to his hip, squeezed. Beneath his dun woolens and beneath his ring mail he wore a woman's scarf. He never took it off. It was faded and it was ragged and it reminded him never to argue with a warlock. It was all he had left of her, who had been the subject of his dispute with a mage.

Long ago in Azehur . . .

He sighed, a rattling sound, in a voice hoarse and gravelly from endless battlefield commands. "Have it your way tonight, then, Wrigglie. And hope you live till morning." He named a price. The storyteller named another. The difference was split.

The old man came close and put his hand on the horse's neck. "The lightning came and the thunder rolled and when it was gone the temple of Ils was no more. The prince has bought the aid of a mighty enchanter, whom even the bravest of the Hell Hounds fears. A woman was washed up naked and half-drowned on the Downwinders' beach and in her hair were pins of diamond."

"Pins?"

"Rods, then."

"Wonderful. What else?"

"The redhead from Amoli's Lily Garden died at moonrise."

He knew very well what whore the old man meant. He did not like the story, so far. He growled. "You had better astound me, quick, for the price you're asking."

"Between the Vulgar Unicorn and the tenement on the corner an entire building appeared on that vacant lot, where once the Black Spire stood—you know the one."

"I know it."

"Astounding?"

"Interesting. What else?"

"It is rather fancy, with a gilded dome. It has two doors, and, above them two signs that read, 'Men,' and, 'Women.' "

Vashanka had kept his word, then.

"Inside it, so the patrons of the Unicorn say, they sell weapons. Very special weapons. And the price is dear."

"What has this to do with me?"

"Some folk who have gone in there have not come out. And some have come out and turned one upon the other, dueling to the death. Some have merely slain whomsoever crossed their paths. Yet, word is spreading, and Ilsigi and Rankan queue up like brothers before its doors. Since some of those who were standing in line were hawk-masks, I thought it good that you should know."

"I am touched, old man. I had no idea you cared." He threw the copper coins to the storyteller's feet and reined the horse sideways so abruptly it reared. When its feet touched the ground, he set it at a collected canter through the crowd, letting the rabble scatter before its iron-shod hooves as best they might.

2

In Sanctuary, enchantment ruled. No sorcerer believed in gods. But they believed in the Law of Correspondences, and they *believed in* evil. Thus, since every negative must have its positive, they implied gods. Give a god an inch and he will take your soul. That was what the commoners and the second-rate prestidigitators lined up outside the weapon shop of Vashanka did not realize, and that was why no respectable magician or Hazard-class enchanter stood among them.

In they filed, men to Tempus' left, toward the Vulgar Unicorn, and women to his right, toward the tenement on the corner.

Personally, Tempus did not feel it wise or dignified for a god to engage in a commercial venture. From across the street, he took notes on who came and went.

Tempus was not sure whether he was going in there, or not.

A shadow joined the queue, disengaged, walked toward the Vulgar Unicorn in the tricky light of fading stars. It saw him, hesitated, took one step back.

Tempus leaned forward, his elbow on his pommel, and crooked a finger. "Hanse, I would like a word with you."

The youth cat-walked toward him, errant torchlight from the Unicorn's open door twinkling on his weapons. From ankle to shoulder, Shadowspawn bristled with armaments.

"What is it with you, Tempus? Always on my tail. There are bigger frogs than this one in Sanctuary's pond."

"Are you not going to buy anything tonight?"

"I'll make do with what I have, thanks. I do *not* swithe with sorcerers."

"Steal something for me?" Tempus whispered, leaning down. The boy had black hair, black eyes, and blacker prospects in this desperadoes' demesne.

"I'm listening."

"Two diamond rods from the lady who came out of the sea tonight."

"Why?"

"I won't ask you how, and you won't ask me why, or we'll forget it." He sat up straight in his saddle.

"Forget it, then," toughed Shadowspawn, deciding he wanted nothing to do with this Hell Hound.

"Call it a prank, a jest at the expense of an old girlfriend."

The thief edged around where Tempus could not see him, into a dapple of deepest dark. He named a price.

The Hell Hound did not argue. Rather, he paid half in advance.

"I've heard you don't really work for Kitty. I've heard your dues to the mercenaries' guild are right up to date, and that Kitty knows better than to give you any orders. If you are not arguing about my price, it must be too low."

Silence.

"Is it true that you roughed up that whore who died tonight? That Amoli is so afraid of you that you do whatever you want in her place and never pay?"

Tempus chuckled, a sound like the cracking of dry ice. "I will take you there, when you deliver, and you can see for yourself what I do."

There was no answer from the shadows, just a skittering of stones.

Yes, I will take you there, young one. And yes, you are right. About everything. You should have asked for more.

3

Tempus lingered there still, eating a boxed lunch from the Unicorn's kitchen, when a voice from above his head said, "The deal is off. That girl is a sorceress, if a pretty one. I'll not chance ensorcellment to lift baubles I don't covet, and for a pittance!"

Girl? The woman was nearly his own age, unless another set of diamond rods existed, and he doubted that. He yawned, not reaching up to take the purse that dangled over the lee of the roof. "I am disappointed. I thought Shadowspawn could steal."

The innuendo was not lost on the invisible thief. The purse was withdrawn. An impalpable something told him he was once again alone, but for the clients of Vashanka's weapon shop. Things would be interesting in Sanctuary, for a good little while to come. He had counted twenty-three purchasers able to walk away with their mystical armaments. Four had died while he watched, intrigued.

It was possible that a career Hell Hound such as Zalbar might have intervened. But Tempus wore Vashanka's amulet about his neck, and, if he did not agree with Him, he would at least bear with his god.

The woman he was waiting for showed there at dusk. He liked dusk; he liked it for killing and he liked it for loving. Sometimes if he was very lucky, the dusk made him tired and he could nap. A man who has been cursed by an archmage and pressed into service by a god does not sleep much. Sleep was something he chased the way other men chased women. Women, in general, bored him, unless they were taken in battle, or unless they were whores.

This woman, her black hair brushing her doeskin-clad shoulders, was an exception.

He called her name, very softly. Then again: "Cime." She turned, and at last he was sure. He had thought Hakiem could mean no other: he had not been wrong.

Her eyes were gray as his horse. Silver shot her hair, but she was yet comely. Her hands rose, hesitated, covered a mouth pretending to hardness and tight with fear. He recognized the aborted motion of her hands: toward her head, forgetful that the rods she sought were no longer there.

He did not move in his saddle, or speak again. He let her decide, glance quickly about the street, then come to him.

When her hand touched the horse's bridle, he said: "It bites."

"Because you taught it to. It will not bite me." She held it by the muzzle, squeezing the pressure points that rode the skin there. The horse raised his head slightly, moaned, and stood shivering.

"What seek you in there?" He inclined his head toward Vashanka's; a lock of copper hair fell over one eye.

"The tools of my trade were stolen."

"Have you money?"

"Some. Not enough."

"Come with me."

"Never again."

"You have kept your vow, then?"

"I slay sorcerers. I cannot suffer any man to touch me except a client. I dare no love; I am chaste of heart."

"All these aching years?"

She smiled. It pulled her mouth in hard at its corners and he saw aging no potion or cosmetic spell could hide. "Every one. And you? You did not take the Blue Star, or I would see it on your brow. What discipline serves your will?"

"None. Revenge is fruitless. The past is only alive in us. I am not meant for sorcery. I love logic too well."

"So, you are yet damned?"

"If that is what you call it, I suppose—yes. I work for the Storm God, sometimes. I do a lot of wars."

"What brought you, here, Cle—"

"Tempus, now. It keeps me in perspective. I am building a temple for Him." He pointed to Vashanka's weapon shop, across the street. His finger shook. He hoped she had not seen. "You must not ply your trade here. I have employment as a Hell Hound. Appearances must be preserved. Do not pit us against one another. It would be too sour a memory."

"For whomever survived? Can it be you love me still?" Her eyes were full of wonder.

"No," he said, but cleared his throat. "Stay out of there. I know His service well. I would not recommend it. I will get you back what you have lost. Meet me at the Lily Garden tonight at midnight, and you will have them. I promise. Just take down no sorcerers between now and then. If you do, I will not return them, and you cannot get others."

"Bitter, are you not? If I do what you are too weak to do, what harm is there in that?" Her right eyebrow raised. It hurt him to watch her.

"We are the harm. And we are the harmed, as well. I am afraid that you may have to break your fast, so be prepared. I will reason with myself, but I promise nothing."

She sighed. "I was wrong. You have not changed one bit."

"Let go of my horse."

She did.

He wanted to tell her to let go of his heart, but he was struck mute. He wheeled his mount and clattered down the street. He had no intention of leaving. He just waited in a nearby alley until she was gone.

Then he hailed a passing soldier, and sent a message to the palace.

When the sun danced above the Vulgar Unicorn's improbably engaged weather vane, support troops arrived, and Kadakithis' new warlock, Aspect, was with them.

"Since last night, and this is the first report you have seen fit to make?" The sorcerer's pale lips flushed. His eyes burned within his shadowed cowl.

"I hope you and Kadakithis had a talk."

"We did, we did. You are not still angry at the world after all these years?"

"I am yet living. I have your kind to blame or thank, whichever."

"Do you not think it strange that we have been thrown together as—equals?"

"I think that is not the right word for it, Aspect. What are you about, here?"

"Now, now, Hell Hound—"

"Tempus—"

"Yes, Tempus. You have not lost your fabled sense of irony. I hope it is a comfort."

"Quite actually. Do not interfere with the gods, guildbrother of my nemesis."

"Our prince is justifiably worried. Those weapons—"

"—equal out the balance between the oppressors and the oppressed. Most of Sanctuary cannot afford your services, or the prices of even the lowliest members of the Enchanters' Guild. Let it be. We will get the weapons back, as their wielders meet their fates."

"I have to report to Kitt—to Kadakithis."

"Then report that I am handling it." Behind the magician, he could see the ranks whispering. Thirty men, the archmage had brought. Too many.

"You and I have more in common than in dispute, Tempus. Let us join forces."

"I would sooner bed an Ilsigi matron."

"Well, I am going in there." The archmage shook his head and the cowl fell back. He was pretty, ageless, a blond. "With or without you."

"Be my guest," Tempus offered.

The archmage looked at him strangely. "We do the same services in the world, you and I. Killing, whether with natural or supernatural weapons, is still killing. You are no better than I."

"Assuredly not, except that I will outlive you. And I will make sure you do not get your requisite burial ritual."

"You would not!"

"Like you said, I yet bear my grudge—against every one of you."

With a curse that made the ranks clap their hands to their helmeted ears, the archmage swished into the street, across it, and through the door marked "Men" without another word. It was his motioned command which made the troops follow.

A waitress Tempus knew came out when the gibbous moon was high, to ask him if he was hungry. She brought him fish and he ate it, watching the doors.

When he had just about finished, a terrible rumble crawled up the street, tremors following in its wake. He slid from his horse and held its muzzle, and the reins up under its bit. The doors of Vashanka's weapon shop grew shimmery, began taking color. Above, the moon went behind a cloud. The little dome on the shop rocked, grew cracks, crazed, steamed. The doors were ruby red, and melting. Awful wails and screams and the smell of sulfur and ozone filled the night.

Patrons began streaming out of the Vulgar Unicorn, drinks in hand. They stayed well back from the rocking building, which howled as it stressed larger, growing turgid, effluescing spectrums which sheeted and snapped and snarled. The doors went molten white; then they were gone. A figure was limned in the left-hand doorway, and it was trying to climb empty air. It flamed and screeched, dancing, crumbling, facing the street but unable to pass the invisible barrier against which it pounded. It stank: the smell of roasting flesh was overwhelming. Behind it, helmets crumpled, dripped onto the contorted faces of soldiers whose mustaches had begun to flare.

The mage who tried to break down the invisible door had no fists; he had pounded them away. The ranks were char and ash in falling effigy of damnation. The doors, which had been invisible, began to cool to white, then to gold, then to red.

The street was utterly silent. Only the snorts of his horse and the squeals of the domed structure could be heard. The squeals fell off to growls and shudders. The doors cooled, turned dark.

People muttered, drifted back into the Unicorn with mumbled wardings, tracing signs and taking many backward looks.

Tempus, who could have saved thirty innocent soldiers and one guilty magician, got out his silver box and sniffed some *krrf*.

He had to be at the Lily Garden soon.

When he got there, the mixed elation of drug and death had faded.

What if Shadowspawn did not appear with the rods? What if the girl Cime did not come to get them back? What if he still could hurt, as he had not hurt for more than three hundred years?

He had had a message from the palace, from Prince Kadakithis himself. He was not going up there, just yet. He did not want to answer any questions about the archmage's demise. He did not want to appear involved. His only chance to help the prince governor effectively lay in working his own way. Those were his terms, and under those terms Kitty's supporters in the Rankan capital had employed him to come down here and play Hell Hound and see what he would do. There were no wars, anywhere. He had been bored, his days stretching out neverending, bleak. So he had concerned himself with Kitty, for something to do. The building of Vashanka's temple he oversaw for himself more than Kadakithis, who understood the necessity of elevating the state cult above the Ilsig gods, but believed only in wizardry, and his noble Ranke blood.

He was not happy about the spectacle at Vashanka's weapon shop. Sloppy business, this sideshow melting and unmelting. The archmage must have been talented, to make his struggles visible to those outside.

Wisdom is to know the thought which steers all things through all things, a friend of his who was a philosopher had once said to him. The thought that was steering all things through Sanctuary was muddled, unclear.

That was the hitch, the catch, the problem with employing the supernatural in a natural milieu. Things got confused. With so many spells at work, the fabric of causality was overly strained. Add the gods, and Evil and Good faced each other across a board game, whose extent was the phenomenal world. He wished the gods would stay in their heavens and the sorcerers in their hells.

Oh, he had heard endless persiflage about simultaneity; iteration—the constant redefining of the now by checking it against the future; alchemical laws of consonance. When he had been a student of philosophy and Cime had been a maiden, he had learned the axiom that Mind is unlimited and self-controlled, but all other things are connected; that nothing is completely separated off from any other thing, nor are things divided one from the other, except Mind.

The sorcerers put it another way: they called the consciousness of all things into service, according to the laws of magic.

Not philosophy, nor theology, nor thaumaturgy held the answer for Tempus; he had turned away from them, each and all. But he could not forget what he had learned.

And none of the Adepts like to admit that no servitor can be hired without wages. The wages of unnatural life are unnatural death.

He wished he could wake up in Azehur, with his family, and know that he had dreamed this impious dream.

But instead he came to Amoli's whorehouse, the Lily Garden. Almost, but not quite, he rode the horse up its stairs. Resisting the temptation, he reflected that in every age he had ever studied, doom-criers abounded. No millennium is attractive to the man immured in it; enough prophecies have been made in antiquity that one who desires, in any age, to take the position that Apocalypse is at hand can easily defend it. He would not join that dour order; he would not worry about anything but Tempus, and the matter awaiting his attention.

Inside Amoli's, Hanse the thief sat in full swagger, a pubescent girl on each knee.

"Ah," he waved. "I have something for you."

Shadowspawn tumbled both girls off of him, and stood, stretching widely, so that every arm dagger and belted sticker and thigh sheath creaked softly. The girls at his feet stayed there, staring up at Tempus wide-eyed. One whimpered to Shadowspawn and clutched his thigh.

"Room key," Tempus snapped to no one in particular, and held out his hand. The concierge, not Amoli, brought it to him.

"Hanse?"

"Coming." He extended a hand to one girl.

"Alone."

"You are not my type," said the thief, suspicious.

"I need just a moment of your evening. You can do what you wish with the rest."

Tempus looked at the key, headed off toward a staircase leading to the room which bore a corresponding number.

He heard the soft tread of Shadowspawn close behind.

When the exchange had been made, the thief departed, satisfied with both his payment and his gratuity, but not quite sure that Tempus appreciated the trouble to which he had put himself, or that he had gotten the best of the bargain they had made.

He saw the woman he had robbed before she saw him, and ended up in a different girl's room than the one he had chosen, in order to avoid a scene. When he had heard her steps pass by, stop before the door behind which the big Hell Hound waited, he made preclusive threats to the woman whose mouth he had stopped with the flat of his hand, and slipped downstairs to spend his money somewhere else, discreetly.

If he had stayed, he might have found out what the diamond rods were really worth; he might have found out what the sour-eyed mercenary with his high brow, suddenly so deeply creased, and his lightly carried mass, which seemed tonight too heavy, was worried about. Or perhaps he could have fathomed Tempus' enigmatic parting words:

"I would help you if I could, backstreeter," Tempus had rumbled. "If I had met you long ago, or if you liked horses, there would be a chance. You have done me a great service. More than that pouch holds. I am seldom in any man's debt, but you, I own, can call me anytime."

"You paid me, Hell Hound. I am content," Hanse had demurred, confused by weakness where he had never imagined it might dwell. Then he saw the Hell Hound fish out a snuffbox of *krrf*, and thought he understood.

But later, he went back to Amoli's and hung around the steps, cautiously petting the big man's horse, the *krrf* he had sniffed making him willing to dodge the beast's square, yellow teeth.

4

She had come to him, had Cime. She was what she was, what she had always been.

It was Tempus who was changed: Vashanka had entered into him, the Storm God who was Lord of Weapons who was Lord of Rape who was Lord of War who was Lord of Death's Gate.

He could not take her, gently. So spoke not his physical impotence, as he might have expected, but the cold wash of wisdom: he would not despoil her; Vashanka would accept no less.

She knocked and entered and said, "Let me see them," so sure he would have the stolen diamonds that her fingers were already busy on the lacings of her Ilsig leathers.

He held up a hide-wrapped bundle; slimmer than her wrist, shorter than her forearm. "Here. How were they thieved?"

"Your voice is hoarser than I have ever heard it," she replied, and: "I needed money; there was this man . . . actually, there were a few, but there was a tough, a street brawler. I should have known—he is half my apparent age. What would such as he want with a middle-aged whore? And he agreed to pay the price I asked, without quibbling. *Then* he robbed me." She looked around, her eyes, as he remembered them, clear windows to her thoughts. She was appalled.

"The low estate into which I have sunk?"

She knew what he meant. Her nostrils shivered, taking in the musty reek of the soiled bedding on which he sprawled fully clothed, smelling easily as foul. "The devolution of us both. That I would be here, under these circumstances, is surely as pathetic as you."

"Thanks. I needed that. Don't."

"I thought you wanted me." She ceased unlacing, looked at him, her tunic open to her waist.

"I did. I don't. Have some *krrf*." On his hips rode her scarf; if she saw it, then she would comprehend his degradation too fully. So he had not removed it, hoping its presence would remind him, if he weakened and his thoughts drowned in lust, that *this* woman he must not violate.

She sat on the quilt, one doe-gloved leg tucked under her.

"You jest," she breathed, then, eyes narrowed, took the *krrf*.

"It will be ill with you, afterward, should I touch you."

Her fingers ran along the flap of hide wrapped over her wands. "I am receiving payment," she tapped the package. "And I may not owe debts."

"The boy who pilfered these, did it at my behest."

"Must you pander for me?"

He winced. "Why do you not go home?" She smelled of salt and honey and he thought desperately that she was here only because he forced the issue: to pay her debt.

She leaned forward, touched his lips with a finger. "For the same reason that you do not. Home is changed, gone to time."

"Do you know that?" He jerked his head away, cracking it against the bed's wooden headboard.

"I believe it."

"I cannot believe anything, anymore. I surely cannot believe that your hand is saying what it seems to be saying."

"I cannot," she said, between kisses at his throat he could not, somehow, fend off, "leave . . . with . . . debts . . . owing."

"Sorry," he said firmly, and got out from under her hands. "I am just not in the mood."

She shrugged, unwrapped the wands, and wound her hair up with them. "Surely, you will regret this, later."

"Maybe you are right," he sighed heavily. "But that is my problem. I release you from any debt. We are even. I remember past gifts, given when you still knew how to give freely." There was no way in the world he was going to hurt her. He would not strip before her. With those two constraints, he had no option. He chased her out of there. He was as cruel about it as he could manage to be, for both their sakes.

Then he yelled downstairs for service.

When he descended the steps in the cool night air, a movement startled him, on the gray's off side.

"It is me, Shadowspawn."

"It is I, Shadowspawn," he corrected, huskily. His face averted, he mounted from the wrong side. The horse whickered disapprovingly. "What is it, snipe?"

As clouds covered the moon, Tempus seemed to pull all night's shadows round him. Hanse might have the name, but this Tempus had the skill. Hanse shivered. There were no Shadow Lords any longer. . . . "I was admiring your horse. Bunch of hawk-masks rode by, saw the horse, looked interested. I looked proprietary. The horse looked mean. The hawk-masks rode away. I just thought I'd see if you showed soon, and let you know."

A movement at the edge of his field of vision warned him, even as the horse's ears twitched at the click of iron on stone. "You should have kept going, it seems," said Tempus quietly, as the first of the hawk-masks edged his horse out past the intersection, and others followed. Two. Three. Four. Two more.

"Mothers," whispered Cudget Swearoath's prodigy, embarrassed at not having realized that he was not the only one waiting for Tempus.

"This is not your fight, junior."

"I'm aware of that. Let's see if they are."

Blue night: blue hawk-masks: the sparking thunder of six sets of hooves rushing toward the two of them. Whickering. The gleam of frothing teeth, and bared weapons: iron clanging in a jumble of shuddering, straining horses. The kill-trained gray's challenge to another stallion: hooves thudding on flesh and great mouths gaped, snapping; a blaring death clarion from a horse whose jugular had been severed. Always watching the boy: keeping the gray between the hawk-masks and a thief who just happened to get involved; who just happened to kill two of them with thrown knives, one through an eye and the other blade, he recalled clearly, sticking out of a slug-white throat. Tempus would remember even the whores' ambivalent screams of thrill and horror, delight and disgust. He had plenty of time to sort it out:

Time to draw his own sword, to target the rider of his choice, feel his hilt go warm and pulsing in his hand. He really did not like to take unfair advantage. The iron sword glowed pink like a baby's skin or a just-born day. Then it began to react in his grip. The gray's reins, wrapped around the pommel, flapped loosely; he told it where he wanted it with gritted words, with a pressing knee, with his shifting weight. One hawk-mask had a greenish tinge to him: protected. Tempus' sword would not listen to such talk: it slit charms like butter, armor like silk. A blue wing whistled above his head, thrown by a compatriot of the man who fell so slowly with his guts pouring out over his saddle like cold molasses. While that hawk-mask's horse was in midair between two strides, Tempus' sword licked up and changed the color of the foe-seeking boomerang. Pink, now, not blue. He was content to let it return its death to the hand that threw it. That left just two.

One had the thief engaged, and the youth had drawn his wicked, twenty-inch Ilbarsi knife, too short to be more than a temporizer against the hawk-mask's sword, too broad to be thrown. Backed against the Lily Garden's wall, there was just time for Tempus to flicker the horse over there and split the hawk-mask's head down to his collarbones. Gray brains splattered him. The thrust of the hawk-mask, undiminished by death, shattered on the flat of the long, curved knife Shadowspawn held up in a two-fisted, desperate block.

"Behind you!"

Tempus had known the one last hawk-mask was there. But this was not the boy's battle. Tempus had made a choice. He ducked and threw his weight sideways, reining the horse down with all his might. The sword, a singing one, sonata'd over his head, shearing hairs. His horse, overbalanced, fell heavily, screaming, pitching, rolling onto his left leg. Pinned for an instant, he saw white anguish; then the last hawk-mask was leaping down to finish him, and the gray scrambled to its feet. "Kill," he shouted, his blade yet at ready, but lying in the dirt. His leg flared once again, then quieted. He tried it, gained his knees, dust in his eyes. The horse reared and lunged. The hawk-mask struck blindly, arm above his head, sword reaching for gray, soft underbelly. He tried to save it. He tried. He tackled the hawk-mask with the singing sword. Too late, too late: horse fluids showered, him. Bellows of agony pealed in his ears. The horse and the hawk-mask and Tempus went down together, thrashing.

When Tempus sorted it out, he allowed that the horse had killed the hawk-mask at the same time the hawk-mask had disemboweled the horse.

But he had to finish it. It lay there thrashing pathetically, deep groans coming from it. He stood over it uncertainly, then knelt and stroked its muzzle. It snapped at him, eyes rolling, demanding to die. He acceded, and the dust in his eyes hurt so much they watered profusely.

Its legs were still kicking weakly when he heard a movement, turned on his good leg, and stared.

Shadowspawn was methodically stripping the hawk-masks of their arms and valuables.

Hanse did not notice Tempus, as he limped away. Or he pretended he did not. Whichever, there was nothing left to say.

5

When he reached the weapon shop, his leg hardly pained him. It was numb; it no longer throbbed. It would heal flawlessly, as any wound he took always healed. Tempus hated it.

Up to the weapon shop's door he strode, as the dawn spilled gore onto Sanctuary's alleys.

He kicked it; it opened wide. How he despised supernal battle, and himself when his preternatural abilities came into play.

"Hear me, Vashanka! I have had enough! Get this sidewalk stand out of here!"

There was no answer. Within, everything was dim as dusk, dim as the pit of unknowingness which spawned day and night and endless striving.

There were no weapons here for him to see, no counter, no proprietor, no rack of armaments pulsing and humming expectantly. But then, he already had his. One to a customer was the rule: one body; one mind; one swing through life.

He trod mists tarnished like the gray horse's coat. He trod a long corridor with light at its ending, pink like new beginnings, pink like his iron sword when Vashanka lifted it by Tempus' hand. He shied away from his duality; a man does not look closely at a curse of his own choosing. He was what he was, vessel of his god. But he had his own body, and that particular body was aching; and he had his own mind, and that particular mind was dank and dark like the dusk and the dusty death he dealt.

"Where are You, Vashanka, O Slaughter Lord?"

Right here, resounded the voice within his head. But Tempus was not going to listen to any internal voice. Tempus wanted confrontation.

"Materialize, you bastard!"

I already have; one body; one mind; one life—in every sphere.

"I am not you!" Tempus screamed through clenched teeth, willing, firm footing beneath his sinking feet.

No, you are not. But I am you, sometimes, said the nimbus-wreathed figure striding toward him over gilt-edged clouds. Vashanka: so very tall with hair the color of yarrow honey and a high brow free from lines.

"Oh, no . . ."

You wanted to see. Me. Look upon Me, servant!

"Not so close, Pillager. Not so much resemblance. Do not torture me, my god! Let me blame it all on you—not *be* you!"

So many years, and you yet seek self-delusion?

"Definitely. As do You, if You think to gather worshipers in this fashion! O Berserker God, You cannot roast their mages before them: they are all dependent on sorcery. You cannot terrify them thusly, and expect them to come to You. Weapons will not woo them; they are not men of the armies. They are thieves, and pirates, and prostitutes! You have gone too far, and not far enough!"

Speaking of prostitutes, did you see your sister? Look at me!

Tempus had to obey. He faced the manifestation of Vashanka, and recalled that he could not take a woman in gentleness, that he could but war. He saw his battles, ranks parading in endless eyes of storm and bloodbath. He saw the Storm God's consort, His own sister whom He raped eternally, moaning on Her couch in anguish that Her blood brother would ravish Her so.

Vashanka laughed.

Tempus snarled wordlessly through frozen lips.

You should have let us have her.

"Never!" Tempus howled. Then: "O God, leave off! You are not increasing your reputation among these mortals, nor mine! This was an ill-considered venture from the outset. Go back to Your heaven and wait. I will build Your temple better without Your maniacal aid. You have lost all sense of proportion. The Sanctuarites will not worship one who makes of their town a battlefield!"

Tempus, do not be wroth with Me. I have My own troubles, you know. I have to get away every now and again. And you have not been warring, whined the god, *for so very long. I am bored and I am lonely.*

"And you have caused the death of my horse!" Tempus spat, and broke free of Vashanka, wrenching his mind loose from the mirror mind of his god with an effort of will greater than any he had ever mounted before. He turned in his steps and began to retrace them. The god called to him over his shoulder, but he did not look back. He put his feet in the smudges they had left in the clouds as he had walked among them, and the farther he trudged, the more substantial those clouds became.

He trekked into lighter darkness, into a soft, new sunrise, into a pink and lavender morning which was almost Sanctuary's. He continued to walk until the smell of dead fish and Downwind pollution assailed his nostrils. He strode on, until a weed tripped him and he fell to his knees in the middle of a damp and vacant lot.

He heard a cruel laugh, and as he looked up he was thinking that he had not made it back at all—that Vashanka was not through punishing him.

But to his right was the Vulgar Unicorn, to his left the palimpsest tenement wall. And before him stood one of the palace eunuchs, come seeking him with a summons from Kittycat to discuss what might be done about the weapon shop said to be manifesting next to the Vulgar Unicorn.

"Tell Kadakithis," said Tempus, arduously gaining his feet, "that I will be there presently. As you can see . . ." He waved around him, where no structure stood or even could be proved ever to have stood. ". . . there is no longer any weapon shop. Therefore, there is no longer any problem, nor any urgency to attend to it. There is, however, one very irritable Hell Hound in this vacant lot who wants to be left alone."

The blue-black eunuch exposed perfect, argent teeth. "Yes, yes, master," he soothed the honey-haired man. "I can see that this is so."

Tempus ignored the eunuch's rosy, outstretched palm, and his sneer at the Hell Hound pretending to negotiate the humpy turf without pain. Accursed Wrigglie!

As the round-rumped eunuch sauntered off, Tempus decided the Vulgar Unicorn would do as well as anyplace to sit and sniff *krrf* and wait for his leg to finish healing. It ought to take about an hour—unless Vashanka was more angry at him that he estimated, in which case it might take a couple of days.

Shying from that dismal prospect, he pursued diverse thoughts. But he fared little better. Where he was going to get another horse like the one he had lost, he could not conjecture, any more than he could recall the exact moment when the last dissolving wisps of Vashanka's weapon shop blurred away into the mists of dawn.

Shadow's Pawn

Andrew Offutt

She was more than attractive and she walked with head high in pride and awareness of her womanhood. The bracelet on her bare arm flashed and seemed to glow with that brightness the gods reserve for polished new gold. She should have been walking amid bright lights illuminating the dancing waters of a fountain, turning its sparkling into a million diamonds and with the aid of a bit of refraction, colorful other gemstones as well.

There was no fountain down here by the fish market, and the few lights were not bright. She did not belong here. She was stupid to be here, walking unescorted so late at night. She was stupid. Stupidity had its penalties; it did not pay.

Still, the watching thief appreciated the stupidity of others. It did pay; it paid him. He made his living by it, by his own cleverness and the stupidity of others. He was about to go to work. Even at the reduced price he would receive from a changer, that serpent-carved bracelet would feed him well. It would keep him, without the necessity of more such hard work as this damnable lurking, waiting, for—oh, probably a month.

Though she was the sort of woman men looked upon with lust, the thief would not have her. He did not see her that way. His lust was not carnal. The waiting thief was no rapist. He was a businessman. He did not even like to kill, and he seldom had to. She passed the doorway in whose shadows he lurked, on the north side of the street.

"G'night Praxy, and thanks again for all that beer," he called to no one, and stepped out onto the planking that bordered the street. He was ten paces behind the quarry. Twelve. "Good thing I'm walking—I'm in no condition to ride a horse t'night!" Fourteen paces.

Laughing giddily, he followed her. The quarry.

She reached the corner of the deserted street and turned north, onto the Street of Odors. Walking around two sides of the Serpentine! She was stupid. The dolt had no business whatever with that fine bracelet. Didn't have proper respect for it. Didn't know how to take care of it. The moment she rounded the corner, the thief stepped off the boardwalk onto the unpaved street, squatted to snatch up his shoes the moment he stepped out of them, and *ran*.

Just at the intersection he stopped as if he had run into a wall, and dropped the shoes. Stepped into them. Nodded affably, drunkenly to the couple who came around off Stink Street—slat and slattern wearing three coppers' worth of clothing and four of "jewelry." He stepped onto the planking, noting that they noted little save each other. How nice. The Street of Odors was empty as far as he could see. Except for the quarry.

"Uhh," he groaned as if in misery. "Lady," he called, not loudly. "My lady?" He slurred a little, not overdoing. Five paces ahead, she paused and looked back. "H—help," he said, right hand clutching at his stomach.

She was too stupid to be down here alone at this time of night, all right. She came back! All solicitous she was, and his hand moved a little to the left and came out with a flat-bladed knife while his left hand clamped her right wrist, the unbraceleted one. The point of the knife touched the knot of her expensive cerulean sash.

"Do not scream. This is a throwing knife. I throw it well, but I *prefer* not to kill. Unless I have to, understand me? All I want is that nice little snake you're wearing."

"Oh!" Her eyes were huge and she tucked in her belly, away from the point of several inches of dull-silvery leaf-shape he held to her middle. "It—it was a gift. . . ."

"I will accept it as a gift. Oh you are smart, very smart not to try yelling. I just hate to have to stick pretty women in the belly. It's messy, and it could give this end of town a bad name. I hate to throw a knife into their backs, for that matter. Do you believe me?"

Her voice was a squeak: "Yes."

"Good." He released her wrist and kept his hand outstretched, palm up. "The bracelet then. I am not so rude as to tear such a pretty bauble off a pretty lady's pretty wrist."

Staring at him as if entranced, she backed a pace. He flipped the knife, caught it by the tip. His left palm remained extended, a waiting receptacle. The right hefted the knife in a throwing attitude and she swiftly twisted off the bracelet. Better than he had thought, he realized with a flash of green and gratification; the serpent's eyes appeared to be nice topazes! All right then, he'd let her keep the expensive sash.

She did not drop the bracelet into his palm; she placed it there. Nice hard cold gold, marvelously weighty. Only slightly warmed from a wrist the color of burnt sienna. Nice, nice. Her eyes leaped, flickered in fear when he flipped the knife to catch it by its leather-wrapped tang. It had no hilt, to keep that end light behind the weighted blade.

"You see?" he said, showing teeth. "I have no desire for your blood, understand me? Only this bauble."

The bracelet remained cold in his palm and when it moved, he jerked his hand instinctively. Fast as he was he was only human, not a striking serpent; the bracelet suddenly became a living snake, drove its fangs into the meaty part of his hand that was the inner part of his thumb. It clung, and it hurt. Oh it hurt.

The thief's smile vanished with his outcry of pain. Yet he saw her smile, and even as he felt the horror within him he raised the throwing knife to stab the filthy bitch who had trapped him.

That is, he tried to raise the knife, tried to shake his bitten hand, to which the serpent clung. He failed. Almost instantly, the bite of that unnatural snake ossified every bone and bit of cartilage in his body and, stiffly, Gath the thief fell down dead.

His victim, still smiling, squatted to retrieve her property. She was shivering in excitement. She slipped the cold hard bracelet of gold onto her wrist. Its eyes, cold hard stones, scintillated. And a tremor ran all through the woman. Her eyes glittered and sparkled.

"Oooohh," she murmured with a shiver, all trembly and tingly with excitement and delight. "It was worth every piece of silver I paid, this lovely bauble from that lovely shop. I'm really glad it was destroyed. Those of us who bought these weapons of the god are so *unique*." She was trembling, excitement high in her and her heart racing with the thrill of danger faced and killing accomplished, and she stroked the bracelet as if it were a lover.

She went home with her head high in pride and continuing excitement, and she was not at all happy when her husband railed at her for being so late and seized her by the left wrist. He went all bright eyed and stiff and fell down dead. She was not at all happy. She had intended to kill only strangers for the thrill of it, those who deserved it.

Somewhere, surely, the god Vashanka smiled.

"The god-damned city's in a mess and busy as a kicked anthill and I think you had more than a whit to do with it," the dark young man said. (Or was he a youth? Streetwise and tough and hooded of eyes and wearing knives as a courtesan wore gems. Hair blacker than black and eyes nearly so above a nose almost meant for a bird of prey.)

" 'God-damned' city, indeed," said the paler, discomfitingly tall man, who was older but not old, and he came close to smiling. "You don't know how near you are to truth, Shadowspawn."

Around them in the charcoal dimness others neither heard nor were overheard. In this place, the trick was not to be overheard. The trick was to talk under everyone else. A bad tavern with a bad reputation in a bad area of a nothing town, the tavern called Vulgar Unicorn was an astonishingly quiet place.

"Just call me Hanse and stop being all cryptic and fatherly," the dark young man said. "I'm not looking for a father. I had one—I'm told. Then I had Cudget Swearoath. Cudget told me all I—all he knew."

The other man heard "fatherly" used to mean "patronizing," and the flash of ego in the tough called Shadowspawn. Chips on his shoulders out to here. The other man did not smile. How to tell Hanse how many Hanses he had known, over so many years?

"Listen. One night a while ago I killed two men." Hanse did not lower his voice for that statement-not-admission; he kept it low. The shadow of a voice.

"Not men, Hanse. Hawk-masks. Jubal's bravos. Hardly men."

"They were men, Tempus. They were all men. So is Hanse and even Kadaki—the prince governor."

"Kittycat."

"I do not call him that," Hanse said, with austerity. Then he said, "It's you I'm not sure of, Tempus. Are you a man?"

"I'm a man," Tempus said, with a sigh that seemed to come from the weight of decades and decades. "Tonight I asked you to call me Thales. Go ahead, Hanse. You killed two men, while helping me. Were you, by the way? Or were you lurking around my horse that night thinking of laying hands on some *krrf*?"

"I use no drugs and little alcohol."

"That isn't what I asked," Tempus said, not bothering to refute.

Dark eyes met Tempus', which impressed him. "Yes. That is why I was there, T—Thales. Why 'Thay-lees'?"

"Since all things are presently full of gods, why not 'Thales'? Thank you, Hanse. I appreciate your honesty. We can—"

"Honesty?" A man, once well built and now wearing his chest all over his broad belt and bulging under it as well had been passing their small round table. "Did I hear something about Hanse's honesty? Hanse?" His laugh was a combination: pushed and genuine.

The lean youth called Shadowspawn moved nothing but his head. "How'd you like a hole in your middle to let out all that hot air, Abohorr?"

"How'd you like a third eye, Abohorr?" Hanse's tablemate said.

Abohorr betook himself elsewhere, muttering—and hurrying. Both Hanse's lean swift hands remained on the tabletop. "You know him, Thales?"

"No."

"You heard me say his name and so you said it right after me."

"Yes."

"You're sharp, Thales. Too . . . smart." Hanse slapped the table's surface. "I've been meeting too many sharp people lately. Sharp as . . ."

"Knives," Tempus said, finishing the complaint of a very very sharp young man. "You were mentioning that you were waiting for me to come out of that house-not-home, Hanse, because you knew I was carrying. And then Jubal's bravos attacked—me—and you took down two."

"I was mentioning that, yes." Hanse developed a seemingly genuine interest in his brown-and-orange Saraprins mug. "How many men have you killed, Thales?"

"Oh *gods*. Do not ask."

"Many."

"Many, yes."

"And no scars on you."

Tempus looked pained. "No scars on me," he said, to his own big hands on the table. Bronzed, they were still more fair than Shadowspawn's. On a sudden thought, he looked up and his expression was of dawning revelation and disbelief. "Hanse? You saved my life that night. I saved yours—but they were after me to begin with. Hanse? How many men have you killed?"

Hanse looked away. Hair like a raven, nose of a young falcon. Profile carved out by a hand-ax sharper than a barber's razor, all planes and angles. A pair of onyxes for eyes, and just that hard. His look away was uncharacteristic and Tempus knew it. Tempus worked out of the palace and had access to confidential reports, one of which not even the prince governor had seen. He wouldn't, either, because it no longer existed. Too, Tempus had dealt with this spawn of Downwind and the shadows. He was here in this murkily lit tavern of humanity's dregs to deal with him again.

Hanse, looking away, said, "You are not to tell anyone."

Tempus knew just what to say. "Do not insult me again."

Hanse's nod was not as long as the thickness of one of his knives. (Were there five, or did he really wear a sixth on one of his thighs? Tempus doubted that; the strap wouldn't stay up.)

At last Hanse answered the question. "Two."

Two men. Tempus nodded, sighing, pushing back to come as close to slumping on his bench as his kind of soldier could. Damn. Who would have thought it? The reputation he had, this dark surly scary (to others, not the man currently calling himself Tempus) youth from the gutters he doubtless thought he had risen so far above. Tempus knew he had wounded a man or two, and he had assumed. Now Shadowspawn said he had never slain! That, from such a one, was an admission. *Because of me he has been blooded*, Tempus mused, and the weary thought followed: *Well, he's not the first. I had my first two, once. I wonder who they were, and where?* (But he knew, he knew. A man did not forget such. Tempus was older than anyone thought; he was not as world-weary old as he thought, or thought he thought.) Just now he wanted to put forth a hand and touch the much younger man. He certainly did not.

He said, "How do you feel about it?"

Hanse continued to gaze assiduously at something else. How could a child of the desert with such long long lashes and that sensuous, almost pretty mouth look so grim and thin-lipped? "I threw up."

"That proves you are human and is what you *did*. How *do* you feel about it?"

Hanse looked at him directly. After a time, he shrugged.

"Yes," Tempus sighed, nodding. He drained his cup. Raised a right arm on high and glanced in the general direction of the tap. The new nightman nodded. Though he had not looked at the fellow, Tempus lowered his arm and looked at Hanse. "I understand," he said.

"Do you? A while ago I told the prince that it is a prince's business to kill, not a thief's. Now I have killed."

"What a wonderful thing to say to a bit of royalty! I wish you weren't so serious right now, so I could laugh aloud. Do not expect any gentle words from me about the kills, my friend. It happens. I didn't ask for your help—or for you to be waiting for me. You won't do that again."

"Not that way, no." Hanse leaned back while whatever-his-name-was (they called him "Two-Thumb") set two newly filled mugs between them. He did not take the other two, or wait for payment. "I think things started when Bourne . . . died, and you came to Thieves' World."

"Thieves' World?"

Again that almost-embarrassed shrug. "It's what we call Sanctuary. Some of us. Now the whole city's in a mess and a turmoil and I think you have to do with that."

"I believe you said that."

"You led me astray, 'Thales.' That temple or store or whatever it was. It . . . collapsed?—erupted, like a volcano? Something. Next the prince—"

"You really do respect him, don't you?"

"I don't work for him though," Hanse pointed out; Tempus did. "He impounded the . . . the god-weapons?—that place sold, or tried to. Hell Hounds paying people for things they bought—or else! *Things!* New wealth in the city, because some of them had been stolen and now are bought from thieves. People are laughing at dealing with the new changer: the palace!"

Changer, Tempus knew, meant fence in this—*city*? O my God Vashanka—this? A city?!

"Two ships sitting out there in the harbor," Hanse went on,

"guarded up to here. I know those Things, those dark weapons of sorcery are being loaded aboard. Then what? Out to sea and straight to the bottom?"

"The very best place for them," Tempus said, turning and slowly turning his glazed earthenware mug. This one was striped garishly in yellow waves. "Believe it. There is too much power in those devices."

"Meanwhile some 'enforcers' from the mageguild have been trying to get hands on them first."

That Tempus also knew. Three of the toughs had been eliminated in the past twenty hours, unless another or two, had been slain tonight, by local watchmen or those special guardsman called Hell Hounds. "Unions will try to protect their members, yes. No matter what. A union is a mindless animal."

"You paid me well—*fair*, to fetch you the diamond wand-things that woman wears in her hair. I did, and she has them back. You gave them back."

Cime. Cime's diamond rods in her fine fine wealth of hair. "Yes. Did I?"

"You did. And strange things are happening in Sanctuary. Those were sorcerous weapons those hawk-masks used against you and me. A poor thief tried to snatch a woman's bracelet the other night, down in—never mind the street. She shouldn't have been there. The bracelet turned into a snake and killed him. I don't know what it did to him. He's dead and they say he weighs about twice as much as he did alive."

"It solidified his bones. It was obtained this morning. And when didn't strange things happen in Sanctuary, my friend?"

"That is twice you have called me that." Hanse's words had the sound of accusation about them.

"So I have. I must mean it, then."

Hanse became visibly uncomfortable. "I am Hanse. I was . . . apprentice to Cudget Swearoath. Prince *Kittycat* had him hanged. I am Shadowspawn. I have breached the palace and because of me a Hell Hound is dead. I have no friends."

And you slip and call him "Kittycat" when you think of your executed mentor, do you? Not seeking a father, eh? Do you know that all men do, and that I have mine, in Vashanka? Ah Hanse how you seek to be enigmatic and so cool—and are about as transparent as a pan of water caught from the sky!

Tempus waved a hand. "Save all that. Just tell me not to be your friend. Not to call you friend."

A silence fell over them like a struck banner and something naked stared out of Hanse's eyes. By the time he knew he must speak into the silence, it was too late. That same silence was Tempus' answer.

"Yes," Tempus said, considerately-cleverly changing the subject. "What old whatsisname Torchholder yammers about is true. Vashanka came, and He claimed Sanctuary. His name is branded into the palace, now. The very temple of Ils lies, in rubble. Vashanka created the weapon shop, from nothing, and—"

"A peddler-*god?*"

"I didn't think much of the tactic myself," Tempus said, hoping Vashanka heard him while noting how good the youth was at sneering. "And the weapon shop destroyed the mage the governor imported to combat him. Vashanka is not to be combated."

Hanse snapped glances, this way and that. "Say such things a time or two more in Sanctuary, *my friend,* and your body will be mourning the loss of its head."

The blond man stared at him. "Do you believe that?"

Hanse let that pass, while he rowed into the current of other conversations in the tavern. A current restless as a thief on a landing outside a window, and conversations just as stealthy and dark. He tuned it out again, stepping out of the flow yet flowing with it. Quietly.

"And how many of those fell Things do you think are still loose?"

"Too many. Two or four? You know our job is to collect them."

"Our?"

"The Hell Hounds."

"Who's your bearded friend, Hanse?"

The speaker stood beside the table, only a bit older than Hanse and just as cocky. Older in years only; he had not benefited from those years and would never be so much as Hanse. Self-consciously he wore self-consciously tight black. Oh, a brilliant thief! About as unobtrusive as hives.

Hanse was staring at Tempus, who was pink and bronze of skin, gold and honey of hair, lengthy and lengthy of legs, and smooth-shaven as a pair of doeskin leggings. Hanse did not take his dark-eyed gaze off the Hell Hound, while his dark hand moved out to close on the (black-bracered) wrist of the other young man.

"What color would you say his beard is, Athavul?"

Athavul moved his arm and proved that his wrist would not come loose. His arrogance and mask of cocky confidence fled him faster than a street girl fled a man revealed poor. Tempus recognized Athavul's chuckle; nervousness and sham. Tempus had heard it a thousand or a million times. What was the difference? He reflected on temporality, even while this boy Athavul temporized.

"You going blind, Shadowspawn? You think myself is, and testing he and I?" With a harsh short laugh and a slap with his other hand on his own chest, Athavul said, "Black as this. Black as this!" He slapped his black leather pants—self-consciously.

Tempus, leaning a bit forward, elbows on the little table, big swordsman's shoulders hunched, continued to gaze directly at Hanse. Into Hanse's eyes. His face looked open because he made it that way. Beardless.

"Same's his hair?" Hanse said, and his voice sounded brittle as very old harness leather. His eyes glittered.

Athavul swallowed. "Hair." He swallowed again, looking from Hanse to Tempus to Hanse. "Ah . . . he's your, ah, friend, Hanse. Let go, will you? You twit him about his . . . head if you want to, but I won't. Sorry I stopped and tried to be civil."

Without looking away from Hanse, Tempus said, "It's all right, Athavul. My name is Thales and I am not sensitive. I've been this bald for years."

Hanse was staring at Tempus, blond Tempus. His hand opened. Athavul yanked his arm back so fast he hit himself in his (nearly inexistent) stomach. He made no pretense of grace; with a dark glance at Hanse, he betook himself elsewhere, sullenly silent.

"Nicely done," Tempus said, showing his teeth.

"Don't smile at me, stranger. What do you look like?"

"Exactly what you see, Hanse. Exactly."

"And . . . what did he see?" Hanse's wave of his arm was as tight as he had become inside. "What do they see here, talking with Hanse?"

"He told you."

"Black beard, no hair."

Blond, beardless Tempus nodded.

Neither had taken his gaze off the other's eyes. "What else?"

"Does it matter? I am in the employ of that person we both know. What you people call a Hell Hound. I would not come here in that appearance! I doubt anyone else would be in this room, if they saw me. I was here when you came in, remember? Waiting for you. You were too cool to ask the obvious."

"They call me spawn of the shadows," Hanse said quietly, slowly, in a low tone. He was leaning back as if to get a few more centimeters between him and the tall man. "You're just a damned shadow!"

"It's fitting. I need your help, Shadowspawn."

Hanse said, enunciating distinctly, "Shit." And rising he added, "Sing for it. Dance in the streets for it." And he turned away, then back to add, "You're paying of course, Baldy," and then he betook himself elsewhere.

Outside, he glanced up and down the vermiform "street" called Serpentine, turned right to walk a few paces north. Automatically, he stepped over the broken plank in the boardwalk. He glanced into the tucked-in courtyard that was too broad and shallow to be dangerous for several hours yet. Denizens of the Maze called it variously the Outhouse, Tick's Vomitory, or, less seriously, Safehaven. From the pointed tail of the short cloak on the man back within that three-sided box, Hanse recognized Poker the cadite. From the wet sounds, he made an assumption as to Poker's activity. The man with the piebald beard glanced around.

"Come on in, Shadowspawn. Not much room left."

"Looking for Athavul. Said he was carrying and said I could join him." Lying was more than easy to Shadowspawn; it was almost instinctive.

"You're not mad at him?" Poker dropped his tunic's hem and turned from the stained rearmost wall.

"No no, nothing like that."

"He went south. Turned in to Slick Walk."

"Thanks, Poker. There's a big-bearded man in the Unicorn with no hair on top. Get him to buy you a cup. Tell him I said."

"Ah. Enemy of yours, Hansey?"

"Right."

Hanse turned and walked a few paces north toward Straight, his back to Slick Walk (which led into the two-block L whose real name no one remembered. Nary a door opened onto it and it stayed dark as a sorcerer's heart. It smelled perpetually sour and was referred to as Vomit Boulevard). When Poker said the weather was sunny, turn up your cloak's hood against rain. When Poker said right, head left.

Hanse cut left through Odd Birt's Dodge, angling around the corner of the tenement owned by Furtwan the dealer in snails for dye—who lived way over on the east side, hardly in tenement conditions. Instantly Hanse vanished into the embrace of his true friend and home. The shadows.

Because he had kept his eyes slitted while he was in the light filtering down from Straight Street, he was able to see. The darkness deepened with each of his gliding westward steps.

He heard the odd tapping sound as he passed Wrong Way Park. What in all the—a blind man? Hanse smiled—keeping his mouth closed against the possible flash of teeth. This was a wonderful place for the blind! They could "see" more in three-quarters of the Maze than anyone with working eyes. He eased along toward the short streetlet called Tanner, hewing the noises from Sly's Place. Then he heard Athavul's voice, out in the open.

"Your pardon, dear lady, but if you don't hand myself your necklace and your wallet I'll put this crossbow bolt through your left gourd."

Hanse eased closer, getting himself nearer the triple "corner" where Tanner sort of intersected with Odd Birt's Dodge and touched the north-south wriggle of the Serpentine as well. Streets in the Maze, it has been said, had been laid out by two love-struck snakes, both soaring on *krrf*. Hanse heard the reply of Ath's intended prey:

"You don't *have* a crossbow, slime lizard, but see what *I* have!"

The scream, in a voice barely recognizable as Athavul's, raised the hairs on the back of Hanse's neck and sent a chill running all the way down his coccyx. He considered freezing in place. He considered the sensible course of turning and running. Curiosity urged him to edge two steps farther and peek around the building housing Sly's. Curiosity won.

By the time he looked, Athavul was whimpering and gibbering. Someone in a long cloak the color of red clay, hood up, stepped around him, and Hanse thought he heard a giggle. Cowering, pleading, gibbering in horribly obvious fear—of what?—Athavul fell to his knees. The cloak swept on along Tanner toward the Street of Odors, and Hanse swallowed with a little effort. A knife had got itself into his hand; he didn't throw it. He edged down a few more steps to see which way the cloak turned. Right. Hanse caught a glimpse of the walking stick. It was white. The way the person in that cloak was moving, though, she was not blind. Nor was she any big woman.

Hanse put up his knife and started toward Athavul.

"No! Please plehehehease!" On his knees, Ath clasped his hands and pleaded. His eyes were wide and glassy with fear. Sweat and tears ran down his face in such profusion that he must soon have salt spots on his black jerkin. His shaking was windblown wash on the line and his face was the color of a priming coat of whitewash.

Hanse stood still. He stared. "What's the matter with you, Ath? I'm not menacing you, you fugitive from a dung-fueled stove! *Athavul!* What's the *matter*'th you?"

"Oh please pleohplease no no oh ohh ohohohono—o—o . . ."

Athavul fell on his knees and his still-clasped hands, bony rump in the air. His shaking had increased to that of a whipped, starved dog.

Such an animal would have moved Hanse to pity. Athavul was just ridiculous. Hanse wanted to kick him. He was also aware that two or three people were peering out of the dump still called Sly's Place though Sly had taken dropsy and died two years back.

"Ath? Did she hurt you? Hey! You little piece of camel dropping— what did she *do* to you?"

At the angry, demanding sound of Hanse's voice, Athavul clutched himself. Weeping loudly, he rolled over against the wall. He left little spots of tears and slobber and a puddle from a spasming sphincter. Hanse swallowed hard. *Sorcery.* That damned Enas Y—no, he didn't work this way. Ath was absolutely terrified. Hanse had always thought him the consistency of sparrow's liver and chicken soup, with bird's eggs between his legs. But *this*—not even this strutting ass could be this hideously possessed by fear without preternatural aid. Just the sight of it was scary. Hanse felt an urge to stomp or stick Ath just to shut him up, and that was awful.

He glanced at the thirty-one strands of dangling Syrese rope (each knotted thirty-one times) that hung in the doorway of Sly's. He saw seven staring eyeballs, six fingers, and several mismatched feet. Even in the Maze, noise attracted attention . . . but people had sense enough not to go running out to see what was amiss.

"BLAAAH!" Hanse shouted, making a horrid face and pouncing at the doorway. Then he rushed past the groveling, weeping Athavul. At the corner he looked up Odors toward Straight, and he was sure he saw the vermilion cloak. Maroon now, in the distance. Yes. Across Straight, heading north now past the tanners' broad open-front sheds, almost to the intersection, with the street called Slippery.

Several people were walking along Odors, just walking, heading south in Hanse's direction. The lone one carried a lanthorn.

All six walkers—three, one, and two—passed him going in the opposite direction. None saw him, though Hanse was hurrying. He heard the couple talking about the hooded blind woman with the white staff. He crossed well-lighted Straight Street when the red-clay cloak was at the place called Harlot's Cross. There Tanner's Row angled in to join the Street of Odors at its mutual intersection with the broad Governor's Walk. He passed the tiny "temple" of Theba and several shops to stop outside the entrance of the diminutive temple of Eshi Virginal—few believed in that—and watched the cloak turn left. Northwest. A woman, all right. Heading past the long sprawl of the farmers' market? Or one of the little dwellings that faced it?

Heading for Red Lantern Street? *A woman who pretends to be blind and who put a spell of terror on Athavul like nothing I ever saw.*

He had to follow her. He was incapable of not following her.

He was not driven only by curiosity. He wanted to know the identity of a woman with such a device, yes. There was also the possibility of obtaining such a useful wand. White, it resembled the walk-tap stick of a sightless woman. Painted, though, it could be the swagger stick of . . . Shadowspawn. Or of someone with a swollen purse who could put it to good use against Hanse's fellow thieves.

He looked out for himself; let them.

Hanse did not follow. He moved to intersect, and could anyone have done it as swiftly and surefootedly, it must have been a child who lived hereabouts and had no supervision.

He ran past Slippery—fading into a fig peddler's doorway while a pair of city watchmen passed—then ran through two vacant lots, a common backyard full of dog droppings and the white patches of older ones, over an outhouse, around a fat tree and then two meat houses and through two hedges—one spiny, which took no note of being cursed by a shadow on silent feet—across a porch and around a rain barrel, over the top of a sleeping black cat that objected with more noise than the two dogs he had aroused—one was still importantly barking, puffed up and hating to leave off—across another porch ("Is that you, Dadisha? Where have you *been*?"), through someone's scraps and—long jump!—over a mulch pile, and around two lovers ("What was that, Wrenny?"), an overturned outhouse, a rain barrel, a cow tethered to a wagon he went under without even slowing down, and three more buildings.

One of the lovers and one of the dogs actually caught sight of the swift-fleeting shadow. No one else. The cow might have wondered.

On one knee beside a fat beanberry bush in the far end of Market Run, he looked out upon the long straight stretch of well-kept street that ran past the market on the other side. He was not winded.

The hooded cloak with the walking stick was just reaching this end of the long, long farmers' market. Hanse crimped his cheeks in a little smile. Oh he was so clever, so speedy! He was just in time to—

—to see the two cloakless but hooded footpads materialize from the deep jet shadows at the building's corner. They pounced. One ran angling, to grasp her from behind, while his fellow came at her face-on with no weapons visible. Ready to snatch what she had, and run. She behaved surprisingly; she lunged to one side and prodded the attacker in front. *Prodded*, that Hanse saw; she did not strike or stab with the white staff.

Instantly the man went to his knees. He was gibbering, pleading, quaking. A butterfly clinging to a twig in a windstorm. Or . . . Athavul.

Swiftly—not professionally fast, but swiftly for her, a civilian, Hanse saw (he was moving)—she turned to the one coming up behind her. He also adjusted rapidly. He went low. The staff whirred over his head while his partner babbled and pleaded in the most abject fear. The footpad had not stopped moving. (Neither had Hanse.) Up came the hooded man from his crouch and his right hand snapped out edge-on to strike her wrist while his other fist leaped to her stomach. That fist glittered in the moonlight, or something glittered in it. That silvery something went into her and she made a puking gagging throaty noise and while she fell the white stick slid from her reflexively opening fingers. He grabbed it.

That was surely ill advised, but his hand closed on the staff's handle without apparent effect on him. He kicked her viciously, angrily—maybe she felt it, gutted, and maybe she did not—and he railed at his comrade. The latter, on his knees, behaved as Athavul had when Hanse shouted at him. He fell over and rolled away, assuming the fetal posture while he wept and pled.

The killer spat several expletives and whirled back to his victim. She was twitching, dying. Yanking open the vermilion cloak, he jerked off her necklace, ripped a twisted silver loop out of each ear, and yanked at the scantling purse on her girdle. It refused to come free. He sliced it with the swift single movement of a practiced expert. Straightening, he glanced in every direction, said something to his partner—who rolled fetally, sobbing.

"Theba take you, then," the thief said, and ran.

Back into the shadows of the market building's west corner he fled, and one of the shadows tripped him. As he fell, an elbow thumped the back of his neck.

"I want what you've got, you murdering bastard," a shadow-voice said from the shadows—while the footpad twisted to roll over. "Your kind gives thieves a bad name."

"Take it then!" The fallen man rammed the white staff into the shadow's thigh as it started to bend over him.

Instantly fear seized Hanse. Vised him; encompassed him; possessed him. Sickening, stomach-fluttering fear. His armpits flooded and his sphincter fluttered.

Unlike the stick's victims he had seen, he was in darkness, and he was Shadowspawn. He did not fall to his knees.

He fled, desperately afraid, sniveling, clutching his gut, babbling. Tears flowed to blind him, but he was in darkness anyhow. Staggering, weeping, horribly and obscenely afraid and even more horribly knowing all the while that he had no reason to be afraid, that this was sorcery; the most demeaning spell that could be laid on a man. He heard the killer laugh, and Hanse tried to run faster. Hoping the man did not pursue to confront him. Accost him. Snarl mean things at him. He could not stand that.

It did not happen that way. The thief who had slain without intending to kill laughed, but he too was scared, and disconcerted. He fled, slinking, in another direction. Hanse stumbled-staggered-sniveled on, on. Instinct was not gone but was heightened; he clung to the shadows as a frightened child to its mother. But he made noise, noise.

Attracted at the same time as she was repulsed by that whining fearful gibbering, Mignureal came upon him. "What—it's Han—*what are you doing?*"

He was seriously considering ending the terror, by ending himself with the knife in his fist. Anything to stop this enveloping, consuming agony of fear. At her voice he dropped the knife and fell weeping to his knees.

"Hanse—*stop that!*"

He did not. He could not. He could assume the fetal. He did. Uncomprehending, the garishly dressed girl acted instinctively to save him. Her mother liked him and to Mignureal he was attractive, a figure of romance. In his state, saving him was easy, even for a thirteen-year-old. Though his hysterical sobbing pleas brought tears to her eyes, for him, Mignureal tied his wrists behind him. The while, she breathed prayers known only to the S'danzo.

"You come along now," she said firmly, leaking tears and gulping. "Come along with me!"

Hanse obeyed.

She went straight along the well-lit Governor's Walk and turned down Shadow Lane, conducting her bound, sniveling captive. At the corner of Shadow and Slippery, a couple of uniformed men accosted her.

"Why it's Moonflower's darter. What'e you got there, Mineral?"

"Mignureal," she corrected. "Someone put a spell on him—over on the Processional," she said, choosing an area far from where she had found him. "My mother can help. Go with Eshi."

"Hmm. A spell of fear, huh? That damned Anus Yorl, I'll wager a cup! Who is it, sniveling under your shawl that way?"

Mignureal considered swiftly. What had happened to Hanse was awful. To have these city watchmen know, and spread it about—that would be insupportable. Again Mignureal lied. It was her brother Antelope, she told them, and they made sympathetic noises and let her be on her way, while they muttered about dam' sorcerers and the nutty names S'danzo gave their get. Both men agreed; they would make a routine check of Awful Alley and stop in at the Alekeep, just down the street.

Mignureal led Hanse a half-block more and went into her parents' shop-and-living-quarters. They were asleep. The tautly overweight Moonflower did not heed summonses and did not make house calls. Furthermore her husband was an irrepressibly randy man who bedded early and insisted on her company. At her daughter's sobbing and shaking her, the seer awoke. That gently named collection of talent and adipose tissue and mammalia sufficient to nurse octuplets, simultaneously, sat erect. She reached comfortingly for her daughter. Soon she had listened, was out of bed and beside Hanse. Mignureal had ordered him to remain on the divan in the shop.

"That just isn't Hanse, Mother!"

"Of course it isn't. Look on sorcery, and hate it."

"Name of Tiana Savior—it's awful, seeing him, hearing him this way. . . ."

"Fetch my shawl," Moonflower said, one by one relieving Hanse of his knives, "and do make some tea, sweetheart."

Moonflower held the quaking young man and crooned. She pillowed his tear-wet face in the vastness of her bosom. She loosed his wrists, drew his hands round, and held their wiry darkness in her large paler dimple-backed ones. And she crooned, and talked low, on and on. Her daughter draped her with the shawl and went to make tea.

The ray of moonlight that fell into the room moved the length of a big man's foot while the seer sat there with him, and more, and Hanse went to sleep, still shivering. She held his hands until he was still but for his breathing. Mignureal hovered close, all bright of eye, and knew the instant her mother went off. Sagging. Glassy-eyed. She began murmuring, a woman small inside and huge without; a gross kitten at her divining.

"A yellow-furred hunting dog? Tall as a tree, old as a tree . . . he hovers and with him is a god not of Ilsig. A god of Ranke—oh, it is a Hell Hound. Oh Hanse it is not wizard-sorcery but god-sorcery! And who is thi—oh. Another god. But why is Theba involved, who has so few adherents here? Oh!"

She shuddered and her daughter started to touch her; desisted.

"I see Ils Himself hiding His face . . . a shadow tall as a tree and another, not nearly so big. A shadow and its pawn? Why it has no head, this smaller shad—oh. It is afraid, that's it; it has no face left. It is Ha—I will not say even though he sleeps. Oh—Mignue, there is a corpse on the street up in front of the farmers' market and—ahhh." Her relief was apparent in that great sigh. "Hanse did not kill her. Another did, and Theba hovers over her. Hmm. I see—I s—I will not say what I s . . . it fades, goes."

Again she sighed and sat still, sweating, overflowing her chair on both sides. Gazing at the sleeping Shadowspawn. "He has spoken with the governor who is the emperor's kinsman, Mignureal my dear, did you know that? He will again. They are not enemies, our governor and Shadowspawn."

"Oh." And Mignureal looked upon him, head to one side. Moonflower saw the look.

"You will go to bed and tomorrow you will tell me what you were doing abroad so late, Mignue. You will *not* come near Hanse again, do you understand?"

"Oh, Mother." Mignureal met the level gaze only briefly. "Yes, Mother. I understand." And she went to bed.

Moonflower did not; she stayed beside Hanse. In the morning he was all right and she told him what she had Seen. He would never be the same again, she knew, he who had met quintessential fear, Lord Terror himself, face-to-face. But he was Hanse again, and not afraid, and Moonflower was sure that within a few hours he would have his gliding swagger back. She did note that he was grim-facedly determined.

The message left at the little watchpost at the corner of Shadow and Lizard's Way suggested that the "tall as a tree Hell Hound take a walk between stinky market and the cat storage" at the time of the fifth night watch "when the shadows are spawning fear in all hearts." The message was delivered to Tempus, who ordered the subprefect to forget it, and looked fierce. The Wrigglie agreed and got thence.

In private, his mind aided by a pinch of his powdered friend, Tempus worked backward at the cipher. The last line had to be the signature: Shadowspawn. Hanse wanted to meet him very privately, an hour past midnight. Good. So . . . *where?* "Stinky market" could mean lots of places. "Cat storage" meant nothing. Cat storage; cat—the granaries?— where cats not only were kept but migrated, drawn by the mice drawn by the grain? No, there was no way to walk between any of the granaries; and anything deserving to be characterized as stinky market beyond any other stenchy place.

What stinks most? Easy, he answered himself. *The tanners—no! Don't be stupid,* second thought told him. *Fish stink worse than anything.* Hmm. The fish market then, down on Red Clay Street—which might as well be called Warehouse Street. So all the natives called it. The stinking fish market then and . . . *cat storage?* He stared at the map.

Oh. Simple. The governor was called Kittycat and a warehouse was a place for storage. The Governor's Warehouse then, down beside the fish market. Not a block from the watchpost at Shadow and Lizard, the rascal! Tempus shook his head, and hours and hours later he was there. He made sure no one tried to "help" him; twice he played thief, to watch his own trail. He was not followed. Wrinkling his nose at the stench and slipping on a discarded fish head, he resolved to get a cleanup detail down here, and recommend a light as well.

"I am glad you look like you," the shadows said, from behind and above him.

"A god has marked me, Hanse," Tempus explained, without turning or looking up. "He helped me, in the Vulgar Unicorn. I didn't care to be seen there, compromising you. Did you leave the message because you have changed your mind?"

"There will be a bargain."

"I can appreciate that. Word is that you have bargained before, with my employer."

"That is as obviously impossible as breaking into the palace."

"Obviously. I am empowered to bargain, Hanse."

"A woman was found dead on Farmer's Run just at the west end of the market," the shadows said quietly. "She wore a cloak the color of red clay."

"Yes."

"She had a walking stick. It has a . . . *horrible* effect on a man. Her killer stole it, after she used it on his partner. He abandoned him."

"No thief's corpse was found."

"It does not kill. Its effect is . . . *obscene*." A pause; while the shadow shuddered? "I saw it happen. They were hooded."

"Do you know who they are?"

"Not now. I can find out easily. Want the stick?"

"Yes."

"How many of those foul things remain in . . . circulation?"

"We think two. A clever fellow has done well for himself by counting the people who came out of the shop with a purchase, and recording the names of those he knew. What is the bargain, Hanse?"

"I had rather deal with him."

"I wish you would trust me. Setting up interviews with him takes time."

"I trust you, Tempus, just as you trust me. Get me something in writing from him, then. Signed. Give it to the seer Moonflower. This is costing me time, pulling me away from my work—"

"Work?"

"—and I shall have to have compensation. Now."

Oh you damned arrogant boy, Tempus thought, and without a word he made three coins clink as he dropped them. He was sure Hanse's ears could distinguish gold from copper or silver by the sound of the clink. He also dropped a short section of pig's intestine, stitched at one end and tied off at the other. He said, "Oops."

"I want assistance in recovering something of mine, Tempus. Just labor, that's all. What's to be recovered is mine, I guarantee it."

"I'll help you myself."

"We'll need tools, a horse, rope, strength. . . ."

"Done. I will get it in writing, but it is done. Deliver and I deliver. We have a bond between us."

"So have he and I. I do want that paper signed and slipped to the S'danzo seer. Very well then, Tempus. We have bargained."

"By midafternoon. Goodnight, spawn of shadows."

"Goodnight, shadow-man. You didn't say 'pawn,' did you?"

"No." And Tempus turned and walked back up between the buildings to light, and less stenchy air. Behind him, soundlessly, the three gold coins and little bag of *krrf* he had dropped vanished, into the shadows.

Next day not long after dawn Hanse gave Moonflower a great hug and pretended to find a gold piece in her ear.

"I Saw for you, not for coin," she told him.

"I understand. I know. Why look, here's another in your other ear, for Mignureal. I give you the gold because I found it, not because you helped me. And a message will be given you today, for me."

Moonflower made both coins disappear beneath her shawl into what she called her treasure chest. "Don't frown; Mignue shall have the one as her very own. Will you do something for me I would prefer to coin, Hanse?"

Very seriously, relaxing for once, he nodded. "Without question."

"My daughter is very young and thinks you are just so romantic a figure. Will you just pretend she is your sister?"

"Oh you would not want *that*, Passionflower," he said, in one of those rare indications of what sort of childhood he must have had. "She is my friend's daughter and I shall call her cousin. Besides, she saw me . . . that way. I may not be able to look her in the eyes again."

She took those lean restless hands of a thief proud never to have hurt any he robbed. "You will, Hanse. You will. It was god-sorcery, and no embarrassment. Will you now be careful?"

"I will."

She studied his eyes. "But you are going to find him."

"I am."

The adherents of the most ancient goddess Theba went hooded to their little temple. This was their way. It also made it easier for the government to keep them under surveillance, and made it easy for Hanse to slip among them. A little tilt to his shoulder, a slight favoring of one leg under the dull brown robe, and he was not the lithely gliding Shadowspawn at all.

The services were dull and he had never liked the odor of incense. It made him want to sneeze and go to sleep, both at once. Insofar as he ever gave thought to religion, he leaned toward a sort of loyalty to the demigod Rander Rehabilitatus. He endured, and he observed. This goddess's worship in Sanctuary included two blind adherents. Both carried staffs. Though only one was white, it was not in the grip of a left-handed man.

Finding his quarry really was as simple as that. On deserting his partner, the murderous thief had sneered "Theba take you," and Moonflower had Seen that goddess, or at least the likeness of her icons and amulets. She had no more than forty worshipers here, and only this one (part-time) temple. The thief had also struck away the terror stick with his right hand and used his left to drive the dagger into his victim—and to use the staff on Hanse.

There came the time of Communing In Her. Hanse watched what the others did. They mingled, and a buzz rose as they said nice silly loving peace-things to each other in the name of Her. The usual meaningless ritual; "peace" was a word and life and its exigencies were another matter. Hanse mingled.

"Peace and love to you, brother," a woman said from within her wine-dark cowl, and her hand slipped into Hanse's robe and he caught her wrist.

"Peace and defter fingers to you, sister," he said quietly, and went around her toward his goal. To be certain, he came cowl-to-cowl with the man with the white stick and, smiling, made a shamefully obscene gesture. The cowl and the staff did not move; a hand moved gently out to touch him.

"Her peace remain on you, my brother," the blind man said in a high voice, and Hanse mouthed words, then turned.

"You rotten slime," a cowl striped in green and red hissed. "Poor blind Sorad has been among us for years and no one ever made such a nasty gesture to him. Who are you, anyhow?"

"One who thinks that other blind man is not blind and not one of us, and was testing—brother. Have you ever seen him before?"

His accoster—burly, in that striped Mrsevadan robe—looked around. "Well . . . no. The one in the gloves?"

"Yes. I think they are because his stick—yes, peace to you too, sister—has just been painted."

"You think it's a disguised weapon? That he's from the . . . palace?"

"No. I think the prince governor couldn't care a rat's whisker about us." Substituting the pronoun was a last-instant thought, and Hanse felt proud of that touch. Playing "I'm just like you but *he* is bad" had got him out of several scrapes. "I do think he is a spy, though. That priest from Ranke, who thinks every temple should be closed down except a glorious new one to Vash—Vashi—whatever they call him. I'll bet that's his spy."

That made the loyal Thebite quiver in rage! He went directly toward the man in the forest green cloak, with the brown stick. Hanse, edging along toward the entrance of what was by day a beltmaker's shop, watched Striped Robe speak to the man with the staff. An answer came, as Hanse moved.

Hanse didn't hear the reply; he heard "May all your days be bright in Her name and She take you when you are tired of life, brother." This from the fat man beside him, in a tent-sized cloak.

"Oh, *thank* you, brother. And on you, peace in Her n—" Hanse broke off when the terrified screaming began.

It was the big fellow in the robe of green and red stripes, and his cowl fell back to show his fear-twisted face. Naturally no one understood, and other cries arose amid the milling of robed, faceless people. Two did understand, and both moved toward the door. One was closer. He hurried forth, running—and outside, cut left out of view of the doorway and swung swiftly back. He already had the little jar of vinegar out of his dull brown robe, and the cork pulled. Inside the temple: clamor.

The man with the gloves and brown walking stick hurried through the door and turned left; had he not, Hanse would have called. The fellow had no time for anything before Hanse sent the vinegar sloshing within his hood.

"*Ah!*" Naturally the man ducked his head as the liquid drenched him and entered both eyes. Since he was not blind and not accustomed to carrying a staff as a part of him, he dropped it to rush both hands to his face. Hanse swallowed hard before snatching up the stick by its handle. He kicked the moaning fellow in the kneecap, and ran. The god-weapon seemed hummingly *alive* in his hand, so much that he wanted to throw it down and keep running. He did not, and it exerted no other effect on him. Just around the corner he paused for an importuning beggar, who soon had the gift of a nice brown, cowled robe. Since it was thrown over him as he sat, he never saw the generous giver. He had been swallowed by the shadows once the beggar got his head free of the encumbering woolen.

"Here, you little lizard, where do you think you're running to, hah?"

That from the brutish swaggering desert tradesman who grabbed at Hanse as he ran by. Well, he was not of the city, and did not know whom he laid a big hand on. Nor was he likely to aught but hie himself out of Sanctuary, once he returned to normal—doubtless robbed. Besides, a test really should be made to be sure, and Hanse poked him.

This was the staff of ensorcellment, all right.

Hurrying on his way, Hanse began to smile.

He had the stick, and the murdering thief who had used it on him would not be too nimble for a long, long time, and the robe he had snitched off a drying line was in the possession of a beggar who would be needing it in a few months, and Hanse had his little message from the prince governor. It avowed—so Hanse was told, as he did not read—that "he you specify shall lend full aid in the endeavor you specify, provided it is legal in full, in return for your returning another wand to us."

Hanse had laughed when he read that last; even a prince had a sense of humor and could allude to Hanse's having stolen his Savankh, rod of authority, some time ago. And now Shadowspawn would have the aid of big strong superlegal Tempus in regaining two bags of silver coin from a well up in the supposedly haunted ruins of Eaglenest. Hanse hoped Prince Kadakithis would appreciate the humor in that, too: the bagged booty had come from him, as ransom for the official baton of his imperial authority in Sanctuary. Even Tempus' *krrf* had brought in a bit of silver.

And now . . . Hanse's grin broadened. Suppose he just went about a second illicit entry of the palace? Suppose a blind man showed up among the swarm of alms seekers to be admitted into the courtyard two days hence, in accord with Kadakithis' people-wooing custom? Shadowspawn would not only hand this awful staff to the prince governor, he would at the same time provide graphic demonstration of the palace's pitiable security.

Unfortunately, Tempus had taken charge of security. The hooded blind beggar was challenged at the gate two days thence, and the Hell Hound Quag suspiciously snatched the staff from him. When the disguised Hanse objected, he was struck with it. Well, at least that way it was proven that he had brought the right stick in good faith, and that way he did get to spend a night in the palace, however unpleasant in his state of terror.

To Guard the Guardians

Robert Lynn Asprin

The Hell Hounds were now a common sight in Sanctuary, so the appearance of one in the bazaar created little stir, save for the concealment of a few smuggled wares and a price increase on everything else. However, when two appeared together, as they did today, it was enough to silence casual conversation and draw uneasy stares, though the more observant vendors noted that the pair were engrossed in their own argument and did not even glance at the stalls they were passing.

"But the man has offended me . . ." the darker of the pair snarled.

"He offends everyone," his companion countered, "it's his way. I tell you, Razkuli, I've heard him say things to the prince himself that would have other men flayed and blinded. You're a fool to take it personally."

"But, Zalbar . . ."

"I know, I know—he offends you; and Quag bores you and Annan is an arrogant braggart. Well this whole town offends me, but that doesn't give me the right to put it to the sword. Nothing Tempus has said to you warrants a blood feud."

"It is done." Razkuli thrust one fist against his other palm as they walked.

"It is *not* done until you act on your promise, and if you do *I'll* move to stop you. I won't have the men in my command killing each other."

The two men walked silently for several moments, each lost in his own dark thoughts.

"Look, my friend," Zalbar sighed, "I've already had one of my men killed under scandalous circumstances. I don't want to answer for another incident—particularly if it involves you. Can't you see Tempus is trying to goad you into a fight?—a fight you can't win."

"No one lives that I've seen over an arrow," Razkuli said ominously, his eyes narrowing on an imaginary target.

"Murder, Razkuli? I never thought I'd see the day you'd sink to being an assassin."

There was a sharp intake of breath and Razkuli faced his comrade with eyes that showed a glint of madness. Then the spark faded and the small man's shoulders relaxed. "You're right, my friend," he said, shaking his head, "I would never do that. Anger speeds my tongue ahead of reason."

"As it did when you vowed blood feud. You've survived countless foes who were mortal; don't try the favor of the gods by seeking an enemy who is not."

"Then the rumors about Tempus are true?" Razkuli asked, his eyes narrowing again.

"I don't know, there are things about him which are difficult to explain by any other logic. Did you see how rapidly his leg healed? We both know men whose soldiering career was ended after they were caught under a horse—yet he was standing duty again within the week."

"Such a man is an affront against Nature."

"Then let Nature take vengeance on him," Zalbar laughed, clapping a friendly hand on his comrade's shoulder, "and free us for more worthwhile pastimes. Come, I'll buy you lunch. It will be a pleasant change from barracks food."

Haakon, the sweetmeats vendor, brightened as the two soldiers approached him and waited patiently while they made their selections from his spiced-meat turnovers.

"That will be three coppers," he smiled through yellowed teeth.

"Three coppers?" Razkuli exclaimed angrily, but Zalbar silenced him with a nudge in the ribs.

"Here, fellow." The Hell Hound commander dropped some coins into

Haakon's outstretched hand. "Take four. Those of us from the capital are used to paying full value for quality goods—though I suppose that this far from civilization you have to adjust the prices to accommodate the poorer folk."

The barb went home and Zalbar was rewarded by a glare of pure hatred before he turned away, drawing Razkuli with him.

"Four coppers! You were being overcharged at three!"

"I know." Zalbar winked. "But I refuse to give them the satisfaction of haggling. I find it's worth the extra copper to see their faces when I imply that they're selling below value—it's one of the few pleasures available in this hellhole."

"I never thought of it that way," Razkuli said with a laugh, "but you're right. My father would have been livid if someone deliberately overpaid him. Do me a favor and let me try it when we buy the wine."

Razkuli's refusal to bargain brought much the same reaction from the wineseller. The dark mood of their conversation as they had entered the bazaar had vanished and they were ready to eat with calm humor.

"You provided the food and drink, so I'll provide the setting," Razkuli declared, tucking the wine flask into his belt. "I know a spot which is both pleasant and relaxing."

"It must be outside the city."

"It is, just outside the Common Gate. Come on, the city won't miss our presence for an hour or so."

Zalbar was easily persuaded though more from curiosity than belief. Except for occasional patrols along the Street of Red Lanterns he rarely got outside Sanctuary's North Wall and had never explored the area to the northwest where Razkuli was leading him.

It was a different world here, almost as if they had stepped through a magic portal into another land. The buildings were scattered, with large open spaces between them, in contrast to the cramped shops and narrow alleys of the city proper. The air was refreshingly free from the stench of unwashed bodies jostling each other in crowded streets. Zalbar relaxed in the peaceful surroundings. The pressures of patrolling the hateful town slipped away like a heavy cloak, allowing him to look forward to an uninterrupted meal in pleasant company.

"Perhaps you could speak to Tempus? We needn't like each other, but if he could find another target for his taunts, it would do much toward easing my hatred."

404 THIEVES' WORLD: FIRST BLOOD

Zalbar shot a wary glance at his comrade but detected none of the blind anger which he had earlier expressed. The question seemed to be an honest attempt on Razkuli's part to find a compromise solution to an intolerable situation.

"I would, if I thought it would help," he sighed reluctantly, "but I fear I have little influence on him. If anything, it would only make matters worse. He would redouble his attacks to prove he wasn't afraid of me either."

"But you're his superior officer," Razkuli argued.

"Officially, perhaps," his friend shrugged, "but we both know there are gaps between what is official and what is true. Tempus has the prince's ear. He's a free agent here and follows my orders only when it suits him."

"You've kept him out of the Aphrodisia House. . . ."

"Only because I had convinced the prince of the necessity of maintaining the goodwill of that House before Tempus arrived," Zalbar countered, shaking his head. "I had to go to the prince to curb Tempus' ill-conduct and earned his hatred for it. You notice he still does what he pleases at the Lily Garden—and the prince looks the other way. No, I wouldn't count on my influence over Tempus. I don't think he would physically attack me because of my position in the prince's bodyguard. I also don't think he would come to my aid if I were hard-pressed in a fight."

Just then Zalbar noticed a small flower garden nestled beside a house not far from their path. A man was at work in the garden, watering and pruning. The sight created a sudden wave of nostalgia in the Hell Hound. How long had it been since he stood outside the Emperor's Palace in the capital, fighting boredom by watching the gardeners pampering the flowered grounds? It seemed like a lifetime. Despite the fact that he was a soldier by profession, or perhaps because he was a soldier, he had always admired the calm beauty of flowers.

"Let's eat there . . . under that tree," he suggested, indicating a spot with a view of the garden. "It's as good a place as any."

Razkuli hesitated, glancing at the gardened house, and started to say something, then shrugged and veered toward the tree. Zalbar saw the mischievous smile flit briefly across his comrade's face, but ignored it, preferring to contemplate the peaceful garden instead.

The pair dined in the manner of hardened, but off-duty, campaigners. Rather than facing each other, or sitting side by side, the two assumed back-to-back positions in the shade of a spreading tree. The earthenware wine flask was carefully placed to one side, but in easy reach of both. Not only did the arrangement give them a full circle of vision to insure that their meal would be uninterrupted, it also allowed a brief illusion of privacy for the individual—a rare commodity to those whose profession required that every moment be shared with at least a dozen colleagues. To further that illusion they ate in silence. Conversation would be neither attempted nor tolerated until both were finished with their meal. It was the stance of men who trusted each other completely.

Although his position allowed him a clear view of the flower garden, Zalbar found his thoughts wandering back to his earlier conversation with Razkuli. Part of his job was to maintain peace among the Hell Hounds, at least to a point where their personal differences did not interfere with the performance of their duties. To that end he had soothed his friend's ruffled feathers and forestalled any open fighting within the force . . . for the time being, at least. With peace thus preserved, Zalbar could admit to himself that he agreed wholeheartedly with Razkuli.

Loudmouthed bullies were nothing new in the army, but Tempus was a breed apart. As a devout believer in discipline and law, Zalbar was disgusted and appalled by Tempus' attitudes and conduct. What was worse, Tempus did have the prince's ear, so Zalbar was powerless to move against him despite the growing rumors of immoral and illegal conduct.

The Hell Hound's brow furrowed as he reflected upon the things he had heard and seen. Tempus openly used *krrf*, both on duty and off. He was rapidly building a reputation for brutality and sadism among the not easily shocked citizens of Sanctuary. There were even rumors that he was methodically hunting and killing the blue-masked sell-swords employed by the ex-gladiator Jubal.

Zalbar had no love for that crime lord, who traded in slaves to mask his more illicit activities, but neither could he tolerate a Hell Hound taking it upon himself to be judge and executioner. But he had been ordered by the prince to allow Tempus free rein and was powerless to even investigate the rumors: a fine state of affairs when the law enforcers became the lawbreakers and the lawgiver only moved to shelter them.

A scream rent the air, interrupting Zalbar's reverie and bringing him to his feet, sword in hand. As he cast about, searching for the source of the noise, he remembered he had heard screams like that before . . . though not on any battlefield. It wasn't a scream of pain, hatred, or terror but the heartless, soulless sound of one without hope and assaulted by horror too great for the mind to comprehend.

The silence was completely shattered by a second scream and this time Zalbar knew the source was the beautifully gardened house. He watched in growing disbelief as the gardener calmly continued his work, not even bothering to look up despite the now frequent screams. Either the man was deaf or Zalbar himself was going mad, reacting to imaginary noises from a best-forgotten past.

Turning to Razkuli for confirmation, Zalbar was outraged to find his friend not only still seated but grinning ear-to-ear.

"Now do you see why I was willing to pass this spot by?" the swarthy Hell Hound said with a laugh. "Perhaps the next time I offer to lead you won't be so quick to exert your rank."

"You were expecting this?" Zalbar demanded, unsoothed by Razkuli's humor.

"Of course, you should be thankful it didn't start until we were nearly finished with our meal."

Zalbar's retort was cut off by a drawn-out piercing cry that rasped against ear and mind and defied human endurance with its length.

"Before you go charging to the rescue," Razkuli commented, ignoring the now fading outburst of pain, "you should know I've already looked into it. What you're hearing is a slave responding to its master's attentive care: a situation entirely within the law and therefore no concern of ours. It might interest you to know that the owner of that building is a . . ."

"Kurd!" Zalbar breathed through taut lips, glaring at the house as if it were an archenemy.

"You know him?"

"We met once, back at the capital. That's why he's here . . . or at least why he's not still there."

"Then you know his business?" Razkuli scowled, a bit deflated that his revelations were no surprise. "I'll admit I find it distasteful, but there's nothing we can do about it."

"We'll see," Zalbar announced darkly, starting toward the house.

"Where're you going?"

"To pay Kurd a visit."

"Then I'll see you back at the barracks." Razkuli shuddered. "I've been inside that house once already, and I'll not enter again unless it's under orders."

Zalbar made no note of his friend's departure though he did sheathe his sword as he approached the house. The impending battle would not require conventional weapons.

"Ho there!" he hailed the gardener. "Tell your master I wish to speak with him."

"He's busy," the man snarled, "can't you hear?"

"Too busy to speak with one of the prince's personal guard?" Zalbar challenged, raising an eyebrow.

"He's spoken to them before and each time they've gone away and I've lost pay for allowing the interruption."

"Tell him it's Zalbar," the Hell Hound ordered. "Your master will speak with me, or would you like to deal with me in his stead?"

Though he made no move toward his weapons Zalbar's voice and stance convinced the gardener to waste no time. The gnomelike man abandoned his chores to disappear into the house.

As he waited Zalbar surveyed the flowers again, but knowledge of Kurd's presence had ruined his appreciation of floral beauty. Instead of lifting his spirits, the bright blossoms seemed a horrifying incongruity, like a gaily colored fungus growing on a rotting corpse.

As Zalbar turned away from the flowers, Kurd emerged into the daylight. Though it had been five years since they had seen each other, the older man was sufficiently unchanged that Zalbar recognized him instantly: the stained disheveled dress of one who sleeps in his clothes, the unwashed, unkempt hair and beard, as well as the cadaverously thin body with its long, skeletal fingers and pasty complexion. Clearly Kurd had not discontinued his habit of neglecting his own body in the pursuit of his work.

"Good day . . . citizen." The Hell Hound's smile did not disguise the sarcasm poisoning his greeting.

"It *is* you," Kurd declared, squinting to study the other's features. "I thought we were done with each other when I left Ranke."

"I think you shall continue to see me until you see fit to change your occupation."

"My work is totally within the limits of the law." The thin man bristled, betraying, for a moment, the strength of will hidden in his outwardly feeble body.

"So you said in Ranke. I still find it offensive, without redeeming merit."

"Without redeeming . . ." Kurd shrieked; then words failed him. His lips tightened, he seized Zalbar by the arm and began pulling him toward the house. "Come with me now," he instructed. "Let me show you my work and explain what I am doing. Perhaps then you will be able to grasp the importance of my studies."

In his career Zalbar had faced death in many guises, and done it unflinchingly. Now, however, he drew back in horror.

"I . . . That won't be necessary," he insisted.

"Then you continue to blindly condemn my actions without allowing me a fair hearing?" Kurd pointed a bent, bony finger at the Hell Hound, a note of triumph in his voice.

Trapped by his own convictions, Zalbar swallowed hard and steeled himself. "Very well, lead on. But, I warn you—my opinions are not easily swayed."

Zalbar's resolve wavered once they entered the building and he was assaulted by the smells of its interior. Then he caught sight of the gardener smirking at him from the doorway and set his face in an expressionless mask as he was led up the stairs to the second floor.

All that the Hell Hound had ever heard or imagined about Kurd's work failed to prepare him for the scene that greeted him when the pale man opened the door to his workshop. Half a dozen large, heavy tables lined the walls, each set at a strange angle so their surfaces were nearly upright. They were not unlike the wooden frames court artists used to hold their work while painting. All the tables were fitted with leather harnesses and straps. The wood and leather, both, showed dried and crusted bloodstains. Four of the tables were occupied.

"Most so-called medical men only repeat what has gone before," Kurd was saying. "The few who do attempt new techniques do so in a slipshod, trial-and-error fashion borne of desperation and ignorance. If the patient dies, it is difficult to determine if the cause was the original affliction, or the new treatment itself. Here, under controlled conditions,

I actually increase our knowledge of the human body and its frailties. Watch your step, please. . . ."

Grooves had been cut in the floor, running along beneath the tables and meeting in a shallow pit at the room's far end. As he stepped over one, Zalbar realized that the system was designed to guide the flow of spilled blood. He shuddered.

There was a naked man on the first table and when he saw them coming he began to writhe against his bonds. One arm was gone from the elbow down and he beat the stump against the tabletop. Gibberings poured from his mouth. Zalbar noted with disgust that the man's tongue had been cut out.

"Here," Kurd announced, pointing to a gaping wound in the man's shoulder, "is an example of my studies."

The man had obviously lost control of his bodily functions. Excretions stained his legs and the table. Kurd paid no attention to this, gesturing Zalbar closer to the table as he used his long fingers to spread the edges of the shoulder wound. "I have identified a point in the body which, if pressure like this . . ."

The man shrieked, his body arching against the restraining straps.

"Stop!" Zalbar shouted, losing any pretense of disinterest.

It was unlikely he could be heard over the tortured sounds of the victim, but Kurd withdrew his bloody finger and the man sagged back on the table.

"Well, did you see it?" the pale man asked eagerly.

"See what?" Zalbar blinked, still shaken by what he had witnessed.

"His stump, man! It stopped moving! Pressure, or damage, to this point can rob a man of the use of his arm. Here, I'll show you again."

"No!" the Hell Hound ordered quickly. "I've seen enough."

"Then you see the value of my discovery?"

"Umm . . . where do you get your . . . subjects?" Zalbar evaded.

"From slavers, of course." Kurd frowned. "You can see the brands quite clearly. If I worked with anything but slaves . . . well, that would be against Rankan law."

"And how do you get them onto the tables? Slaves or not, I should think they would fight to the death rather than submit to your knives."

"There is an herbalist in town," the pale man explained, "he supplies me with a mild potion that renders them senseless. When they awaken, it's too late for effective resistance."

Zalbar started to ask another question, but Kurd held up a restraining hand. "You still haven't answered my question: do you now see the value of my work?"

The Hell Hound forced himself to look around the room again. "I see that you genuinely believe the knowledge you seek is worthwhile," he said carefully, "but I still feel subjecting men and women to this, even if they are slaves, is too high a price."

"But it's legal!" Kurd insisted. "What I do here breaks no Rankan laws."

"Ranke has many laws, you should remember that from our last meeting. Few live within all of them, and while there is some discretion exercised between which laws are enforced and which are overlooked, I tell you now that I will be personally watching for anything which will allow me to move against you. It would be easier on both of us if you simply moved on now . . . for I won't rest while you are within my patrol range."

"I am a law-abiding citizen." The pale man glared, drawing himself up. "I won't be driven from my home like a common criminal."

"So you said before." The Hell Hound smiled as he turned to go. "But, you are no longer in Ranke—remember that."

"That's right," Kurd shouted after him, "we are no longer in Ranke. Remember that yourself, Hell Hound."

Four days later Zalbar's confidence had ebbed considerably. Finishing his night patrol of the city, he turned down the Processional toward the wharves. This was becoming a habit with him now, a final off-duty stretch-of-the-legs to organize his thoughts in solitude before retiring to the crowded barracks. Though there was still activity back in the Maze, this portion of town had been long asleep and it was easy for the Hell Hound to lose himself in his ponderings as he paced slowly along the moon-shadowed street.

The prince had rejected his appeal, pointing out that harassing a relatively honest citizen was a poor use of time, particularly with the wave of killings sweeping Sanctuary. Zalbar could not argue with the prince's logic. Ever since that weapon shop had appeared, suddenly, in the Maze to dispense its deadly brand of magic, killings were not only more frequent but of an uglier nature than usual. Perhaps now that the shop had disappeared the madness would ease, but in the meantime he could ill afford the time to pursue Kurd with the vigor necessary to drive the vivisectionist from town.

For a moment Kurd's empassioned defense of his work flashed across Zalbar's mind, only to be quickly repressed. New medical knowledge was worth having, but slaves were still people. The systematic torture of another being in the name of knowledge was . . .

"Cover!"

Zalbar was prone on the ground before the cry had fully registered in his mind. Reflexes honed by years in service to the empire had him rolling, crawling, scrabbling along the dirt in search of shelter without pausing to identify the source of the warning. Twice, before he reached the shadows of an alley, he heard the unmistakable *hisss-pock* of arrows striking nearby: ample proof that the danger was not imaginary.

Finally, in the alley's relative security, he snaked his sword from its scabbard and breathlessly scanned the rooftops for the bowman assassin. A flicker of movement atop a building across the street caught his eyes, but it failed to repeat itself. He strained to penetrate the darkness. There was a crying moan, ending in a cough; moments later, a poor imitation of a night bird's whistle.

Though he was sure someone had just died, Zalbar didn't twitch a muscle, holding his position like a hunting cat. Who had died? The assassin? Or the person whose call had warned him of danger? Even if it were the assassin there might still be an accomplice lurking nearby.

As if in answer to this last thought a figure detached itself from a darkened doorway and moved to the center of the street. It paused, placed hands on hips, and hailed the alley wherein Zalbar had taken refuge.

"It's safe now, Hell Hound. We've rescued you from your own carelessness."

Regaining his feet, Zalbar sheathed his sword and stepped into the open. Even before being hailed he had recognized the dark figure. A blue hawk-mask and cloak could not hide the size or coloring of his rescuer, and if they had, the Hell Hound would have known the smooth grace of those movements anywhere.

"What carelessness is that, Jubal?" he asked, hiding his own annoyance.

"You have used this route three nights in a row, now," the ex-gladiator announced. "That's all the pattern an assassin needs."

The Negro crime lord did not seem surprised or annoyed that his disguise had been penetrated. If anything, Jubal gave an impression of being pleased with himself as he bantered with the Hell Hound.

Zalbar realized that Jubal was right: on duty or off, a predictable pattern was an invitation for ambush. He was spared the embarrassment of making this admission, however, as the unseen savior on the rooftops chose this moment to dump the assassin's body to the street. The two men studied it with disdain.

"Though I appreciate your intervention," the Hell Hound commented dryly, "it would have been nice to take him alive. I'll admit a passing curiosity as to who sent him."

"I can tell you that." The hawk-masked figure smiled grimly. "It's Kurd's money that filled that assassin's purse, though it puzzles me why he would bear you such a grudge."

"You knew about this in advance?"

"One of my informants overheard the hiring in the Vulgar Unicorn. It's amazing how many normally careful people forget that a man can hear as well as talk."

"Why didn't you send word to warn me in advance?"

"I had no proof." The black man shrugged. "It's doubtful my witness would be willing to testify in court. Besides, I still owed you a debt from our last meeting . . . or have you forgotten you saved my life once?"

"I haven't forgotten. As I told you then, I was only doing my duty. You owed me nothing."

". . . And I was only doing my duty as a Rankan citizen in assisting you tonight." Jubal's teeth flashed in the moonlight.

"Well, whatever your motive, you have my thanks."

Jubal was silent a moment. "If you truly wish to express your gratitude," he said at last, "would you join me now for a drink? There's something I would like to discuss with you."

"I . . . I'm afraid I can't. It's a long walk to your house and I have duties tomorrow."

"I was thinking of the Vulgar Unicorn."

"The Vulgar Unicorn?" Zalbar stammered, genuinely astonished. "Where my assassination was planned. I can't go in there."

"Why not?"

"Well . . . if for no other reason that I am a Hell Hound. It would do neither of us any good to be seen together publicly, much less in the Vulgar Unicorn."

"You could wear my mask and cloak. That would hide your uniform and face. Then, to any onlooker it would only appear that I was having a drink with one of my men."

For a moment, Zalbar wavered in indecision; then the audacity of a Hell Hound in a blue hawk-mask seized his fancy and he laughed aloud. "Why not?" he agreed, reaching for the offered disguise. "I've always wondered what the inside of that place looked like."

Zalbar had not realized how bright the moonlight was until he stepped through the door of the Vulgar Unicorn. A few small oil lamps were the only illumination, and those were shielded toward the wall, leaving most of the interior in heavy shadow. Though he could see figures huddled at several tables as he followed Jubal into the main room, he could not make out any individual's features.

There was one, however, whose face he did not need to see, the unmistakably gaunt form of Hakiem the storyteller slouched at a central table. A small bowl of wine sat before him, apparently forgotten, as the talespinner nodded in near-slumber. Zalbar harbored a secret liking for the ancient character and would have passed the table quietly, but Jubal caught the Hell Hound's eye and winked broadly. Withdrawing a coin from his sword belt, the slaver tossed it in an easy arch toward the storyteller's table.

Hakiem's hand moved like a flicker of light and the coin disappeared in midflight. His drowsy manner remained unchanged.

"That's payment enough for a hundred stories, old man," Jubal rumbled softly, "but tell them somewhere else . . . and about someone else."

Moving with quiet dignity, the storyteller rose to his feet, bestowed a withering gaze on both of them, and stalked regally from the room. His bowl of wine had disappeared with his departure.

In the brief moment that their eyes met, Zalbar had felt an intense intelligence and was certain that the old man had penetrated both mask and cloak to coldly observe his true identity. Hastily revising his opinion of the gaunt tale-spinner, the Hell Hound recalled Jubal's description of an informant whom people forgot could hear as well as see and knew whose spying had truly saved his life.

The slaver sank down at the recently vacated table and immediately received two unordered goblets of expensive qualis. Settling next to him, Zalbar noted that this table had a clear view of all entrances and exits of the tavern and his estimation of Hakiem went up yet another notch.

"If I had thought of it sooner, I would have suggested that your man on the rooftop join us," the Hell Hound commented. "I feel I owe him a drink of thanks."

"That man is a woman, Moria; she works the darkness better than I do . . . and without the benefits of protective coloration."

"Well, I'd still like to thank her."

"I'd advise against it." The slaver grinned. "She hates Rankans, and the Hell Hounds in particular. She only intervened at my orders."

"You remind me of several questions." Zalbar set his goblet down. "Why did you act on my behalf tonight? And how is it that you know the cry the army uses to warn of archers?"

"In good time. First you must answer a question of mine. I'm not used to giving out information for free, and since I told you the identity of your enemy, perhaps now you can tell me why Kurd would set an assassin on your trail?"

After taking a thoughtful sip of his drink, Zalbar began to explain the situation between himself and Kurd. As the story unfolded, the Hell Hound found he was saying more than was necessary, and was puzzled as to why he would reveal to Jubal the anger and bitterness he had kept secret even from his own force. Perhaps it was because, unlike his comrades, whom he respected, Zalbar saw the slaver as a man so corrupt that his own darkest thoughts and doubts would seem commonplace by comparison.

Jubal listened in silence until the Hell Hound was finished, then nodded, slowly. "Yes, that makes sense now," he murmured.

"The irony is that at the moment of attack I was bemoaning my inability to do anything about Kurd. For a while, at least, an assassin is unnecessary. I am under orders to leave Kurd alone."

Instead of laughing, Jubal studied his opposite thoughtfully. "Strange you should say that." He spoke with measured care. "I also have a problem I am currently unable to deal with. Perhaps we can solve each other's problems."

"Is that what you wanted to talk to me about?" Zalbar asked, suddenly suspicious.

"In a way. Actually this is better. Now, in return for the favor I must ask, I can offer something you want. If you address yourself to my problem, I'll put an end to Kurd's practice for you."

"I assume that what you want is illegal. If you really think I'd . . ."

"It is not illegal!" Jubal spat with venom. "I don't need your help to break the law, that's easy enough to do despite the efforts of your so-called elite force. No, Hell Hound, I find it necessary to offer you a bribe to do your job—to enforce the law."

"Any citizen can appeal to any Hell Hound for assistance." Zalbar felt his own anger grow. "If it is indeed within the law, you don't have to . . ."

"Fine!" the slaver interrupted. "Then, as a Rankan citizen I ask you to investigate and stop a wave of murders—someone is killing my people; hunting blue-masks through the streets as if they were diseased animals."

"I . . . I see."

"And I see that this comes as no surprise," Jubal snarled. "Well, Hell Hound, do your duty. I make no pretense about my people, but they are being executed without a trial or hearing. That's murder. Or do you hesitate because it's one of your own who's doing the killing?"

Zalbar's head came up with a snap and Jubal met his stare with a humorless smile.

"That's right, I know the murderer, not that it's been difficult to learn. Tempus has been open enough with his bragging."

"Actually," Zalbar mused dryly, "I was wondering why you haven't dealt with him yourself if you know he's guilty. I've heard hawk-masks have killed transgressors when their offense was far less certain."

Now it was Jubal who averted his eyes in discomfort. "We've tried," he admitted. "Tempus seems exceptionally hard to down. Some of my men went against my orders and used magical weapons. The result was four more bloody masks to his credit."

The Hell Hound could hear the desperate appeal in the slaver's confession.

"I cannot allow him to continue his sport, but the price of stopping him grows fearfully high. I'm reduced to asking for your intervention. You more than the others have prided yourself in performing your duties in strict adherence to the codes of justice. Tell me, doesn't the law apply equally to everyone?"

A dozen excuses and explanations leapt to Zalbar's lips; then a cold wave of anger swept them away. "You're right, though I never thought you'd be the one to point out my duty to me. A killer in uniform is still a killer and should be punished for his crimes . . . all of them. If Tempus is your murderer, I'll personally see to it that he's dealt with."

"Very well." Jubal nodded. "And in return, I'll fill my end of the bargain—Kurd will no longer work in Sanctuary."

Zalbar opened his mouth to protest. The temptation was almost too great—if Jubal could make good his promise—but, no, "I'd have to insist that your actions remain within the law," he murmured reluctantly. "I can't ask you to do anything illegal."

"Not only is it legal, it's done! Kurd is out of business as of now."

"What do you mean?"

"Kurd can't work without subjects," the slaver smiled, "and I'm his supplier—or I was. Not only have I ended his supply of slaves, I'll spread the word to the other slavers that if they deal with him I'll undercut their prices in the other markets and drive them out of town as well."

Zalbar smiled with new distaste beneath his mask. "You knew what he was doing with the slaves and you dealt with him anyway?"

"Killing slaves for knowledge is no worse than having slaves kill each other in the arena for entertainment. Either is an unpleasant reality in our world."

Zalbar winced at the sarcasm in the slaver's voice, but was unwilling to abandon his position.

"We have different views of fighting. You were forced into the arena as a gladiator while I freely enlisted in the army. Still, we share a common experience: however terrible the battle, however frightful the odds, we had a chance. We could fight back and survive—or at least take our foemen with us as we fell. Being trussed up like a sacrificial animal, helpless to do anything but watch your enemy—no, not your enemy—your tormentor's weapon descend on you again and again . . . No being, slave or freedman, should be forced into that. I cannot think of an enemy I hate enough to condemn to such a fate."

"I can think of a few," Jubal murmured, "but then, I've never shared your ideals. Though we both believe in justice we seek it in different ways."

"Justice?" the Hell Hound sneered. "That's the second time you've used that word tonight. I must admit it sounds strange coming from your lips."

"Does it?" the slaver asked. "I've always dealt fairly with my own or with those who do business with me. We both acknowledge the corruption in our world, Hell Hound. The difference is that, unlike yourself, I don't try to protect the world—I'm hard-pressed to protect myself and my own."

Zalbar set down his unfinished drink. "I'll leave your mask and cloak outside," he said levelly. "I fear that the difference is too great for us to enjoy a drink together."

Anger flashed in the slaver's eyes. "But you will investigate the murders?"

"I will," the Hell Hound promised, "and as the complaining citizen you'll be informed of the results of my investigation."

Tempus was working on his sword when Zalbar and Razkuli approached him. They had deliberately waited to confront him here in the barracks rather than at his favored haunt, the Lily Garden. Despite everything that had or might occur, they were all Army and what was to be said should not be heard by civilians outside their elite club.

Tempus favored them with a sullen glare, then brazenly returned his attention to his work. It was an unmistakable affront, as he was occupied only with filing a series of sawlike teeth into one edge of his sword, a project that should run a poor second to speaking with the Hell Hound's captain.

"I would have a word with you, Tempus," Zalbar announced, swallowing his anger.

"It's your prerogative," the other replied without looking up.

Razkuli shifted his feet, but a look from his friend stilled him.

"I have had a complaint entered against you," Zalbar continued. "A complaint which has been confirmed by numerous witnesses. I felt it only fair to hear your side of the story before I went to Kadakithis with it."

At the mention of the prince's name, Tempus raised his head and ceased his filing. "And the nature of the complaint?" he asked darkly.

"It is said you're committing wanton murder during your off-duty hours."

"Oh, that. It's not wanton. I only hunt hawk-masks."

Zalbar had been prepared for many possible responses to his accusations: angry denial, a mad dash for freedom, a demand for proof or witnesses. This easy admission, however, caught him totally off-balance. "You . . . you admit your guilt?" he managed at last, surprise robbing him of his composure.

"Certainly. I'm only surprised anyone has bothered to complain. No one should miss the killers I've taken . . . least of all you."

"Well, it's true I hold no love for Jubal, or his sell-swords," Zalbar admitted, "but, there are still due processes of law to be followed. If you want to see them brought to justice you should have . . ."

"Justice?" Tempus laughed. "Justice has nothing to do with it."

"Then why hunt them?"

"For practice," Tempus informed them, studying his serrated sword once more. "An unexercised sword grows slow. I like to keep a hand in whenever possible and supposedly the sell-swords Jubal hires are the best in town—though, to tell the truth, if the ones I've faced are any example, he's being cheated."

"That's all?" Razkuli burst out, unable to contain himself any longer. "That's all the reason you need to disgrace your uniform?"

Zalbar held up a warning hand, but Tempus only laughed at the two of them.

"That's right, Zalbar, better keep a leash on your dog there. If you can't stop his yapping, I'll do it for you."

For a moment Zalbar thought he might have to restrain his friend, but Razkuli had passed explosive rage. The swarthy Hell Hound glared at Tempus with a deep, glowering hatred that Zalbar knew could not be dimmed now, with reason or threats. Grappling with his own anger, Zalbar turned, at last, to Tempus.

"Will you be as arrogant when the prince asks you to explain your actions?" he demanded.

"I won't have to." Tempus grinned again. "Kittycat will never call me to task for anything. You got your way on the Street of Red Lanterns, but that was before the prince fully comprehended my position here. He'd even reverse that decision if he hadn't taken a public stance on it."

Zalbar was frozen by anger and frustration as he realized the truth of Tempus' words. "And just what is your position here?"

"If you have to ask," Tempus laughed, "I can't explain. But you must realize that you can't count on the prince to support your charges. Save yourselves a lot of grief by accepting me as someone outside the law's jurisdiction." He rose, sheathed his sword, and started to leave, but Zalbar blocked his path.

"You may be right. You may indeed be above the law, but if there is a god—any god—watching over us now, the time is not far off when your sword will miss and we'll be rid of you. Justice is a natural process. It can't be swayed for long by a prince's whims."

"Don't call upon the gods unless you're ready to accept their interference." Tempus grimaced. "You'd do well to heed that warning from one who knows."

Before Zalbar could react, Razkuli was lunging forward, his slim wrist dagger darting for Tempus' throat. It was too late for the Hell Hound captain to intervene either physically or verbally, but then Tempus did not seem to require outside help.

Moving with lazy ease, Tempus slapped his left hand over the speeding point, his palm taking the full impact of Razkuli's vengance. The blade emerged from the back of his hand and blood spurted freely for a moment, but Tempus seemed not to notice. A quick wrench with the already wounded hand and the knife was twisted from Razkuli's grip. Then Tempus' right hand closed like a vise on the throat of his dumbfounded attacker, lifting him, turning him, slamming him against a wall and pinning him there with his toes barely touching the floor.

"Tempus!" Zalbar barked, his friend's danger breaking through the momentary paralysis brought on by the sudden explosion of action.

"Don't worry, Captain," Tempus responded in a calm voice. "If you would be so kind?"

He extended his bloody hand toward Zalbar, and the tall Hell Hound gingerly withdrew the dagger from the awful wound. As the knife came clear, the clotting ooze of blood erupted into a steady stream. Tempus studied the scarlet cascade with distaste, then thrust his hand against Razkuli's face.

"Lick it, dog," he ordered. "Lick it clean, and be thankful I don't make you lick the floor as well!"

Helpless and fighting for each breath, the pinned man hesitated only a moment before extending his tongue in a feeble effort to comply with the demand. Quickly impatient, Tempus wiped his hand in a bloody smear across Razkuli's face and mouth, then examined his wound again.

As Zalbar watched, horrified, the seepage from the wound slowed from flow to trickle and finally to a slow ooze—all in a matter of seconds.

Apparently satisfied with the healing process, Tempus turned dark eyes to his captain. "Every dog gets one bite—but the next time your pet crosses me, I'll take him down and neither you nor the prince will be able to stop me."

With that he wrenched Razkuli from the wall and dashed him to the floor at Zalbar's feet. With both Hell Hounds held motionless by his brutality, he strode from the room without a backward glance.

The suddenness and intensity of the exchange had shocked even Zalbar's battlefield reflexes into immobility, but with Tempus' departure, control flooded back into his limbs as if he had been released from a spell. Kneeling beside his friend, he hoisted Razkuli into a sitting position to aid his labored breathing.

"Don't try to talk," he ordered, reaching to wipe the blood smear from Razkuli's face, but the grasping man jerked his head back and forth, refusing both the order and the help.

Gathering his legs under him, the short Hell Hound surged to his feet and retained the upright position, though he had to cling to the wall for support. For several moments, his head sagged weakly as he drew breath in long ragged gasps, then he lifted his gaze to meet Zalbar's.

"I must kill him. I cannot . . . live in the same world and . . . breathe the same air with one who . . . shamed me so . . . and still call myself a man."

For a moment, Razkuli swayed as if speaking had drained him of all energy; then he carefully lowered himself onto a bench, propping his back against the wall.

"I must kill him," he repeated, his voice steadying. "Even if it means fighting you."

"You won't have to fight me, my friend." Zalbar sat beside him. "Instead accept me as a partner. Tempus must be stopped, and I fear it will take both of us to do it. Even then we may not be enough."

The swarthy Hell Hound nodded in slow agreement. "Perhaps if we acquired one of those hellish weapons that have been causing so much trouble in the Maze?" he suggested.

"I'd rather bed a viper. From the reports I've heard they cause more havoc for the wielder than for the victim. No, the plan I have in mind is of an entirely different nature."

The bright flowers danced gaily in the breeze as Zalbar finished his lunch. Razkuli was not guarding his back today: that individual was back at the barracks enjoying a much earned rest after their night's labors. Though he shared his friend's fatigue, Zalbar indulged himself with this last pleasure before retiring.

"You sent for me, Hell Hound?"

Zalbar didn't need to turn his head to identify his visitor. He had been watching him from the corner of his eyes throughout his dusty approach.

"Sit down, Jubal," he instructed. "I thought you'd like to hear about my investigations."

"It's about time," the slaver grumbled, sinking to the ground. "It's been a week—I was starting to doubt the seriousness of your pledge. Now, tell me why you couldn't find the killer."

The Hell Hound ignored the sneer in Jubal's voice. "Tempus is the killer, just as you said," he answered casually.

"You've confirmed it? When is he being brought to trial?"

Before Zalbar could answer a terrible scream broke the calm afternoon. The Hell Hound remained unmoved, but Jubal spun toward the sound. "What was that?" he demanded.

"That," Zalbar explained, "is the noise a man makes when Kurd goes looking for knowledge."

"But I thought . . . I swear to you, this is not my doing!"

"Don't worry about it, Jubal." The Hell Hound smiled and waited for the slaver to sit down again. "You were asking about Tempus' trial?"

"That's right," the black man agreed, though visibly shaken.

"He'll never come to trial."

"Because of that?" Jubal pointed to the house. "I can stop . . ."

"Will you be quiet and listen! The court will never see Tempus because the prince protects him. That's why I hadn't investigated him before your complaint!"

"Royal protection!" the slaver spat. "So he's free to hunt my people still."

"Not exactly." Zalbar indulged in an extravagant yawn.

"But you said . . ."

"I said I'd deal with him, and in your words 'it's done.' Tempus won't be reporting for duty today . . . or ever."

Jubal started to ask something, but another scream drowned out his words. Surging to his feet, he glared at Kurd's house. "I'm going to find out where that slave came from, and when I do . . ."

"It came from me, and if you value your people you won't insist on his release."

The slaver turned to gape at the seated Hell Hound. "You mean . . ."

"Tempus," Zalbar nodded. "Kurd told me of a drug he used to subdue his slaves, so I got some from Stulwig and put it in my comrade's *krrf*. He almost woke up when we branded him . . . but Kurd was willing to accept my little peace offering with no questions asked. We even cut out his tongue as an extra measure of friendship."

Another scream came—a low animal moan that lingered in the air as the two men listened.

"I couldn't ask for a more fitting revenge," Jubal said at last, extending his hand. "He'll be a long time dying."

"If he dies at all," Zalbar commented, accepting the handshake. "He heals very fast, you know."

With that the two men parted company, mindless of the shrieks that followed them.

The Lady of the Winds

Poul Anderson

Southward the mountains lifted to make a wall across a heaven still hard and blue. Snow whitened their peaks and dappled the slopes below. Even this far under the pass, patches of it lay on sere grass, among strewn boulders—too early in the season, fatally too early. Dry motes blew off in glittery streaks, borne on a wind that whittered and whirled. Its chill searched deep. Westward, clouds were piling up higher than the heights they shrouded, full of darkness and further storm.

A snow devil spun toward Cappen Varra, thickening as it went. Never had he known of the like. Well, he had gone forth to find whatever Power was here. He clutched the little harp with numbered fingers as if it were his courage. The gyre stopped before him and congealed. It became the form of a woman taller than himself. She poised utterly beautiful, but hueless as the snow, save for faint blue shadows along the curves of her and eyes like upland lakes. The long, tossing hair and a thin vortex of ice dust half clothed her nakedness. Somehow she seemed to quiver, a wind that could not ever come altogether to rest.

"My lady!" broke from him in the tongue of his homeland.

He could have tried to stammer on with words heard in this country,

THIEVES' WORLD: FIRST BLOOD

but she answered him likewise, singing more than speaking, maybe whistling more than singing: "What fate do you seek, who dared so to call on me?"

"I—I don't know," he got out, truly enough. "That lies with my lady. Yet it seemed right to bring her what poor gift was mine to offer."

He could not tell whether he heard scorn or a slight, wicked mirth. "A free gift, with nothing to ask in return?"

Cappen drew breath. The keen air seemed to whip up his wits. He had dealt with the mighty often before now—none such as her, no, but whatever hope he had lay with supposing that power makes for a certain way of feeling, be it human or overhuman. He swept his headgear off, holding it against his breast while he bowed very deeply. "Who am I to petition my lady? I can merely join all other men in praising her largesse and mercy, exalting her name forever."

The faintest of smiles touched her lips. "Because of what you brought, I will hear you out." It ceased. Impatience edged her voice. The wind strengthened, the frosty tresses billowed more wildly. "I think I know your wish. I do not think I will grant it. However, speak."

He had meant to depart from Sanctuary, but not so hastily. After some three years in that famous, infamous city, he remembered how much more there was to the wide world. Besides, while he had made friends high in its life, as well as among the low and raffish—with whom he generally felt easier—he had also made enemies of either kind. Whether by arrest on some capital charge or, likelier, by a knife in some nighted alley, one of them might well eventually make an end of him. He had survived three attempts, but the need to stay ever alert grew wearisome when hardly anything remained here that was new to him.

For a time after an adventure into which he fell, rescuing a noble lady from captivity in another universe and, perhaps, this world from the sikkintairs, he indulged in pleasures he could now afford. Sanctuary provided them in rich variety. But his tastes did not run to every conceivable kind, and presently those he enjoyed took on a surprising sameness. "Could it be that the gods of vice, even the gods of luxury, have less imagination than the gods of virtue and wholesomeness?" he wondered. The thought appalled.

Yet it wakened a dream that surprised him when he recognized it for what it was. He had been supposing his inborn restlessness and curiosity would send him on toward fresh horizons. Instead, memories welled up, and longing sharpened until it felt like unrequited love. Westward his wish ran, across plains, over mountains, through great forests and tumultuous kingdoms, the whole way home to Caronne. He remembered not only gleaming walls, soaring spires, bustling marts and streets; not only broad estates, greensward and greenwood, flowerbeds ablaze, lively men and livelier women; he harked back to the common folk, his folk, their speech and songs and ways. A peasant girl or tavern wench could be as fair as any highborn maiden, and often more fun. He remembered seaports, odors of tar and fish and cargo bales, masts and spars raking the sky, and beyond them the water a-glitter beneath a Southern sun, vast and blue where it reached outward and became Ocean.

Enough remained of his share of Molin Torchholder's reward for the exploit. He need not return as a footloose, hand-to-mouth minstrel, showman, gambler, and whatever-else, the disinherited and rather disgraced younger son of a petty baron. No, if he could get shrewd advice about investments—he knew himself for a much better versifier than money manager—he would become a merchant prince in Croy or Seilles at the very least. Or so he trusted.

Summer was dying away into autumn. The last trader caravans of the year would soon be gone. One was bound as far as Arinberg. That was a goodly distance, well beyond the western border of this empire, and the town said to be an enjoyable place to spend a winter. Cappen bought two horses, camp gear, and supplies from the master. The traders were still trading here, and did not plan to proceed for another week. Cappen had the interval idle on his hands.

And so it came about that he perforce left Sanctuary earlier than intended.

Candlelight glowed over velvet. Fragrances of incense, of Peridis' warmth and disheveled midnight locks, of lovemaking lately come to a pause, mingled with the sweet notes of a gold-and-diamond songbird crafted by some cunning artificer. No noise or chill or stench from the streets outside won through windows barred, glazed, and curtained. Nerigo, third priest of Ils, housed his newest leman well.

Perhaps if he visited her oftener she would not have heeded the blandishments of a young man who encountered her in the gaudy chaos of Midyear Fair and made occasions to pursue the acquaintance. At least,

they might have lacked opportunity. But although Nerigo was not without vigor, much of it went in the pursuit of arcane knowledge, which
included practices both spiritually and physically demanding. Today he
had indicated to Peridis, as often before, that he would be engaged with
dark and dangerous powers until dawn, and then must need sleep in his
own house; thereafter, duties at the temple would keep him busy for an
indefinite span.

So she sent a note to Cappen Varra at the inn where he lodged. It went
by public messenger. As she had made usual, her few servants retired to a
dormitory shed behind the house when she had supped. If she needed
any, she could ring a bell. Besides, like servants generally in Sanctuary,
these cultivated a selective blindness and deafness.

After all, she must shortly bid her lover farewell. It would probably
take a while to find another. She might never find another so satisfactory.

"You have asked about some things here," she murmured. "I never
dared show you them. Not that you would have betrayed me, but what
you didn't know couldn't be gotten out of you, were he to become suspicious. Now, though, when, alas, you are leaving for aye—" She sighed,
fluttered her eyelashes, and cast him a wistful smile. "It will take my
mind off that, while we rest before our next hour of delight."

"The wait will not be long, since it's you I'm waiting for," he purred.

"Ah, but, my dear, I am less accustomed than I . . . was . . . before
that man persuaded me hither." With gold, Cappen knew, and the luxury everywhere around, and, he gathered, occasional tales and glimpses
of marvels. "Let me rest an hour, to be the readier for you. Meanwhile,
there are other, more rare entertainments."

A long silken shift rippled and shimmered as she undulated over to a
cabinet of ebony inlaid with ivory in enigmatic patterns. Her single, curious modesty was not to be unclad unless in bath or bed. Having nothing
else along, Cappen gratified it by resuming blouse and breeks, even his
soft shoes. When she opened the cabinet, he saw shelves filled with
objects. Most he couldn't at once identify, but books were among them,
scrolls and codices. She paused, considering, then smiled again and took
out a small, slim volume bound in paper, one of perhaps a dozen. "These
amuse me," she said. "Let me in turn beguile you. Come, sit beside me."

He was somewhat smugly aware of how her gaze followed him as he
joined her on the sofa. Speech and manner counted most with women,

but good looks helped. He was of medium size, slim, lithe and muscular because hitherto he had seldom been able to lead the indolent life he would have preferred. Black hair, banged over the brow and above the shoulders, framed straight-cut features and vividly blue eyes. It also helped to have quite a musical voice.

She handed him the book. He beheld letters totally unfamiliar, laid it on his lap, and opened it. She reached to turn the pages, one by one.

Plain text mingled with lines that must be verse—songs, because it seemed the opening parts were under staffs of what he guessed was a musical notation equally strange. There were pictures too, showing people outlandishly clad, drawn with an antic humor that tickled his fancy. "What is this?" he wondered.

"The script for a rollicking comedic performance," she answered.

"When done? Where? How do you know?"

"Well, now, that is a story of its own," she said, savoring his attention. He knew she was not stupid, and wanted to be more to him than simply another female body. Indeed, that was among her attractions. "See you, Nerigo's wizardly questings go into different worlds from ours, alike in some ways, alien in more. Different universes, he says, coexistent with this one on many planes, as the leaves of this tome lie side by side. But I can't really understand his meaning there. Can you?"

Cappen frowned, abruptly uneasy. "Much too well," he muttered.

"What's wrong? I feel you go taut."

"Oh, nothing, really." Cappen made himself relax. He didn't care to speak of the business, if only because that would spoil the mood here. It was, after all, safely behind him, the gate destroyed, the sikkintairs confined to their own skies.

And yet, raced through his mind, that gate had been in the temple of Ils, where the high flamen made nefarious use of it. He had heard that, subsequently, the priests of the cult disavowed and severely discouraged such lore. They could have found themselves endangered. Yet search through the temple archives might well turn up further information. Yes, that would explain why Nerigo was secretive, and stored his gains in this house, where nobody would likely think to search.

"He only lusts for knowledge," Peridis reassured. Her tone implied she wished that were not his primary lust. "He does not venture into the Beyond. He simply opens windows for short whiles, observes, and, when he can, reaches through to snatch small things for later study. Is that so terrible? But the hierarchy would make trouble for him if they knew, and . . . it might strike at me as well."

She brightened. "He shares with me, a little. I have looked with him into his mirror that is not a mirror, at things of glamour or mirth. I have seen this very work performed on a stage far elsewhere, and a few more akin to it. True, the language was foreign to both of us, but he could discern that the story, for instance, concerns a love intrigue. It was partly at my wish that he hunted about until he found a shop where the books are sold, and cast spells to draw copies into his arcanum. Since then I've often taken them out when I'm alone, to call back memories of the pleasure. Now let me explain and share it with you as well as I'm able." Heavy-lidded, her glance smoldered on him. "It does tell of lovers who at last come together."

He thrust his qualms aside. The thing was in fact fascinating. They began to go through it page by page, her finger tracing out each illustration while she tried to convey what understanding she had of it. His free arm slid behind her.

A thud sounded from the vestibule. Hinges whined. A chill gust bore smells of the street in. Peridis screamed. Cappen knew stabbingly that the bolt on the main door had flung back at the command of its master. The book fell from their hands and they read no more that night.

A lean, grizzle-bearded, squinting man, clad in a silvery robe, entered. At his back hulked another, red-skinned, seven feet tall, so broad and thick as to seem squat, armed with steel cap, leather cuirass, and unfairly large scimitar. Cappen did not need Peridis' gasp to inform him that they were Nerigo and a Makali bodyguard.

The woman sprang to her feet. As the bard did, the little volume slid off his lap. Almost without thinking, he snatched it and tucked it down his half-open blouse. A bargaining counter—?

For an endless instant, silence held them all.

When Nerigo then spoke, it was quite softly, even impersonally. "I somewhat hoped I would prove mistaken. But you realize, Peridis, I cannot afford blind trust in anyone. A sortilege indicated you were receiving a visitor in my absences."

She stepped back, lifting her hands, helpless and imploring. Nerigo shook his head. Did ruefulness tinge his words? "Oh, fear not, my cuddly. From the beginning, I knew you for what you are. It's not rational to wax angry when a cat steals cream or a monkey disarrays documents. One simply makes provision against further untowardness. Why should I deny myself the pleasure that is you? No, you will merely be careful in future, very careful. If you are, then when I want novelty you shall go your way freely, unharmed, with only a minor spell on you to lock your lips against ever letting slip anything about me or my doings."

Cappen heard how she caught her breath and broke into sobs. At the back of his mind, he felt a burden drop off himself. He would have hated being the instrument of harm to her. Not that she had been much more to him than frolic; yet a man wishes well-being for his friends. Besides, killing beautiful young women was a terrible waste.

Hope flickered up amidst his dismay. He bowed low. "My lord, most reverend sir," he began, "your magnanimity surpasses belief. No, say rather that it demonstrates, in actual incarnation, the divine benevolence of those gods in whose service you so distinguish yourself. Unworthy though I be, my own humble but overwhelming gratitude—"

Nerigo cut him off. "You need not exercise that flattering tongue which has become notorious throughout Sanctuary," the sorcerer-priest said, now coldly impersonal. "You are no wayward pet of mine, you are a brazen intruder. I cannot possibly let you go unpunished; my demons would lose all respect for me. Furthermore, this is an opportunity first to extract from you everything you know. I think especially about the eminent Molin Torchholder and his temple of Vashanka, but doubtless other bits of information can prove useful too. Take him, Yaman."

"No, no, I beg you!" Peridis shrieked, but scrambled aside as the giant advanced.

If he was hustled off to a crypt, Cappen knew, he would welcome death when at last it came. He retreated, drawing the knife at his belt. Yaman grinned. The scimitar hissed forth. "Take him alive," Nerigo called, "but I've ways to stanch wounds once he's disabled."

Cappen was no bravo or brawler. Wits were always his weapon of choice. However, sometimes he had not been granted the choice. Thus he went prepared. His knife was not just the article of clothing and minor tool commonly carried by men. It was razor-honed, as balanced as a hawk on the wing. When in his wanderings he earned some coins by a show of prestidigitation, it had often figured in the act.

He poised, took aim, and threw.

A hoarse, gurgling bellow broke from Yaman. He lurched, dropped his weapon, and went to his knees. Blood spurted. The blade had gone into his throat below the chin. If Nerigo wanted to keep his henchman, he'd be busy for a while. Mainly, Cappen's way out was clear. He blew Peridis a kiss and darted off.

A yell pursued him. "You'll not escape, Varra! I'll have you hounded to the ends of the empire. If they're imperial troopers who find you, they'll have orders to cut you down on sight. But first demons will be on your trail—"

By then he was in the vestibule, retrieving his rapier and cloak, whence he slipped forth into the street. Walls and roofs loomed black along its narrowness. A strip of stars between barely gave light to grope by. Oh, lovely gloom! He kept to one side, where the dark was thickest and there was less muck to step in, and fled as deftly as a thief.

What to do? tumbled through his head. The inconspicuous silver amulet hanging on his breast ought to baffle Nerigo's afreets or whatever they were. It protected him against any supernatural forces of less than divine status. At least, so the wizard who gave it to him years ago had said, and so it had seemed to work on two or three occasions since. Of course, that might have been happenstance and the wizard a liar, but he had plenty of worries without adding hypothetical ones.

Equally of course, if such a being did come upon him, it could seize him or tear him apart. Physical strength was a physical quality. Likewise for human hunters.

Yes, Nerigo would have those out after him, while messengers sped north, south, east, and west bearing his description to castles, cantonments, garrisons, and watchposts. Once he had aroused the indignation of his colleagues, Nerigo would have ample influence to get such an order issued. Cappen's connections to Molin were too slight—how he wished now that he hadn't thought it best to play down his role in that rescue—for the high priest of Vashanka to give him asylum and safeguard across the border. Relations between the temples were strained enough already.

The westbound caravan wouldn't leave for days. Well before then, Nerigo would learn that Cappen had engaged a place in it. There were several others, readying to go in their various directions. He could find temporary refuge and get information in one of the disreputable inns he knew. With luck, he could slink to the master of whichever was depart-

ing first, give him a false name and a plausible story, and be off with it—
maybe even tomorrow.

That would cost, especially if a bit of a bribe proved advisable. Cappen had deposited his money with a reliable usurer, making withdrawals
as desired. Suddenly it might as well be on the moon. He was back to
what lay in his pouch. It might barely stretch to getting him away.

He suppressed a groan and shrugged. If his most recent memories
were dearly bought, still, they'd be something to enjoy on an otherwise
dismal journey.

It was a long annual trek that Deghred im Dalagh and his followers
made. Northward they fared from Temanhassa in Arechoum, laden with
spices, aromatics, intoxicant herbs, pearls, rich fabrics, cunningly
wrought metal things, and the like, the merchants and hucksters among
them trading as they went. The route zigzagged through desert and
sown, village and town, across dunes and rivers, by highroad and cairn-
marked trail, over the Uryuk Ubur and thence the cultivated plains of the
empire, Sanctuary its terminus. That city produced little other than
crime and politics, often indistinguishable, but goods of every kind
flowed to its marts and profitable exchanges could be made. The return
journey was faster, as direct as possible, to get beyond the mountains
before their early winter closed the passes.

Well, Cappen consoled himself, this was not the destination he had
had in mind, but needs must, he had never yet seen yonder exotic lands,
and maybe he could improve his luck there.

It could stand improvement, his thoughts continued. Instead of the
comforts he paid for and forfeited, he had a single scrawny mule, which
he must frequently relieve by turning to shank's mare; a greasy thirdhand
bedroll; two similar changes of clothes and a towel; ill-fitting boots; a
cheap knife, spoon, and tin bowl; and leave to eat with the choreboys,
not the drovers.

However, he remained alive and at large. That was ample cause for
cheerfulness, most of the time. Making friends came naturally to him.
Before long his tales, japes, and songs generated a liveliness that drew the
attention of the merchants. Not long after that, they invited him into
their mess. Deghred gave him a decent kaftan to wear while they ate,
drank, and talked; everybody concerned was fluent in the Ilsig language,

as well as others. "I think you have possibilities, lad," the caravan master said. "I'll lodge you for a while after we come to Temanhassa and introduce you to certain people." He waved his hand. "No, no, not alms. A modest venture, which in the course of time may bring me a modest profit."

Cappen knew he had better not seem a daydreamer or a fool. "The tongue of Arechoum is foreign to me, sir. Your men can scarcely teach me along the way."

"You're quick to pick things up, I've seen. Until you do, belike I can help."

Cappen understood from the drawl and the bearded smile that Deghred meant also to profit from that help, perhaps considerably. Not that he was ever unnecessarily unkind or hostile. Cappen rather liked him. But business was business. At the moment, nothing better was in sight.

Beasts and men plodded on. The land rose in bleakening hills. Now and then, when by himself, Cappen took from his meager baggage the book he had borne from Peridis' house and paged through it, puzzling over the text and staffs, smiling at the pictures, mainly recalling her and their nights. Thence he harked back to earlier recollections and forward to speculations about the future. It bore him away from the trek.

At a lonely fortress on a stony ridge, the commander routinely let them cross the frontier. Cappen drew a long breath. Yet, he realized, that frontier was ill-defined, and Nerigo's agents might still find him. He would not feel altogether safe until he was on the far side of the Uryuk Ubur.

Those mountains reared like a horse. Mile by mile the trails grew more toilsome, the land more cold and stark. Unseasonably so, Deghred said, and burned some incense to his little private gods. Nevertheless the winds lashed, yelled, and bit, clouds raced ragged, snow flurried.

Thus they came to the hamlet Khangaii and heard that if they went ahead, they would almost surely die.

A storm roared about the huts. Sleet hissed on the blast. Moss-chinked stone walls and turf roof muffled the noise, a dung fire and crowded bodies kept the dwelling of headman Bulak odorously warm, but somehow that sharpened the feeling of being trapped.

"Aiala is angry," he said. "We have prayed, we have sacrificed a prime ewe—not in feast, but casting it into a crevasse of Numurga Glacier—yet she rages ever worse."

"Nor has she sent me a dream to tell why, though I ate well-nigh all the sacred *ulaku* left us and lay swooned through two sunrises." His elder wife, who was by way of being the tribal priestess, shuddered. "Instead, nightmares full of furious screams."

Flames flickered low on the hearth and guttered in clay lamps. Smoke dimmed what light they gave and blurred uneasy shadows. From the gloom beyond gleamed the frightened stares of Bulak's younger wife and children, huddled on the sheepskins that covered the sleeping dais. Three favored dogs gnawed mutton bones tossed them after the company had eaten. Several men and the senior woman sat cross-legged around the fire, drinking fermented milk from cow horns refilled out of a jug. They were as many as could well have been crowded in, Deghred and such of the merchants as he picked. The rest of the travelers were housed elsewhere. Even in this bad time, hospitality was sacred. Cappen had persuaded the caravan master that he, come from afar, might conceivably have some new insight to offer.

He was beginning to regret the mix of cockiness and curiosity that led him to do so. He had more or less gotten to ignoring the stench, but his eyes stung and he kept choking back the coughs that would have been impolite. Not that things were likely any better in any other hut. Well, maybe he could have slept. It was a strain trying to follow the talk. Bulak knew some Ilsigi, and some of the guests had a smattering of his language. Between stumbling pidgin and awkward translations, conversation did not exactly flow.

At least, though, the slowness and the pauses gave him a chance to infer what he could not directly follow, correcting his mistakes when context revealed them to him. It became almost as if he listened to ordinary speech. He wasn't sure whether or not the drink helped, if only by dulling his discomfort. Foul stuff, but by now his palate was as stunned as his nose and he readily accepted recharges.

"Have you not gods to appeal to other than this—this Aiala?" asked the merchant Haran im Zeyin.

Deghred frowned at the brashness and shook his head. The wife caught her breath and drew a sign which smoke-swirls traced. Bulak took it stolidly. "She rules the air over the Uryuk Ubur," he answered.

Light wavered across the broad, seamed face, almond eyes, and thin beard. "What shall they of the Fire, the Earth, and the Water do?"

"It may be she is even at odds with them, somehow, and this is what keeps her wrathful," whispered the woman. "There is a song among the olden songs that tells of such a time, long ago, when most of the High Folk died before she grew mild again—but I must not sing any of those songs here."

"So it could worsen things to call on them," said Deghred with careful gravity. "Yet—may she and you bear with an ignorant outsider who wishes only to understand—why should she make you suffer? Surely you are blameless."

Bulak half-shrugged. "How else shall she vent her anger than in tempest and chill?"

Irreverence grinned within Cappen. He remembered infuriated women who threw things. The grin died. Men were apt to do worse when beside themselves, and be harder to bring to reason. More to the point, he happened to be on the receiving end.

The headman's stoicism gave way for a moment. "I have had my day. Our tribe will live through the winter—enough of us—I think—and may hope that then she has calmed—"

"For she is not cruel," the priestess said as if chanting. "Her snows melt beneath her springtime breezes and fill the streams, while the pastures turn green and starry with tiny flowers and lambs frisk in the sunshine. She brings the fullness of summer, the garnered riches of autumn, and when her snows have returned we have been snug and gladsome."

Isn't that the sort of thing a goddess or god is supposed to do? thought Cappen.

"—but how many of our young will freeze or starve, how many of our littlest ones?" croaked Bulak. He stiffened his lips. "We must wait and see."

And, Cappen reflected, *few gods are noted for tender solicitude. In fact, they often have nasty tempers.*

If this is even a goddess, properly speaking. Maybe she ranks only as a sylph or something, though with considerable local power. That could make matters even worse. Minor functionaries are notoriously touchy.

Supposing, of course, there is anything in what I've been hearing.

Deghred said it for him: "Again I pray pardon. No impertinence is meant. But is it not possible that what we have met is merely a freak, a flaw in the weather, nothing for the Lady Aiala to take heed of, and very soon, perhaps already tomorrow, it will go back to what it should be?"

Bulak shook his head. "Never in living memory have we suffered aught like this so early: as well you should know, who have passed through here, to and fro, for year after year. But there is the sacred song. . . . Push on if you will. The higher you go, the harder it will be. Unless we get respite within the next three or four days, I tell you that you will find the passes choked with snow and yourselves in a blizzard, unable even to go back. If afterward your bodies are found, we will make an offering for your souls." His smile held scant mirth. "Not that I'm at all sure 'we' means anyone here tonight."

"What, then, do you counsel we should do?"

"Why, retreat while still you are able. Tomorrow, I'd say. We cannot keep you through such a winter as is upon us. Barely will we be able to keep ourselves—some of ourselves. Go back north into the lowlands and wait. Could we High Folk do likewise, we might well, but if naught else, the empire would seize on the chance to make us impoverished clients. We have had dealings with it ere now. Better that a remnant of us stay free. You, though, need but wait the evil out."

"At cutthroat cost," muttered Haran.

"Better to lose our gains than our lives," retorted Deghred. His tone gentled. "And yet, Bulak, we are old friends, you and I. A man should not turn his back on a friend. Might we, your guests, be able to do something? Maybe, even, as foreigners, give reverence and some unique sacrifice to the Lady, and thus please her—?" His voice trailed off.

"How shall we speak to her? In our broken Uryuk?" wondered another merchant. "Would that not be an insult?"

"She is of the winds," said Bulak. "She and her kind ken every tongue in the world, for the winds hear and carry the knowledge to each other." He turned to his elder wife. "Is that not so?" She nodded.

Deghred brightened. "Then she will understand us when we pray and make offerings."

The priestess pinched her lips together above the few teeth left her. "Why should she heed you, who are outlanders, lowlanders, have never before done her homage, and clearly are now appealing only to save— not even your lives, for you can still escape, but your mongers' profits?"

"Treasure? We have jewelry of gold, silver, and gemstones, we have garments fit for queens—"

"What are such things to Air?"

"To Earth, maybe," Bulak put in. "Aromatic woods might please Fire, spices and sweetmeats Water. Yet with them, too, I fear you would be unwise." Shrewdly: "For in no case will you offer your entire freight, when you can better withdraw and come back with most of it several months hence. It is . . . not well to try to bargain with the Powers."

That depended on which Powers, Cappen thought. He knew of some—but they were elsewhere, gods and tutelaries of lands less stark than this.

The drink was buzzing in his head. Dismay shocked through. *Why am I jesting? It's my life on the table tonight!*

Slowly, Deghred nodded. The one sensible thing for his caravan to do was retreat, wait out the winter, and cut its losses as much as might be. Wasn't it?

And absolute lunacy for Cappen Varra. Once he was back in the empire, he himself would not bet a counterfeit lead bawbee on his chance of getting away again. The alert was out for him. If nobody else noticed first, one or another of his fellow travelers was bound soon to hear the description and betray him for the reward. Fleeing into the hinterlands or diving into some thieves' den would hardly buy enough time. Though his amulet might keep Nerigo's demons off his direct track, they could invisibly watch and listen to others, everywhere, and report everything suspicious to the sorcerer.

Stay here in Khangaii? Surely the villagers could feed one extra mouth. He'd pay them well, with arts and shows, entertainments such as they'd never enjoyed before, keeping heart in them through the grim time ahead.

Maybe they'd agree. Then maybe he'd starve or freeze to death along with so many of them. Or maybe Nerigo would get word of a vagabond who'd joined the men of Arechoum and stayed behind when they returned. He was not yet too far beyond the imperial marches for a squad to come after him as soon as the ways became at all passable.

Deghred barked a harsh laugh. "Yes, most certainly not to dicker and quibble with a female already incensed," he said. "That would be to throw oil on a fire." He sighed. "Very well, we'll load up again tomorrow and betake ourselves hence. May we find it well with the High Folk when we come back."

The younger wife moaned softly in the shadows and clutched two of the children to her.

Let her live, Cappen thought wildly. *She's beautiful. Several of them that I've spied here are, in their way. Though I don't suppose I can beguile any—*

His heart leaped. His legs followed. The others stared as he sprang to his feet. "No, wait!" he cried. "Wait only a little span. A few days more at most. I've an idea to save us!"

"What, you?" demanded Deghred, while his traders gaped and Bulak scowled. "Has a *yawanna* taken your wits? Or have you not understood what we were saying, how easily we can give the Lady offense and bring her fury straight against us?"

"I have, I have," Cappen answered frantically. "My thought is nothing like that. Any risk will be wholly my own, I swear. Only hearken to me."

Risk indeed. A notion born out of half-drunken desperation, maybe. But maybe, also, sired by experience.

He called up coolness, to be a wellspring for a spate of eager, cozening words such as a bard and showman had better always be able to produce.

Day came bleak and bright. Washed clean, newly smooth-shaven, wearing the finest warm raiment to be found in the caravan's goods—plumed cap of purple satin, scarlet cloak, green tunic embroidered with gold and trimmed with sable, dark blue hose, buskins of tooled leather—with a small harp in his hand from the same source, he left the village behind and made his way on up the path toward the heights. Wind whistled. Far overhead, a hawk rode it. The chill whipped his face. He hardly felt it, nor any weariness after sleepless hours. He was strung too taut.

But when he reached the cairn they had told him of, from which rose a pole and flew an often-renewed white banner, while a narrow trail wound off to the left, an abrupt sense of how alone he was hollowed him out. Though he seldom thought about it, his wish was to die, sometime in the distant future, with a comrade or two and a girl or three to appreciate his gallantry and his last quip.

He stiffened his sinews and summoned up his blood. He must not seem to be afraid, so best was to convince himself that he wasn't. Think rather of this as a unique challenge.

The trail went across the mountainside, near the edge of a cliff sheer-

THIEVES' WORLD: FIRST BLOOD

ing down into dizzy depths. Elsewhere the land reached vast and tilted, here and there a meadow amidst the rock. A waterfall gleamed like a sword across the gorge. Its booming came faintly through the wind.

Before long he reached the altar where they prayed and sacrificed to Aiala, a great boulder squared off and graven with eroded symbols. Cappen saw few if any other traces of man. No sacred smoke, but thin gust-borne streamers of dry snow blew past. Here, though, if anywhere, she should quickly discern any worshiper.

He took stance before the block and turned his gaze aloft. Give her a short time to see, perhaps to wonder, perhaps even to admire.

The air shrilled.

Cappen tucked gloves into belt and positioned the harp. His fingers evoked the first chord. He began to sing.

It was a song he had used more than once over the years, usually to good effect. Of course, it must be adapted to each occasion, even rendered into a different language, and he had lain awake working on it. However, if she really did know all human tongues, he could simplify the task by staying with the original Caronnais. If not, or if he was mistaken about her femaleness—he wouldn't weaken his delivery by fretting about that. He sang loud and clear:

> Be merciful, I pray, and hear my cry
> Into the winds that you command. I know
> That I am overbold, but even so
> Adore the one whose queendom is the sky,
> In awe of whom the moonlit night-clouds fly,
> Who dances in the sunlight and the snow,
> Who brings the springtime, when the freshets flow
> And all the world goes green beneath her eye.
> Yet worship is not that which makes me call
> Upon you here, and offer up my heart.
> Although I, mortal, surely cannot woo
> As man to maiden, still, I have seen all—
> No, just a little, but at least a part—
> Of that alive enchantment which is you.

And she came to him.

"—However, speak," she said.

He suppressed a shiver. Now he must be as glib as ever in his life. "First, will my lady permit that I resume my cap and gloves and pull my cloak around me? It's mortal cold for a mortal."

Again something like amusement flickered briefly. She nodded. "Then say what is your name, your home, and your errand."

"May it please my lady, the caravaneers I travel with know me as Peor Sardan of Lorace." He was clearly from such parts. "But you of the high heavens surely recognize that this cannot be quite so." *Really? Well, anyhow, outright prevarication could be hazardous and should be unnecessary. She won't deign to give me away. If she chooses to destroy me, she'll do it herself. Battered to death by hailstones*—? "My motherland is farther west and south, the kingdom of Caronne, and I hight Cappen Varra, born to the noble house of Dordain. As for my errand, I have none fixed, being a wanderer—in spite of the birth I mentioned—who wishes to see something of the world and better his fortune before turning home. Rather, that was my only wish until this happy day."

"Yes, I've spied the pack train," said Aiala scornfully. "You hope I'll grant you better weather."

"Oh, my lady! Forgive me, but no. Who am I to petition you? Nor am I in their enterprise. I simply took what appeared to be an opportunity to visit their country, of which go many fabulous accounts. Now I see this for the velleity it was." He made his look upon her half shy, half aglow. "Here I find the fulfillment of my true and lifelong desire."

Was she taken a bit aback? At any rate, her manner grew less forbidding. "What do you mean?"

Cappen gestured from beneath his cloak. "Why, my lady, what else than the praise of Woman? She, the flower of earthly creation, in her thousandfold dear incarnations, no wine so sweet or heady as her presence, she is the meaning of my existence and my poor verses in her honor are its justification. Yes, I have found her and sung to her in many a land, from the soft vales of Caronne to the stern fjords of Norren, from a fisher hut on Ocean shore to a palace in Sanctuary, and my thought was to seek her anew in yonder realm, perhaps some innocent maiden, perhaps some wise enchantress, how can I know before she has kindled my heart?"

"You are . . . a flighty one, then." She did not sound disapproving—what constancy has the wind?—but as though intrigued, even puzzled.

"Also, my very love drives me onward. For see you, my lady, it is Woman herself for whom I quest. While often wondrous, no one woman is more than mortal. She has, at most, a few aspects of perfection, and they changeable as sun-sparkles on the river that is time. Otherwise, the flaws of flesh, the infirmities of insight, the narrowness of dailiness belong to being human. And I, all too human, lack strength and patience to endure such thwarting of the dream for long. The yearning overtakes me and I must be off again in search of that prize which common sense tells me is unattainable but the spirit will not ever quite let me despair of."

Not bad, Cappen thought. By now he half-believed it.

"I told you to speak in few words." Aiala didn't say that quite firmly.

"Ah, would that I could give you obedience in this as I shall in all else whatsoever," Cappen sighed into the wind. "Dismiss me, and of course I will depart, grieving and yet gladsome over what has been vouchsafed me. But until then I can no more curb my tongue than I can quell my heart. For I have glimpsed the gates of my goal, loftier and more precious than any knight before me can have beheld, and I jubilate."

"And never before have I—" escaped from her. She recalled her savage dignity. "Clarify this. I'll not stand here the whole day."

"Certainly not. The heights and the heavens await your coming. But since you command me, I can relate quite plainly that, hitherbound, I heard tell of my lady. Beyond, perhaps over and above her majesty and mightiness, the tales were of visions, dazzlements, seen by an incredibly fortunate few through the centuries, beauty well-nigh too great to bear—and, more than that, a spirit lordly and loving, terrible and tender, mysterious and merry, life-bearing and life-nourishing—in short, Woman."

"You . . . had not seen me . . . earlier," Aiala murmured.

"But I had, fleetingly, fragmentarily, in dreams and longings. Here, I thought, must be Truth. For although there are doubtless other goddesses of whom something similar can be said, and I imply no least disrespect for any, still, Truth is One, is it not? Thus I strove to infer a little of the immortally living miracle I heard of. I wove these inferences into a humble tribute. I brought it to your halidom as my offering.

"To do worship is an end and a reward in itself. I dared hope for no more. Now—my lady, I have seen that, however inadequate, my verse was not altogether wide of the mark. What better can an artist win than such a knowledge, for an hour of his few years on Earth? My lady, I can die content, and I thank you."

"You—need not die. Not soon. Go back to the plains."

"So we had decided, the caravaneers and I, for never would we defy our lady's righteous wrath. Thence I will seek to regain my faraway birthland, that my countrymen too may be enriched by a hint of your glory. If I fall by the wayside—" Cappen shrugged. "Well, as I said, today my life has had overflowing measure."

She raised her brows. "Your road is dangerous?"

"It is long, my lady, and at the outset—I left certain difficulties behind me in the empire—trivial, but some people overreact. My plan had been to circumvent them by going roundabout through Arechoum. No matter. If the cosmic cycle requires that my lady decree an early winter throughout her mountains, I shall nevertheless praise her while blood beats within me."

"It's not that." Aiala bridled. The wind snarled. "No! I am not bound to a wheel! This is my will."

"Your wisdom."

"My anger!" she yelled. The storm in the west mounted swiftly higher. "I'll show them! They'll be sorry!"

"They?" asked Cappen low.

"Aye, they'll mourn for that they mocked me, when the waters of Vanis lie frozen past the turning of the springtime, and the earth of Orun remains barren, and the fires of Lua smolder out because no dwellers are left alive to tend them." Under his cloak, Cappen suppressed a shudder. *Yes*, he thought, *human rulers don't take their subjects much into account either.* "Then they'll come to me begging my mercy, and I will grant it to them for a song."

I'm on the track. "But is it not my lady of the winds who sings to the world?" Cappen pursued, carefully, carefully.

"So they'll discover, when I laugh at their effort."

"I am bewildered. How could any being, divine or not, possibly quarrel with my lady?"

Aiala paced to and fro. The wind strengthened, the dark clouds drew closer. After a stark minute she halted, looked straight at him, and said, "The gods fall out with each other now and then." He forbore to mention that he well knew that. His need was for her to unburden herself. His notion that she was lonelier than she realized seemed the more likely when her tone calmed somewhat. "This—" She actually hesitated. "You may understand. You are a maker of songs."

"I am when inspired, my lady, as I was today." Or whenever called for, but that was beside the immediate point.

"You did well. Not that *they* could have appreciated it."

"A song was wanted among the gods?"

Locks streamed and tumbled the more wildly as she nodded. "For a wedding, a divine marriage. Your countrymen must perceive it otherwise, but in these uplands it is Khaiantai who wakens at the winter solstice from her sleep, a virgin, to welcome Hurultan the Lightbearer, her bridegroom; and great is the rejoicing in Heaven and on earth."

On earth in better years, Cappen thought. *Yes, the mythic event, forever new and forever recurrent.* A chill passed up his spine. He concealed it as best he was able. "But . . . the occasion is not always the same?"

"No. Is one day the same as the last? Time would come to a stop."

"So—the feast and"—his mind leaped—"gifts to the happy pair?"

"Just so. Of us Four, Orun may bring fruits or gold, Vanis a fountain or a rainbow, Lua an undying lamp or a victorious sword—such things as pertain to them—while I have given an eagle or a fragrance or—we go there together; for we are the Four."

"But now lately—?"

Her reasonableness began to break. "I had in mind a hymeneal song, like none heard before in those halls but often to be again. They agreed this would be a splendid gift. I created it. And then—" Elemental rage screamed through an icy blast.

"And they did not comprehend it," Cappen proposed.

"They scoffed! They said it was so unworthy they would not come to the feast in my company if I brought it. They *dare!*"

Cappen waited out the ensuing whirlwind. When Aiala had quieted down a grim trifle, he ventured, "My lady, this is often the fate of artists. I have learned how eloquence is meaningless to the word-blind, music and meter to the tone-deaf, subtlety to the blunt-brained, and profundity to the unlearned."

"Good names for these, Cappen Varra."

"I refer to no gods or other high Powers, my lady," he made haste to reply. One never knew who or what might be listening. "No irreverence. Absolutely never! I speak merely of my small human experience and of people whom I actually pity more than despise—except, to be sure, when they set themselves up as critics. Yet even persons of unimpeachable taste and discernment can have differences of opinion. This is an unfortunate fact of life, to which I have become resigned."

"I will not be. Moreover, word has gotten about. If I come lamely in with something else than a song— No!" Aiala yowled. "They'll learn respect when I avenge my pride with disasters like none since Chaos rebelled in the beginning."

"Ah—may that perhaps conceivably be just a minim extreme, my lady? Not that I can judge. Indeed, I am baffled to grasp how your colleagues could reject your epithalamium. The music of the wind pervades the world, lulling breeze, sough in forests, laughterful rainsquall, trumpeting gale, oh, infinite is its variety, and its very hushes are a part of the composition," said Cappen with another sweeping gesture.

She nearly thawed. "You, though, you understand me—" she breathed. "For the first time ever, someone—"

He intended to go on in this vein until he had softened her mood enough for her to stop punishing the land. But she paused, then exclaimed, "Hear what I have made, and judge."

"Oh, my lady, I cannot!" gasped Cappen, aghast. "I'm totally unworthy, unfit, disqualified."

She smiled. "Be not afraid," she said quite gently. "Only tell me what you think. I won't take offense."

Too many others had insisted on declaiming their verses to him. "But, my lady, I don't know, I cannot know the language of the gods, and surely your work would lose much in translation."

"Actually," she said, "it's in classical Xandran, as we're wont to use when elegance is the aim."

He remembered white temples and exquisite sculptures in the South and West, too often ruinous, yet still an ideal for all successor peoples. Evidently the local deities felt that, while their worshipers might be barbarians, they themselves ought to display refinement. "But I also fear—I regret—my lady, I was not very dedicated to my schooling. My knowledge of Xandran was slight at best, and has largely rusted out of me." True enough.

Impulsive as her winds, she smiled afresh. "You shall have it back, and more."

"That would, er, take a while."

"No. Hear me. All tongues spoken by men anywhere are open to me."

Yes, so Bulak had said. How remote and unreal the Uryuk hut felt.

"For the sake of your courteous words, Cappen Varra, and your doubtless keen judgment, I will bestow this on you."

He gaped. "How—how— And how can this weak little head of mine hold so overwhelmingly much?"

"It need not. Whenever you hear or read a language, you will be able to use it like a native. Afterward and until next time, there will be only whatever you choose to keep and can, as with ordinary memories."

"My lady, I repeat, I'm wholly unworthy—"

"Hold still." Imperious, she trod over to him, laid hands on his cheeks, and kissed him.

He lurched, half stunned. A forefinger slid into either ear. He noted vaguely amidst the tempest that this was a caress worth trying in future, if he had a future.

She released him and stepped back. His daze faded and he could pay close heed to what he said. "I, I never dreamed that Woman herself would— For that instant I was like unto a god."

Her hand chopped the air, impatient. "Now you are ready to hear me."

He braced for it.

Gaze expectant upon him, she cleared her throat and launched into her song. Fantastically, the Xandran lyrics rang Caronnais-clear. He wished they didn't. As for the melody, she possessed a marvelous voice, but these notes took a drunkard's walk from key to key.

> The universe has looked forward with breath baited,
> Not only earth but the underworld and the starry sky,
> For this day so well-known, even celebrated,
> When all of us assembled see eye to eye
> About the union of our shiny Hurultan, whose ability
> It is the daylight forward to bring,
> And dear Khaiantai, who will respond with agility.
> So that between them they become parents of the spring—

Cappen thanked the years that had taught him acting, in this case the role of a gravely attentive listener.

Aiala finished: " '—And thus let us join together in chorusing my song.' There! What do you think of that?"

"It is remarkable, my lady," Cappen achieved.

"I didn't just dash it off, you know. I weighed and shaped every word. For instance, that line '*Birds also will warble as soon as they hatch from the egg.*' That did not come easily."

"An unusual concept, yes. In fact, I've never heard anything like it."

"Be frank. Tell me truly, could I make a few little improvements? Perhaps—I've considered—instead of '*as ardent as a prize bull,*' what about '*as vigorous as a stud horse*'?"

"Either simile is striking, my lady. I would be hard put to suggest any possible significant changes."

Aiala flared anew. "Then *why* do Orun, Vanis, and Lua sneer? How can they?"

"Sneering comes easily to some persons, my lady. It is not uncommonly an expression of envy. But to repeat myself, I do not propose that that applies in the present case. Tastes do differ. Far be it from me to imagine how your distinguished kindred might perceive a piece like this. Appropriateness to an occasion need have nothing to do with the quality of a work. It may merely happen to not quite fit in—like, say, a stately funeral dirge in a series of short-haul chanties. Or vice versa. Professionals like me," said Cappen forbearingly, "must needs learn to supply what may be demanded, and reserve our true art for connoisseurs."

He failed to mollify her. Instead, she stiffened and glared. "So! I'm unskilled, am I? I suppose you can do better?"

Cappen lifted his palms with a defensiveness not entirely feigned. "Oh, absolutely not. I simply meant—"

"I know. You make excuses for them on behalf of your own feelings."

"My lady, you urged me to be forthright. I hint at nothing but a conceivable, quite possibly hypothetical reconsideration of intent, in view of the context."

Indignation relieved him by yielding to haughtiness. "I told you how I would lose honor did I by now give anything but a song. Rather will I stay home and make them sorry."

Cappen's mind leaped like a hungry cat at a mouse. "Ah, but perhaps there is a third and better way out of this deplorable situation. Could you bring a different paean? I know many that have enjoyed great success at nuptial gatherings."

"And the gods will know, or in time they'll discover, that it is not new in the world. Shall I bring used goods to the sacred wedding—*I*?"

"Well, no, my lady, of course not."

Aiala sniffed. "I daresay you can provide something original that will be good enough."

"Not to compare with my lady's. Much, much less exalted. Thereby, however, more readily blending into revelry, where the climate is really not conducive to concentrated attention. Grant me time, for indeed the standard to be met is heaven-high—"

She reached a decision. "Very well. A day and a night."

"Already tomorrow?" protested Cappen, appalled.

"*They* shall not think I waver weakly between creativity and vengeance. Tomorrow. In classical Xandran. Fresh and joyous. It had better be."

"But—but—"

"Then I will give you my opinion, freely and frankly."

"My lady, this is too sudden for imperfect flesh and feeble intelligence. I beg you—"

"Silence. It's more than I think I would grant anyone else, for the sake of your respectful words and song. I begin to have my suspicions about it, but will overlook them if you bring me one that is acceptable and that my winds can tell me has never been heard before on this earth or in its skies. Fail me, and your caravan will not get back to the plains, nor you to anywhere. Go!"

In a whirl of white, she vanished. The wind shrieked louder and colder, the storm clouds drew nearer.

Villagers and caravaneers spied him trudging back down the path and, except for those out forlornly herding the sheep, swarmed together to meet him. Their babble surfed around his ears. He gestured vainly for silence. Bulak roared for it. As it fell, mumble by mumble, he and Deghred trod forward. "What did you do yonder?" he asked, less impassively than became a headman.

Cappen had donned his sternest face. "These be mysteries not to be spoken of until their completion," he declared. "Tomorrow shall see my return to them."

He dared not spend hours relating and explaining, when he had so few. Nor did it seem wise to admit that thus far, in all likelihood, he had made matters worse, especially for the travelers.

Bulak stood foursquare. Deghred gave the bard a searching and skeptical look. The rest murmured, fingered prayer beads or josses, and otherwise registered an awe that was useful at the moment but, if disappointed, could well turn murderously vengeful.

Cappen went on headlong. "I must meditate, commune with high Powers, and work my special magianisms," he said. "For this I require to be alone, well sheltered, with writing materials and, uh, whatever else I may require."

Bulak stared. "Suddenly you speak as if born amidst us."

"Take that as a token of how deep and powerful the mysteries are." Cappen forgot to keep his voice slowly tolling. "But, but does anybody here know Xandran?"

Wind whistled, clouds swallowed the sun, three ravens flew by like forerunners of darkness.

"I have some command of the tongue," said Deghred, almost as if he suspected a trap.

"Classical Xandran?" cried Cappen.

"No. Who does but a few scholars? I mean what they use in those parts nowadays—that is, the traders and sailors I've had to do with. And, yes, once a crew of pirates; but I think that was a different dialect."

The foolish, fire-on-ice hope died. Still—"I may want to call on what knowledge you have. That will depend on what my divinations reveal to me. Hold yourself prepared. Meanwhile, what of my immediate needs?"

"We have a place," Bulak said. "Lowly, but all we can offer."

"The spirits take small account of earthly grandeur," his elder wife assured them, for whatever that was worth.

Thus Cappen found himself and his few possessions in the village storehouse. It was a single room, mainly underground, with just enough walls beneath the sod roof to allow an entryway. After the door was closed, a lamp gave the only light. While the space was fairly large, very little was available, for it was crammed with roots, dried meat, sheepskins, and other odorous goods. The air hung thick and dank. However, it was out of the wind, and private.

Too private, maybe. Cappen had nothing to take his mind off his thoughts.

He settled in, a pair of skins between him and the floor, one over his shoulders. Besides the lamp, he had been given food, a crock of wine, a goblet, a crock for somewhat different purposes, and his tools—a bottle of ink, several quill pens, and a sheaf of paper, articles such as merchants used in their own work. Now he began wondering, more and more frantically, what to do with them.

Ordinarily he could have dashed something off. But a canticle in classical Xandran, suitable for a marriage made in heaven? Especially when the cost of its proving unsatisfactory would be widespread death, including his? He did not feel inspired.

The language requirement was obstacle enough. His wits twisted to and fro, hunting for a way, any way, around it. Through Deghred, he could now get a doubtless very limited acquaintance with the present-day speech. He recalled hearing that it descended directly from the antique, so much of it must be similar. How would pronunciation have changed, though, and grammar, and even vocabulary? In his days at home he had read certain famous poems five or six hundred years old. It had been difficult; only a lexicon made it possible at all; and the archaic idiom of the Rojan hillmen suggested how alien the verses would have sounded.

He glugged a mouthful of wine. It hit an empty stomach and thence sent a faint glow to his head. He did have a bit more to go on. When he concentrated, he could drag scraps of the proper classical up from the forgetfulness in which they had lain. Maybe his newly acquired facility helped with that. But they were just scraps. He had yawned through a year of this as part of the education that even a bastard son of a minor nobleman was supposed to receive, but declensions, conjugations, moods, tenses, and the dismal rest set his attention adrift in the direction of girls, flowery forests, rowdy friends, composing a song of his own that might seduce a girl, or almost anything else. What stayed with him had done so randomly, like snatches of his aunt's moralizings when he was a child and couldn't escape.

And then he had Aiala's lyrics. That wasn't by design. Every word clung to him, like the memory of every bit of a certain meal years ago that he had had to eat and praise because the cook was a formidable witch. He feared he would never get rid of either. Still, the thing gave him a partial but presumably trustworthy model, a basis for comparison and thus for a guesswork sort of reconstruction.

He drank again. His blood started to buzz faintly, agreeably. Of course, he'd need his reason unimpaired when—if—he got to that task. But "if" was the doomful word. First he needed the poesy, the winged fancy, concepts evoking words that in turn made the concepts live. Anxiety, to give it a euphemistic name, held his imagination in a swamp of glue. And wasn't that metaphor a repulsive symptom of his condition? Anything he might force out of himself would belong in yonder crock.

So he must lift his heart, free his spirit. Then he could hope his genius would soar. After which he could perhaps render the Caronnais into Xandran without mutilating it beyond recognition. The basic difficulty was that to create under these circumstances he must get drunk, no good condition for a translator. He suspected the necessary degree of drunkenness was such that when he awoke he wouldn't care whether he lived or died—until much too late. The lady of the winds did not expect to be kept waiting.

Besides—he spat a string of expletives—she demanded not only words but music. The two must go together as naturally as breath and heartbeat, or the song was a botch and a mockery. This meant they must grow side by side, intertwining, shaping one another, as he worked. Oh, usually he could find an existing melody that fitted a poem he had in process, or vice versa. Neither was admissible in this case; both must never have been heard before in the world. He could attempt a double originality, but that, he knew, would only be possible with the Caronnais native to him. To force the subsequent translation into that mold—well, give him a week or two and maybe he might, but since he had only until tomorrow—

He glugged again. He would doubtless be wise to ballast the wine with food. It wasn't the worst imaginable food, caravaneers' rations, smoked meat and fish, butter, cheese, hardtack, rice cold but lately boiled with leeks and garlic, dried figs and apricots and— On the other hand, he lacked appetite. What use wisdom anyway? He glugged again.

If this was the end of his wanderings, he thought, it was not quite what he had visualized and certainly far too early. Not that he did well to pity himself. Think of his waymates, think of the poor innocent dwellers throughout these mountains. Surely he had enjoyed much more than them, much more colorful. It behooved a minstrel, a knight of the road, to hark back, as gladly as the wine enabled.

Most recently, yes, to Sanctuary. He had had his troubles there, but the same was true of every place, and the multifarious pleasures much outnumbered them. Ending with delicious Peridis—may she fare always well—and their last, so unfortunately interrupted moment—

He stirred on his sheepskins. By all the nymphs of joy, it happened he had brought away a souvenir of it! There he could for a while take refuge from his troubles, other than in drink. And perhaps, said practicality, this would liberate his genius.

Groping about, shivering in the chill, he found the book. Cross-legged, he opened it on his lap and peered through the dim, smoky, smelly lamplight.

The words leaped out at him. They were in no language he had ever heard of, nor was it anywhere named; but he read it as easily as he did his own, instantly understanding what everything he came upon referred to. Not that that brought full knowledge. The world he found was an abstraction, a bubble, floating cheerfully free in a space and a time beyond his ken. No matter. He guessed it was almost as airy there.

The musical notation stood equally clear to him, tunes lilting while he scanned them. Their scale was not too different from that common in the Westlands. He would need only a little practice before singing and strumming them in a way that everybody he met ought to like. What exoticism there was should lend piquancy. Yes, for his future career—

Future!

He sprang to his feet. His head banged against a rafter.

Hastily fetched through biting wind and gathering murk, Deghred im Dalagh hunkered down and peered at Cappen Varra. "Well, what do you crave of me?" he asked.

"In a minute, I pray you." Himself sitting tailor-fashion, the bard tried to arrange paper, inkpot, and open book for use. Bloody awkward. No help at all to the image of a knowing and confident rescuer.

"I've a feeling you're none too sure either," Deghred murmured.

"But I am! I simply need a bit of assistance. Who doesn't ever? The craftsman his apprentices, the priest his acolytes, and you a whole gang of underlings. I want no more than a brief . . . consultation."

"To what end?" Deghred paused. "They're growing dubious of you. What kind of Powers are you trying to deal with? What could come of it?"

"The good of everybody."

"Or the ruin?"

"I haven't time to argue." *If I did, I suspect you'd be utterly appalled and make me cease and desist. Then you'd offer an extravagant sacrifice to a being that no such thing will likely appease—for you haven't met her as I have.*

Deghred's voice harshened. "Be warned. If you don't do what you promised—"

"Well, I didn't exactly *promise*—"

"My men won't let you leave with us, and I suspect the villagers will cast you out. They fear you'll carry a curse."

Cappen was not much surprised. "Suppose, instead, I gain clemency, weather as it ought to be, and the passes open for you. Will they give me anything better than thanks? I'm taking a considerable personal risk, you know."

"Ah, should you succeed, that's different. Although these dwellers be poor folk, I don't doubt they'd heap skins and pelts at your feet. I'll show you how to sell the stuff at good prices in Temanhassa."

"You and your fellow traders are not poor men," said Cappen pointedly.

"Naturally, you'd find us, ah, not ungenerous."

"Shall we say a tenth share of the profit from your expedition?"

"A tenth? How can you jest like that in an hour like this?"

"Retreating to winter in the empire would cost more. As you must well know, who've had to cope year after year with its taxes, bribes, and extortionate suppliers." Getting snowed in here would be still worse, but Cappen thought it imprudent to explain that that had become a distinct possibility.

"We are not misers or ingrates. Nor are we unreasonable. Three percent is, indeed, lavish."

"Let us not lose precious time in haggling. Seven and a half."

"Five, and my friendship, protection, and recommendations to influential persons in Temanhassa."

"Done!" said Cappen. He sensed the trader's surprise and a certain instinctive disappointment. But the need to get on with the work was very real, and the bargain not a bad one.

Meanwhile he had arranged his things just barely well enough that he could begin. Dipping pen in ink, he said, "This is a strange work I must do, and potent forces are afoot. As yet I cannot tell of it, save to pledge

THIEVES' WORLD: FIRST BLOOD

that there is nothing of evil. As I write, I want you to talk to me in Xandran. Naught else."

Deghred gaped, remembered his dignity, and replied, "May I wonder why? You do not know that tongue, and I have only some smatterings."

"You may wonder if you choose. What you must do is talk."

"But what about?"

"Anything. Merely keep the words flowing."

Deghred groped for a minute. Such an order is not as simple as one might think. Almost desperately, he began: "I have these fine seasonings. They were shipped to me from distant lands at great expense. To you and you alone will I offer them at ridiculously low wholesale prices, because I hold you in such high esteem. Behold, for an ounce of pungent peppercorn, a mere ten zirgats. I look on this not as a loss to me, although it is, but a gift of goodwill."

Cappen scribbled. While he listened, the meanings came clear to him. He even mentally made up for the stumblings, hesitations, and thick accent. The language was his to the extent that it was the other man's; and he could have replied with fluency. What slowed him was the search in his mind for words that weren't spoken. "Knot" and "insoluble," for instance. How would one say them? . . . Ah, yes. Assuming that what he pseudo-remembered was correct. Maybe the connotations were strictly of a rope and of minerals that didn't melt in water. He jotted them down provisionally, but he wanted more context.

Deghred stopped. "Go on," Cappen urged.

"Well, uh—O barefaced brazen robber! Ten zirgats? If this withered and moldy lot went for two in the bazaar, I would be astounded. Yet, since I too am prepared to take a loss for the sake of our relationship, I will offer three—"

"Uh, could you give me something else?" Cappen interrupted. "Speech not so, m-m, commercial?"

"What can it be? My dealings with Xandrans are all commercial."

"Oh, surely not all. Doing business in itself involves sociability, the cultivation of friendly feelings, does it not? Tell me what might be said at a shared meal over a cup of wine."

Deghred pondered before he tried: "How did your sea voyage go? I hope you're not troubled by the heat. It is seldom so hot here at this time of year."

"Nothing more—more intimate? Don't men like these ever talk of their families? Of love and marriage?"

"Not much. I can't converse with them easily, you know. Women, yes."

"Say on."

"Well, I remember telling one fellow, when he asked, that the best whorehouse in the city is the Purple Lotus. Especially if you can get Zerasa. By Kalat's cloven hoof, what a wench! Plump and sweet as a juicy plum, sizzling as a spitted rump roast, and the tricks she knows—" Deghred reminisced in considerable detail.

It wasn't quite what Cappen had meant. Still, association evoked words also amorous, but apparently decorous. His pen flew, scrawling, scratching out, spattering the paper and his tunic. When Deghred ended with a gusty sigh, Cappen had enough.

"Good," he said. "My thanks—albeit this is toward the end of saving your own well-being and prosperity too. You may go now. Five percent, remember."

The merchant rose and stretched himself as well as the roof allowed. "If naught else, that was a small respite from reality. Ah, well. You do have hopes? Are you coming along?"

"No," said Cappen. "My labors are just beginning."

Day broke still and cloudless but cruelly cold. Breath smoked white, feet crunched ice. When he emerged at midmorning, Cappen found very few folk outdoors. Those stared at him out of their own frozen silence. The rest were huddled inside, keeping warm while they waited to learn their fate. It was as if the whole gigantic land held its breath.

He felt no weariness, he could not. He seemed almost detached from himself, his head light but sky-clear. His left arm cradled the harp. Tucked into his belt was a folded sheet of paper, but he didn't expect any need to refer to it. The words thereon were graven into him, together with their music. They certainly should be. The gods of minstrelsy knew—or would have known, if they weren't so remote from this wild highland—how he had toiled over the lyrics, searching about, throwing away effort after effort, inch by inch finding his way to a translation that fitted the notes and was not grossly false to the original, and at last, not satisfied but with time on his heels, had rehearsed over and over and over for his audience of turnips and sheepskins.

Now he must see how well it played for a more critical listener.

If it succeeded, if he survived, the first part of the reward he'd claim was to be let to sleep undisturbed until next sunrise. How remotely that bliss glimmered!

He trudged onward, scarcely thinking about anything, until he came to the altar. There he took stance, gazed across the abyss to peaks sword-sharp against heaven, and said, "My lady, here I am in obedience to your command."

It sounded unnaturally loud. No echo responded, no wings soared overhead, he stood alone in the middle of aloneness.

After a while, he said, "I repeat, begging my lady's pardon, that here I am with that which I promised you."

The least of breezes stirred. It went like liquid across his face and into his nostrils. In so vast a silence, he heard it whisper.

"I humbly hope my offering will please you and all the gods," he said.

And there she was, awesome and beautiful before him. A phantom wind tossed her hair and whirled snow-sparkles around her whiteness. "Well?" she snapped.

Could she too, even she, have been under strain? He doffed his cap and bowed low. "If my lady will deign to heed, I've created an epithalamium such as she desires, and have the incomparable honor of rendering it unto her, to be known forever after as her unique gift at the turning of the winter."

"That was quick, after you protested you could not."

"The thought of you inspired me as never ere now have I been inspired."

"To make it out of nothing?"

"Oh, no, my lady. Out of experience, and whatever talent is mine, and, above all else, as I confessed, the shining vision of my lady. I swear, and take for granted you can immediately verify, that neither melody nor lyrics were ever heard in this world, heaven or earth or the elsewhere, before I prepared them for you."

He doubted that she could in fact scan space and time at once, so thoroughly. But no matter. He did not doubt that Nerigo kept his half-illicit arcanum and whatever came to it through his mirror that was not a mirror well sealed against observation human and nonhuman. Whatever gods had the scope and power to spy on him must also have much better things to do.

Aiala's glance lingered more than it pierced. "I do not really wish to destroy you, Cappen Varra," she told him slowly. "You have a rather charming way about you. But—should you disappoint me—you will understand that one does have one's position to maintain."

"Oh, absolutely. And how better could a man perish than in striving to serve such a lady? Yet I dare suggest that you will find my ditty acceptable."

The glorious eyes widened. The slight mercurial shivers almost ceased. "Sing, then," she said low.

"Allow me first to lay forth what the purpose is. Unless I am grievously mistaken, it is to provide an ode to nuptial joy. Now, my thought was that this is best expressed in the voice of the bride. The groom is inevitably impatient for nightfall. She, though, however happy, may at the same time be a little fearful, certain of loving kindness yet, in her purity, unsure what to await and what she can do toward making the union rapturous. Khaiantai is otherwise. She is a goddess, and here is an annual renewal. My song expresses her rapture in tones of unbounded gladness."

Aiala nodded. "That's not a bad theme," she said, perhaps a trifle wistfully.

"Therefore, my lady, pray bear with my conceit, in the poetic sense, that she sings with restrained abandon, in colloquial terms of revelry, not always classically correct. For we have nothing to go on about that save the writings of the learned, do we? There must have been more familiar speech among lesser folk, commoners, farmers, herders, artisans, lowly but still the majority, the backbone of the nation and the salt of the earth. To them too, to the Life Force that is in them, should the paean appeal."

"You may be right," said Aiala with a tinge of exasperation. "Let me hear."

While he talked, Cappen Varra, in the presence of one who fully knew the language, mentally made revisions. Translating, he had chosen phrasings that lent themselves to it.

The moment was upon him. He took off his gloves, gripped the harp, strummed it, and cleared his throat.

"We begin with a chorus," he said. Therewith he launched into song.

> *Bridegroom and bride!*
> *Knot that's insoluble,*
> *Voices all voluble,*
> *Hail it with pride.—*

She hearkened. Her bosom rose and fell.
Now the bride herself sings.

When a merry maiden marries,
Sorrow goes and pleasure tarries;
Every sound becomes a song,
All is right, and nothing's wrong!—

He saw he had captured her, and continued to the bacchanalian end.

Sullen night is laughing day—
All the year is merry May!

The chords rang into stillness. Cappen waited. But he knew. A huge, warm easing rose in him like a tide.

"That is wonderful," Aiala breathed. "Nothing of the kind, ever before—"

"It is my lady's," he said with another bow, while he resumed his cap and gloves.

She straightened into majesty. "You have earned what you shall have. Henceforward until the proper winter, the weather shall smile, the dwellers shall prosper, and you and your comrades shall cross my mountains free of all hindrance."

"My lady overwhelms me," he thought it expedient to reply.

For a heartbeat, her grandeur gave way, ever so slightly. "I could almost wish that you— But no. Farewell, funny mortal."

She leaned over. Her lips brushed his. He felt as if struck by soft lightning. Then she was gone. It seemed to him that already the air grew more mild.

For a short while before starting back with his news he stood silent beneath the sky, suddenly dazed. His free hand strayed to the paper at his belt. Doubtless he would never know more about this than he now did. Yet he wished that someday, somehow, if only in another theatrical performance, he could see the gracefully gliding boats of the Caronnais gondoliers.

The Lighter Side of Sanctuary

Robert Asprin

The reader response to the first volume of *Thieves' World* has been overwhelming and heartwarming. (For those of you who were not aware of it: you can write to me or any other author in care of their publisher.) The volume of correspondence helped to sell volumes two and three and prompted a *Thieves' World* wargame soon to be released from the Chaosium. It seems that none of of our *Thieves' World* readers realize that anthologies in general don't sell and that fantasy anthologies specifically are sudden death.

While the letters received have been brimming with enthusiasm and praise, there has been one comment/criticism which has recurred in much of the correspondence. Specifically, people have noted that Sanctuary is incredibly grim. It seems that the citizens of the town never laugh, or when they do it is forcefully stifled . . . like the time Kittycat spilled wine down the front of his tunic while trying to toast the health of his brother, the emperor.

This is a valid gripe. First of all because no town is totally dismal. Second, because those readers familiar with my other works are accustomed to finding some humor buried in the pages—even in a genocidal war between lizards and bugs. What's worse, in reviewing the stories in this second volume, I am painfully aware that the downward spiral of Sanctuary has continued rather than reversing itself.

As such I have taken it upon myself as editor to provide the reader with a brief glimpse of the bright side of the town—the benefits and advantages of living in the worst hellhole in the empire.

To this end let us turn to a seldom seen, never quoted document issued by the Sanctuary Chamber of Commerce shortly before it went out of business. The fact that Kittycat insisted the brochure contain some modicum of truth doubtless contributed to the document's lack of success. Nonetheless, for your enjoyment and edification, here are selected excerpts from

Sanctuary
Vacation Capital
of the Rankan Empire

Every year tourists flock to Sanctuary by the tens, drawn by the rumors of adventure and excitement which flourish in every dark corner of the empire. They are never disappointed that they chose Sanctuary. Our city is everything it is rumored to be—and more! Many visitors never leave and those that do can testify that the lives to which they return seem dull in comparison with the heart-stopping action they found in this personable town.

If you, as a merchant, are looking to expand or relocate your business, consider scenic Sanctuary. Where else can you find all these features in one locale?

Business Opportunities

Property—Land in Sanctuary in cheap! Whether you want to build in the swamplands to the west of town, or east in the desert fringes, you'll find large parcels of land available at temptingly low prices. If you seek a more central location for your business, just ask. Most shop owners in Sanctuary are willing to surrender their building, stock and staff for the price of a one-way passage out of town.

Labor—There is no shortage of willing workers in Sanctuary. You'll find most citizens are for hire and will do anything for a price. Moreover, the array of talents and skills available in our city is nothing short of startling. Abilities you never thought were marketable are bought and sold freely in Sanctuary—and the price is always right!

For those who prefer slave labor, the selection available in Sanctuary is diverse and plentiful. You'll be as surprised as the slaves themselves are by who shows up on the auction block. There, as everywhere in Sanctuary, bargains abound for one with a sharp eye . . . or sword.

Materials—If the remoteness of the town's location makes you hesitate—never fear. Anything of value in the empire is sold in Sanctuary. In fact, commodities you may have been told were not for sale often appear in the stalls and shops of this amazing town. Don't bother asking the seller how he got his stock. Just rest assured that in Sanctuary no one will ask how you came by yours, either.

Lifestyles

Social Life—As the ancients say, one does not live by bread alone. Similarly, a citizen of the Rankan Empire requires an active social life to balance his business activity. Here is where Sanctuary truly excels. It has often been said that day-to-day life in Sanctuary is an adventure without parallel.

Religions—For those with an eye for the afterlife, the religious offerings in a given area must withstand close scrutiny. Well, our town welcomes such scrutinizers with open arms. Every Rankan deity and cult is represented in Sanctuary, as well as many not in open evidence elsewhere in the empire. Old gods and forgotten rites exist and flourish alongside the more accepted traditions, adding to the town's quaint charm. Nor are our temples reserved for devout true believers only. Most shrines welcome visitors of other beliefs and many allow—nay, require—audience participation in their curious native rituals.

Night Life—Unlike many cities in the empire which roll up their streets with the setting sun, Sanctuary comes to life at night. In fact, many of its citizens exist for the night life to a point where you seldom see them by the light of day. However conservative or jaded your taste in entertainment might be, you'll have the time of your life in the shadows of Sanctuary. Our Street of Red Lanterns alone offers a wide array of amusements, from the quiet elegance of the Aphrodisia House to the more bizarre pleasures available at the House of Whips. If slumming is your pleasure, you need look no further than your own doorstep.

Social Status—Let's face it: everybody likes to feel superior to somebody. Well, nowhere is superiority as easy to come by as it is in Sanctuary. A Rankan citizen of moderate means is a wealthy man by Sanctuary standards, and will be treated as such by its inhabitants. Envious eyes will follow your passing and people will note your movements and customs with flattering attentiveness. Even if your funds are less than adequate in your own opinion, it is still easy to feel that you are better off than the average citizen of Sanctuary—if only on a moral scale. We can guarantee, without reservation, that however low your opinion of yourself might be, there will be somebody in Sanctuary you will be superior to.

A Word About Crime—You have probably heard rumors of the high crime rate in Sanctuary. We admit to having had our problems in the past, but that's behind us now. One need only look at the huge crowds that gather to watch the daily hangings and impalements to realize that the support of the citizens of Sanctuary for law and order is at an all-time high. As a result of the new governor's anticrime program, we are pleased to announce that last year the rate of reported crime, per day, in Sanctuary was not greater than that of cities twice our size.

In Summary

Sanctuary is a place of opportunity for a far-thinking opportunist. Now is the time to move. Now, while property values are plummeting and the economy and the people are depressed. Where better to invest your money, your energies, and your life than in this rapidly growing city of the future? Even our worst critics acknowledge the potential of Sanctuary when they describe it as a "town with nowhere to go but up"!